THIS IS WHAT IT FEELS LIKE

RAE LLOYD

To eleven-year-old me who wrote her first book that no one saw. I'm gonna make sure that people see this one.

To my husband, who, when I told him I had completed the book, asked me, "Just how descriptive were you?" And I love him for that.

To my daughters, I love you, but please don't read this.

And to the thousands of books that I have read by the brave authors who gave me an escape into the world that they created, even if it was just for a moment, it was everything to me when I needed it. So, thank you.

TRIGGER WARNINGS

This book contains references to alcohol and marijuana consumption, panic attacks, off-page rape, abortion, religious trauma, adoption, and parental abandonment. Please read with care to your mental health.

feel it. the thing you don't want to feel. feel it. and be free.
Nayyirah Waheed

PLAYLIST

I decided to put together a playlist of the songs I listened to while I wrote this book. They don't necessarily have to do with the theme of the book, but they were what I listened to incessantly on repeat through every word. Listen to it while you read, and we'll connect through the music.

With All My Heart by ILLENIUM (with JVKE)
Crazy by gavn!
Where You Go by Kiana Ledé & Khalid
Save Me (From Myself) by NURKO
Reasons to Leave by Suriel Hess
Sun Will Shine by Robin Schulz & Tom Walker
The Hard Way by PNAU & Khalid
i looked into your eyes by Sky McCreery
Loved By You by Justin Bieber (ft. Burna Boy)
lifejacket by Matt Hansen
The Feels by Labrinth
June by Chris Lanson (ft. Eluera)
Wasted Love by Ofenbach (ft. Lagique)
You by Regard, Troye Sivan, Tate McRae

Questions by Lost Frequencies & James Arthur
closure by Henry Moodie
Hunger by Ross Copperman
dead the day ur gone by Matt Hansen
Caroline by Boy In Space
I Go Dancing by Frank Walker (ft. Ella Henderson)
Dancing When I Die by Heather Janssen
Blind by Corey Harper
Me On You by Nicky Romero & Taio Cruz

1

I had perfected the art of being an emotional chameleon all the way back in second grade when a girl named Tara Simon asked me why I looked sad all the time. Instead of explaining that I was being raised by my twenty-three-year-old mother who worked the night shift as a nurse and was not home in time to get me ready for school. Instead of saying that I had no idea who my father was. Instead of telling Tara that it had been twenty days since someone had hugged me and that person was a teacher, not my mom, I smiled and told her that I wasn't sad, I was just tired. Tara seemed pacified, and I learned a new set of rules. Don't let people see it on my face because they will ask questions. Questions that, honestly, at eight years old, I had no idea how to answer.

Now, years later, in fact, I was only thirty days away from graduating high school, and I still made sure no one saw my feelings on my face. I didn't want them to know that, at times, I still felt sad and alone. I didn't want anyone to see how confusing life felt for me sometimes. To make it easier to fake it in public, I got really good at stuffing all of my feelings down super deep in private. If I couldn't feel it, then certainly no one would see it on my face either.

I got out of bed, shaking off the not-so-fond memories, and looked at the time on my phone: 6:52. Shit, I had wasted so much time in my head that I was going to miss my bus, which either meant walking and being late to school or laying out money for an Uber, which I definitely didn't want to do. I was saving every dollar I made at my part-time job at the dog shelter to buy a car so I would have a form of my own transportation once I graduated. My best friend Liam always offered to pick me up, but I had been stubborn since it had gotten warmer out and told him not to come by, that I wanted to get my steps in. Really, I just hated relying on people, even the ones closest to me. Tossing my hair up into a high bun, I turned on the shower to take a really quick, no hair included, shower before starting my thirty-minute walk to school.

When my slightly lukewarm shower was complete, I ran a brush through my long, thick, dirty-blonde hair and then pulled half of it back with a claw clip. As I threw my makeup wipe into the garbage, I noticed two tied-off, used condoms haphazardly shoved under some tissues. It made me upset knowing that while I was in school, my mom came home from her night shift at the hospital and had sex. She had plenty of time for these men who I had never met, but she never had any time for me, I thought angrily. We were literally two passing ships in the night. Depending on her shift schedule, I could go six to ten days at a time without seeing her. It wasn't that she didn't like me; it just felt like she had never come to terms with the fact that at fifteen years old, she had become a mother. I knew no details about how I was conceived or who my father was, as she refused to talk about it. But I guessed that was how she felt about it because she had continued to live her life with herself as the main priority, and I had to learn to live mine without a maternal figure guiding me. My hand shook as the anger manifested itself through my body, and my mascara wand left a black streak of makeup on my cheekbone.

"Fuck," I muttered loudly at my reflection in the mirror. My bright green eyes looked so irritated and hurt. Deep breaths, Shaen, I told myself. Do not let these unnecessary feelings mess up your day. I calmed myself down by shutting all of my feelings off. Numbing myself out was not a healthy coping mechanism, but it was one I turned to often. I finished doing my makeup and went back to my room to choose something to wear, shoving those disgusting used condoms into the deep recesses of my mind. This, all of this fuck up of a life, was why I was going to avoid having sex for as long as possible.

It was a decision I came to when I first learned how babies were made from my best friend, Liam Hennessy, in the fourth grade. I was ten years old at the time and was two years into making myself peanut butter and jelly sandwiches on my own and putting myself on the bus in the morning. One day in December, on the way home from school, Liam sat down next to me on the bus and asked if I knew where babies came from. Wide-eyed I had shaken my head no, so Liam launched into a long rendition about sperm, penises, vaginas, and eggs. Apparently, his mother had announced her pregnancy to him and his brothers, which had come with a birds and the bees speech, so now I found myself lucky enough to be included in the coming-of-age talk. At a very young age, I knew that my mother had given birth to me while she was still in high school, but my grandmother, on her rare visits, really liked to point out how hard having me had been for her daughter. I never knew what to say to her when she would go on her rant about how difficult life had become for my mother after I was born. It wasn't like I had asked to be her kid; in fact, given a choice, I probably would have chosen someone more like Liam's mother. It was in that moment of Liam telling me how sperm got into a girl's vagina that I decided I just wouldn't let sperm anywhere near my eggs till I had my entire life figured out. Because I couldn't risk putting a kid through what I was currently going through.

It was 7:30 when I left the house, shoving a protein bar in my mouth and slinging my backpack over one shoulder. If I walked quickly, I would get to school at eight, which was about fifteen minutes after the first bell rang. At eighteen, the secretary let me sign myself in without asking to talk to my mom about why I was late. I had done enough dodging questions about why my mom was never at PTA, never sent in permission slips, and would never answer the phone when I was late to last an actual lifetime.

As I began walking briskly toward school, I put one AirPod into my ear and turned the music on my phone onto shuffle mode. I never wore both headphones at the same time when I was out because I knew I needed to be safe. I received the AirPods as a gift from my bosses at the dog shelter last Christmas. I had been so grateful to swap out my string headphones from CVS for an Apple product that if I hadn't had seventeen years of practice of numbing myself out by then, I would have definitely cried when they handed them to me. The problem with numbing pain and sadness was that happiness got numbed out too. It was a casualty of war, as I liked to tell myself.

I had made it halfway to school when I heard someone call out my name. Startled, I took the AirPod out my ear and turned to look where I had heard the shout come from. It was Liam, yes, how-babies-were-made Liam. We had stayed best friends all these years, even though he had no idea how much his sperm and egg talk had scarred me for life. Liam had definitely grown up since fourth grade and was now over six feet tall and was on the school football team. As much as he jokingly flirted with me, we were just friends, and therefore by proxy, I was forced to hear all of his sexcapade stories. Although they had calmed down a bit since he had started dating my friend, Lia. Clearly, the egg and sperm trauma hadn't affected him the same way it had me.

"Shaen, get your fine ass in the car," Liam shouted from across the intersection. I wanted to ignore him and keep walking, but I knew he would just keep yelling until I listened. The reason I wanted to ignore him was sitting in the back seat of Liam's green jeep and staring at me through the open window: Remi Taylor.

Remi, short for Remiel, who had apparently been some angel in the Bible, was Liam's cousin who had suddenly moved in with his aunt and uncle at the start of twelfth grade and switched to our school. His family only lived a town over, and his father was a well-known pastor in a megachurch there. To my knowledge, Remi had yet to visit his family since he'd moved here in August, and it was now the beginning of June. He never talked about why he had made the sudden switch, but Liam had made an off-handed comment to me about Remi no longer wearing his purity ring and not participating in the conversation when Liam's dad would say anything related to religion at the dinner table. I figured one plus one probably equaled some sort of falling out with Remi's famous pastor dad or God or maybe both.

Liam and I were best friends, so by default, Remi and I were friends, but we had never really hung out, just the two of us. We had maybe had a handful of real, deep conversations in the entire ten months since he had moved into Liam's house. Most of the time, we just joked around and fake flirted in our group chat. To be honest, I was scared of him. Why? Well, Remi Taylor made me feel things. Not just a tightening in my groin whenever I got a whiff of his cologne mixed with whatever natural spice he had going on, but he just made me *feel* in general. I would get a little blip of the heart when I would look up and find him watching me with those deep, dark eyes. I felt excited when Liam would get me good seats at their football games because then I could watch six-foot-three Remi in his tight little football pants running up and down the field. I felt both thrilled and nervous when Liam would offer me a ride home from school because usually, his girlfriend Lia would sit in the front, which meant I had to sit next to Remi in the back. Now, Remi was a big guy. Not just tall but really broad with big shoulders and arms. He also had a whole bunch of thigh muscles going on. I had seen him without a shirt on multiple occasions when I would go over to Liam's house to swim, and while Remi was a big dude, he was not the kind of gym bro who worked out too much. It was obvious that football kept him in shape, and of course, he spent time in the school gym with the team. Although he had a flat stomach, he didn't have an overly obvious six-pack, which I secretly really loved. My friend Eva's boyfriend, who was also in our friend group, was obsessed with his six-pack and was always drinking protein shakes and counting macros. I found Remi's more natural-looking body refreshing because although he was big, muscular, and strong, his body was probably cozier to lay on than Carter, who was all hard muscle. Yeah, it was thoughts like these that meant I had to stay away from him. I began to cross the street, knowing exactly what the drive to school was going to be like. Remi took up a lot of the back seat, so I would try to become one with the door and would then spend the ten minutes it took to get to school trying not to breathe in his scent because, to be super honest, it made me wet. And wet was bad. Because wet equaled feelings all up in my body, and I, Shaen Collins, didn't do feelings. I couldn't afford to. I had to get my life in order first. Then, I would defrost my frozen heart and maybe let myself be happy with someone.

As I approached Liam's jeep, I put on my happy, peppy face and answered Liam and Lia's calls of good morning. I risked a glance at Remi and confirmed that he was still, in fact, staring at me from under his unfairly long lashes that all the boys naturally had, and the girls paid so much money to get. I went around to the other side of the car, braced myself, and opened the door. Remi was sitting with his thighs spread because, quite frankly, he wouldn't fit otherwise, and I watched him put his backpack onto his lap to make room for me.

"Hurry up bitch, we're already late," Lia called.

"Okay, drama. No one asked you guys to stop. I was doing just fine getting my steps in," I joked back. For a feelingless virgin, I could dish it as good as the rest of them. Lia laughed and turned around in her seat, complimenting me on how nice my hair looked.

"Why are you guys late anyway?" I asked as I buckled myself and then tried to flatten my five-foot-three body as far away from Remi as possible.

Remi mumbled something, at which Liam laughed loudly as he pulled back onto the road.

"I didn't catch that," I told him, looking over at his side profile. His cheeks were covered in a warm shadow of hair, telling me that he hadn't bothered shaving this morning. His lips were full, and they were pulled back in a grin. His hair was a dark brown color, and it fell in messy waves on his forehead.

"They were fucking. That's why we're late," Remi repeated, turning to look at me full-on.

I blinked. I rarely heard Remi talk like that. He would sometimes join in on Liam's locker room talk stories in a halfhearted way. I never really saw him drink, and no one in the friend group could confirm if he himself was having sex with anyone. If he was, he kept it so well on the down-low that no one knew about it.

"Huh?" I felt slow. I knew what he had said, but my brain was suddenly feeling really foggy hearing those words coming out of his mouth. He grinned, showing me his straight white teeth because, of course they were.

"They were fornicating. Doing the dirty. Making looove," he almost crooned, leaning forward and smacking Liam upside the head as he said it.

Liam tried to swat him back while keeping his eyes on the road and turning onto the street where our school was.

"Hey!" Liam protested, laughing. Remi just shrugged, keeping his eyes on me.

"It's true," Lia admitted, a blush dotting her cheeks. "Sorry, not sorry."

Liam looked over at her. "I'm certainly not sorry, babe. That thing you did with your..."

"La la la," I sang, putting my fingers in my ears. "I cannot hear what my friend did to my other friend's dick this early in the day."

Liam cracked up again as he pulled into a parking spot and said, "Okay, we'll save all the dirty details for the ride home."

"We'll see. I have a bio test, and I might run late, so don't wait for me. I'm happy to take the bus," I replied, hurriedly trying to grab my stuff and get out of the car before I gave in to my body and nuzzled up into Remi's chest to take a sniff of his intoxicating smell.

"Okay, babe." Liam came around to give me a quick one-armed hug while opening the door for Lia. "I'll see you at lunch."

"Yeah, see you." I slung my backpack back onto one shoulder and started to shut the car door. As I did, I caught Remi's brown gaze again, and he gave me a slight nod, one I would have missed if I hadn't looked up when I did. Tingles ran down my spine. God, he was so hot, and it was so unfair because I was on a dick ban until the foreseeable future. I blinked in his direction, took a deep breath, and firmly shut the door.

I had thirty more days and one summer left until Remi, Liam, and all of my friends would be headed off to college, and I would be left behind. Lonely was a familiar feeling to me and one I would be shoving down deep with the rest of my feelings. Feelings were a weakness, and I could not afford to be weak. Their leaving would keep me safe. Safe and free from weak decisions that included letting myself ponder why my body tingled when Remi looked at me.

Lunch came quicker than I would have liked because all I had packed was a cup of soup and a water bottle, which meant most of my lunch hour would be spent avoiding looking at and smelling Remi instead of eating. I considered skipping and going to the library to give my ovaries a rest, but the rumbling in my belly convinced me to go to the lunchroom to get myself some hot water for my soup. My group of friends included Liam and Lia, who I had gone to elementary school with, Eva, Carter, her boyfriend, who was included only because they were dating, Rachel, and Dee, who had joined the group in ninth grade because they had gone to a different elementary school then the rest of us had. And, of course, Remi was now in the group as well, being that he was Liam's cousin and on the football team with Liam and Carter. Lia, Eva, and Rachel were cheerleaders. Dee, short for Deidre, and I both chose to stay out of that endeavor. Dee because she had zero rhythm and me because, besides not being able to afford the uniform, I couldn't sign up for something that would keep me late after school, making me miss the bus as I had no other ride home, and I didn't want to rely on Liam.

As I walked up to our table, carefully holding my cup of soup that was now filled with piping hot water, Rachel and Dee looked up from where they were whispering excitedly over something on their phone.

"Oh my fucking God, you are never going to believe this, Shaen," they said in unison.

"Oh my fucking God, what?" I mimicked their tone, putting my backpack down by my feet and sliding onto the bench of the lunchroom table. I laughed at myself sometimes because somehow, I had managed to get all the way through high school being well-liked, in a great group of loyal friends with very little drama, and getting good grades, and yet my home life was the complete opposite. My mother barely talked to me. I lived in a small two-bedroom apartment, and I had to work at an animal shelter to be able to afford my clothes, food, and phone bill. My home self and my school self were so different. I marveled at my ability to manage them both and never have my school friends meet my home self because, honestly, I worried my home self wouldn't really fit in.

"Okay, so you know Aile from eleventh grade?" Dee asked in a hushed tone. I paused and pictured the tall, thin girl with really long black hair and nodded.

"Okay, so Shantell, who takes art with me is in Aile's class, and Shantell's brother Derrick works in a gym right near Planned Parenthood, and he swears he saw Aile and Jackson Morris leaving the building last Saturday!" Dee paused with a dramatic flair.

Rachel nodded, looking excitedly aghast at what Dee had just shared.

"Okay, well, maybe they were going to get birth control?" I offered while peeling the top of my soup cup off and mixing the noodles around with a plastic spoon, watching the little freeze-dried bits of veggie floating around the top.

"Bruh, Jackson Morris is a sophomore in college, and his dad is loaded," Rachel told me as Liam, Lia, and Remi joined us at the table, with Eva and Carter trailing right behind them, holding hands. "No way would they need to go to Planned Parenthood for birth control."

"Exactly," Dee whispered loudly. "Rumor on the street is that Jackson got Aile pregnant, her parents don't know, and he took her to take care of it before anyone would find out."

"If that's true, then Jackson needs to learn to wrap his dick up," Liam chimed in loudly while biting into his turkey sandwich.

"Who said he doesn't?" Carter said as he sat down and pulled Eva into his lap. "I bet he just knows how much better it feels bare, right baby?" Carter nipped at Eva's earlobe, and she blushed and pushed him away.

"Shut up, Carter," she told him. "No one wants to hear about how you beg to do it bare."

That had everyone laughing except me and, apparently, also Remi, who barely smiled as he sat down in front of me. I knew I was a virgin by choice, but I found the constant talk of sex, cum, and bareback riding to be tiresome because, truthfully, it sounded fun, but it was a fun I didn't allow myself to partake in. Remi, on the other hand, could have the pick of any girl he wanted. I often wondered why he didn't participate in any of the "whose dick is bigger than whose" kind of talk that our friend group often defaulted to. I took a sip of my soup, which tasted more like cheap chemicals than actual soup, and felt a knee knock into my knee, followed by a frisson of energy that ran up my leg and ended as a dull ache in my crotch. I looked up at Remi, but he was laughing over something Liam had said while unwrapping his own sandwich and seemed not to notice that he was basically playing footsie with me under the table. It didn't happen again, so I chalked it up to him being six-three and having no room for his long legs. I spent lunch finishing my soup and half listening to the chatter around me while making a list in my head of things I needed to remind my mom to do. Like, pay the rent. As a nurse, I assumed she made decent money, but between paying for rent, utilities, her car, a bare-bones health insurance plan through her hospital, and a monthly stock-up grocery run, I knew there wasn't much wiggle room. However, a rent notice had shown up on the door this morning, and I needed to make sure she left me a check to run down to the super tonight. I crunched up my now empty cup of soup and pushed it away from me slightly while I pulled out my phone.

"Hey, rent was due. Can you leave me a check to give to Bob tonight?" I texted her. She was saved as "Amy" in my phone because I couldn't bring myself to write "Mom" when she had never earned the title. I placed the phone back down in front of me, feeling a headache coming on. I rubbed my temples, hoping it wouldn't get worse before I could get home and pop a Motrin. My phone screen lit up, and I saw that my mom had left a thumbs-up on my message. That meant she would leave a check, but it also meant that she couldn't be bothered to say anything else to me. I rubbed at my head again as the stress of managing my life and her life began to weigh on me. I looked up to find Remi's eyes on me. His stare turned my insides to lava. I hated it and loved it at the same time. I had read enough romance novels to know that sex was good, forbidden for me, but it seemed so good all the same. For a brief moment, I let myself stare back, wondering what those kinds of activities would feel like with big, cuddly Remiel Taylor. Was everything about him big? Would he moan with that deep, rumbling voice of his? What would the scruff on his cheeks feel like between my legs? I squeezed said legs together as the dull ache I had felt earlier turned into a wetter, more insistent throb. Get it the fuck together, Shaen, I thought angrily to myself. When my eyes refocused and made contact with Remi's stare again, I noticed that he looked more flustered than before. There was a bit of a flush showing up on his face above his five o'clock shadow, and he seemed to be fidgeting in his seat. Awareness seemed to push all the air out of my lungs, and I took a deep breath as I wondered if cool, calm, collected Remi was as affected by me as I was by him. We played stare-down for a couple more seconds before he blinked and looked away. He then pulled his big body up from the bench, took his backpack in one hand, gathered up his garbage along with mine with his other hand, and left the table without looking at me again. It was such a simple thing, but it felt like the nicest thing someone could do for me.

2

———

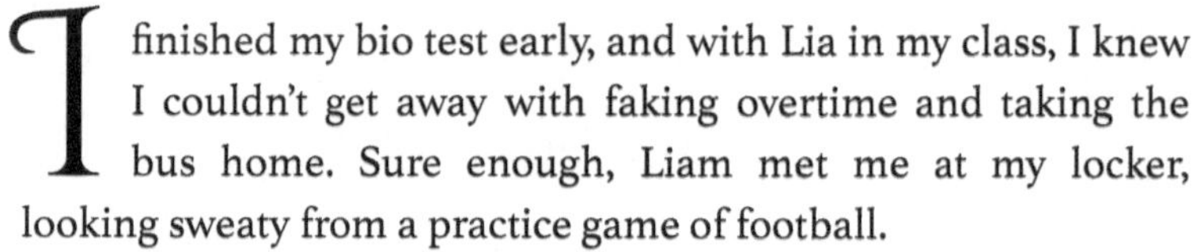

I finished my bio test early, and with Lia in my class, I knew I couldn't get away with faking overtime and taking the bus home. Sure enough, Liam met me at my locker, looking sweaty from a practice game of football.

"You okay, babe?" he asked me, taking my backpack from me and putting his hand on my shoulder. I nodded, shoving the sudden desire to cry and ask for help all the way down until I didn't feel that lump in my throat anymore. I was so tired of coming home to an empty apartment where I did my own laundry, cooked my own dinner, worked for my own money, and felt generally lonely and abandoned until I finally fell asleep to then wake up and do it all over again the next day. My mother never hugged me. We had no photos on the walls in our little apartment. She never asked me how my day was. I didn't feel cared for. I knew my friends cared about me, but to what extent if I didn't let them fully in? They knew that my mom was only thirty-three, but they didn't know how little we interacted with each other. They knew that I loved to thrift, but I wasn't sure if they realized it was because I couldn't shop new. They didn't know that I was tired of taking care of myself. That I would give anything to have a man hold my hand like Carter did with Eva or have so much sex like Liam and Lia that they were late to school because passion overtook their priorities. I wanted to wake up and feel like I mattered to someone's life. Not just as friends but truly deeply mattered to someone. I craved it so badly that it scared me because it was the opposite of the path and the plan I had laid out for myself. The plan was to finish school. Stay a virgin. Buy a car. Work as hard as possible at the shelter until I could figure out how to open my own. Find a man to love me and fuck me. In that order. And by all means possible, do not get pregnant.

"I'm good. I'm just getting a bit of a headache." I turned to close my locker and let Liam sling his arm over my shoulder while he held Lia's hand and led us both out of the school building.

A wind-blown-looking Remi was leaning on the side of the car; the front of his gray T-shirt had sweat marks on it, meaning he had come straight from practice instead of showering first.

Fuckkkkk, I groaned in my head. A clean Remi smelled delicious, but a sweaty, post-practice Remi had me seeing images in my head of me climbing up his body like a Goddamn tree.

"Remi, you drive. I wanna sit in the back with my girl," Liam shouted as we got closer to the car. Remi looked up from where he was clutching his phone in such a tight grip that I worried he would break it. He nodded wordlessly, and Liam tossed him the keys. Liam and Lia immediately started making out in the backseat, and I resigned myself to a very uncomfortable drive home.

Remi started the car and flipped the cap he was wearing from facing front to sitting backward on his head. I presumed it was so he could see better, though I wouldn't know because although I had my license, I basically had no driving hours, being that I didn't own a car yet. My ovaries did a little jump at the sight of him all sweaty, the muscles in his arms popping as he shifted the car into reverse with his backward hat on. I let out a little sigh, to which Remi shot me a look that I did not understand. Halfway through the drive, things got weirder.

"Lia, can you stop tongue fucking my cousin for just a second?" Remi suddenly said, sounding almost aggravated. We all looked at him, surprised, as we had all seen quiet Remi, determined Remi, tired Remi, and excited Remi, but we had never seen a straight-up angry Remi.

"What's up, bro?" Liam asked, pulling his face away from Lia. Remi paused and seemed to be weighing some sort of list of pros and cons out in his head as he drove rather quickly further away from the school.

"Apparently, my dad has shown up at your house," Remi finally said. We all remained quiet until Liam corrected him quietly, "Our house."

Remi grunted out an, "Our house" back at Liam. I was surprised because I had never heard Remi say anything about his personal life. Ever. We kind of had that in common. Lia and I made eye contact, and both gave each other a "holy shit" look.

"So, what do you want to do?" Liam asked Remi. Remi let out a deep breath and gripped the steering wheel as he turned onto my street.

"I cannot go home until he leaves," he said quietly. Liam looked at me. I looked back at Liam. I had never let any of my friends into my apartment. Back in ninth grade, I had told them that my mom worked the night shift, and I couldn't have people over, and the topic never came back up. I knew what Liam was silently asking me. I didn't know any details of Remi's issues with his dad. Actually, I basically didn't know anything about Remi's life before he had come here, and now, with only thirty days left till I could escape the possibility of any unnecessary scrutiny from my school friends if they ever saw my at home persona, I could hear myself saying, "Do you want to come to my place until Liam's parents get rid of your dad?"

Remi's head turned so fast, and I could see the look of raw surprise on his face.

"Oh, I wouldn't want to bother your mom..." he started.

"She has already left to go back to work," I interjected. He parked outside my building, still holding onto the steering wheel for what looked like dear life. I could practically see the cogs turning in his head as he again weighed the pros and cons of going into an apartment with a girl he had never hung out with alone without the buffer of our friends or going home to face his dad; which clearly by the tense muscles in his back and face, he did not seem to like that option at all. He sighed again and then very quietly asked, "You sure?"

I was not sure at all. I could imagine his big body taking up all the oxygen in my tiny, impersonal-looking apartment. His delicious, sweaty smell would permeate the air long after he left. I felt so anxious at the idea, but I nodded again and said, "Definitely."

He nodded back at me and looked over at Liam.

"Can you text me when the coast is clear?"

Liam rested a hand on his cousin's shoulder for a second and replied, "Hell yeah, I will, bro."

Remi looked at me again as if he wanted to say something else, but instead, he turned off the car and opened the driver's door to get out. Lia and Liam were both looking kind of surprised at how things were playing out, but I just shrugged and made a text-me motion with my fingers. They nodded, and then I also got out of the car.

My building had no elevator, and I was acutely aware of what an eyeful of my ass Remi must be getting as he took the stairs behind me to the fourth floor. He waited patiently as I tapped in the code on the door and felt super relieved that I had already thrown out the late rent notice that morning because I would have been mortified if Remi had seen it. I began to open the door and hesitated, looking over at Remi's emotionless face. I thought of Liam's big house with its white kitchen and top-of-the-line pool. Although I had never seen it, I imagined that Remi's room alone was probably the size of my whole apartment. I wasn't ashamed of how I lived as much as it was a situation that would lead to questions that I had no energy to answer.

"It's kinda small," I said quietly, looking up at Remi. He seemed so much taller and more intimidating in my building's hallway with its threadbare carpets and the faint, always-present smell of pot. Remi made my whole body tremble when he patted my shoulder.

"It's okay, Shaen. I'm just grateful I have somewhere to hang."

I didn't think I had ever heard him say my name like that before, and on hearing it, my tiny little crush bloomed uncomfortably larger in my chest. I nodded and opened the door.

I walked into the small living room that led into a smaller kitchen and waited while Remi came in behind me and then shut the door, locking it. He turned, and we looked at each other until I broke the silence and asked, "Do you like pizza? I think I'm going to order pizza."

To which he grinned and replied, "Who doesn't like pizza?"

"Carter," I retorted, and I was rewarded with a real laugh. I felt the sound of it throughout my whole body. Remi shook his head, put his backpack down, and followed me into the kitchen, where I went to pull out a pile of restaurant menus.

"Order the pizza, Shaen," he said in that low, deep tone of his. There was my name again; I physically shivered. I was so embarrassed at how my body rejected every mature thought I had about the direction I wanted my life to go in and, instead, basically melted every time this man spoke.

While we waited for Uber Eats to deliver our pizza, which Remi had insisted on covering the cost of, I sat us down in the living room which had two large chairs and a decent-sized coffee table that we used as an actual table. No couches because that took up too much unnecessary space. The rest of the room was lined with three bookshelves that I had filled with raunchy romance novels. If Remi noticed, he didn't say anything. We sat there quietly, me freaking out at how awkward the silence was and him seemingly comfortable with it until his phone buzzed, and he said, "Well, shit." I looked up as he turned the screen for me to see a text from Liam that said, "Sorry!" And then his phone rang, and Liam's name popped up as the caller.

"Coast clear yet?" was how Remi answered the phone, but instead of Liam's voice coming through the phone, an authoritative, deep voice barked.

"Remiel?!"

I watched the energy get sucked from Remi's body, and his posture seemed to collapse into the chair he was sitting on. He looked at me, and I bit my lip anxiously, waiting to see how this would play out.

"What?" Remi suddenly sounded cold and guarded.

"Remiel, I had to get another pastor to run tonight's sermon so I could drive all the way out here, and you don't respect my time enough to come meet with me?" The man on the other line sounded really pissed in a quiet, controlled way which honestly felt scarier than if he was yelling.

"I have nothing to say to you," Remi replied through clenched teeth.

His father sighed loudly into the phone.

"Your mother and I have let this little game go on long enough. You wanted to go live with your cousins? Okay, we allowed it and have left you alone in hopes that God would lead you in the right direction."

Remi visibly flinched.

"But now we find out that you withdrew yourself from the pastoral college that we registered you at for next year? Your mother is hysterical, and I am extremely concerned as to how you have been spending your time spiritually this year, son."

Remi rolled his eyes. I got a little flutter in my stomach when he did that, and I had to hold back a laugh.

"Dad, I'm not going to a Christian college to become a pastor. I told you that when I moved out. And as far as how I have been spending my time, I'll tell you what I haven't been doing—I have not been spending time between the legs of a woman who is not my wife, Dad. That's where I have not been. Go home. I have nothing more to say to you." And with that, Remi hung up the phone.

The air was thick with my unasked questions and his unspoken answers. He stared at his phone for a moment longer and then held the side button down and slid the prompt on the screen to shut it off completely.

"Do you have alcohol?" he suddenly asked. I stared at him for a moment until I unfolded myself from the oversized living room chair and went to the fridge.

"My mom has a bunch of Trulys in here," I called out to him from behind the fridge door.

"That'll work. Bring the bunch," he called back. So I did.

He was three cans in when the pizza came. I had ordered half a meat lover's pie for him and half a mushroom pie for me. We sat in my living room over my secondhand coffee table, eating oily, cheesy pizza, while he drank Trulys like they were water. At one point, Remi had asked me for my phone and my password, which I promptly gave him, and he found my music app and put on one of my playlists. The apartment, which always felt cold, clinical, and empty, was suddenly my favorite place to be because he was here, taking up all the oxygen in the best way possible. In fact, his big body made the oversized chair look small. As he finished his last slice of pizza and began to work on his fifth Truly, my phone rang. It was Liam.

"Hello?" I answered as Remi left his chair and began to crowd me in mine, trying to lean in to hear what Liam was saying. Apparently, Trulys made Remi kinda touchy-feely. I put a hand on his chest to push him back, and he ended up falling backward till he was sitting on the floor in between my legs, pawing at my phone. I was enthralled since I had never seen Remi drink this much, let alone get as playful and happy as he was acting right now.

"Shhh," I admonished him, laughing. "Stop it, I'll put it on speaker," I whispered. He nodded, finishing his drink and popping the tab on the sixth can of the night. Four more remained on the coffee table; a fifth sat half-finished in my hand.

"Shaen?"

I could hear Liam calling my name, so I quickly switched the call to speaker and said, "What's up?"

"Is Remi still there, babe? I can't reach him. His phone keeps going to voicemail, and it's been three hours since the call with his dad. And I'm sorry for that. He just took my phone. I had no say. I swear I didn't say anything about anything... Do you know where he is?" Liam was uncharacteristically babbling; his anxiety that his cousin might be mad at him was showing.

"Liam... Liam... calm down," I interrupted. "Remi is still here..."

Remi's back straightened when I said his name, and his whole body seemed to grow still. His legs that were in between mine shifted, and his knee was suddenly resting on mine. My legs felt hot, and the heat was traveling up from where his body was touching me all the way up to my face, which I swore was probably bright red now.

"He's fine. He's not mad?" I looked at Remi with that statement, and he nodded in agreement. "He's not mad," I repeated with more confidence. "At least not with you."

Liam let out a sound of relief.

"Okay, good. Shit, what a clusterfuck. His dad literally just left. Does he want me to come pick him up?"

I looked at Remi, who had now chugged his sixth drink. His gaze seemed to latch onto mine, and suddenly, his fingers were touching my ankle. So gently, I barely felt it, but the clench my body made as my underwear grew damp had my breath picking up in faster puffs as my lungs suddenly seemed desperate for air.

Remi slowly shook his head. I covered the phone with one hand and leaned my head down toward his.

"You don't want him to pick you up yet?"

He shook his head.

"I don't want him to pick me up at all."

My body stilled at his words.

"But what will you do?" I asked slowly, trying to process that a drunk Remi was half leaning on the side of the coffee table and half resting on my thigh while his hand had now started working its way gently up from my ankle to my knee in soft, warm strokes. I needed to do something, or I was going to combust or come right here in my living room.

"Remi." I tried to get his attention again. His words were muffled against my leggings when he said, "I'll shower, and I'll sleep, and he can bring me clothes tomorrow when he picks us up for school." He paused and then looked up at me with those annoyingly beautiful brown eyes of his.

"If that's okay with you, Shaen."

Fuckkkkk, my brain thought. How was I going to hide this beast of a linebacker in my apartment on the off chance my mom decides to get home before I leave for school for the first time in my entire school career? Where would he sleep? I only had my bed and my mom's bed. We didn't have any blow-up mattresses or even a couch, for that matter.

"Shaen? Am I coming to get him now?" Liam broke the silence and my racing anxious thoughts. Remi shook his head against my leg again.

"No," I breathed out quickly. "Can you bring him more clothes tomorrow when you come pick us up in the morning?"

Remi made a pumping movement in the air with his fist, which made me laugh.

"Okaaaay." Liam sounded unsure. "I'll tell my mom he's with Carter, and we'll figure it out tomorrow. Are you sure you're okay with this?"

Remi's hand was back to holding my ankle, and I gulped out, "Yeah, it's fine. Happy to help a friend."

As Liam disconnected the call, Remi mumbled, "Are we just friends, Shaen?"

3

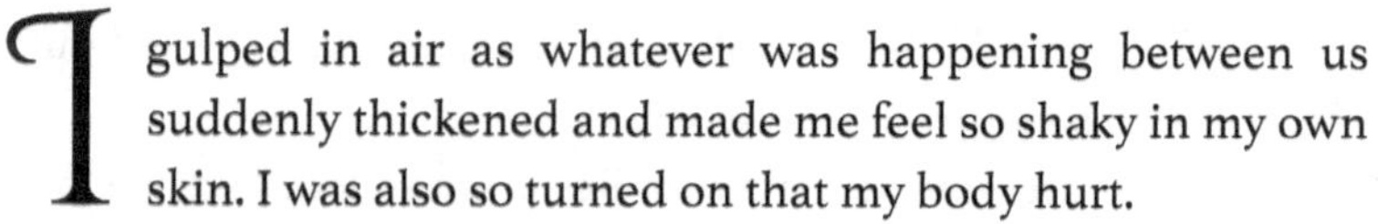

I gulped in air as whatever was happening between us suddenly thickened and made me feel so shaky in my own skin. I was also so turned on that my body hurt.

"I mean, yeah," I said shakily. "We're friends..." My voice trailed off as Remi lifted up his head to look at me.

"My dad drilled into me that believing in God was literally the only way to live. Men of the church don't drink..." He snorted at that and made a "cheers" gesture in the air with his seventh can. "I haven't drunk a lot of alcohol until now because I was told for years what a sin it was, and old habits die hard, ya know?" He locked eyes with me then, and I had to stop myself from reaching out to pat his cheek.

"He told me that I had to remain pure till marriage. That the evil people go to hell unless they're saved, and that's how we have entry to heaven..." He sighed and closed his eyes for a second. "Not only did he threaten me with hell and fiery brimstone if I had premarital sex..."

I sucked in a breath when he said *sex*.

"But also, a godly man doesn't masturbate."

My whole body went cold and felt like it had been lit on fire at the same time.

Remi looked at me with sad eyes. He didn't seem embarrassed, but I figured maybe he was too many Trulys in to notice what he had just said until he continued talking.

"For years, I would ignore the urges. I felt so ashamed when I would get hard, and of course, I never did anything about it because I wanted to please God. I would end up just coming in my sleep, and I was so horrified at not being able to control this sin." His voice trailed off, and I thought he had fallen asleep, but then he started his story back up again.

"Last year, I was going through some documents to find my social security card to apply for a summer job as a lifeguard at church camp, and I found something that I'll never be able to unsee, and it changed my whole life."

He let out a pained half breath, half sob. At this point, I finally reached out, and instead of rubbing his face like a weirdo, I took his hand. His huge hand engulfed my tiny one, and he squeezed it gently while I waited for him to keep talking.

"I found a letter from a woman, a girl really, telling my father that she had given birth to his baby instead of aborting it like he had told her to. She had a baby two months after I was born, but the kicker is that in the letter, she said she was just a teenager. When I was born, my dad was twenty-six." He whispered that last part, and I could see the pain in his eyes when he remembered becoming aware that everything he thought was true was actually a lie.

Remi covered his face with his other hand for a second, and when he removed it, I could see the tears in his eyes. As someone who shoved all tears and feelings back to where they came from, I was shocked at how vulnerable he was being with me.

"I gave it all up in that moment. How can God be real if the pastor, who all of these people are coming to listen to in order to get closer to God, had sex with a teenager while his wife was pregnant and then told her to go get an abortion? An abortion that I have heard him preach about, saying how terrible they are! I'm not allowed to jerk off, but he's off fucking teenagers?"

I had never seen Remi so angry. I took my other hand and ran it through his hair. He stilled and leaned his head back into my palm. I still said nothing.

"When I confronted him, he got so angry and told me to strengthen my relationship with the Lord, and how dare I question him? So I secretly did a DNA test on that anonymous website that does the DNA match thing..." His voice trailed off again, and his eyes closed. I waited with bated breath.

"But no matches came up. I don't know where my sister or brother is, but they're out there somewhere, and my dad abandoned them and their mom." His shoulders shuddered. "I haven't told anyone any of this. Just you, Shaen. Last year, when school was over, I just packed up my shit and told my parents that I wanted to go live with my mom's sister, who is Liam's mom." His words were starting to slur, and yet I felt so honored to know that I was the only one in the world whom he had trusted with his secret. "So here I am. I'm furious at my dad. I don't know what I believe anymore, and I'm horny as fuck because every time I try to jerk off, I can't finish because I keep hearing my dad's voice telling me to be pure and God-like, but I don't want to be pure anymore, especially when every day I see you..."

Remi's head fell to my leg, and he seemed to be fully asleep at this point. However, I was completely frozen after hearing what he had just said.

"I don't want to be pure when every day I see you..." What did that mean? I realized I had continued to absentmindedly run my fingers through his thick, wavy hair, so I stilled my hand

and looked around at the mess in my living room, trying to figure out how I was going to clean it up and get this massive man-boy into bed. And into what bed?

Suddenly, I heard Remi say, "Don't stop, that feels good."

I was confused for a second, and then it occurred to me that he was talking about my hand in his hair.

"Remi..." I whispered. "I need to clean up, and I think you should go to bed." I knew I hadn't acknowledged everything he had just confessed to me, but I needed time to process it, plus I wasn't even sure if he was fully aware of what he had just said.

He sat up, seeming unsteady.

"Can I shower first?" he asked, as if just realizing that he was still in his sweat-soaked shirt from earlier today.

I cringed as I thought about a big, muscular Remi in my small bathroom with the pink shower curtain, low water pressure, and my mother's lover's cum-filled condoms in the small garbage can. Despite that, I nodded and stood up. So did Remi. He towered over me and reached out to take my hand. I had gone so long without affectionate touch that; for a moment, I felt like my nervous system had short-circuited. I regained my composure and took him to the one bathroom in my apartment. I handed him a towel, which would definitely be too small, as he said, "I have a pair of sweatpants in my bag. Do you mind getting them for me?"

Wordlessly, I went back to the living room, rummaged through his gym bag, and found the pair of gray sweatpants he was referring to. I brought them back to the bathroom and pushed the door open. As expected, Remi had turned the water on, but what I did not expect was to see him fully naked, his cock jutting out from his body, looking angry and redder than I imagined a penis would be. But what was worse was he was staring wordlessly at the garbage, and at that moment, I realized he was looking at the condoms. Despite him being naked, I rushed into the bathroom, covering my eyes with his sweat-pants, saying desperately, "Those are not mine!"

I peeked over the sweatpants to find him standing unsteadily, looking at me. His eyes were bloodshot. His hair was a complete mess from my fingers. And the hair on his face was gradually going from a forgot-to-shave look to a full-on shadow of a beard. Yet he had never looked more beautiful to me than he did right now.

"Whose are they?" he asked, looking back at those disgusting condoms.

"My mom's," I answered. Remi seemed taken aback for a second.

"Oh," was all he responded at first. "Well, that's good," he added. "I wouldn't want to wake up to your angry boyfriend."

"You know I don't have a boyfriend." I scoffed and turned to leave the bathroom, holding out his sweatpants as I looked away from him. Remi took the sweatpants from me with one hand and turned me back around with his other hand. I stood there making eye contact with his chest because of his sheer height until he tilted my chin up with his fingers so I would look at his eyes instead. His chest was lightly coated with dark hair that then led to a happy trail that then led to, gulp... his hand was now on his big cock. I had never seen a penis in real life before, given my strict *no penis near me* rule, but I imagined his was bigger than the usual. He tugged at the head of his dick, and a bead of liquid dripped out. My eyes widened.

"I would be way too afraid to ask you this sober. And I'll be honest, I'm shocked it only took me seven girly drinks to take me down in my first time really drinking, but I've been hard for you all year, Shaen. Like every time I see you or sit near you or hear your cute little laugh, I'm in pain, Shaen. I want to come for you so bad, but the messed up devil bullshit my dad put into my head won't let me. Can you help me, Shaen?"

He all but begged; his eyes were slightly glazed over, but he still seemed to know where he was and what he was asking of me.

I couldn't breathe. Between the bathroom getting all hazy and humid from the steam filling the room and this beautiful, drunk, sad, messed-up man in my bathroom asking me to help him masturbate for the first time, I was a mess. My legs were jello, my heart was racing, and I was soaking between my legs.

"I'm sorry, Shaen, I don't know what came over me. I should have never..." Remi was starting to backtrack in his confidence. To which I absolutely shocked myself by blurting, "Like just my hand, right? Not my mouth or...?"

Did I just insinuate giving a blow job to Remiel Taylor?

I must have because his eyes darkened as he stared at me.

"I mean, for now, I'm just referring to your hand, baby," he confirmed.

He called me baby. I'm going to die, I thought. I'm going to pass out. What in the fuck is happening?

"Remi, I have to tell you something." I took a step closer, and he leaned down. "I'm a virgin."

His eyes flared with an emotion I couldn't decipher.

"My mom had me very young, and I put a no-sex ban on myself. I don't believe in God. This is not a religious thing for me, it's a safety thing. I need to get myself on my feet. With a job and my own place. I can't be worrying about when I'm ovulating and your sperm going places it shouldn't..."

I just said sperm to Remi Taylor. Motherfucker. I tried to turn my face away as my babbling got the best of me, but to my surprise, Remi didn't laugh. Instead, he kneeled down in front of me, took my face in his big, rough hands, and said, "You astonish me, Shaen Collins. And I respect your rules. Honestly, sex is the furthest thing on my mind when I can't even use my own hand to make myself come." He seemed embarrassed now. "But if it's too much to ask of you, I completely understand, and I'll even walk home."

I snickered at that because there was no way he could make it home in his current state, but I loved that he offered in an attempt to make me feel safe.

"I don't want to scare you. I just think you're so sweet and so beautiful, and I..." His voice trailed off again, my face still in his hands. He took his thumb and rubbed it gently over my lips. As he did this, my jumbled thoughts concluded that I couldn't get pregnant from kissing or having a man come in my hand, so I changed my rule to no sex, but other stuff was okay.

"I've only kissed a few people," Remi whispered, his face getting closer to mine. "So I might not be very good at it yet."

"I actually never let anyone kiss me at all," I admitted. He looked so shocked.

"I don't know how that's possible. You are so beautiful and sweet, baby."

There was that word again. For a pretty inexperienced virgin, he certainly knew how to get the blood thrumming through my veins.

"Can I kiss you now, Shaen?"

I nodded wordlessly. I was kind of enthralled that only this morning, I was bemoaning my fate looking at the two used condoms in the garbage, and now I was standing here in the same spot, nipples hard, hair wet from the steam, clit aching, being touched by a very naked and very hard Remi Taylor. I could not have made up this turn of events if I had tried.

He leaned in, closing the space between us, took my face in his hands again, and put his lips on mine. His first attempt was chaste. Dry. Just a peck from him to me. Then he came back for more. And this time, he blew my mind as he angled his mouth and ran his tongue over my lips. I shocked myself by sucking his tongue into my mouth. We completely lost ourselves in each other as we nibbled, sucked, and licked our way into each other's mouths. At one point, our teeth hit, but he just laughed and dove back in. His hands were in my hair, pulling on the brink of beautiful pain and pleasure. I could feel myself dripping down my legs, and I could feel his dick poking me in the stomach. We both came up for air, and I rested one hand on his chest and slowly brought the other hand down to meet where his hand was tugging at his dick. The moan that left this man's chest when my small hand touched the head of his cock went straight between my legs.

"I don't know what I'm doing," I admitted over the sound of the shower.

"Fuck, honestly, I don't either," Remi told me against my mouth, and we both started laughing at how ludicrous all of this was.

"I mean, I've jerked it plenty," Remi divulged. "I just get soft before I can come because all I can hear in my head is my dad telling me how mad God will be at me and how I will burn in hell for all eternity. I don't even believe in any of that stuff anymore, but it's somehow keeping a hold on me, and I know if I can break out of it once, I'll be free of it."

"Yeah, your dad does not sound like the best turn-on," I laughed. Remi half laughed, half groaned.

"That he is not," he agreed. His eyes were half-mast, and in the shitty lighting of my bathroom, his long lashes cast shadows on his cheeks. He looked up to find me watching him, and he smiled slightly.

"Do you like what you see, little Shaen?" His voice was deeper than usual, and I literally shivered. I was turning into a clichéd mess. I bit my lip, and his eyes stalked the movement.

"I always have." I paused, then revealed, "I really like the way you smell."

He faltered at that. His body shifted away from me slightly, and the hand on his dick stopped moving.

"The way I smell?"

I nodded.

"I don't know what cologne you wear, but every ride to school is torture." I let out a shy laugh, bringing my hand up to cover my mouth as the embarrassment of my confession got the best of me.

"And here I thought you couldn't stand me." Remi ran a large hand over his face, suddenly looking exhausted.

"Couldn't stand you?" I repeated. "Why?"

"Have you seen how close you sit to the door in the car? It's like you want to be as far away from me as possible." His eyes showed me a glimpse of pain, and I felt guilty as it seemed I was responsible for putting it there. I moved closer to him and looked up.

"I'm sorry it came across that way. It wasn't like that at all. It's because you make my no-sex ban very hard to follow. If I didn't plaster myself to the car door, I would have been climbing up your very big..." I ran my hands over his sweaty arms. "Very hot..." Now, my fingers were coming down his chest. "Very sexy body." I encircled his dick with both of my hands and began to move them up and down in unison. I may not have ever physically done this before, but between hearing my friends talk and all of the smut I read, I was far from prude. He groaned and leaned his head forward till it rested on the top of mine.

His cock was super hot in my hands, and as hard and stiff as it was, the skin around it was also velvety soft. I had no idea if I was doing this right because Remi had both his hands on my shoulders, squeezing really tight. His eyes were closed, his mouth hung open slightly, and he was barely making a sound. I ran my hand down the shaft and used my fingers to squeeze gently around the head that was leaking what I assumed was pre-cum. I had read about it plenty in my smutty books, but I had never come up close and personal with it until tonight. I used my thumb to gather up some of the wetness and then ran it over the slit.

"Fuuuuuck, Shaen." His voice sounded strained.

"Good?" I asked innocently.

"Are you kidding? I'm doing math problems in my head right now because otherwise, I'm going to embarrass myself." He opened his eyes and grinned at me sheepishly.

"Go ahead and embarrass yourself. I want to help you. I don't want you to stop it," I told him. He hesitated.

"What?" My hand slowed, but I kept my fingers wrapped around him.

"I kind of want to make it last because I don't know when I'll ever get to experience this again," he confessed. He was back to making eye contact with me in a way that had me saying stupid things. Like inviting him up to my house in the first place. Like letting him drink so much. Like ending up in the bathroom with all of my clothes still on, him stark naked, and his big hard penis in my hand.

"Do you plan on this being a one-and-done thing?" I teased. I laughed at myself in my head because as confident and as chill as I was pretending to be with my funny one-liners, I was actually freaking the fuck out. Remi had only been in my apartment for a few hours. He was drunk and frankly going through some shit with his dad right now. I couldn't quite explain how we had ended up here doing what we were doing, but my abandonment fears began to rise as my mind began to race. Maybe he wasn't into me the way I was into him. Maybe he just saw me as a quick opportunity for a hand job. Maybe the way his eyes looked at me, like they could see my every secret, was simply just how he looked at people. Maybe this was really just a way for him to see if he could finally come without all of his hang-ups stopping him. I began to move my hand away from his body, but he reached down, closing his own hand around mine, and held it there.

"What just happened, Shaen?" he asked softly. I tried to respond, but it felt like all of my breath was stuck in my chest, and I realized that I was beginning to have a panic attack. I used to get them a lot in middle school when my mom was never home; we lived in a worse neighborhood, and every little noise kept me up all night. Between the lack of sleep, my hormones running amok because I was beginning to go through puberty, and my developing awareness that not all was right with the world when it came to my life, I began experiencing what I had later self-diagnosed as a panic attack. I would get dizzy and would feel like I couldn't get a breath in or out of my lungs. My body would get all tight, and all I could do was wait it out until the moment would pass, and I could take a deep breath again. They had stopped coming so frequently when I got a phone in ninth grade and was able to search up panic attacks online. I learned a lot about the nervous system, mental health, and ways to support myself with things like meditation, yoga, and deep breathing. And in the event that I felt a panic attack coming on, if I could, I would put ice on my vagus nerve to help regulate myself through it. I was so mortified that this was going to happen in front of my crush thirty days before I would finally be done with the charade of having to pretend I was okay every day. I had managed to hide this side of my mental health for so long. Why was my body failing me now? And why did it have to be in front of him and his very naked body? I could feel tears prick up in my eyes, and I was horrified at the full-on breakdown my system was having. I slowly slid down the vanity until I sat on the tiles of the bathroom floor and put my head between my legs as I begged my body to let me take a full breath in. All I could manage now was a bunch of short breaths, which I knew were not helping the situation.

"Fuck," I panted out. "I'm so sorry," I managed in between breaths, angrily wiping away the tears that were forcing their way through my closed eyelids. I felt the air shift as Remi sat down in front of me, his big body crowding me in and surrounding me. His hands were on my arms, and his voice was soft in my ear.

"Tell me what to do to help you, Shaen. Do you have panic attacks often? That is what's happening, right?"

I nodded, unable to get another word out, as my brain tried to force my body to breathe, and my body refused to cooperate. Remi tilted my head up, and my arms came around my legs, under my knees in a way that looked like I was hugging myself, mainly to support my body but also to self-soothe. I tried to bend my head back down, but Remi held my chin steady in his strong hands.

"I want you to mimic my breath, baby. Can you do that for me?"

There was that word again. My heart skipped a beat, and I wasn't sure if it was from the lack of oxygen or because his words and his trying to help me affected me so much. I nodded. He began to take in long, deep breaths through his nose and then would push them out through his mouth in successions of three. At first, I couldn't get into rhythm with him, but after a minute or two, my body relaxed, and I began to copy his breathing pattern. After another minute or so, I felt the tension of the panic attack completely release, and I was able to take an even deeper breath in. My body and mind felt so tired that I just wanted to curl up on the floor and sleep. Between the embarrassment of the moment and the shame I felt that Remi just wasn't that into me, I could barely look at him.

"Don't do that," I heard him say from above me. I hid my face behind my hair and stared at my chipped nail polish.

"I can't believe you saw that," I managed.

"Shaen. Look at me." He was starting to sound more sober at this point, and his tone was so commanding that I looked up.

"Do not hide from me. What happened is not okay, but you are okay now, and I'm happy I was here to help. We are definitely going to talk about that later, but right now, I want to know what brought it on. Was it something I did? Did we move too fast? I don't want to scare you." He looked genuinely concerned.

"It's nothing you did," I told him. "I just... I just think I like you more than you like me, and I have very little, actually, I have zero experience managing this kind of dynamic." I gestured between my fully clothed body and his very naked one. "And it just overwhelmed my system. I'll be fine though. Don't worry about me." I gave him a forced smile and fought the desire to just run away to my room and wait for him to leave. Maybe I could skip the rest of school and avoid seeing him ever again. Yes, the avoidant side of my brain loved that idea. Before my thoughts could take over again, Remi laughed. I looked up at him, confused and starting to feel a little annoyed at his reaction.

"You think you like me more than I like you?" he said in between laughter. "I literally just told you that I'm afraid this will only happen one time. I'm scared I'll get to experience something amazing with you, and you won't want to do it again. I have no idea what I'm doing here, Shaen, but all I do know is tonight, when you ordered me pizza and sat by me when my dad was being an ass and told Liam not to pick me up... I've never felt more comfortable being myself in front of someone than I did tonight. I've never told anyone what my dad did or why I moved away. I've never trusted anyone with..." He gestured to his body. "I'm scared you're going to reject me, but on the off chance that you don't, I want you to know that I like you. I like you a lot, and I'm sorry that I waited till the end of the school year to tell you, but... Fuck, I'm fucking this up, aren't I?" His voice faltered, and he anxiously ran his hands through his hair, making it even messier than it had been before.

I had never heard so many words come out of Remi's mouth all at once. I had also never felt so seen by someone, cared for even. My brain did not know what to make of the situation, but my body decided for us. I got up, still feeling weak from my episode, and sat myself down in Remi's lap.

"You're not fucking this up," I told him, and then I leaned my head down and kissed him with everything I had.

"Oh fuck," he moaned, running his hands up my legs, my ass, and then gripping my waist. "I was so worried I scared you away," he admitted into my mouth. I kissed him into silence, and we sat there entangled in each other's arms, making out until the water of the shower ran cold.

When I noticed that the air was cooling, I sat up in Remi's arms and held myself up with my hands on his chest. The V of my legs was directly lined up with his groin, and the only thing separating us was my thin leggings and underwear. I swallowed thickly and said, "Why don't you take that shower, and we can move this to somewhere more comfortable?"

He raised an eyebrow at me. "And where would that be?"

"Uh... my b-bed," I stuttered out. Remi laughed and messed up my hair with his hand.

"Your bed sounds perfect." He reached a hand behind the shower curtain. "And a cold shower is just what I need right now," he added sarcastically. I snickered as I refolded the towel I had brought in for him and placed it on the back of the toilet.

"Well, whose fault is it that the water is cold?" I asked jokingly. He pretended to look hurt as he got into the shower and closed the curtain behind him.

"That would be your ass," he told me as I made my way out of the bathroom. "And your sexy mouth," he called after me. I shut the door behind me and made my way to my room. What the hell was going on? I needed time to process what was happening. I had spent so many years alone, and as much as I adored my friends, I still kept a lot of people at arm's length, so this entire experience was short-circuiting my brain. Did Remi Taylor say he likes me?

4

"What the actual fuck?" I muttered under my breath, opening my pajama drawer and pulling out a tank top set. I thought better of it and instead took out an oversized T-shirt and shorts. I didn't want to look too desperate. I did my skin care routine in the kitchen sink so I wouldn't have to go back into the bathroom, plugged my phone into the charger by my bed, cleaned up the living room, hiding all of the evidence that anything had ever happened so my mom would never know, and then went back into my room as I heard the bathroom door open.

"In here," I called, standing awkwardly by the end of my bed, which was thankfully a queen size. The person who had lived in the apartment before us had been evicted, and when we moved in, we had found this brand new, still in the plastic mattress leaning against the wall in my room. My mom had told me to keep it and said she would take the full-sized bed that we had brought with us from our previous apartment. It was one of the nicer memories that I had of her.

Remi peeked his head around the door and then made his way into my room. He was still shirtless, but he was now wearing his gray sweatpants, which left very little to the imagination. My friends Eva and Rachel were always laughing about how pornographic gray sweatpants were, and now I understood why. Remi put his bag in the corner of my room and took his phone out.

"I should probably turn this back on," he said, sounding remorseful, for what I wasn't completely sure. I offered him the other phone plug that sat on my dresser, and Remi made short work of turning his phone on and plugging it in. It was now buzzing with messages that we both tried to ignore.

"Sooooo," he said. I looked at him, feeling shy again. "Bedtime?" He winked at me, and I felt his wink all over my body.

"Great idea." I hurried over to pull the blanket back, and then I went back over to my bedroom door to lock it.

"My mom never comes in here, but just in case..." I said in explanation. He looked like he wanted to say something, but he stayed quiet. I turned off the light but left the fan on and then climbed into bed. I couldn't see him so well in the dark, but I could hear his breathing as he got into my bed, and I was suddenly hot all over again. I felt his leg on my leg and his arm touching my arm as we both lay down on our backs and stayed in awkward silence until I felt his head turn toward me, and he asked, "Can I kiss you again, Shaen?"

The way my name sounded with his deep tone made my loins clench. Do people say loins anymore? My brain panicked as I nodded and then realized he couldn't see me.

"Y-yes. Yes. Kiss me, Remi," I told him, feeling a little bit breathless. With a groan, he rolled over so his arms were on either side of my head, caging me in, and his body was raised over me. I could detect the heat of him all over me. He leaned down growing closer to me. I could feel his breath on my lips and my chin, but he just stayed like that for a few seconds till I felt like I had to break free because the anticipation was too much.

"Fucking do it, Remi," I breathed out, and he made a cross between a moan and a laugh again and then slammed his mouth onto mine.

I felt like I could breathe again. How had I ever lived without his body over mine, his tongue in my mouth, or his fingers gripping the sides of my hips? I didn't know. I could feel his erection, insistent, against my leg. I shifted.

"Ignore him. He's stupid," Remi muttered against my mouth. I laughed.

"What if I don't want to ignore him?"

Remi's whole body stilled above me.

I took advantage of the situation and slid my hand past the waistband of his very scandalous gray sweatpants. He wasn't wearing any underwear. Oh, Remi, you're so hot, my brain thought.

"Thank you," he said above me. Fuck, I was saying my thoughts again.

"For the record, you make me so hard, Shaen. I think you're so sexy. Your body. Your face. These boobs..." He groaned, and his body jerked above me as my hand closed over his shaft.

"You were saying..." I teased.

"You're so hot," he panted. "I am so attracted to you."

I began to move my hand in earnest, up and down, hoping that I was applying enough pressure. Apparently, I wasn't because Remi said, "Squeeze it tighter, you won't break it."

That made both of us laugh, yet as I squeezed his dick tighter, he wasn't laughing anymore.

"Oh f-fuck, that's good, baby. Yeah, just like that. Squeeze it. Oh my God, that's so good," he stuttered out. If I weren't so turned on, I would have laughed at how easy it was to turn big, strong, football player Remi into a pile of mush. He was breathing heavily in my ear; half his body was on me, and half he was holding up with one arm so he didn't squash me. I imagined that couldn't be so comfortable, so I half sat up and gently pushed him over so he was lying on his back. Then I reached over to my night table, where I kept a tissue box, and I took a few tissues with me as I crawled back to climb over him. My thighs were on either side of his, and his cock was jutting out proudly from his body.

"I don't think I have ever been this hard," he admitted when he saw me looking at it. I felt some bravery come over me, and I said softly, "Do you think you'll be able to come for me?" I cupped his balls with one hand, and with my other hand, I ran my pointer finger over his slit where pre-cum was now leaking in earnest.

"Oh J-Jesus..." he moaned, his hips lifting off the bed in their desire to seek more pressure from my hand.

"Is that a yes?" I teased as I began to jack his cock in rhythm with his hips.

"Y-yessss. Yes, baby, I'm going to come for you." His eyes were squeezed shut, and he almost looked like he was in pain. I was enthralled with how Remi's body was reacting to me. He had sweat beading on his lightly-haired chest, and the muscles in his arms were flexing as he opened and closed his fists on my sheets. His lips looked puffy from kissing me, and his wavy hair was an absolute wreck, yet it turned me on so much. I could feel my wetness leaking down my thighs, and I worried that I was leaving a stain on his sweatpants that were now pulled halfway down his legs.

"Oh God, tighter, tighter," he begged. His eyes flew open and met mine. At this point, I knew he was sober, but his eyes looked wild and kind of unfocused again. My newfound ability to disarm this man made me feel all sorts of warm feelings within my chest, making the emotionally numb side of me feel slightly panicked, but I pushed the whole mess away and chose to stay focused on Remi's heavy breathing, the stuttering movements of his hips, the moans coming out of his mouth, and the way his glassy eyes were fixed on mine.

"I'm gonna come. I'm gonna come," he chanted, his eyes widening in what could only be described as awe. I knew this moment meant a lot for him because not only was it a big "fuck-you" to the trauma religion had given him, but I also knew that other than what happened in his sleep, he had never been able to finish on his own. I didn't know it was possible, but his dick started to feel thicker and harder in my hand, and his movements started to feel more erratic. His breathing grew louder, and one of his hands snaked around us to hold tightly onto my hips, where I found myself grinding against his thigh. I hadn't even realized I was doing that. His fingers were gripping so tight that I was going to have a bruise, I thought. And something about that felt good and right. I paused for a second and did what I had read someone do in a book. I spit into my palm and then put my hand back on his dick, so now everything was warm and wet.

"Oh my God, Shaen. I'm coming, I'm coming for you, baby!" He half shouted; half sobbed. I was enthralled. I kept jacking him as thick ropes of cum seemed to burst from his cock and got all over my hand, some on my arm, and some ended up on his stomach. I stopped moving my hand once his dick started to soften. With his chest heaving like he had just run a marathon, he shuddered as I ran my fingers through the cum that was pooled on his stomach.

"Was that as good as you thought it would be?" I asked, taking a tissue and gently cleaning us both up. He nodded frantically, seemingly still at a loss for words. I stilled in his arms and grinned.

"I'm weirdly excited for you," I admitted to him. The grip he had on my hip tightened.

"You really don't know what that meant to me," were the first words he could manage as his breathing and heart rate came back to normal.

"But I want you to keep doing that." He gestured to the lower half of my body.

"Doing what?" I tried to shift my hips off of him, but he held me down so that my pussy, only covered by my boy shorts pajama bottoms, was directly on his thick hard thigh.

"You were rubbing on me. You're getting me all wet." He grinned.

"Oh my God, that's so embarrassing." I tried to scramble off him again, but I was no match for how strong he was, and his arms kept me right where he wanted me.

"Embarrassing, Shaen? It's so fucking hot I'm getting hard again," he basically growled in my ear. He sat us up now, and with his back against the headboard of my bed, he was holding my body directly over his now bare thigh. I looked down, and he was, in fact, getting hard again.

"I didn't know you could recover that fast," I told him, wide-eyed.

"I didn't either." He laughed, making fun of himself. "But don't change the subject. I want you to come on me. Do you touch yourself, baby?" He was practically whispering now, his breath making the skin on my neck and chest so sensitive. I met his eyes, and I nodded.

"Goddamn that's so hot. Do you use your fingers, or do you have any toys?" he asked, and I could almost laugh at how curious he was.

"Usually just my fingers, but Lia bought me a vibrator as a joke for my birthday, so sometimes I use that," I admitted. I couldn't feel shy when this man was looking at me like I was the sun, moon, and stars.

"I want to watch you touch yourself next time, but tonight I want you to keep rubbing your pussy on me like you were before, and I will hold you while you do it." He was panting now as my hips started to move achingly slow, my clit felt so swollen, and my lips felt so wet.

"Will there be a next time?" I asked as I began to move faster now.

"There better be. I might die if I can't touch you again after this." He said this so dramatically that I laughed as I moaned.

"There it is, baby, take what you need. I can't wait to watch you come." His words spurred me on. Remi's hands on my hips were so tight. His chest was rubbing against my sensitive nipples. I was so close to the precipice but couldn't quite get there. One of his hands moved to my ass, and I moaned again loudly.

"What do you need?" he asked, out of breath again. "Let me help you."

I might die of embarrassment, but I admitted, "Can you talk to me?"

His hand that was on my ass was moving up to my breast, and as he found his way under my big T-shirt, he said, "Like dirty talk?"

I bit my bottom lip, feeling my cheeks heat up, and I stopped grinding on him.

"Don't get shy on me now," he admonished. "Not with my cum drying in your hand and yours all over my thigh." He laughed at how self-conscious I got from him saying that. He leaned in to kiss me.

"You're so funny 'cause you get so shy, but you also want me to say dirty, dirty things to you."

I shrugged. "I'm a conundrum," I joked.

"You really are," he agreed. His hand closed around my breast, and his thumb began to rub my nipple. "I am brand new to this, baby, so we're going to have to learn together. If you don't like something, please tell me."

I nodded. "I like that."

He laughed and bent down to lick my nipple through my T-shirt.

"This?" He looked up at me, my cotton-covered nipple now in his mouth.

"Y-yes." My hips started to move again. I was on fire. Why did I have a penis ban again? At the moment, I genuinely couldn't remember. My nipple popped out of his mouth, and he leaned in so his mouth was by my ear.

"You are so sexy when you make those noises for me, Shaen. You make my cock so hard. I came so hard for you I thought I was going to pass out."

That made me giggle, but I quickly stopped when he rasped into my ear, "Are you gonna be a good girl and come on my leg, baby?"

The praise did it for me. I combusted; my body got all tight and achy, my clit felt so sensitive, and my pussy felt so empty as it contracted through the waves of what was most definitely the strongest orgasm I had ever had. And all just from rubbing myself on his leg.

"Oh yeah, baby, let it out, let me hear you, what a good girl," Remi was saying encouragingly in my ear. His hand was back on my breast, and I was moaning and writhing in his arms. Slowly, the blood rushed back to my brain, and I came down from the euphoria of the moment. I tried to climb off of him, but he held me against his chest as he laid down on his pillow, taking me with him and pulling the blanket over both of us.

"So my girl has a praise kink, huh?" He laughed, his voice sounding husky. I hit his chest. "Hey, stop it."

He just laughed again. "Oh, I like knowing that. Trust me. That was so hot." He yawned, and his eyes closed, as did mine, and I snuggled into his chest.

Was I his girl? The thought flitted through my brain as I fell asleep.

5

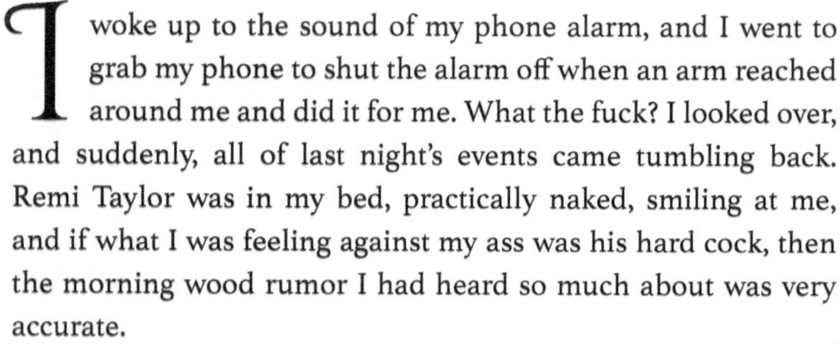

I woke up to the sound of my phone alarm, and I went to grab my phone to shut the alarm off when an arm reached around me and did it for me. What the fuck? I looked over, and suddenly, all of last night's events came tumbling back. Remi Taylor was in my bed, practically naked, smiling at me, and if what I was feeling against my ass was his hard cock, then the morning wood rumor I had heard so much about was very accurate.

"Good morning." He leaned down and kissed the top of my head.

"Um." Did I have morning breath? Was my hair a mess? What did I look like? Oh my God, I felt the panic rise in me, and it felt paralyzing not knowing what I was supposed to do next.

"Is your mom home?" he whispered.

"Not yet. She finishes work around now, but her hospital is like an hour away, so I'm always gone before she gets back," I told him, throwing the blanket off me and sitting up to get ready for school.

"Okay, good, so we can be as loud as we want then." He snaked his arm around me and pulled me back against his chest.

"Remi!" I shrieked. "We have school. Let go." But I was laughing as he tickled my sides and kissed his way down my face.

"I'll be quick," he said as he nipped along my chin. He filled his hands with my ass, and I knew my pajama bottoms had ridden up as I slept, so it was basically handfuls of bare skin.

"Fuckkkkk," he moaned out as he made my ass jiggle. "I swear your ass is just perfection."

I rolled my eyes.

"Hey, can you wear that little green skirt you wore to one of my games? Goddamn, your butt looked fine in it." He was back to kissing his way down my face and then began sucking on my neck.

"I wore that in February," I told him, feeling surprised that he remembered such a small detail like what I had worn months ago.

"Oh. I know. It's been burnt in my memory ever since," he told me as he lifted my T-shirt and put his mouth on my nipple. This time directly on my skin.

"R-Remi. We do not have time. Liam is going to be here in thirty minutes," I groaned out.

"How long do you need to get ready?" My nipple slipped out of his mouth, and I saw how shiny he had made it.

"Like all thirty minutes," I admitted.

"Well, I can't argue with that." He rolled over and slapped my butt as he did. "Let's go to school. We'll pick this up another time." He winked at me. I gestured to his obvious hard-on and said, "Sorry."

He laughed as he stretched, then unplugged his phone.

"Babe, I am so used to this, just ignore him." Then he unlocked the door and went to the bathroom, where I heard the shower start up.

I texted Liam to remind him to bring clothes up for Remi,

and then I went to my closet, taking out the flared, short green skirt that Remi apparently liked so much and a white short-sleeved scoop-neck T-shirt that said: "I'm not shy, I just don't like you" on the front in black letters. I did my skin care routine in the kitchen again and went back to my room to do my makeup. Remi walked in with a towel around his waist and his hair all wet as I was finishing up my hair.

"Fuck, babe, you look so hot." He literally stopped in his tracks to look at me. I giggled and did a little spin.

"You like?"

"Very much," he said, sounding really serious. My phone buzzed, and I saw it was Liam saying he was at the front door.

"Liam is here. Act normal," I warned him quietly and went to open the front door. I was so anxious about what was happening with Remi that I didn't have any room left to panic that Liam would now be seeing my apartment for the first time too. As I opened the door, Liam rushed in, looking overly concerned and holding a shopping bag which I assumed contained Remi's clothing. He gave me a quick hug and then said, "Shaen, the drama is bad. His dad threatened my dad. My mom was literally livid... where is he?" Liam tried to catch me up quickly, yet his concern turned to shock when he saw Remi coming out of my room clad in only a blue towel.

"Da fuck?" He looked at Remi and then looked back at me. "Shaen Collins, is that a motherfucking hickey on your neck?!"

Was it? I didn't know. I didn't answer. Which probably made it worse.

"Oh my God, you whores!" Liam seemed more excited than either of us at this turn of events. "Remi, you can't be sucking on a girl's neck like that. Where are your manners?" Liam scolded his cousin while laughing. Remi actually looked kind of ashamed of himself as Liam snapped a photo on his phone and showed me that I did, in fact, have a large bruise on the side of my neck.

"Oh fuck." I rushed back to my makeup bag and took out a color corrector and concealer. "Come here and help me. I can't see it well enough to cover it," I called out to the boys in my living room. Remi had gone into the bathroom to get dressed, so Liam came over and helped me dab on the product until he said it wasn't noticeable anymore.

"Are we gonna talk about this, Shay Shay?" Liam asked as I grabbed my bag, turned off my light, and went into the kitchen to make all of us peanut butter and jelly sandwiches.

"Talk about what?" I asked innocently, licking peanut butter off my fingers as I put each of our sandwiches on a paper plate.

"Uh, that you fucked my cousin!" Liam looked at me like I was stupid.

"I didn't fuck her," Remi corrected as he left the bathroom wearing a black T-shirt and washed-out jeans. Liam scowled at me, trying to figure out if we were lying, and then looked over at his cousin.

"Okay, we do not have the motherfucking time for this, let's go to the car. Lia had a doctor's appointment, so you're up front, big guy. We have to leave now if we're gonna make it in time." Liam handed Remi his breakfast and took a big bite out of his own sandwich as he rushed us out the door like a mother hen. I turned around to lock the door and followed the boys down the four flights of stairs to where Liam's car was parked. Remi was silent the entire time, and I was starting to feel super weird about the whole thing. Remi opened the car door for me and waited till I was inside to shut it. Then he got into the front seat as Liam started the car.

"Best breakfast ever, babe," Liam thanked me around a big bite of bread and Jiffy. The *babe* sounded different coming from him than it did when I heard it from Remi. Liam had been my best friend for so long, and I had never felt anything but platonic feelings for him, while Remi sent my whole system into overdrive.

"Did you guys study for the lit test?" Liam asked as he stopped at a red light. I knew exactly what he was doing. He was biding his time, but I knew the minute he had me alone, he would be grilling me for details. There was no way he was going to let it go this easy.

"Nope," I heard Remi's deep voice respond. Liam looked at me in the rearview mirror and laughed.

"I'll be fine. It's just an essay. I've never had an issue with essays," I said, giving Liam a "shut the fuck up" look with my eyes. He winked and looked back at the road as the light turned green. I stared out the window, taking in the scenery as I tried to calm myself down from all the anxious thoughts that were filling me. I hadn't processed anything that had happened since last night, and I was starting to really freak out. As if Remi could hear the noise in my head, I suddenly felt his hand on me. He had reached behind him through the space between his seat and the door, and his fingers were making small circles on my ankle. I let out a shuddering breath. He wasn't looking at me. He had barely said a word since we got into the car, but I had never felt more seen in my life.

So this is what not feeling alone feels like.

THE BELL WAS RINGING JUST as we ran into school, so with some hurried goodbyes and some serious eye contact from Remi, we split ways and went to our different classes. I saw the boys when we sat for our literature test, but I didn't see them again until lunch. When I walked into the lunchroom, I saw that Lia was back from her doctor's appointment, and she was sitting next to

Liam, eating fries off of his plate. Everyone had a burger except Carter, who was opening up his container of weighed-out chicken and broccoli. It looked like I had missed a "what do you want to eat" message in the group chat. Fuck me. I sat next to Rachel, who had her head down and was resting her eyes, as she called it, but it was really a full-on nap that she tended to take during lunch.

"Scoot over." Remi was standing next to me, holding two burgers. I moved over quickly, causing Rachel to jolt out of her nap, but she just laid her head down again and went back to sleep. Remi sat down next to me, and I was uncomfortably aware of how warm he was with his side pressed to my side and his thigh touching mine. Liam turned and gave me a look as the rest of the table paused to stare. Remi never sat next to me, let alone this close. I could feel my cheeks heating up, and I avoided looking at anyone for too long.

"What?" I heard Remi ask when Eva and Dee wouldn't stop looking at us.

"Absolutely nothing," Eva replied around a bite of fries. But she was grinning, and Dee was making kissing faces at us.

"You can all go fuck yourselves," I announced. "I don't know what Liam has said to you, but it is false."

"Mm-hmm," Lia mumbled around a mouthful of milkshake.

"You wanna swallow and say that again? Being that you're so good at that, it shouldn't be too hard for you," I snapped, but I had a smile on my face. I heard and felt Remi let out a laugh next to me.

"Oh damn." Carter laughed as well and leaned over the table to high-five me.

"Yeah, yeah, fuck off." Lia took another big sip of her drink and swallowed in an overly exaggerated way. I had managed to divert the group's attention for now, and I felt relieved as I unzipped my bag to pull out my water bottle because, in the chaos of the morning, I had forgotten to pack myself lunch. It was then that Remi pushed one of the burgers in front of him over to me. I looked up at him, and he shrugged, a small smile playing on his lips.

"Lia said she didn't see an order from you, so I got what I thought you'd like," he told me, talking quietly.

"That is so nice. You didn't have to do that," I told him as I unwrapped the burger and bit into it because I was so famished. "How much do I owe you?"

He stared at me for a moment and then took a bite of his burger without answering. When did Remi eating become hot, I wondered, watching his throat and Adam's apple move as he chewed. Fuck me, I was in trouble. I didn't join the conversation but rather let it all float over me as I ate. I heard Remi joking around with some of the team that passed by our table and stopped to hype him up for the game they were playing tonight. The official season had ended, but the school had all the sports teams keep playing until the school year was over. Liam and Lia were talking quietly to each other, and he had his arm around her, holding her back to his front. Eva and Carter had left lunch early to study for Carter's math final. Carter was in eleventh grade, while Eva would be graduating with the rest of us. Rachel was still sleeping, and Dee had gone over to another table to talk to a girl she thought was cute. I was feeling kind of hot due to being stuck between a sleeping Rachel and a very warm Remi. I also noticed that I felt well-rested, which I usually never felt. I was sitting in a bit of a blissful state from the intensity of the orgasm I had last night, and I just felt sort of... happy. Happiness scared me because it always felt like it was something that could be taken away from me at any moment, but for now, I let myself have it. I would deal with shoving the feelings back down later. As I finished my burger, I felt Remi shift in his seat, and I knew he had to be looking down at me.

"Was it good?" I heard him ask.

"Was what good?" I responded without looking at him.

"Your burger? What else would I be asking about?"

I heard the grin in his voice, and I shrugged, trying not to let my thoughts go to the fact that I now knew what he sounded like when he came.

"Yes, it was good. Thank you. I still need to pay you back," I told him as I put my water bottle back in my backpack.

"You don't owe me anything," he responded, his jaw flexing as he drank his electrolyte water. He grabbed my garbage together with his again and got up from the table.

"See you later, baby," he said so quietly as he walked off that I almost thought I had imagined it.

6

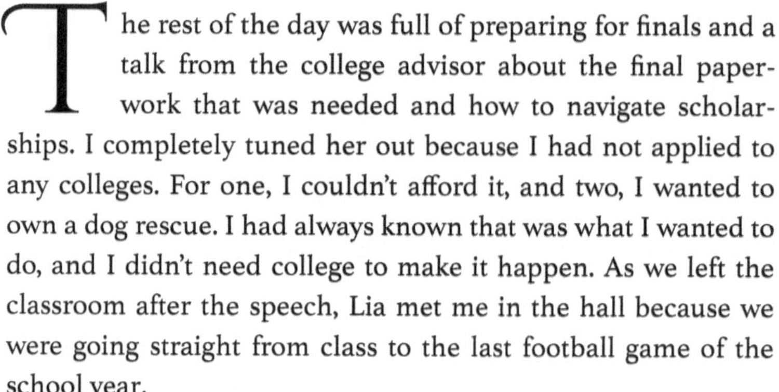

The rest of the day was full of preparing for finals and a talk from the college advisor about the final paperwork that was needed and how to navigate scholarships. I completely tuned her out because I had not applied to any colleges. For one, I couldn't afford it, and two, I wanted to own a dog rescue. I had always known that was what I wanted to do, and I didn't need college to make it happen. As we left the classroom after the speech, Lia met me in the hall because we were going straight from class to the last football game of the school year.

"Oh my God, your outfit is so damn cute today. I didn't get to see it fully yet. Let me look. Girl, your boobs look bangin' in this shirt." Lia was a master of giving compliments and a master at talking in general.

"They do look bangin', Collins," A guy named Travis, who was friendly with Carter, called out as he passed us in the hallway.

"I didn't ask," I called back, and everyone around us laughed as we made our way to our lockers.

"I bet Remi is gonna play better with you in the stands tonight." Lia poked me in the ribs.

"Stop. You are all being crazy. What did Liam tell you?" I shoved my books back in my locker, touched up my makeup in my pocket-sized mirror, and ran a brush through my hair.

"He said that you had a hickey on your neck, that Remi never came home last night, and when he came to pick you two up, Remi was in your room basically naked," Lia told me as she pulled Liam's jersey over her shirt in preparation for the game.

"And that means that..." I encouraged her to finish her train of thought.

"That y'all finally fucked." Lia sounded very confident in the conclusion of her story. "Is he big? Is he a good kisser? How big was he? Is it a solid ten incher? Oh my God, I bet he's huge."

"Lia, good lord girl, stop talking." I shoved her gently in the shoulder as we walked toward the football field. "First of all, do you know that even when aroused, the average vagina is only like four inches deep? What the actual fuck would a girl do with a ten-inch penis?" I was being louder than necessary, and although I surmised that Remi had to be larger than the norm, I seriously found all of the eleven-inch dicks in the dirty novels I read to be so unrealistic. "Second of all, that is your boyfriend's cousin's dick that you are salivating over. Keep it in your pants!" We both burst out laughing. "And lastly, I already told you I'm not gonna have sex with someone until I'm good and ready, so no, we didn't fuck."

"Okay, but you definitely did something because that hickey didn't get there on its own." She gave me a long look, but I didn't answer as I was saved when we entered the noisy football field and began looking for the seats that Liam had saved for us.

Usually, at the football games that I attended, I tried my hardest not to look anywhere in Remi's direction because I had been doing my *don't let Remi turn you on* thing. But now that I actually knew what it felt like to let Remi turn me on, I couldn't keep my eyes off of him. There were no cheerleaders at tonight's game, so all of my friends were sitting with us. Eva was to the right of me, Rachel and Dee were sitting to the left of Lia. Being that the school year was almost over and it was the last game of the year, all of the seats were full because the whole town came to support the seniors on the team who were graduating and moving on. I was aware that Remi was an offensive lineman, but I really knew very little about football as a whole. So I just cheered and shrieked with Lia every time the boys did anything that we thought was good. This game started to feel different as soon as I noticed that Remi kept looking at me as much as I was looking at him. It was making me feel things, which was throwing me off because I was usually very good at keeping all of my feelings completely bottled up.

"I don't know what is going on between you and Mr. McHotness, but he is eye fucking the shit out of you, Shaen," Dee said loudly.

"Yeah, he is. It's even making *me* wet," Rachel chimed in as she pulled some mini bottles of vodka out of her bag and started pouring shots into our cups of Sprite. I usually said no to her offers of alcohol, but tonight, I was fully in for getting a little tipsy and shutting off all of the noise in my brain. As I sipped on my now vodka soda, Lia noticed two tenth graders in front of us who were screaming out Remi's name in between every play and were waving around a sign.

"What does that say?" she asked when she noticed that Liam was laughing hysterically on the sidelines and was playfully punching a very embarrassed-looking Remi. The girls turned their sign around so the rest of us could see it. The sign said: "Remi, put your babies in us." The crowd around us roared with laughter as the two girls got escorted out by our very angry assistant principal. Eva leaned over and shouted, "I'm pretty sure the only person that Remi wants to put his babies into is you, Shaen."

My soda went down the wrong pipe, and Lia had to pound me on the back while I coughed it back out.

"Do you all know something I don't?" I asked when I could finally breathe again.

"Honey, that boy has been half in love with you since the start of the school year. I'm surprised it took him this long to make a move," Eva shouted over all of the noise from the game. I scoffed. "No, he isn't. And he didn't make a move."

"You have a hickey on your neck," Rachel pointed out, leaning over Lia and pouring more vodka into my cup.

"Who said it's from him?" I took a big gulp of my drink, which was now more vodka than soda.

"I certainly hope it's from him," Dee said. "That boy looks like he could rock your world."

"You're gay, Dee," I pointed out, reminding her of the obvious.

"All the more reason to trust me." Dee knocked back a shot and grinned. "I'm a fan of women, and even I can tell that Remi Taylor has a magical penis."

Lia snorted and put my cup back up to my lips.

"Keep drinking, girl. There is an after-party tonight, and at this rate, you will need to be pretty drunk to handle all of our nosey friends."

So I did just that.

By the time the game was over and the boys had won, my friends and I were thoroughly inebriated. Lia and I were holding hands as we sang "We Are the Champions" at the top of our lungs, and Dee had Rachel on her back as we made our way to the car. After agreeing to meet at the after-party being held at the quarterback's house, Eva and Carter took Dee in Eva's car, and Lia, Rachel, and I piled into the back of the green jeep. Liam and Remi were in the front. Remi's hair was wet, which meant he had showered after the game. He was wearing a loose black tank top and a pair of workout pants. Liam leaned over to give Lia a kiss.

"Holy shit, you smell like a bar." He grimaced. "You taste like one too."

"We're all drunk. It was a great game, and we kept drinking every time you got a home run," Rachel explained. Remi let out a short laugh.

"Rachel, you're a cheerleader, and you still don't know that saying home run is definitely referring to the wrong sport?"

Rachel just shrugged and went back to braiding Lia's hair. Remi looked at me briefly but didn't say anything. I didn't like this unknown territory that we were in. Everyone else seemed to think he was madly in love with me and wouldn't stop rubbing the hickey in my face, yet the man in question seemed to be pretty chill around me even though not even twenty-four hours ago he had come all over my hand. I didn't need a marriage proposal, I just wanted to know what was up with us.

"Hun, put on Justin Bieber," Lia told Liam as she took his jersey off and then knotted up the shirt underneath, turning her school-appropriate shirt into a cute midriff look.

"I am not listening to Justin Bieber right now, babe," Liam moaned. "Did you not see the game we just played? We have testosterone oozing out of us. It will be ruined if I have to listen to Justin Bieber."

Remi laughed as he half turned to me and asked, "Do you want to listen to the Beebs, Shaen?"

I nodded excitedly and bounced in my seat. Alcohol always made me less inhibited, and with the amount I had drank tonight, I was as chill and as playful as I ever would be.

"Put it on, Liam," Remi told his cousin.

"Fuck my life," Liam grumbled, but he knew he had lost the

fight and handed his phone over to Lia, who immediately put on the song "Baby," and exactly as Liam feared, the three of us screamed and sang along to it the entire way to the party.

When we got there, Liam parked down the street since the driveway and front of the house were already packed with cars. Remi got out and opened my door. I basically fell out and started laughing hysterically as Remi had to put his hand on my arm to steady me.

"How much did you drink, Shaen?" I heard his voice whisper in my ear, and I got chills up and down my body as I reacted to his nearness, his smell, and the warmth of his hand on my arm.

"Just a bit." I hiccuped as I finally stopped laughing and moved out of the way for Lia to get out of the car too.

"Okay. Well, I won't be drinking because I'm the DD tonight, so I'll be able to keep an eye on you," he told me. He was walking next to me as we all made our way toward the back of the house where the party was happening.

"Oh my God, you don't have to look out for me, Remi." I grinned up at him. Everything was looking a tad bright, and I felt like I was talking a bit too loud, but I also loved the lack of my anxious thoughts and overthinking in general when I drank.

"Yes, I do." He laughed like I was missing something and kept a gentle hold on my arm, guiding me toward the back patio where music was already blaring, and people were gathered.

Eva and Carter were there and were already dancing. Dee was playing poker with a bunch of the football team. Lia and Liam went to make us more drinks, and Rachel had disappeared into the house, leaving Remi and me to find a place for all of us to sit. We found a spot on the porch with a bunch of lounge chairs and a hanging egg chair, which I immediately jumped into and then instantly regretted because the movement started to make me dizzy. I crawled back out of the chair and took the drink that Lia had brought and was holding out for me. Remi watched me but didn't say anything as I downed it and then wiped my mouth on the back of my hand.

"What was that?" I made a face because it had been incredibly sour.

"That was an amaretto sour, my darling." Liam came up the steps of the porch carrying three more and a water for Remi.

"Ew," I said as I swiped Remi's water and took a mouthful to chase the drink down with.

"You just have a little baby girl taste in drinks, Shaen. Welcome to adulthood," Liam retorted jokingly, chugging two of the drinks he held. "Okay, maybe I was a little heavy-handed with the lemon juice," he said, making a face.

"Welcome to adulthood, bitch," Remi said as he drank his water, teasing his cousin.

"Oh burn," Lia laughed, planting a kiss on Liam's face. "It's okay, baby, I liked it."

"Oh yeah, show me how much," Liam said, walking Lia backward and holding onto her waist while continuing to drink his admittedly too-sour drink with his other hand.

"Barf. Get a room, you two." Dee announced her arrival holding a drink of her own with her other arm wrapped around a tall girl who I was positive did not go to our school. "Guys, this is Kerri. Kerri, these are my friends."

Kerri waved, and we all said hi. Liam asked if she wanted a drink, and we all cracked up because he really wasn't that good at making them.

I could feel the amaretto making its way through my veins, or at least that's what it felt like, and I heard a song that I really liked come on.

"We should dance!" I announced.

"Oh man, I was hoping you wouldn't say that," Dee lamented, being that she looked like a baby horse who had no balance when she tried to dance. Kerri laughed and told Dee that she would lead and Dee could follow. We all made our way down to the makeshift dance floor, which was really the area around the pool, and as a group, we began to move to the beat. This included jumping up and down in one place and singing in each other's faces, all holding hands and prancing around in a circle, drinking more and spilling them on our shirts. Then, as the rhythm changed, each of my friends broke off into couples and began to grind up on each other. This left Remi and I standing there surrounded by our friends but also alone for the first time tonight. I was unsure of what to do with my body, but then he inched closer to me and put my hands around his waist.

"Oh, so it's like that, huh?" I was feeling very brave with all this alcohol running through me. He just nodded and said, "Shut up and dance with me, Shaen."

It turned out that Remi could really dance. I know they definitely did not teach him these moves at his Christian school, so I assumed he was just a natural at moving his muscular body. The lights were flashing, the music was blaring, the dancers were really pumping to the beat by now, and we were crowded in close together by how many people were around us.

"Three, six, nine, damn you fine," I screamed and then got really low to the ground as the whole group shouted in unison, "Get low, get low, get low, get low!" As I stood back up, I ground my butt up against Remi's crotch, and I felt a tingle of pride go through my body when I found him hard. I turned around and began to dance and rub up on him while holding onto his shoulders. I smirked up at him. "Looks like little Remi wants to play." Remi sighed and shrugged, completely unashamed. "First of all, he is not little. As you well know." I blushed.

"And I told you last night that he always wants to play when you're around. And to be honest, I would have to be absolutely gay not to have a hard-on right now while watching your ass shake in that little skirt."

"It's true," a guy from our science class leaned over and agreed with Remi. "Your ass is looking real fine tonight, Shaen."

"Shut the fuck up, Miller." Remi's voice had a lighthearted tone to it, but I saw his jaw clench as he waited for Jed Miller to get the point and go back to dancing with his friends. When Miller just winked in response and then left us alone, Remi glanced back down at me and sighed once more.

"Sorry for bringing it up, Dad. Sheesh." I felt like he was disappointed with me somehow. It was almost like he was the mature, responsible one, and I was out here getting drunk and embarrassing him. Not that it mattered because I still had no idea what I meant to him or what any of this meant altogether. With twenty-nine days to go, it probably wasn't worth trying to figure out anyway. As I felt the usual anxious thoughts creeping back in, I decided that was my cue to go get another drink.

"I'll be right back," I told Remi and darted off to find some vodka shots. They were easy and got me feeling good real quick. However, after finding myself two shots, I never did make it back to the dance floor. Instead, I had gotten looped in with a group of girls who were baking, and I found myself in the kitchen preparing chocolate chip cookies.

"I need vanilla extract!" I announced to the room.

"It's in the cabinet above the oven," the quarterback's sister, who was passing by, told me. Sure enough, it was there, but it was way too high for me to reach. I tried jumping to knock it down, but that didn't work either. Suddenly, I felt a body behind me and heard Remi's voice. "What do you need, tiny pixie?"

"Well, for one, I am not tiny. You're just huge. And secondly, I need the vanilla extract."

He peered inside the cabinet but couldn't find what I wanted, so he just put his hands on my waist and lifted me up. So much better than a step stool, I laughed to myself. I may have said it out loud because I felt his hand tighten on my hip.

"Found it!" I held the elusive vanilla extract up in the air as Remi gently lowered me back down. I measured it out, poured it into the bowl, and began mixing it in.

"Can you turn the oven on to three seventy-five?" I asked him. I heard some beeping behind me. "Thank you. You're the best," I said really loudly. I heard him chuckle. One of the girls I was baking with prepped the pans, and we began shaping the cookie dough and putting it into rows on the parchment paper. As they would fill up, Remi would take the pan from me and stick it in the oven.

"Fifteen minutes and then take them out, Rem. Okay?"

"Gotcha, boss," he said back. We kept this going for a half hour and ended up making one hundred cookies. Of course, they got demolished in about five minutes, but I had managed to hoard ten cookies for myself and Remi. Remi took my hand and led me to the living room where a crowd of people were watching a baseball game. One of Remi's teammates made room on the couch, but only enough for one person, so Remi sat down and pulled me into his lap. I was drunk enough not to fight him even when I heard some girls behind us talking about it and asking if anyone knew if we were "official." I held out a cookie for him, but instead of letting me hand it to him, Remi leaned closer and took a bite directly from my hand.

"So good," he mumbled around the cookie.

"Don't talk with your mouth full," I admonished, reaching out to brush a crumb off his lip.

"Okay, Mom." He mimicked me from earlier when I had called him Dad. I rolled my eyes.

"You're kinda sassy when you drink this much," he told me.

"I'm sassy all the time; it just usually stays in my head," I corrected him.

"Duly noted." He took another bite of the cookie in my hand, and this time, I felt his lips on my fingers, and a shiver ran down my back. He was watching me to see if I was going to react to that very forward act, especially with all of our classmates and friends milling about, but I didn't say anything. Instead, I just got another cookie out of my bag and took a bite myself.

"Damn, these are so good." I made a moaning sound as I chewed, and I heard Liam laugh from above me. I looked up, and he said, "Now Remi won't be able to get up for a hot minute after you made that noise."

"Shut up, Liam." Remi smacked Liam's arm, but his cousin just kept laughing and turned away to set up a game of pool with Lia. Remi leaned forward and whispered in my ear, "Jokes on him 'cause I've been hard since you touched me on the dance floor. Although I wouldn't mind if you were a good girl and made that noise again for me later."

I squirmed in his lap, but he pretended that he hadn't just flooded my underwear and started yelling at the TV.

"Catch it, you motherfucker. Fuck…" Then the whole room erupted into cheers when I guess the motherfucker did, in fact, catch the ball. Time passed as we ate our cookies, watched the game, and hung out with our friends. People kept coming over to talk to Remi as he was popular from being on the winning team as well as actually being a really nice guy. He was pretty funny too. He kept fucking with Liam every time he tried to make a shot during his game of pool, and Liam ended up losing the game because of it. The whole time, his hand was just at the edge of my skirt, rubbing circles around on my exposed thigh. Between the alcohol keeping me free of my anxious thoughts, the warm cookies in my belly, his fingers moving on my thigh, and hearing Remi telling me to be a "good girl" earlier, I was positively aching. I wondered what I needed to do to get him to take me upstairs and find an empty room. It was pretty funny how I had gone from a totally uninterested virgin to wondering how I could seduce this beautiful man in public. I started by running my foot up Remi's leg a few times, and although I felt him readjusting himself in his pants once or twice, he kept talking to the guy next to him about the game. So I switched to gently massaging his shoulders or whatever I could reach of them while sitting in front of him. He smiled at me but kept talking. So I leaned forward and licked his earlobe. That got his attention. His body jerked slightly, and he made a "what?" face at me. I squirmed in his lap again, feeling his erection against my butt.

"Shaen." His tone sounded like he was giving me a warning. "What are you doing?"

I made a face back at him. "I'm bored."

"Well, by all means, give me a lap dance in front of my whole team then." He laughed and tugged at a piece of hair that had fallen in front of my face. I went silent.

"You know I'm joking, right?" He suddenly looked panicked at the idea that I might be mad.

"I'm not gonna give you a lap dance in front of your team. I know a joke when I hear one, but maybe I won't be so bored if you let me give you one in private." I smiled in what I hoped looked sexy instead of creepy, but with the amount of alcohol I had consumed, it was plenty possible that I looked creepy as fuck right about now as I had zero experience in the world of seduction.

"H-here?"

Apparently, my suggestion rattled him. My cool, calm, and collected man was looking a little flushed all of a sudden. Perhaps my plan was working after all. I nodded.

"Shit, Shaen... um." He was looking at my lips now, and I moved my hips in his lap again to be encouraging. His hands moved to my waist again, and he held me still.

"Baby, you absolutely have to stop doing that, or I am going to be very embarrassed. You don't want to do that to me, right?"

He was whispering in my ear and sounded chill in his tone, but I also knew that I was no longer playing fair. So I got up and straightened out my skirt.

"I'm going to pee," I announced.

"Have fun," Lia slurred at me.

"Yes, good luck." Liam waved. I laughed at how dumb my friends got when they drank, and I made my way through the crowd, not looking back to see if Remi was following.

Upstairs, I found an empty room that had an en suite bathroom attached to it, so I peed in there. It always fascinated me how hard peeing was when I was drunk. I thought I heard the door open when I flushed and wondered if Remi had joined me. As I washed my hands, I avoided looking in the mirror because seeing my drunk self always freaked me out for some reason. My phone buzzed, but I didn't bother looking at it as I shut off the light and started to cross the room to leave.

"Where are you going, sexy?" a voice said to me from the bed. Immediately, I knew that it was not Remi, and I instantly felt sober. I quickly made my way to the door as best I could in the dark and said, "I'm actually leaving right now. My boyfriend is waiting for me."

"Oh yeah. Where's he at? I bet he won't mind sharing." The man got up from the bed and started to walk toward me.

My heart sank in my chest and began to beat faster at the same time. This house was big, really big. And between the loud music and TV volume being so high, I doubted anyone would hear me if I screamed. I reached for the door handle and pulled the door open just as the stranger slammed it shut again.

"I just want a little taste." He leered at me.

"Leave me alone!" I shouted and banged on the door with my fists. The man, who I still could not fully see in the dark, slapped me across the face.

"Shut up, you little brat." His breath reeked of whiskey, and he smelled sweaty, and not in a good way. I stood there frozen for a second, processing that this creep had just hit me! I lunged for the door handle, and this time, I got the door fully open before he tried to grab me again.

"Get away from me!" I screamed just as Remi came running down the hall, followed by a furious-looking Liam, Carter, and three other guys from the team. Apparently, someone had heard me.

"Get the fuck away from her!" Remi shouted and almost pushed me out of the way as he barged into the bedroom and punched the guy so hard in the face that he fell down, completely knocked out.

"Fuckkkkk, my hand!" Remi was now cradling his right fist as he turned to me, wild-eyed.

"What the hell happened, Shaen?!" He wrapped the arm with his good hand around me as I stood shivering in the doorway. "Did he hurt you?"

I slowly shook my head.

"Did he try?" Carter demanded.

I nodded.

"Motherfucker!" Remi sounded so furious that I didn't know what to make of it. I had never seen him this worked up about anything before; even last night with his dad, he was more calm and collected.

"Who the hell is this piece of shit?" Liam shouted from inside the room where the guy was starting to wake up. His nose was bleeding, and his right eye was beginning to swell.

"We should call the police." Carter started to take his phone out of his jeans pocket, but that's when I started to freak out.

"No, no police. I don't want to start with that. He didn't even do anything that he could get arrested for. Just take me home. I want to go home." I was babbling and feeling really panicked. Remi had handed me off to Lia when she came rushing into the room as the news of what had happened spread. He looked conflicted at my request to let the guy go, but he nodded to Lia.

"Get her in the car. We'll take care of this, and then we'll meet you there."

Liam handed his keys to Lia and turned back to the guy on the floor. But before she could lead me away, I stepped further into the room, feeling a strong desire to never be the victim. He looked at me, blood streaming steadily out of his nose, and I shouted, "You asked me if my man was open to sharing me? Well, I think you got your answer now." And I pointed to Remi. The guy's eyes widened when he took in Remi's sheer size and the furious look on his face.

"Bro, I was just kidding," he started to say.

"It didn't feel so funny when you slapped me across my fucking face," I interrupted.

Now Remi looked even angrier if that was possible. I left the room with my pride reinstated as Liam hauled the guy up by his shirt, and I heard the sound of a fist hitting something solid, and the guy calling out again, "Bro, I said I was joking."

"Shut the fuck up," I heard Remi all but growl, and then I went downstairs and walked back to the car with Lia leading the way.

So this is what being protected feels like.

7

____

About a half hour later, Liam and Remi came running to the car where Lia and I were listening to music, finishing my cookies, and not talking about it. Just how I preferred it to be. Consider all my feelings about tonight completely shoved down. Remi's knuckles had several cuts on them, and his hand was obviously swollen. Liam was holding a bag of frozen peas that I assumed was supposed to be on Remi's hand but somehow hadn't made it there yet. As soon as Remi opened the driver's seat door, I blurted out, "I don't want to talk about it. I'm fine."

He opened his mouth to say something but then closed it again and got into the car, looking unhappy about my request but resigned to respect it. He turned the car on and then took the peas from Liam and laid them over his hand. I wanted to ask him how his hand was, but I had just announced that we were not talking about it, and I wasn't going to disrespect my own rule. As a result, the car remained silent as Remi drove until Liam said, "Drop us off first and then drop Shaen off so you can..." His voice trailed off as I shot him the stink eye. "Make sure she gets home safe. Jesus, Shaen, don't pinch me!"

"You squeal like a girl," I retorted, and everyone laughed. The energy in the car shifted, and Remi turned up the music. As we got closer to Liam's neighborhood, I noticed that Liam's phone lit up with a text, and he leaned closer to Remi and muttered, "All taken care of."

To which Remi nodded and then purposefully didn't look at me.

"Good night, my loves," Lia sang as Liam led her across the grass to the door by the garage so they could hopefully sneak in without waking up the whole house. She was holding an overnight bag as they had clearly planned a sleepover. Remi waited for them to get inside, but he didn't pull out of the driveway until Liam came back outside with a black bag and handed it to Remi. He then came around the car to my side with an ice pack and handed it to me, simply saying, "For your face." And he walked away. He knew me well enough that when I said I was fine, he just let it be and didn't push.

"Good night," I called out from the open window. He lifted his hand up and waved but didn't turn back around. I held the ice to my sore face as Remi began driving back to my place.

"So, we're a mess." I broke the silence jokingly. "Broken hand, broken face..."

"It's not broken," Remi said gruffly, moving his fingers under his bag of peas. "It's just bruised."

"Okay, that's good," I said brightly. "It was a fun party. We should..."

"Can you cut the shit, Shaen?" His voice sounded angry. "Don't do this with me. I get it if you want to be strong in front of everyone else, but now you don't have to. It's just me." He looked over at me as we turned into my building's parking lot, and I saw the pain and anger in his eyes. I swallowed the lump that had risen up in my throat and retorted with my best defense mechanism: pushing people away.

"I know you think you're special somehow because we had a moment yesterday, but you're not closer to me than the rest of them are. Okay? So don't act like you know me better than my other friends because they knew not to force me to talk about it when I didn't want to. Just stop. Thanks for the ride, but I've got it from here." I grabbed my backpack and went to open the door. I heard the lock click in place. I spun around and demanded, "Open the door, Remi."

"No. Not until you listen." He was so quiet, and that was making me madder.

"What the fuck?" I spat at him. "We literally kissed like two times. You can't tell me what to do."

"You called me your man." He was looking at me intently now.

"Yeah, and so what? I said what I needed to say to show that piece of shit that he didn't scare me," I shouted back at him. "It didn't mean anything!" That's when tears began to roll down my cheeks. Tears that I was absolutely horrified were happening.

"It meant something to me," Remi uttered, the vulnerability of his words were clear on his face. I sniffed angrily, wiping the tears off my face. "I know that you feel like we barely know each other, but I really hope that's not true. Because I know you. I've been getting to know you for the last ten months. I know that you keep your feelings buried and don't let a lot of people in. I know that you love to read and that dirty books are your favorite genre. I know that you love animals. I know that you are an amazing and loyal friend. I know that when you laugh hard enough, sometimes you snort."

I took offense to that one, but I started to laugh, which made the tears dry up faster, and the worried look on Remi's face begin to go away.

"I know that your favorite color for your nails is blue, and I know that your favorite drink from Starbucks is an iced vanilla chai tea latte with sweet cream foam."

My eyes widened at that one because that was such a sweet little detail for him to have remembered.

"And maybe those aren't enough things about you to really know the real you, but it makes me want to get to know the real you. Because the parts of you that I do know, I really, really like. And I know you have gone through some shit and are working through it, but so have I, and I get you, I understand you, I want to protect you, and I know it's kind of fast but I really want to be your man if you'll have me."

I felt all of the stress melt out of my body as I listened to him. I had been so alone for so long that I didn't really know what it was like to have someone take care of me. I had my friends, sure, but this man was barging right through the walls I had built around myself, so to speak, and was asking for a chance to know the truest form of me.

"So, be my man like you're my boyfriend or what...?" My voice sounded tentative and a little hoarse from all the yelling and singing I had done today.

"Yes, baby, I want you to be my girlfriend if that's okay." He smiled at me but didn't make a move to touch me. After a few minutes of silence with me thinking and him watching me, I said, "I guess that would be okay."

He grinned, but I put a finger on his lips to shush him.

"But no sex. I am not changing my mind about that."

"But other stuff is on the table?" He appeared his age with that question, and it made me laugh.

"Yes, other stuff is on the table."

"I can handle the no-sex thing until you tell me you're ready." He looked so serious that I had to lean over and kiss him quickly on the mouth. He seemed mollified by that and then informed me that his peas were melting so we should go inside, and I agreed.

The only sign that my mother had been home was an empty bottle of orange juice in the small recycling bin, and the light above the oven had been left on.

"Are you hungry?" I asked Remi as I poured us both a glass of water.

"No. I'm too tired to be hungry." He took the water and drank it down in three gulps. I filled it up again and then led him to my room.

"Can I sleep here?" he asked as I pulled a pair of pajamas out of my drawer.

"I thought we already decided that you were when Liam gave you clothes for tomorrow," I teased him. He laughed.

"If it helps, I was just hopeful, but I didn't assume anything." He pulled off his tank top and rummaged through his bag for something.

"Well, I'm glad you did," I told him as I left the room to go shower the day off of me. When I opened the shower curtain, he was standing there shaving over the sink.

"You better clean that up real good, or my mom will definitely know I had a grizzly in here." I poked him teasingly.

"And don't shave off too much, I always liked a little scruff."

He looked at me in the mirror.

"Oh yeah. Why's that?"

"You'll see." I grinned and left the room. I may not have ever done it yet, but I certainly read enough books where the girl really liked the extra scruff on the guy's face when it was between her legs and his mouth was on her. I hoped one day I would know what that was like for myself.

I had turned the light off and was already in bed by the time Remi came back into the room and crawled in next to me.

"Today feels like it was freaking seventy-two hours long." I yawned. "I'm glad there is no school tomorrow."

He stiffened next to me.

"Won't that mean your mom will be home?"

"Nah, she works another job on the weekends that she sleeps at. She's honestly rarely home." I felt my eyes closing, and I reached for his hand so I could touch him as I drifted off.

"Oh, okay. So we can play house tomorrow, girlfriend?" he asked jokingly.

"We can definitely play house tomorrow, boyfriend." I could feel how happy he was with that response, and as I drifted off to sleep, I thought, so this is what safety feels like.

8
____

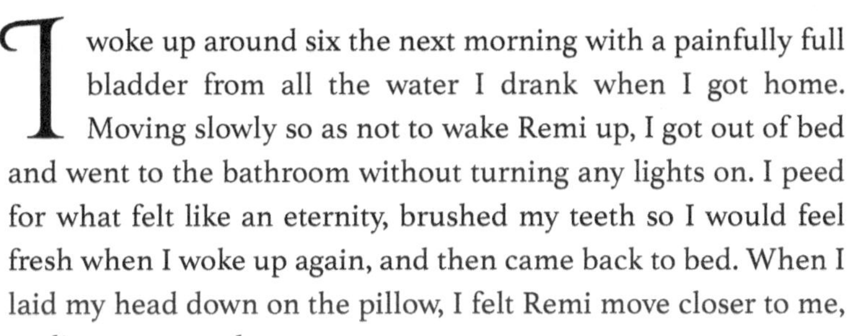

I woke up around six the next morning with a painfully full bladder from all the water I drank when I got home. Moving slowly so as not to wake Remi up, I got out of bed and went to the bathroom without turning any lights on. I peed for what felt like an eternity, brushed my teeth so I would feel fresh when I woke up again, and then came back to bed. When I laid my head down on the pillow, I felt Remi move closer to me, curling up around me.

"Why are you awake, pretty girl?" His voice was groggy with sleep, so I whispered,

"I had to pee so bad."

He laughed quietly at that.

"Your liver finally processed all that alcohol," he murmured against my hair. His hand came up along my ribs, and his fingers found their way under my thin tank top. He soon realized that I was not wearing a bra. I giggled as I heard the sharp intake of his breath.

"Oh, I like this." His fingers were rubbing the underside of my breast and then moved up to rub my nipple.

"If you've never done anything like this before, how are

you so good at it?" I moaned as his mouth closed over the nipple that his fingers weren't playing with. He paused and looked up at me, his mouth sliding off my breast with a soft "pop."

"Well, I have done some stuff," he admitted. "I just never came with them or even by myself before you. And I've also grown up around Liam." We both laughed at that statement because before dating Lia, Liam would literally fuck a girl while you were in the same room with him. He literally didn't care and was super comfortable with the topic of sex.

"I've also watched a lot of porn, and before you tell me how not real it all is, trust me, I know, but it was still fully educational." He laughed.

"Yeah, that makes sense. Sometimes I watch porn too, fully for the educational side of things," I joked, trying to sound serious, but he burst out laughing.

"We should watch something together sometime and then reenact it," I suggested. His eyebrows shot up at that.

"I'm so down to do that."

I could feel how down he was by the way his cock had lengthened up against me. I leaned up to catch his mouth in mine, and we spent the next few minutes kissing. First slow, then more desperate, then back to slow. Remi found the bottom of my tank top and waited for me to nod before pulling it up and off of me.

"You are just..." He palmed my breast, which, although I wore a full C or sometimes a D cup, looked tiny in his huge hand. He let out a low groan. "I can't wait to learn everything that you love." He was so earnest about it that it made me that much more turned on as he lowered his head and began kissing his way down my rib cage and then whispered kisses across my belly button. Physically, I really wanted his mouth there so badly, but emotionally, I didn't feel ready.

"I'm not ready for that yet, Remi," I whispered as he kissed his way over my hips. He sat up quickly as he nodded.

"I wasn't going to, but I also understand."

We sat quietly for a second, with me worrying that I had completely ruined the moment when he asked, "Is it okay if I touch you? With my fingers...?"

I nodded quickly, and he grinned at my obvious enthusiasm. I was feeling so needy and wet already, but when he pressed his body onto mine and began to kiss me, I quickly pulled my underwear down and kicked it off my leg onto the floor some-where. Remi took that as an invitation to run his hand down my pubic bone and faltered when he felt that I was bare.

"Baby...?"

"Lia and I get Brazilian waxes," I explained.

"I mean, I could have done without knowing that about Lia, but I like this." His words were coming out in pants now, and his fingers seemed to be hovering over me but not quite touching me. I gyrated my hips greedily, but he still didn't move.

"Remi?" He bit his lower lip and squeezed my leg gently.

"I'm gonna need a really quick anatomy lesson 'cause I know where it all is theoretically, but not on you if that makes sense, and I just really don't wanna fuck this up."

He was so cute that I laughed.

"That is the sweetest thing anyone has ever said to me," I told him, grinning, as I reached down and took his hand. I moved it down and heard him take a deep breath in. I took one of his fingers and rubbed it over my clit as fireworks seemed to go off in my pelvic area. "This is my..."

"Clit. Yes, I can feel that." He smiled, but he looked intense as he watched me lead his hand around my body. I moved him lower and let go. He rubbed my lips and muttered, almost to himself, "Labia."

That made me laugh again, but it was cut off by a moan

when his finger found my entrance, and he ran it around all of the wetness that had gathered there.

"You are soaked." He stated the obvious, and I panted as he tentatively worked the tip of his finger into me. "You're so tight," he moaned.

"You're so good at this anatomy class," I joked as he got his finger all wet with me and then moved it up to my clit. He rubbed it over me right where I was feeling very sensitive and swollen.

"Oh my Godddd," I ground out as his finger began to move faster, and I grew even wetter. I opened my eyes to find him staring at me.

"You are so beautiful." He bent down to kiss me as his finger continued to move. He alternated between fast up and down movements and slower circular movements. Every now and then, he would move down to gather more of my wetness and work it up to my clit. I was almost there; my legs were feeling so tense, and the sounds coming out of me were getting louder and more desperate.

"Oh my God, I want to come, I just..." I moaned, feeling frustrated with why it was taking me so long. Remi suddenly laid down on his side, his elbow and shoulder holding him up as he continued to rub my clit, his finger making wet slurping noises because, at this point, I was completely soaked and then some. His mouth came close to my ear, and in his gruff, deep voice, he said, "Look how good you're taking it, baby. Be a good girl and come for me."

That was all it took for me to absolutely explode. I swear I saw lights behind my eyelids, and my body felt like it was levitating off the bed for a second. My pussy was pulsing, and my abs were strung so tight as I rode out the waves of this epic orgasm.

"Remi, oh my God. Oh my God. Remi..." I chanted, and he

kept whispering in my ear what a good girl I was, how wet I felt on his finger, and how hard I had made him. When I finally came down, I was breathing so heavily and felt so wrung out in the best way possible. I watched him, both intrigued and horrified, as Remi took his fingers that were now shining with my wetness and stuck them in his mouth.

"Oooh, fuck," he moaned around his fingers. "You taste so good." And before I had a chance to say no, he kissed me. He was desperate, a little sloppy, and a whole lot horny. I tasted a tang in his mouth that had to be from me, and I shivered at the idea of it.

"I love that you need praise. It makes me so hard, it's insane," he said against my mouth.

"I honestly had no idea," I admitted. "I'm a little confused by it."

"I'm super turned on by it." He laughed as his hand was now moving against the side of my body, and I saw that he had reached down and was jerking himself off. I watched, alarmed at how tight he was holding it and intrigued by how rough he seemed to be with himself.

"Can I come on you?" He was breathing heavily now, his hand moving so quickly. I nodded, feeling a little freaked out at his intensity but mainly super turned on as I continued to watch. He got up on his knees and continued jerking his hand quickly up and down his shaft. His movements became a little more erratic until I watched him bend over slightly as the power of his orgasm overtook him. His face was, again, squeezed tight in what looked like pain, but I knew was actually from pleasure. His chest was heaving and sweaty, and his moans were so hot as cum shot out of his penis and coated mainly my stomach, but a little got on my right breast. When he was done, he stared at me, covered in his cum, and seemed not to know what to say.

Remi continued to look a little shaky when he got up to get a small hand towel from the bathroom that he had wet with warm water. He was quiet while he gently wiped all of himself off of me. Then he retrieved my underwear, pulled it up my legs, and helped me put my tank top back on. As he laid back down next to me, he gathered me up in his arms and whispered, "Go back to sleep, beautiful. I'll be here when you wake up."

We didn't talk about it, but to be honest, we really didn't need to.

"WE'RE MOVING TOO FAST," I announced. Remi opened one eye as I abruptly woke him up with my anxiety.

"Hmm?" He yawned and closed his eye, scratching his chest. "What time is it?"

"We've been friends for almost a year, and suddenly, we're going out and sleeping in the same bed for two nights in a row! I don't know enough about you! You could be a serial killer for all I know!"

"A serial killer?" He scoffed. "I mean, sure, I guess between school, church, and football, I could have fit that in." Both eyes were open now, and he looked adorably disheveled and confused. I pulled the blanket tighter around my body as his eyes made their way down and seemed to get stuck staring at my boobs.

"It's not funny. I let you touch my…"

"I know. I was there." He seemed to think this conversation was pretty entertaining.

"No, I'm being serious, Remi, this is too much. I have a plan, and the plan must be followed. We're what, twenty-eight days from graduating? I cannot mess this up. I don't know how we went from hanging in the same friend group one day to telling each other our secrets and swapping saliva the next day."

I felt bad when he genuinely looked offended.

"I mean, swapping saliva is kind of a gross description for what we did, Shaen."

"Ugh. I know, and I'm sorry. I'm just freaking the fuck out right now, and I'm not exactly amazing at sharing my feelings with others." I buried my face in my hands and tried to take some deep breaths. I didn't want to hurt his feelings, but since we went back to sleep earlier this morning, I had tossed and turned and panicked, and now I had to let it out, or it would ruin my whole day. I felt his hand come up and rub my back for a second before he said,

"I would never ruin your plan, Shaen. I promise. I just like you, and I want to get to know you better. But if you need to, we will stop and go back to just being friends, or we can go super slow and get to know each other without swapping saliva, or we can keep going as is and see where it takes us and make changes as you need. I swear I'm not asking for anything else from you." His voice was still husky from sleep, and I did love hearing him say my name. I let his words wash over me, and I weighed out what he was offering in my mind.

"I mean, it is nice having someone tall around," I acquiesced, referencing when he helped me get the vanilla extract.

"I'm happy to be your tall someone." He smiled.

"And it's kinda cool not being alone at home all the time," I added.

"I like that for you too." He was watching me, almost studying me, and I knew that my sudden mood swings were probably confusing for him. Honestly, they were confusing for me too.

"I think I would like to see where this goes... slowly, with no saliva swapping for a bit, if that's okay with you? I know that might be awkward, but it's confusing for me..." I was feeling less panicked hearing that he wasn't going to mess with the plan; maybe he could even enhance the plan.

He moved away from me just slightly and took his hand off my back.

"I will go as slow as you need."

I let out a deep breath that I hadn't realized I'd been holding and gave him a big smile.

"You sure? I feel bad. It just feels like we skipped some important steps. I know you as Liam's cousin, I know you're a nice guy, I know you're a good football player and all the basic stuff, but I don't know other things, like do you have a middle name, what are your plans for after we graduate, what do you do for fun, and what is your favorite food? I'm just thinking maybe we could just hold hands at lunch without also touching each other's private parts."

At that, Remi burst out laughing.

"For someone who reads a lot of smut, you seem to have a very limited vocabulary for describing my dick."

I ducked my head, feeling embarrassed, but I also started snickering at myself.

"My middle name is nothing because my dad thought Remiel was the perfect name for his perfect baby who would one day take over pastoring at his perfect church. As far as what I'm doing after we graduate, well, up until last week, I was registered to start at a pastoral Christian college in the fall, but as you know"— he rolled his eyes— "I called and withdrew so that is still up in the air, but I promise I will tell you as soon as I figure it out. Um, let's see, for fun, I play football, I play a crazy game of Fortnite, I enjoy learning about cars, and I love to eat."

"Eating is not for fun," I interrupted.

"If it's not fun, you're doing it wrong, babe." He laughed. "Speaking of food, my favorite food is lasagna, and my favorite dessert is pie. Really any pie but a pie with a cream filling—booooy, the things I would do for that pie...”

I giggled, honestly thrilled to be learning more about him. They were such silly little details, but they somehow made me feel more comfortable going down this unknown road that could possibly shake up my plan.

“As much as I am loving this little pow-wow”— Remi winked at me— “I need a quick bathroom break.”

While he was out of the room, I quickly pulled on a pair of faded lululemon leggings that I had found at Goodwill and a black oversized shirt that said, “Today is a good day to leave me alone.” I washed my face in the kitchen sink yet again and put on a fresh “no-makeup” makeup look. Pulling my long hair into two braids, I sat back down on the bed and made a quick grocery order. Remi’s phone was buzzing off the hook. I glanced over to see who was so insistent on reaching him, and I saw that the caller ID said “MOM.” I wondered what that was about and if his relationship with his mom was as tumultuous as it was with his dad.

I was scrolling through social media when Remi finally came back into the room, freshly showered and fully dressed in what looked to be gym clothes.

“Sorry that I took so long,” he said, putting his laundry into his overnight bag. “I decided to shower too.”

“Totes fine.”

“Totes?” He laughed.

“Yup.” I grinned. “Soooo, I have a grocery order coming. I figured I could cook us lunch?”

“Sounds perfect to me.” He was looking at my braids but didn’t say anything about them. I worried I may have pushed him away too hard, but I was also looking forward to seeing how this would progress more organically.

“Also, your mom has been calling nonstop.”

He groaned. "That's awesome." He picked up his phone. I went back to my own phone to catch up on the girls' group chat.

LIA

What are you bitches wearing to graduation?

DEE

clothes prob

RACHEL

Dunno - wanna shop???

LIA

hell ya

RACHEL

I'll pick you up at 2

LIA

thanks bestie

Then I switched to the entire friend group chat.

LIAM

did anyone catch the bio hw?

CARTER

hitting the gym anyone joining?

RACHEL

Do you mean you need a ride?

CARTER

I need a ride

RACHEL

laughing face emoji

CARTER

middle finger emoji

LIAM

I'll pick u up in 10 with my moms car cuz Remi has my jeep

CARTER

sweet

EVA

I need the bio homework. Anyone have it?

LIA

Rachel and I are going to the mall at 2 if anyone wants to come

DEE

why are Shaen and Remi so quiet?

LIAM

cuz they're fucking

REMI

we are not fucking

LIAM

stop texting while ur fucking it's rude dick head

LIA

says you

RACHEL

Are you guys being safe?

REMI

guys. We.are.not.fucking

Remi left the room with his phone, so I turned on some

meditation music and sat by the window in my room to catch some sun rays. He had said he wasn't going to get in the way of my plan, so I decided that I was going to stick to my Saturday morning routine. I sat cross-legged and did some deep breathing. I had learned about the power of mediation in my quest to heal my panic attacks. I loved this part of my weekend because it quieted all of the chaos in my mind and allowed me to just be in the moment with no to-do lists, no absent mothers, no sweet, horny, hot, tall football players, and no worries about the future — just a pocket of peace and quiet. After twenty minutes of stillness and gentle introspection, I took some more breaths and opened my eyes, blinking at the sudden intrusion of light. Remi was sitting on the edge of the bed, watching me. I smiled.

"Sorry," I told him.

"Don't be sorry." He was smiling gently at me. I got up and shut off the meditation music.

"So, I'm gonna hit the gym with the boys, but I'll be back. If that's cool?" he said, stretching.

I wasn't sure if he was asking if it was cool if he left to go to the gym or if it was okay if he came back after. But I did not ask for clarification. All I said back was, "Sure. Have fun."

He looked like he wanted to say more, but he just grabbed his Beats headphones from his bag along with a protein bar. As he left, I got a notification that the grocery delivery service had dropped off my groceries. So I got started on making lasagna and lemon meringue pie.

9

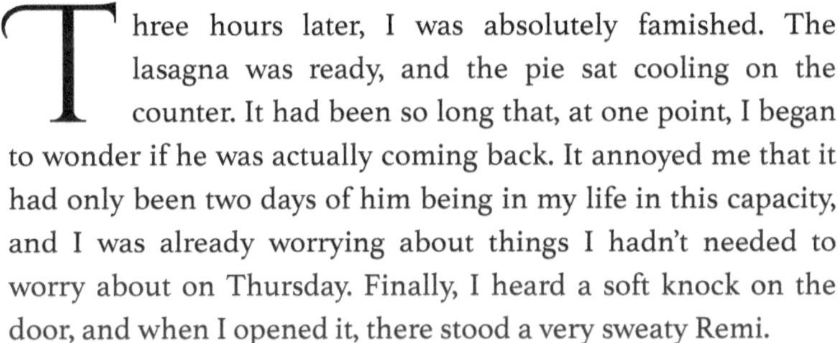

Three hours later, I was absolutely famished. The lasagna was ready, and the pie sat cooling on the counter. It had been so long that, at one point, I began to wonder if he was actually coming back. It annoyed me that it had only been two days of him being in my life in this capacity, and I was already worrying about things I hadn't needed to worry about on Thursday. Finally, I heard a soft knock on the door, and when I opened it, there stood a very sweaty Remi.

"Sorry that took so long, mother fucking Liam put us through the wringer today."

"That's okay." I got a whiff of his natural spice as he came inside. Yummm, my body thought. Down girl, my brain retorted.

"I'm gonna have to shower again. I'm gross," he told me.

I bit my lip so I wouldn't say that he wasn't gross, that actually, he looked absolutely edible. We were going slow. I reminded my libido. No spit-swapping behavior allowed.

"Waiiiit. I smell pasta." He turned around and came back into the kitchen. "Shaen..."

"What?" I asked innocently.

"Is this lasagna and pie for me?"

"I believe it is. Hey, get your finger out of there!" I swatted him away from the pie.

"Oh my God, you are a queen! A literal queen. I hope you're ready for me to demolish that entire pan of lasagna. Holy shit!" He backed out of the kitchen, looking so excited as he took his shirt off with that hot one-handed move boys did.

As Remi showered again, I made us plates of food and brought them over to the coffee table. I put the TV on to make some background noise when my phone vibrated.

LIAM

photo

I opened the text, and it was a picture of a very shirtless, very sweaty Remi lifting weights, muscles bulging.

SHAEN

you're aware that he's your cousin right?

LIAM

& ur my bff. Figured you could use that for your spank bank

SHAEN

Something is wrong with you

LIAM

facts.

SHAEN

thanks though

LIAM

I knew it

SHAEN

you know nothing John Snow

LIAM

I know that ur FUCKING!

SHAEN

nope

Then, in retaliation, I sent him a photo of the lasagna and pie.

LIAM

did u bake my fucking cousin lasagna and pie?

SHAEN

from scratch

LIAM

I hate u

SHAEN

suck it bitch

LIAM

deleted photo

SHAEN

I already saved it to my phone

LIAM

I hate u again

SHAEN

I saved you a piece I'll send it home with R

LIAM

I love u

Remi sat down across from me and took the biggest bite of lasagna that I had ever seen someone take.

"Holy fuck, this is so good." His eyes were closed, and he seemed to be having a whole moment with his food.

"Stop talking with your mouth full." I giggled, loving how much he was appreciating what I had made him.

He just laughed and shoveled more food into his mouth.

"I literally cannot believe you did this. Okay, but now I need to know more about you. What is your middle name?" He stopped to drink some of the water that I had put in front of him.

"I don't have one."

"Okay, okay, what do you do for fun?"

"Read."

"Dirty, dirty smut?"

"Dirty, dirty smut," I confirmed, grinning. "I also like to hang out with our friends. Listen to music and play with the dogs at the shelter that I work at."

"Do you work today?"

I looked at my phone to check the time.

"Yeah, I go in at three."

"Okay, cool, I'll drop you off." Remi finished his first slice of lasagna and went to the kitchen for more.

"Hey, I'm a growing boy," he joked when he came back into the living room.

"I hope not. You're tall enough," I joked back. He shrugged.

"I don't even know how. My dad is like five-eleven, and my mom is five-five. You're still tinier than her, though." He was quickly making his way through his second piece. I sincerely loved how much he was enjoying eating it.

"That's not hard, I'm only five-three."

"You're so tiny and cute. Okay, what about your favorite food?"

I had finished my piece of lasagna and went to the kitchen to cut two slices of pie. I made sure Remi's was extremely generous.

"Hmm…" I licked some meringue off of my fingers and watched his eyes follow the movements of my mouth. We're going slow, Shaen, I told myself. Slow.

"I really like grilled cheese; I also like taco salads, and I consider Nutella a whole-ass food group." I grinned, and he nodded.

"I hear that. It's an important staple."

I loved our semi-sarcastic banter. Remi leaned back and patted his stomach.

"Good lord, woman, I am stuffed."

"I'm so glad you liked it." So much so that I was thinking about what I could bake him next. "Sooo, what did your mom want?" I asked as I began cleaning up the coffee table. I planned on packing up some food for Remi to take home, and then I would save some to have later for dinner when I got back from work.

"I didn't call her back yet. She's probably sick of hearing my dad rant about what a sinner I am and is calling to play good cop." He stood up and came into the kitchen. "Do you need help?"

"You can wash the pan if you want," I told him from where I was packing up a Tupperware for Liam. He turned the sink on and started washing out the glass pan I had used to bake the lasagna in.

"Look at us playing house," he joked. It was his first reference to the girlfriend-boyfriend conversation we had last night, and then when I had put the brakes on us moving so fast, I had been wondering if we would still do titles.

"Washing dishes is a good look for you," I quipped, avoiding the heavier part of the conversation as my survival mechanisms kicked in.

"Thank you. I'm happy to do it if you keep feeding me like that." He winked.

Both of our phones buzzed, and I saw the group chat pop up on my phone screen.

LIAM

photo

LIAM

isn't this the bitch who hit you last night Shaen???

It was a mugshot of the man who had assaulted me last night. I swallowed heavily, my throat suddenly feeling tight.

CARTER

That's definitely him. Remi you really ducked up his face. Look at him!

CARTER

fucked

RACHEL

Omg what?

LIAM

apparently after we roughed him up and kicked him out he got pulled over for a DUI. Check out this link

EVA

Good, he's a piece of shit

RACHEL

what was he doing at our school party?

LIAM

looks like he goes to college nearby. I guess he just crashed?

EVA

how is your face Shaen?

SHAEN

guys I'm fine. I swear

REMI

types…. stops typing

I met his eyes from over my phone.

"Still don't want to talk about it?" He looked pretty serious.

"You're catching on quick." I faked a chill tone in my voice and handed him three Tupperware containers. "Okay, this pie is for Liam. The other piece is for you, and I gave you some more lasagna for when you're hungry again later."

"Why does Liam get pie?"

"He sent me something, so it's his prize." I went to my room to grab my bag and charger and put on sneakers for work.

"What did he send you?" Remi was leaning in the doorway of my room, his bag slung over his chest, the keys to Liam's jeep in his hand.

I hesitated and then unlocked my phone to pull up the photo Liam had sent me. I had already set it to be Remi's contact photo on my phone. Remi laughed when he saw it. I loved how his personality was a mix of both humility and confidence.

"You like?" He was clearly flirting now, but he hadn't touched me since our conversation this morning, which I appreciated and missed at the same time.

"I like," I confirmed. He beamed.

"I need a photo of you now," he told me as we left the apartment.

"I don't go to the gym," I joked.

"I'm gonna need a pic, Shaen," he repeated.

"Mm-hmm." I clicked my seat belt and gave Remi the

address of the dog shelter where I worked. We listened to music the whole drive there. Why was he so sexy when he drove? I watched his hand on the wheel and wished he had it on my thigh right now. I always thought that possessive move was kind of hot. You made the rules, Shaen, I reminded myself as Remi pulled up in front of my work and unlocked the door.

"Thank you so much for lunch, Shaen, it was so good," he told me again as I grabbed my phone and bag. I hesitated before I opened the door, wondering if I should at least give him a hug or something. I decided against it and smiled.

"Thanks for the ride."

He nodded.

"Talk to you later."

He didn't drive away until I was safely inside. We were definitely in some awkward territory. It's like we had jumped into the deep end of the pool, and now I had dragged us back to the shallow. We just needed to get to know each other better; that would allow me to feel more secure about the whole thing, and then I'd be happy to swim in the deep end with him again. I blushed at what that innuendo meant to me. My phone buzzed.

REMI

I'm gonna need that photo

I said hi to one of my bosses, Margo, and then got busy processing paperwork for the three new dogs that had come in earlier this week and the two dogs that had been adopted. My bosses were a married couple who lived in the apartment above the shelter. They had hired me two years ago. At first, I had just manned the desk and phones, but now they trusted me to do a lot more, like managing the groomer's schedule and posting on the rescue's social media. I took the three new dogs who had come in this week and brought them into a gated area where I had set up a gray velvet doggy bed and a background that I had made out of wrapping paper and taped up on the wall behind the little doggy couch. I had a bow tie collar for the boys and a hair bow for the girls. I would pose them and try to get shots of the dogs that would get them adopted really quickly. I would then post the photos and the dog's bio on our social media accounts. I absolutely loved my job, and usually, it was full of happily ever after stories, but sometimes we had sad stories, and they always wrecked me. We had gotten in a one-year-old pit bull named Rex, who had a beautiful tan and white coat and a huge pitty smile. We also had received a black lab who had been found roaming a Walmart parking lot, so we weren't sure exactly how old she was, but the vet thought she was around two or three. I had chosen her name to be Midnight, since we didn't know what her previous one was. Last, was a tiny six-month-old white Maltipoo named Tigger, who I immediately fell in love with. I knew he would go quickly. People loved the fluffy, tiny babies. I took shots of each dog in several poses. When I was done, I rewarded each of them with treats and belly rubs. I was lying on the floor with Tigger snuggled on my chest, Midnight lying curled up by my head, and Rex resting his big face on my belly. I grabbed my phone and snapped a selfie with them, and before I could chicken out, I texted it over to Remi.

REMI

you're adorable

I hearted his response.

I began editing the photos and preparing the posts for social media. Then, I fed all of the dogs dinner and let them run around outside in the gated yard before bedtime. The four hours of my shift flew by, and it was time for me to leave.

"See you tomorrow," I called to Margo. She waved but didn't say anything because she was talking to someone on the phone. I had requested an Uber ten minutes prior, and it was pulling up as I stepped outside. During the day, I would walk the twenty minutes home, but when my shift ended in the evenings, I would lay out some hard-earned money for an Uber. I couldn't wait to get my own car. I had some decent cash saved since I had never missed a shift in two years. I worked three to seven on Saturdays and ten to four on Sundays. My bosses paid me fifteen dollars an hour. Sometimes, I would edit photos at home or answer social media messages, but I never logged those hours. I did that for my doggy friends. Every time one of them went to their "furever" home, I wanted to cry from sheer happiness. I didn't actually cry since I had pushed that deep down, but I wanted to. I grimaced at my thoughts, wishing I had better coping skills than numbing out so much of my life. On the car ride home, the group chat got active again.

EVA

I still need the bio homework. Did anyone track it down?

LIAM

Seth just sent it to me I'll email it to u

EVA

you're the best thank you *heart emoji*

CARTER

I mean...

EVA

simmer down

I snickered. I loved watching Eva put Carter in his place.

DEE

link to a video.

DEE

guys I'm literally dying. You must watch this. It's
so funny

RACHEL

I don't get it

DEE

sigh

LIAM

did u finish work yet Shaen?

SHAEN

on my way home now

SHAEN

photo of Tigger

RACHEL

omg my ovaries !

LIAM

that's a dog Rachel. U cannot birth a puppy

RACHEL

wtv i lit love him

REMI

if you think that's cute check this out

REMI

photo

He had sent the selfie of me and the three new dogs. I froze. Why did he do that? Our friends were going to have a field day with it.

RACHEL

does that mean what I think it means??

EVA

Shaen you have the best job like everrr

LIAM

$100 they're ducking

LIAM

fucking

CARTER

I'll take that bet

REMI

we are NOT fucking

Liam reacted to his message with an angry face emoji.

When I got home, my mom was actually in her room, which was surprising as she usually worked on Saturday nights. I could hear her on the phone as I warmed up the leftover lasagna in the microwave. I went into my room to eat and shut the door. I started reading a new book as I ate, and then when I finished, I did the bio homework that Eva had forwarded to me. At around ten, I began getting ready for bed, and I heard my mom leave her room.

"Hey, Shaen," she called.

"Hey," I answered back.

"I see you made pie."

"Yup. You can have a piece if you want."

"Thanks. You going to bed?"

"Yup."

"Good night." I heard her in the kitchen cutting herself some pie.

"Good night," I muttered. She really had no idea how to be a mother. She wasn't a bad person; she had just never grown up. She did the best she could, but mostly her best wasn't enough.

I was dozing off to sleep when I heard my phone buzz on my night table.

REMI

good night

I smiled and noticed that my heart rate had picked up. Crap, I really was into him, wasn't I? I couldn't tell you how this had evolved so quickly, but it was already feeling so nice to matter to someone. To matter to him.

SHAEN

night x

REMI

with tongue?

I reacted to his message with a laughing emoji and went to sleep.

10

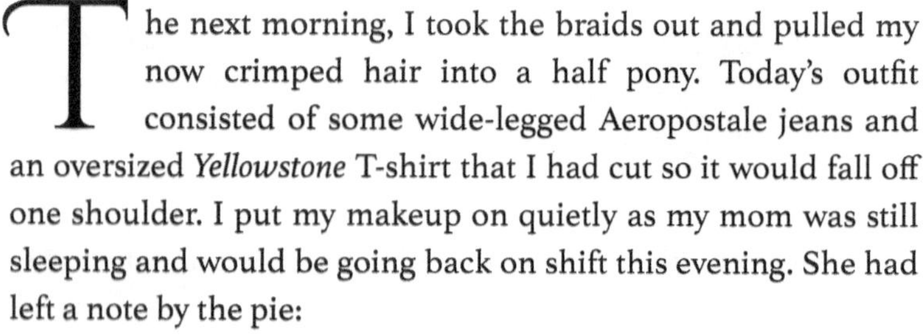

The next morning, I took the braids out and pulled my now crimped hair into a half pony. Today's outfit consisted of some wide-legged Aeropostale jeans and an oversized *Yellowstone* T-shirt that I had cut so it would fall off one shoulder. I put my makeup on quietly as my mom was still sleeping and would be going back on shift this evening. She had left a note by the pie:

"This was delicious. XO."

I wanted to let it make me happy. I wanted to believe that this meant that she cared about me, but I had gotten my hopes up so many times before, and the disappointment that followed was worse than just protecting my heart against any nice little gesture she made because it never lasted. I crumbled up the note, threw it out, and then helped myself to a slice of pie for breakfast.

At nine-thirty, I set out for my walk to work, putting one AirPod in to listen to music. Halfway there, I got a notification from Siri.

"Text message from Remi. Would you like me to read it?"

I looked down at my phone and swiped open my message app.

REMI

guess what

SHAEN

what

REMI

I *eggplant emoji* *droplets of water emoji* all by myself!

SHAEN

ew

REMI

And here I thought you'd be proud

SHAEN

you're so weird lmao

REMI

hey this is a big deal for mankind

SHAEN

so I guess you finally didn't hear your dad while you did it? Lol

REMI

nope I heard you

This man! I ignored the tingles erupting in my underwear, shoved my phone into my pocket, and walked into work. My day consisted of two more adoptions, lots of phone calls, and tons and tons of doggy kisses. At three-thirty, Margo's husband Eddie showed up to take the second shift, and I got ready to leave.

"All good?" Eddie started unpacking a dog food order that had been delivered today.

"Yep! Gordy and Lacy got picked up by their new families. Speaking of, we need to make more take-home bags," I informed him. Last year, I proposed the idea of making a bag for newly adopted dogs to send home with them and their families. In it, we put a container of their current food— so if the families wanted to get them on something new, they could transition the dog off properly— a bowl with their name on it, a toy that smelled like the shelter, and all of their paperwork in a folder that was covered in paw prints.

"We need to order more bags and folders. I'll do that tonight, and when they come, we'll pack up some more," he agreed. I had lucked out when it came to bosses. Both Eddie and Margo were generous and kind and always treated me with respect. They would be giving me more hours once I graduated, and I was so grateful that they had allowed me the option for extended hours because I had been dreading finding a new job when I loved my current one so much.

"I'm gonna go do a poop clean up outside, and then I'll head out."

"Aight, see you next week." Eddie passed me the pooper scooper, and I went outside.

I finally had a chance to look at my phone again on my walk home. The chat was so full that I had to scroll back to catch up on all my friends' bullshit. I smiled at my phone because truly I loved them, but while I worked, that chat had blown up because no one else needed a job like I did. Liam's parents were very wealthy. His dad was a surgeon, and his mom was a nurse who owned two aesthetics and injections spas. I assumed Remi's parents were taking care of him financially, but if they weren't, then Liam's parents would want him to focus on school and would never put him in a position of needing a job. Lia's parents were divorced, and her dad basically just sent a bunch of money every month to assuage his guilt for cheating on her mom and abandoning the family. Eva was an only child to older parents. Her dad had already retired from some big tech job, and her mother was an artist whose work went for a lot of money. Rachel and Dee were both more middle class. Rachel's dad was a police officer, and her mom was a principal, and both of Dee's fathers owned their own businesses. One owned a hair salon, and the other owned a bee farm where he raised bees for organic honey and other honey products. They were honestly what I considered to be upper middle class because both of them would get summer jobs, but they didn't need to work during the year to afford clothes or their phone bill like I did. Carter's parents owned multiple gyms around the country. His mom had even competed in a Miss USA pageant before she had him, hence his obsession with his physique. He spent his summers traveling and would come home with a tan, talking about yachts this and Cartier bracelets that. I wasn't jealous of them; I was just sad for myself. I usually had what I needed, but it took so much effort on my part to make sure that I did. By the time I had caught up on the chat, more messages had come in.

LIAM

my mom is bbq'ing. Pools open. Hookah is lit
let's gooooo

RACHEL

I'm with Jake can he come?

LIAM

of course

Jake was a year ahead of us and was going to a local college. He and Rachel would hang out a lot, but he had never quite gotten past the friend zone.

DEE

omw

LIA

I'm baking muffins with Julia, hurry up before I
eat them all

Julia was Liam's mom, and she was so beautiful and so fun to be around. I loved hanging out at Liam's house not only because he had so many siblings, a pool, a theater room, and a walk-in pantry but because Julia always made me feel welcome and a part of the family.

CARTER

Eva is getting a pedicure we'll come by after
she finishes

REMI

that's what she said

LIAM

Shaen are you done work?

SHAEN

walking home now

REMI

I'll come pick you up

LIAM

my keys are on my night table

LIAM

near the condoms if you need any

REMI

middle finger emoji

When I got home, I was sweaty and covered in dog hair. I quickly tore all of my clothes off and chose a green, strapless one-piece bathing suit that had an oval cutout on one side. I had gotten it thrifting, and it had come with the protective crotch liner and tags still on it. I literally loved it when rich people just discarded new things in my size. Then I paired it with a pair of white flip-flops from Charlotte Russe and a thin, gauzy black dress that doubled as a pool cover-up. I was freshening up my makeup and deodorant when Remi texted me that he was outside. I shoved a bra, underwear, sweatpants, tank top, and a brush into my beach bag and ran downstairs. I knew my friends were on to us for real because Remi would have never offered to pick me up by himself before. I was also still trying to find my footing around him since I had made my rules yesterday. Well, my head had made the rules, my libido and heart were not happy about them at all. Remi leaned over to open the door for me, and I hopped in, quickly adapting to my super chill, every-thing is absolutely fine vibe. He was smiling, and his skin was kind of flushed with the beginnings of a tan, hinting that he had already spent the day outside.

"How was work?" he asked, pulling out of the parking lot.

"Great!" I was back to avoiding full eye contact because I was feeling so anxious, not knowing exactly how he felt about what we had done, what we were doing, and how slowly we were now doing it in comparison.

"You okay?"

"I'm great." I flashed him another one of my "everything is wonderful" grins that I had perfected over the years. He didn't look so convinced, but he changed the subject.

"I hope you're hungry because Julia overdid it with the food."

"Of course she did." I finally gave a genuine laugh. "She doesn't know anything other than over the top."

"Facts," he agreed as we pulled into the circular driveway in front of Liam's large home. I found Julia in the front hallway of the house putting floaty wings onto her six-year-old.

"Hi, lovie." She stood up and gave me a big hug. "I'm so happy you could make it. You look stunning. Doesn't she look stunning, Remiel?" She didn't wait for him to answer; instead, she turned and opened up a bag with her business's logo on it. "Honey, I brought this home for you. New samples came in, and I absolutely need you to try them." She showed me a lash growth serum, a moisturizer, and a tinted lip balm that also claimed to plump. She was always doing stuff like this, and it filled the empty hole inside of me that wanted to have a mom to do girly things with. I hugged her again.

"Julia, thank you so much. I will let you know how I like them."

She smiled.

"Take selfies. I wanna post your gorgeous face on my page."

Two more of Liam's younger brothers went running down the hall dripping pool water, and Julia excused herself to chase after them. I felt a soft touch on my shoulder as Remi moved me in the direction of the kitchen, which led to the patio down to the massive pool. As soon as we walked outside, I was hit with the sounds of loud music, the voices of all of my friends floating up from the pool, and the bubbles from the Jacuzzi. I immediately felt the tension leave my body, and I found a lounge chair to put my stuff down on. I took off my dress and threw my hair up in a high bun. When I turned around, Remi was staring. He cleared his throat and turned away.

"Are you hungry? I can make you a plate," he asked, still not looking at me, as he gestured to the huge table laden with food.

"Shaen, get into the pool!" Lia's voice interrupted our little awkward moment. I nodded at him and shrugged. "Sure, I'll take whatever, thank you," I told him as I took the stairs down to the pool.

"Grab me a drink, babe," Liam called, so I snagged him and myself a White Claw and came to sit at the edge of the pool. Julia wouldn't let us have anything other than canned, low-alcoholic drinks at our parties because, other than Liam's two older brothers, we were all underage. Remi was the oldest; he was turning nineteen in July, and I wouldn't be nineteen until September.

"Get in," Liam encouraged.

"I will. I'm just catching some sun." I stuck my feet in the water and wiggled my toes around, loving the feeling of summer coming early even though we weren't quite yet there. Lia swam up and rested her arms on the side of the pool next to me.

"Guess what? Rachel brought a karaoke machine!" She was so excited that I laughed.

"What's so funny?" Remi came over, holding a plate of food for me. He had changed into his bathing suit, which was sitting low on his hips, his muscular body in full view.

I quickly looked away so no one would see me staring, but Lia had caught me, and she grinned mischievously but didn't say anything.

"Nothing's funny. I'm just very excited because Rachel brought karaoke, and we're going to have so much fun with it later," Lia explained. Remi sat down next to me and put his feet in the water. His thigh was dangerously close to mine, but I knew if I scooted away even an inch, everyone would notice and would give me shit about it.

"I'll sing." Remi handed me my plate. He had given me salad, fries, a hotdog, a hamburger with all the toppings, chicken, cut-up fruit, and a piece of apple cobbler.

"Thank you, but how much do you think I can eat?" I asked, taking the fork that he held out for me. He had also cracked open my White Claw and put it down next to me.

"Whatever you don't eat, I'll finish," he told me. Lia and Liam looked like they were going to implode from not saying their usual "see, they're fucking" comments. I must admit I was enjoying their discomfort from it all. I stuck my fork into the cobbler and took a generous bite.

"Oh damn." I gave a little moan. "This is so good."

"My mom outdid herself." Liam swam away with a little splash. I noticed Remi watching me out of the corner of my eye. As I got to the last bite of cobbler, I held it out on my fork for him.

"Saved the best for last," I joked. He maintained eye contact, leaned forward, and ate it. As cliche as it sounded, I literally shivered. But I was the queen of pretending like everything was fine, so I continued to do just that. I kept pretending that I wasn't affected by him and dug into the rest of my food. Sure enough, Remi took my plate when I felt full and cleared it for me. I was now two White Claws in and not tipsy but definitely feeling less stressed about our situationship as I got into the pool. It was now getting dark, and all of the twinkle lights around the pool were glowing against the water. Lia was on Liam's shoulders, Eva on Carter's, Rachel had climbed up on Jake, and Dee was the only one not in the water because she was managing the playlist and getting the s'mores ready. Remi came up from behind me.

"Get up here."

"How? You're like eleven feet taller than me," I protested.

"Twelve inches, but okay." He knelt down, picked me up, and literally placed me on his shoulders.

"Holy shit!" I squealed as he stood up. I quickly tightened my thighs around his neck and then held on to his hands that he was holding up for me.

"If I die," he wheezed, "tell them it was for a good cause."

"Oh my God, I'm sorry. I'm just so scared that I'm going to fall." I loosened the death grip my thighs had on him.

"I will not let you fall," I heard him say as he walked closer to where our friends were bouncing around in the pool, each girl trying to knock the other one off the shoulders of the guy she sat on. I ended up winning because Remi was so damn tall and quick that no one had a chance of dunking me. I was out of breath from laughing so hard and was feeling so in the moment, which I loved because it kept my toxic, anxious thoughts away. Everyone was getting out and getting dried off to make s'mores and sing karaoke, and as Remi got to the stairs of the pool to let me off his shoulders, he turned ever so slightly and placed a quick kiss on my inner thigh. Then he lifted me off his shoulders and laughed when I stumbled up the stairs.

"You shut up." I pretended to be mad. He lifted his hands up in defense.

"Hey, I didn't say anything." Then he winked. I wanted to hold his hand so badly as we walked up to the patio, where the firepit was crackling and giving off delicious warmth, but I kept my hands to myself.

In the bathroom, I quickly changed out of my wet bathing suit and got into my sweatpants and tank top. My nipples were pebbled up from the cold air that had come with the sun going down, and when I came back out to join my friends, I could see Remi pretending he hadn't noticed them. We all made a ton of s'mores, and then we finally did karaoke. We each chose a song and took turns singing. Liam did a pretty good rap, Rachel and Dee sang Justin Bieber, of course, and Lia chose a song from the movie *Frozen*. Carter did backup for Eva, who sang Britney Spears. I sang "Under the Sea" from *The Little Mermaid*, which was fun, and then it was Remi's turn. He chose a song called "Say It Back" by Ross Harris, which I had never heard before, but as soon as he started singing, we all froze.

"What the fuck?" Liam was absolutely shocked.

"He can sing?" Lia was just as shocked. I was literally speechless. Apparently, Remiel Taylor had the voice of an angel, like his actual namesake. It was deep and husky at the lower parts, but he was able to climb and hold his tone beautifully at the higher parts.

"I have goosebumps," Rachel announced, showing us her arm. Dee had her phone out and was videoing him. Remi's eyes had stayed closed the whole song, but at the very last part, he opened them and looked right at me. Everyone started clapping, and Carter and Jake were whooping. Liam got up to give him that slap-hug on the back that guys do.

"Please explain to me how I didn't know that my cousin had the voice of Apollo himself," he demanded.

Remi shrugged modestly.

"I guess I have some PTSD from being forced to sing in the church choir when I was younger, so I don't sing much anymore." He laughed it off, but I could hear the pang of truth in his words.

"Wait, like, for real?" Lia asked.

"Yeah, like, *Our God is an awesome God. He reigns from heaven above. With wisdom, power, and love. Our God is an awesome God.*" Remi belted the song out, sounding every bit the pastor's son in that moment. Liam was now absolutely hysterically laughing, Rachel was wiping away tears, and Lia was just looking confused.

"I'm so confused," she confirmed.

I kept laughing at how disoriented she seemed. Remi shrugged and handed the mic to Jake, who was getting ready to sing something from *The Lion King*. Then he got a hookah and brought it over to where I was sitting.

"Wow," I said as he got the coal sparked.

"No biggie." He seemed almost embarrassed.

"Uh, when you sound like that, it's a biggie, Rem. I'm adding the song to my playlist right now."

Remi shrugged once again as he took a pull of the hookah

and then offered it to me as he blew the smoke out through his nose. He looked so hot, it was downright illegal, I thought to myself as I took a hit. He had used a blueberry flavor, and it was really good. I took another pull because I loved the head rush the tobacco hitting my system gave me, and then I handed it back so he could get another pull himself. Afterward, we passed the hookah over to Liam and Lia, who couldn't stop making out. Then I moved over to sit on the hammock chair that Remi was sitting on. I had intended on sitting next to him, but the curve of the hammock kind of put me directly in his lap. I froze, trying to quickly decide if I was going to stand up and pretend like that never happened or take the opportunity the universe had given me and stay put. Remi quickly pulled his arm up and laid it across the back of the hammock. I leaned back tentatively till my back was on his chest, and then I felt him let out a big sigh and give in to what he had clearly been grappling with since my freak-out yesterday. His arm came down to gently rest on my shoulders, and his hand began playing with a bit of my hair, which I had taken down from the bun earlier.

"This okay?" I heard him whisper as all of our friends came to join us in the other hammock chairs. I nodded. I felt him lean down and kiss my hair. Something shifted in me at that moment. I knew that we had started off in a weird setting: Him being my bff's cousin, and the fact that we didn't really attempt to get to know each other outside the context of being friends until he got drunk the other night and spilled the beans on his weird church trauma, we made out, and then things escalated physically. But since yesterday, he had been showing me that this was a lot more than just a damaged church kid trying to figure his shit out with the nearest available girl. It actually felt like he cared about me, whether he was allowed to touch me or not. He admittedly had been super respectful of my boundaries. He was sweet. Attentive. Always making sure I had what I needed, like giving me a towel after we got out of the pool or roasting an extra marshmallow for me when mine fell into the fire. He had even wiped the gooey marshmallow residue off my chin with his thumb. I leaned back more firmly on his chest and pulled my legs up so they intertwined with his.

"What are you doing? Everyone can see you," he muttered quietly in my ear. I smiled up at him. "I'm not ashamed of you."

He held eye contact with me.

"I didn't say you were ashamed."

"We're not a secret." I changed my wording to appease him. He smiled at that. "So, there's a we?" he asked.

"What are you two whispering about?" Rachel interrupted our little figuring-out-our-shit session.

"They're figuring out when they can fuck next." Of course Carter would say that. I sat up and looked at all of my friends.

"We are not fucking. But..."

"But...?" Dee said gleefully.

"We are getting to know each other," I finished.

"Like dating?" Rachel pushed. I felt Remi's hand close around my hip and gently squeeze.

"Yeah, like dating... But like super slow and..." I trailed off as all of my friends erupted into cheers.

"I knew it!" Liam shouted. "You guys are going to make the cutest babies."

"Oh my God, Liam," I groaned and leaned up in protest. Remi pulled me back onto his chest and proceeded to rock the hammock with his long legs.

"He's just excited," Remi told me, seeming like he hoped I wouldn't go back to my anxious place where I inevitably pushed him away.

"I know he is, but take it down a notch, crazy pants."

Remi snorted but didn't say anything further about it.

By nine, the girls were getting all of the food put away inside with Liam. Remi was outside cleaning the grill, Carter was putting out the fire pit, and Jake was assisting with the hookahs. I yawned.

"I'm so not in the mood for school tomorrow," I said out loud.

"Ugh, same though." Rachel looked up from where she was putting all of the cut-up fruit into containers.

"Just a few more weeks, and we'll be done." Liam came up to me and slung his arm around my shoulder. "I'm really happy," he whispered into my hair. "Remi is such a good guy, and you know you're my favorite person."

"For real, we're going so slow…" I looked up at him. Liam wasn't as tall as Remi, but it wasn't that hard for anyone to tower over me.

"I know, babe. We're all just joking around," Liam reassured me.

"I'm just scared that if it doesn't work out, we'll ruin the whole friend group." I told him one of the fears I had been having since I decided I wanted to get to know Remi better.

"Then we won't allow that to happen." Liam sounded very confident. "If it doesn't work, then we figure it out. We go back to just being a friend group. I will never ever pick between you two if that's what you're worried about. You're gonna be my best woman at my wedding one day, Shaen. And he's my cousin. These friendships are for life, no matter what happens. Okay?"

"Okay." I nodded, trying to be comforted by Liam's easy-going confidence, but I thought, if only it were that easy.

When the pool was completely cleaned up and everyone was ready to leave, Eva and Carter offered to take me home, but Remi came up behind us and said, "I'll take her. You guys are headed in the opposite direction."

Eva gave me a knowing look but didn't say anything as she hugged me goodbye. I gave everyone else hugs as if we weren't all going to see each other again tomorrow. Lia whispered in my ear that we definitely were going to talk about this turn of events later. I laughed and gently pushed her back in Liam's direction. Remi took my bag and opened the front door.

"Remi, I can carry my own stuff," I protested.

"Yeah, but why should you when I can do it?" He unlocked the jeep. "After you. Pixie."

I stuck my tongue out at him.

"Careful what you do with that." He laughed. As he drove out of the driveway, he asked, "So, we're dating, huh?"

"Are you mad? I probably should have discussed it with you again before I just said that in front of all of our friends."

"I'm not mad," he replied softly. "I'll be honest, though; I'm having a hard time keeping up."

My heart sank. I knew exactly what he meant because I had a hard time keeping up with my rapidly changing emotions most of the time too.

"Hey, hey." He put a hand on my knee. "I will navigate every mood swing with you if it means I get to date you. I'm just going to need to figure you out a little bit better. That's all, baby. Okay?"

"I'm not crazy. I'm just confused. I've been taking care of myself by myself for literally years now, and I just need to figure out how to include someone in that who is more than a friend."

"I know, honey. I have plenty to figure out too. We'll do it together."

I warmed at his use of the word *honey* as he parked the car in front of my apartment building.

"Can I come up to say good night?" he asked. I should just say good night here, I thought, but my traitorous body nodded. His eyes brightened, and I giggled.

"No funny business," he promised.

"Mm-hmm." I did not believe him one bit, and to be honest,

my body was primed and ready for him anyway. He reached for my hand as we walked up to the apartment, and touching him again sent tingles rippling through me.

Once we got inside, he waited in the living room while I showered the salt water from Liam's fancy pool off of me and got into pajamas. I had chosen a silky set of tiny boy shorts and a small, revealing top that, without my bra on, clung to every curve of my breasts. They felt so heavy and full from how turned on I was. I had been ever since he texted me this morning that he had jerked off, basically, in his words, to the thought of me. I came out of the bathroom trying to maintain a very innocent look on my face. When Remi saw me, he groaned and covered his eyes with his hand.

"Shaen, Shaen, how am I supposed to behave when you fucking look like that?" He peeked at me through his fingers and shook his head. "Good lord, girl, you overestimate my self-control."

I didn't say anything, I just turned to go to my room, and in what I hoped looked sexy, I gave him a little "come here" motion with my finger. I've never seen him run faster than at a football game. He scooped me up in his arms, so I had to wrap my legs around his waist to hold myself up. I was laughing and let out a bit of a shriek as he shut off the light and closed my door.

"Oh, you sneaky, naughty girl." His hands were rubbing all over my ass. I grabbed onto his hair to pull his face up to me, and I attacked his mouth. He moaned into mine and began to kiss me in earnest. I could feel him harden against me where I was being held up on him. I wriggled my hips and rubbed my crotch against his body.

"Oh God, yes." He came up for air and looked at me, his hair an absolute mess from my hands and his eyes a bit out of focus. "Is this a sign to do more or...?" He seemed so unsure that I felt bad about all the mixed signals I had been giving out lately.

"This is a sign, Remi. Please, please..." I couldn't form words anymore because he had slipped his fingers into my shorts and was feeling how wet I was.

"You're soaked. Is that for me, baby?" He sounded breathless. I nodded quickly.

"What a good girl."

I melted at the praise. He took his fingers out of my shorts, slick with me, and then wiped some of it on my lips. Before I could even react, he was licking my essence off my mouth. I decided that I loved that based on just how wild it had made Remi.

"Oh my God." He gave me one more deep kiss and then laid me down on my bed. He stared at me for a second, my chest heaving, my breasts super sensitive, my pussy throbbing with desire.

"How did I get so lucky?" He took off his shirt and shorts. He was wearing boxer briefs underneath, and his erection looked huge behind the black cotton. I honestly had no idea how it would fit in me one day. Remi then came over to the bed to lay above me. He kissed me all over my chest and then helped me take off my clothes. I was completely naked now. I had tried to cover myself with my hands, but Remi had taken both of my wrists in one of his hands and held them above me, saying something about not hiding from him. After thoroughly feasting on my nipples and kissing his way all over my stomach, he stopped suddenly and asked, "Where is your vibrator?"

I stilled. "My what?"

"Your toy. Be a good girl and get it for me."

Excitement rose in my chest. I was so turned on right now I would probably come the minute it touched me.

I crawled over to my night table, which earned me a slight slap on my ass. I grabbed the pink bullet and brought it back. Remi sat up against my headboard.

"Come here." He motioned for me to sit in his lap, my legs around his waist, my breasts brushing up against his chest. I could feel him throbbing in his underwear now. We sat face to face for a second when he questioned, "How many orgasms have you had in one night?"

"O-one," I stuttered. "I get so sensitive that I have to stop."

"We're going for three tonight." He seemed determined, and I squirmed in his lap.

"I can't do that."

"We'll see." His eyes were on me when he turned the vibrator on and placed it between my legs.

"Oooh," I moaned so loudly that I clapped my hand over my mouth, afraid the neighbor would hear me.

"Keep your eyes on me." I had noticed that horny Remi was really bossy.

"I can't," I moaned, but I did it anyway. Making eye contact while naked and writhing felt so uncomfortably vulnerable for me. "I'm gonna come. Oh my God, you're making me come!" I called out as a borderline aggressive orgasm hit me. I was now leaning back on Remi's knees, my hips lifted in the air as the orgasm ripped through me, taking all of the strength out of my arms and legs.

"Oh, good girl, give it to me," he crooned. Once I was done, he did not move the vibrator. My body felt like it was on fire.

"Remi, I can't, I can't." I felt like I was going to cry. I was on a dopamine overload, and my body felt every little touch ten times over.

"You can. You can do it." He turned the speed up, and I felt my toes curl. I was now sitting in his lap, my chest pressed against his, and our lips fused as I was licking my way into his mouth. I was soaking his hand; I could feel how slippery everything was. The second orgasm gave me no warning. It had no lead-up, it just hit me out of nowhere.

"Fuuuuuuck," I moaned, closing my eyes and gripping Remi's shoulders. "Ah, ah, ah, ah."

"Breathe, babe," he ordered. I took a deep breath and slowed my hips. I felt drunk. I was so sweaty too, so much for that shower.

"I can't handle another one. I'm going to die," I sobbed, kissing the side of his now prickly cheek.

"You can," he said, moving the toy back in place on my clit. I jerked at how sensitive I was; my nerve endings were short-circuiting.

"Remi, don't make me." I was begging as my hips moved on their own accord. My whole body quivered in his lap.

"You are so stunning." Remi took his other hand and pushed some hair out of my face. I could feel how flushed my face was, and I was certain my eyes looked crazy at this point. I must have had two orgasms in a span of ten minutes, but this next one was taking longer to get its grip on me.

"I'm taking too long," I told him after a while of him moving the vibrator on me.

"I'll go all night for you." He would not give up. I wondered how an eighteen-year-old boy who grew up in the church knew how to give his brand new girlfriend multiple orgasms in a row. Remi dipped the tip of the toy into the mess I had made between my legs and then moved it back up to my clit. He made circular movements that had me sobbing his name. At the same time, getting to this place of pleasure had me feeling so beautiful and revered. It felt so sensual just noticing how hot it was to have his hand grip my hip, how gentle his lips were over my throat, and how good his tongue felt on my breast. I held his face there, reaching down to feel where his tongue was licking my beaded nipple. His mouth closed over my fingers together with my nipple, and he looked up at me.

"You. Taste. So. Good.," he enunciated. "Give me some of it."

In my frenzy, I couldn't understand. He motioned to my pussy. "Give me some to taste."

Holy fuck, he was so kinky. I couldn't wrap my head around how I felt about it while my heart was going a million beats a minute. As my sweat was mixing with his, and my body was chasing it's third orgasm, I slowed the movements of my hips and reached my hand down. I was literally pooling wetness. It had gone completely down both of my thighs and was soaking Remi's underwear.

"Oh, oh my God," I moaned. I got two of my fingers wet to the knuckle and brought them back up in between our mouths. He leaned in and licked up one side of my finger.

"Oh Jesus," he moaned appreciatively. "You're such a good girl for giving this to me."

My pussy clenched at his words. I could feel the wave of an orgasm coming closer, and I began to move my body faster, saying things like, "Yes, yes, do it like that. Harder. Oh my God, this is so good. Ooooh, Remi."

He kept eye contact while he put both of my wet fingers inside his mouth and sucked. My body was instantly in sensory overload again.

"Let go, honey. Let yourself get there." He was holding a hand on my lower back now, helping my hips move against the vibrator. He was kissing me, talking to me in between kisses.

"I never imagined I could get so lucky. You are so hot. Yes, fuck my hand, baby. Fuck it. Oh yes, you're making me so hot. Do you like it? Do you want to come again? Can you do it for me?"

I wanted to so badly, but I couldn't quite get there. Suddenly, he bit the edge of my lip, giving me a pinch of pain, and then he licked it to soothe the bite.

"Be a good girl and come. Look how good you're taking me."

His words made me think of him actually fucking me and

what that would look like, and that is what finally tipped me over the edge. The orgasm ripped from me, and it had me screaming and crying.

"Shh." Remi held me tight against him as he removed the toy and shut it off. "Your neighbors are going to call the police." He laughed huskily. I was limp, spent, and exhausted. Our bodies were stuck together with sweat. I couldn't move even if I wanted to.

"I think you broke me," I muttered against his chest.

"I hope so." I felt his laughter under my cheek. I could feel his hard dick against my stomach.

"I want to help you..." I gestured to his erection. He shook his head, kissing my temple.

"You sleep, baby." Remi pulled the blanket over me, and that was the last thing I remembered till I woke up the next morning. Alone.

I ached in such a blissful way, and as I straddled the place of being fully awake and fully asleep, I wondered why I felt so relaxed until reality smacked me in the face like the bitch she was. All the orgasms! Remi! I ran my hand over the other side of my bed and came up empty. I turned over and saw that he wasn't there. I peeked under the blanket. Yup, I was still stark naked. I wondered if he was in the shower, so I jumped out of bed, but I found the bathroom empty too. In fact, the whole apartment was dark. No one was here but me. I trudged back to the bathroom feeling a little abandoned and started the shower because I could still feel the sticky sweat that had dried on me and the smell of sex that lingered on my body. Well, maybe not sex, but whatever described the place that we had gone to last night. Or, rather, the place that I had gone to. I flushed, remembering that I had been greedy with my orgasms, and he hadn't even had one. I took the time to fully shave my whole body, and then once I got out, I moisturized as well. Then, I chose a vintage button-down shirt that I had just gotten at the thrift store. It had a maroon and gray paisley print on it, and I tucked just the front of it into a pair of washed-out jeans and left a few of the top buttons undone. As I did my hair and makeup, I wondered why my phone was so quiet. Actually, I didn't even know what time it was. It was then that I discovered that my phone was nowhere to be found; my plug hung empty on my night table. After a little bit of panic and a lot of searching, I found my phone under my bed, dead.

"Fuck!" I quickly plugged it in, and as it turned on, a flood of messages from last night came in. I was happy to find that it was only six forty-five. I was so grateful that my body had woken me up early because I could have just kept sleeping without my alarm on to wake me up. I opened up my message app.

> **REMI**
>
> I can't find your phone or pen and paper and I don't want to wake you but I have to leave.

That had been sent at 12:33 a.m., so he had only slept next to me for a few hours. What happened? Why did he have to go? I opened up the group chat, hoping to get more answers.

> **LIA**
>
> @remi where is Shaen? I keep calling her but it goes straight to voicemail

> **REMI**
>
> she's sleeping. I don't know where her phone is. @liam did she leave it by you?

> **LIAM**
>
> I don't see it here

> **LIA**
>
> why is she sleeping at 11:30??

> **CARTER**
>
> you know why he wore her out *tongue out laughing emoji*

LIA

if she wakes up soon tell her to call me

REMI

k

Then at 12:30 a.m., Remi had sent:

REMI

guys my grandfather just had a stroke. I have to leave. If you don't hear from Shaen by 7 am can one of you go check on her? Her alarm won't be on cuz I can't find her ducking phone

REMI

fucking. FUCK

LIAM

shit. take my car bro. I'll take care of Shaen.

Remi didn't answer until 3:30 a.m. when he said:

REMI

thank you. He didn't make it

What?? My heart skipped a beat. It must be his father's father because if it had been the grandfather he and Liam shared, then Liam and his mother would have also gone. I texted the chat with shaky fingers.

SHAEN

I found my phone.

LIAM

I'm picking u up in my moms car. Eta 7:20. U ready?

Then I messaged Remi privately.

He didn't respond.

Liam looked tired as I got into his car. Lia wasn't there. I assumed she had another doctor's appointment. She had Lyme disease and saw a lot of holistic doctors to try to heal it naturally.

"What the hell is going on?" I asked.

"The funeral is on Thursday. You coming?" Liam didn't answer my question but provided me with the info that I wanted.

"I mean... do you think he'll want me there?" I was holding a protein shake for breakfast, but I couldn't even stomach a sip. I felt so anxious and also so sad for Remi. Liam looked at me.

"Uh, yeah, I'm sure he'll want you there."

"We literally have only been doing whatever it is that we're doing for like three days. Maybe it's too much."

"Shaen, he's liked you since last year when he met you at my mom's grand opening party," Liam corrected me. I was shocked to hear this. Last summer, Julia opened up a second location for her injections and aesthetics spa, and she threw a big grand opening party. Liam's aunt and cousin came, and I remember thinking how hot the cousin was. We had barely spoken, although Liam had introduced me as his best friend, and Remi had said, "Nice to meet you, Shaen," while shaking my hand. Then, later on, I had been getting a water from the open bar, and he had been standing behind me waiting to order a drink. When I turned around to walk away, I tripped, and some water spilled from my glass and had gotten on his shirt. I was so morti-fied and kept apologizing, and he just said, "It's really fine. Don't worry about it."

That was the only interaction we had. I wasn't sure how that had made enough of an impression on him for Liam to confi-dently say he had liked me since then, but maybe what was happening between us now wasn't as sudden and out of left field as I had originally thought, at least not for him.

"If you want to come, let me know. We'll drive in on Wednesday night, and we'll leave on Thursday after the funeral, so we only miss one day of school. My mom will talk to the school so we can reschedule our global final." Liam parked in the student parking lot and shut off the car.

"Okay, I'll let you know by lunch." I took my backpack and my phone, which was attached to a portable charger since it was still only at twenty percent.

"Okay, babe. Listen, I know it's only been a few days, but don't underestimate how quickly you can mean something to someone. Sometimes, the best thing you can do is be there for them when they need it. 'kay?" Liam gave me a quick hug, and we went our separate ways.

I could not focus on anything my teachers were saying. I just kept sneaking looks at my phone to see if Remi had answered me. I was scared of how big my feelings were already becoming for him. I was anxious because I missed him, and it had only been a few days of us being together. I worried that maybe his grief would push us apart. I didn't want to be a burden to him either. I wanted to be there for him. I wanted to be with him. I didn't know how to navigate this, not only because I had never been in a relationship before but because I also had never expe-rienced the natural, normal course of life in which grief happened. I had no idea who my father was, so I was born missing an entire family and a guiding paternal energy in my upbringing. My mother had no siblings, and her father passed when I was too little to remember him. Her mother had stopped visiting when I was about ten or eleven. She had not been loving or kind, so losing her from my life literally meant nothing other than another person not being around. I honestly didn't feel like I knew how to be loved properly, but I desperately wanted to. And I wanted to give it in return. I knew we weren't there yet, not even close, but I already knew I was in too deep not to go to the funeral with Liam. That much I knew.

I was spending my free period alone in the library when my phone finally buzzed, and Remi's name showed up on my screen. My heart literally double-tapped inside my chest; mainly because I was so worried about how he was holding up but also because I missed talking to him.

REMI

Shaen?

SHAEN

hi

REMI

are you in class?

SHAEN

no I have a free period now

REMI

k

REMI

I'm sorry I left you

SHAEN

please don't be. How are you?

REMI

typing…

I waited a good five minutes, watching the little blue bubbles popping up and then going away as if he didn't know what to say.

SHAEN

It's ok if you're not ok. And it's ok if you don't want to talk about it. I'm here either way

REMI

I miss you

REMI

I don't want to ask but I'm asking: can you come here?

SHAEN

I'm driving in Wednesday night with Liam

REMI

if I sent a car would you come today?

REMI

i hate being here and being here for this makes it worse and being here for this without you makes it so much worse. I sound crazy. I know we just started going out…

REMI

hey. I don't want to make this complicated im just exhausted I don't even know what I'm saying

I felt the overwhelming need to cry for him. Vulnerable Remi was not something I had seen, even when we were just navigating being in the same friend group. And other than that one night when he drank at my house, he always seemed happy, sure of himself, confident, and strong. Yet here I was, getting a glimpse of a very different side of him. Sure, it was being brought out by his exhaustion and his grief, but he was turning to me instead of shutting me out and bearing it alone, and I wanted to hold onto that.

SHAEN

what do you mean send a car?

REMI

im sorry babe that was a lot. My dad is stressing me out so much. It's too much to ask of you. They won't even let us stay in the same room if you come

SHAEN

so I'll stay in the guest room

He didn't answer for fifteen minutes.

REMI

voice note

I turned the volume of my phone down really low and listened to it.

REMI

"I'm coming back to you. I'm in the car already. I don't know why I'm still here if he's dead already, and all my father is doing is verbally harassing me. The funeral is on Thursday, so I told them that I have school and I'll come back with you guys on Wednesday night. I'm an hour away. I'll pick you up from school. Okay?"

His "okay" sounded so tired and broken. It felt like his grand-father had meant a lot to him, and I was hoping he would tell me more about him eventually. I couldn't send a voice note back because I was in the library, so I sent him a quick "okay" back with a heart emoji.

During my last class of the day, I sent a text to update Liam, letting him know that Remi was coming back and would be getting me from school. At lunch, I told him that I would be joining his family for the funeral, and this turn of events really solidified my decision. The second the bell rang, I jumped up from my seat and ran to my locker to shove my books inside and put my study guide into my backpack so I could study for finals. When? I wasn't sure, but sometime or other, I would squeeze it in. Earlier, I had gathered up all of Remi's work from his teachers, and I put that in my backpack as well. When I got outside, I saw that Remi was waiting for me in his car parked behind the bus zone. He was looking down at his phone; his hair was messy, his face was kind of pale, and he looked tired. I knocked gently on the window on the driver's side, and he looked up, startled. When he saw it was me, he opened the door and got out of the car. I got up on my tippy toes and tried to wrap as much of him up in my arms as I could. He buried his face in my shoulder, and I could feel him heaving with silent sobs. I ran my hand up and down his back, trying to be soothing and comforting.

"I'm sorry," I heard him whisper after about ten minutes of us standing near his car. When he straightened up, I saw that his eyes were red and his lashes were wet.

"Don't be sorry for that. Ever," I said firmly.

"I think I got snot on your shirt," he said once we were both in the car.

"I'll get a new shirt." I held his gaze, trying to will him to believe that I didn't care and I was here to support him.

"Okay." His voice sounded hoarse. I reached for his hand as he started driving. He held on tight, his thumb making circles on my hand. "I need to go home first."

"Okay."

He gave me a soft smile. "I missed you."

"It's been like twelve hours," I teased.

"I missed you for all twelve of them." He smiled, too, but he sounded so serious. "Is that coming on too strong?" He sounded worried. "It probably is, but even though my grandfather was eighty-two, it feels like, in the scheme of things, life is super short, and I really hate wasting that precious time pretending I'm not as into you as I am." He looked over at me. "Do not laugh at me for going all soft on you. I'll replenish my manliness on Friday." He laughed softly at himself, and I squeezed his hand.

"You're not less manly to me because you have feelings," I told him. "And to be honest, I was kinda freaked out at how much I missed you today too. It feels so fast, but I guess if it's right... it's right."

He nodded. "Wait, you were freaked out? Like good or bad?"

"Not bad. It was just weird 'cause I'm so used to doing things on my own, and suddenly, out of the blue, I'm wondering why you're not in my bed or sad that you're not in school..." I explained.

"Yeah, last night was a bit crazy. I was trying to study for a test while you slept, and suddenly, my mom called, which really freaked me out because it was the middle of the night. And she told me that my father had run to the hospital, and I needed to come home." A weird look crossed over his face, but he didn't say anything further. I chose to stay in the car while Remi ran in to get his school stuff and more clothes for tonight and tomorrow. Suddenly, it dawned on me that my mother would be home when we got there. Well fuck. I thought about telling Remi that we should just stay at his place so we could avoid her, but I wasn't sure what Julia would think of that. I knew that Lia slept over pretty often, but I felt like I didn't want to disappoint Julia, which made no sense because I knew how much Julia liked me.

After mulling over both options, I decided to go home, and if my mother wasn't happy about it, I would let her know what was what. She had never given me any rules before, and I wasn't going to let her start now. My phone buzzed, and the group chat was active again now that class was out.

LIA

We love you Remi

EVA

yes! We're so sorry Rem *heart emoji*

CARTER

here for you man

DEE

Remi let us know what you need

RACHEL

so sorry to hear Remi. We'll see you on Thursday

LIAM

I have my moms car so use the jeep as long as you need. We got you cuz

REMI

love you guys too

I hearted his message before I could overthink it. The words love you were practically vibrating in my mind when Remi came back to the car.

"Do you have your license on you?" he asked as he put an overnight bag and his backpack in the backseat.

"Yup." I showed it to him.

"Can you drive? I'm beat," he asked, coming around to the passenger's side and opening my door.

"Ummmm." I really had so few hours driving that I was scared I'd majorly fuck this up. Remi put his hands on either side of my face and leaned in to kiss me gently on the lips.

"Hi," he whispered.

"Hi," I whispered back.

"You can do this," he encouraged me. I sighed and crawled over to the driver's seat. Remi made fun of how much I had to move the seat up.

"I'm not even that short; honestly, you're just absurdly tall." I joked back at him as I anxiously left the driveway.

"Okay, pixie." He always seemed to be slightly amused at how tiny I was next to him.

By the time we got to my parking lot, Remi was looking like he regretted giving me the keys.

"I'm pretty sure you went ninety all the way here."

I laughed. "I can't drive slow. It's boring."

"Stop signs are not suggestions, babe." He took the keys out of my hands, shaking his head, pretending to be annoyed.

"Hey, I stopped!" I protested.

"Yeah, for like three seconds." He took my bag with his and reached for my hand as we started up the stairs.

"Why do I need to stop longer when it's clearly an empty street? It makes no sense." I felt strongly about that.

"Okay, note to self, my girlfriend is a menace on the streets," Remi said, tucking the keys into his pocket.

I tingled at the word girlfriend. Then I poked him in the ribs.

"I am not a menace."

"A tiny pixie menace," he insisted. We were cracking up as I unlocked the door, but I instantly sobered as we walked inside my apartment because my mother's moans were clear as could be coming from her bedroom where her door stood open.

"Holy fuck." My face instantly heated, and I froze. Remi quickly shut the door and ushered us into my room, where he locked the door and immediately pressed play on a playlist on his phone.

"Remi!" I hissed. "Turn it off. She'll know I'm here."

"That's the point." He looked pissed. "Listen, I don't really understand it, but the only acceptable excuse she has for being an absentee mother is that she's a single mom and she works a lot, and you're eighteen... but this? This is not okay. She knows you come home now! This is just not cool. And her door is open! She didn't even try to be appropriately discreet."

I went over to him and hugged him so hard that he bent down and placed a kiss on my head.

"I have never had someone care about me like you do," I mumbled into his shirt.

"What?" He didn't understand me, so instead, I just said, "I said thank you for caring."

The noise had stopped, and then we heard a man's voice laughing, the water in the bathroom turn on, and then the toilet flushing. A few moments later, someone rapped on my bedroom door, so Remi turned off the music. I stood up to crack my door open, and he got right behind me. My mother stood there in her slightly gaping bathrobe. Her hair was a mess, and her makeup was smudged. She was beautiful, but she was bitter, and it showed.

"Lost track of time, sorry," she said begrudgingly, as if I purposefully ruined her little romp in the sheets. "Who are you?" She motioned to Remi.

"This is Remi. We're studying for finals, and then he's sleeping over, so if you order dinner, get enough for him too. Also, I'll be going with him on Wednesday to his hometown for his grandfather's funeral, so I won't be home till Thursday night," I snapped. I was usually overly forgiving with my mother, but seeing the situation through Remi's eyes was suddenly giving me a backbone. I felt Remi's hand on my lower back as if to say, *I'm here.*

My mother blinked at me, and then she reached up to pull her robe closed a little bit more.

"I'm Amy." She didn't smile, but she did introduce herself. "I'm sorry about your grandfather..." Her voice trailed off.

"Thanks," Remi replied tersely. She blinked again, then turned away.

"I'm ordering Taco Bell. I'll text you when it's here."

I heard the faceless man from her room calling her name and her saying to hold on, that she needed to order food. I closed the door and let out the breath I had been holding.

"Are you okay?" Remi sat down next to me on my bed. I nodded but then shook my head.

"She didn't even care enough to tell me that you couldn't sleep over," I whispered, as the lump in my throat grew, threatening to choke me. Remi side-hugged me.

"I'm sorry."

"No, I'm sorry you had to hear any of that; she's so embarrassing." I sniffled. He laid down with his head in my lap, his body across the rest of the bed, hands resting on his stomach.

"Wait till you meet my dad." He closed his eyes and fell asleep almost immediately. I put a soft throw blanket on top of him. It didn't cover all of him, but I tried. I heard him make a soft snore, and I loved that I was a safe enough place for him to just pass out like that.

Half an hour later, my mother texted me that the Taco Bell bag was by my door. When I tried to sneak my body out from under Remi's head, he woke up looking disoriented.

"I'm here, baby," I told him softly, running my hands through his hair.

"Aw." His eyes met mine. "You called me baby."

"I haven't said that before?" I looked confused.

"No, ma'am. I would have remembered if you did." He leaned up and caught my mouth in his. We kissed Spider-Man fashion until his stomach grumbled. He chuckled.

"Sorry."

I got off the bed and retrieved the food. We ate, sitting on my floor, talking and listening to music. I felt like I had known him forever at this point. He had filled a space in my life that I couldn't imagine being empty again. The best part was I felt so comfortable being myself that I didn't keep feeling like I had to stuff my feelings down and fake it. He had even met my mother, whom I had never introduced to my friends before. I licked my fingers as I took the last bite of my taco bowl.

"Good?" he asked, his eyes on my mouth.

"Good," I confirmed. "I'm gonna get changed, and then we'll study?"

"Let's do it." His phone rang, but he silenced it almost immediately. I didn't ask questions. Instead, I took off the clothes I had worn to school and pulled on my oversized T-shirt with a picture of Rip from *Yellowstone* on it.

"A Rip fan, I see?" He cocked an eyebrow.

"Well, since you're my Rip now, get me a shirt with your face on it, and I'll wear it," I joked.

"Will do." He seemed serious, which made me laugh. We got back on the bed after Remi put on a tank top and basketball shorts, and we started studying for our tests. He helped me memorize vocabulary flashcards, and I tested him for his science exam. An hour later, he yawned.

"I'm running on empty, babe."

"Let's go to sleep." I cleaned up our school stuff, and we took turns getting ready for bed in the bathroom. I could hear the TV on in my mother's room, but it didn't do much to hide the sound of her mattress springs creaking. I guess she was trying harder to mask it. I'd give her that.

As we got into bed, Remi buried his head in my shoulder. He smelled like a mix of Remi and mint toothpaste.

"He was more of a dad to me than my real dad," I heard him murmur against my skin. I didn't say anything. I just gave him space to talk.

"When my dad would go on and on in his Sunday sermons, my Pops would play hangman with me on the back of the church schedule." I could feel him smile against me. "We would go fishing and hiking every summer until his hip went out. He loved Starbucks shaken espressos, and even when his nurse said he couldn't have them anymore because of his blood pressure, he still made me sneak them in for him." Remi made a noise that sounded like a mix of a laugh and a sob. I felt a tear fall onto my arm, and then Remi's fingers quickly wiped it away. "I'd driven up to visit him six times since I moved here in September, but I feel bad that it wasn't more." His voice went hoarse. My throat burned with unshed tears for him and his obvious pain.

"I'm sure he knew you loved him so, so much." I rubbed the back of his neck, and his arms tightened around me.

"When I heard that he had a stroke, my brain immediately thought that maybe God was punishing me for... doing what I, we... what I did. I know I don't really believe that jerking off is a sin, but I still can't stop myself from thinking that maybe..."

The pain of the trauma he was holding onto was palpable. I took a deep breath and asked, "Do you still believe in God, Remi?"

He hesitated. "N-no. I don't think so." He sounded unsure.

"Okay, well, let's just say for argument's sake that there is one." I didn't believe in God myself and had never been religious, but I was trying to be very understanding and I wanted to use examples that he could relate to. "Do you think this hypothetical being that created you loves you or wants to hurt you?"

"Loves me?" he responded like it was a question.

"Okay, so say he's an all-encompassing love. Do you think he or she would punish you for finding happiness? For making your girlfriend feel so cared for and safe? For doing something every healthy man does? Having a relationship with yourself and self-pleasure is actually very important mentally and physically. And if there is a God out there, then he wouldn't be very loving if he took your grandfather as a punishment for an orgasm." I was out of breath by the time I finished my little speech. Remi was looking up at me with so much emotion in his overflowing eyes that I felt my eyes well up too.

"Don't cry, baby," he whispered, wiping them off my cheeks.

"And if there is no God…" I hiccupped. "Then this is just the natural way the circle of life goes. Honestly, I prefer to think that I am not at the mercy of an angry man in the sky, but rather, I, myself, am a representation of happiness. I am love, I am peace, I am goodness. I don't need a book or a God to tell me how to be those things. I am self-actualizing. I am not a sinner; I am whole, and I have nothing to prove. And I believe that neither do you, no matter what you were raised to believe. Your beliefs can change, and as they do, you no longer have to believe that the universe is conspiring to punish you for being human." I patted his chest, and he caught my hand in both of his and held it over his rapidly beating heart.

"I think I could love you one day, Shaen," he said, his voice sounding deep and husky. My heart fluttered.

"I think I could love you one day too," I whispered. His mouth found mine, and we held onto each other, murmuring little thoughts and comforting words until we fell asleep, my cheek on Remi's chest, his hand in my hair.

This is what healing feels like.

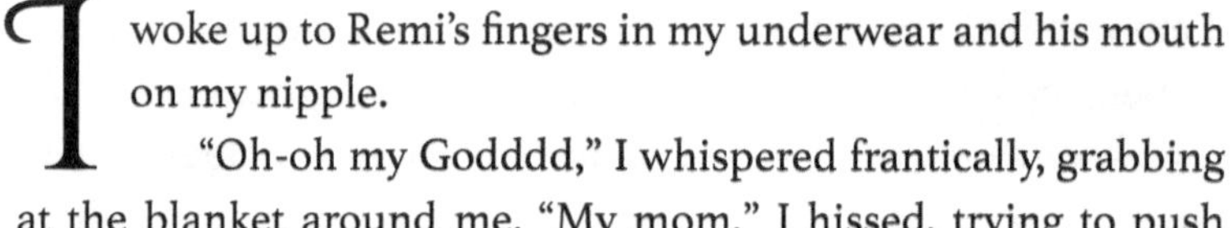

I woke up to Remi's fingers in my underwear and his mouth on my nipple.

"Oh-oh my Godddd," I whispered frantically, grabbing at the blanket around me. "My mom," I hissed, trying to push Remi's mouth off me.

"She left for work," he mumbled around my nipple.

"Huh. What time is it?" I fumbled around, trying to feel for my phone.

"It's 8 a.m., but remember, we only go in for one test today, so we don't have to be there till twelve," Remi reminded me. "So we have lots of time for activities." He grinned up at me as he sat himself up next to me, leaning on his elbow.

"What kind of activities?" I smirked as he began to pull my shorts and underwear off.

"The naked kind, of course."

"I hear that's the best kind." I tried to be funny, but then I moaned as he stuck a finger inside of me. He had never done that before.

"Holy fuck, you're tight," he groaned. I loved how verbal he was. Rachel had told me that one time she was having sex with a guy, and he had been so silent the whole time that it had freaked her out.

"Is this okay, Shaen?"

I nodded.

"Y-yes. It's okay," I mewled as he twisted his finger and found a spot in me that sent shocks throughout my body. He snickered as I gasped.

"What... what are you doing?" I panted, curling my toes into the bed.

"I'm gonna go out on a limb and guess it might be your G-spot." Remi was looking very proud of himself. He was such a conundrum because, on the one hand, he was almost as inexperienced as I was, but on the other, he was so natural at dirty talk and seemed to know exactly what to do with his hands and mouth.

"Oh my God." My hips started to lift up off the bed to match the ministrations of his finger.

"I can feel you squeezing me." He sounded awed. I could see him imagining what that would feel like around his cock. To be honest, the fonder I grew of him, the less my resolve not to have sex became. He took his other hand and rubbed my wetness up to and around my clit.

"Holy shit." I went wild for that. My whole body was on high alert, and every nerve ending was waiting for the waves of pleasure to crash over me. His finger started to move faster in and out of me, and I could hear the squelch of his movements, showing how wet I was.

"That's sooo hot, Shaen," he growled as I made an embarrassed face.

"Do you like knowing how hard you make me?"

I nodded frantically.

"Well, that's how much I like knowing how wet I make you. I mean, I did this to you, right? You're wet for me?"

"I'm so wet for you," I sobbed as his thumb on my clit and his finger in my pussy took me over the edge. I soared with this orgasm; feeling full while I came was not something I had ever experienced before, and I really liked it. According to the shaking in my legs, I liked it a lot. I opened my eyes to see him pull his fingers out and suck me off of them. He maintained eye contact while he did it, and I shivered. I wanted to do something new for him too. Every time he made me come, he had tried something different, and each time was a new experience for me. I wanted the same thing for him. I obviously had no idea what I was doing, and I was feeling really shy, but seeing his erection tenting his shorts made me want to be brave. My tank top and bra were pushed up around my neck, so I reached up to pull them off. Then I laid back down and said, "Come here," as I encouraged him to straddle me. He looked confused. I pushed my breasts together.

"Fuck me here," I told him. I watched as his eyes dilated and his jaw went slack.

"Are you serious?" He was so adorably horny yet also still so respectful. I nodded. He bent down, fully straddling me. I felt his balls brush against my rib cage as he placed his big, hard cock in between my breasts. I squeezed them tighter to create a tight valley. He moved slowly at first, groaning. I watched the angry red head disappearing and then reappearing as he moved. Then he began to pick up the pace, as he genuinely began to fuck this space I had made for him. He was shaking my body and my bed with the movement. I felt so much emotion well up inside me as he moaned and moved above me. Partially because watching him abandon the stupid things his father and the church had drilled into him was beautiful. I knew how much I liked hearing him talk to me, so I began to encourage him verbally as well.

"Yes, baby. Like that. That's so good. Fuck me."

Oh, he really liked that. I could tell by how much his cock was swelling up against my skin and the way his hips stuttered.

"I'm gonna come."

"Give it to me." I squeezed my breasts tighter, and he fucked his way to completion. He spurted all over my neck and chest, and some even got on my chin. He was out of breath as he clambered off of me and sat back, his dick softening between his legs. Remi looked down at me, reaching over to rub the cum off of my chin.

"I'm gonna need you to stay with me forever."

"'Cause I let you fuck my boobs?" I giggled.

"I mean, yes." He laughed at himself. "But also because I feel whole when I'm with you. I cannot explain it. I know it sounds nuts, but I feel like whatever was missing for me before, I have found it with you."

"Babyyy," I hummed, happiness thrumming through my veins. He reached over for his phone.

"Okay... so not to ruin the moment or anything, but can I take a picture of you before my cum dries?" The grin on his face reminded me that he was still a teenage boy.

"Remiel!" I was horrified and also turned on by his question.

"It's obviously just for me, baby. I swear no one will ever see it," he promised. He watched me with his dark eyes, some hair falling across his forehead, and I watched him back, weighing my options in my head. I knew I could say no. I knew if I said no, he would respect it. But did I want to say no? I took a deep breath in, then replied, "I feel crazy saying this, but okay."

His eyes lit up. "Oh my God." He swiped into his camera app, and I hoped I looked sexy as he took a few shots.

"Can I see?" I sat up, pulling the sheet up over me.

"Are you going to make me delete it?" he asked, holding the phone turned away from me.

"I hope not."

He turned his phone around. There I lay, my dirty-blonde hair spread out behind me, my baby hairs curling up around my temple from the sweat drying in it. My lips were red and puffy from making out, and they were turned up in a tiny smirk. My cheeks were flushed, and my eyes looked incredibly green. My chest had some red rub marks on it, and I was covered in him. My nipples were rosy and beaded. I looked hot. I looked like I had just come. I looked happy. I looked like I was in love. I startled at that last thought. Oh no. Where had that come from?

"I love it," he murmured, staring at the screen.

"I…" *love you*, my brain blurted. I squelched the thought again. "Just save it somewhere safe," I finished awkwardly. "I don't want Liam accidentally coming across it." There was no way those feelings were real, I thought to myself, feeling panicked all of a sudden. This was obviously misplaced trauma. I was trauma bonding with him because my father never loved me. That's what this was. He was nice and kind and good to me, but this was not love. Not yet. That was just impossible.

"I can almost hear you freaking out." Remi had gotten a wet washcloth from the bathroom and proceeded to clean me up with it before he pulled the covers over us again and pulled me into his arms. "What's got you so hot and bothered other than me, of course?" He winked. I considered lying and pushing my feelings down. I thought about playing it off like it wasn't a big deal. I almost said, "I'm fine." But I was honestly getting so sick of faking it. It had only been five days, and my mind was insanely aware of how crazy this was. We went from inexperienced virgins, one with abandoned daddy issues and the other with Jesus daddy issues who had never hung out one-on-one, to bonding way too fast and coming all over each other multiple times. But it just felt so easy, and I could not deny that. It felt deep, like my soul knew his soul or some cosmic shit like that. I felt safe, cared for, and seen. So seen. Like Remi had said last night, life was so short; why should I spend it faking anything? I wanted to see where my chips would fall, so to speak. I took a deep breath before saying, "I really, really like you." My voice sounded more strained than I even felt. Remi lifted himself up on one arm.

"And that's bad because?"

"Well, it's fast," I started. He looked disappointed, almost like he was thinking, not this conversation again. But I continued, "Yet somehow, I feel ready to be all in. I feel like I am jumping into the deep end of the pool with you, but I'm also okay with it. I cannot explain what it is, but it's like I can feel how much you care about me. And it feels like you really do listen when I talk, and I want to hear everything you have to say. I know I'm safe when you're around. It makes me not want to think about it being only five days. It makes me want to think of you as a permanent thing for me. And I'll be honest, I'm scared I'll get hurt or that I'll annoy you and you'll regret this, but I'm willing to risk it because this thing feels right. I know we're young, but hey, my mom had me at fifteen so I'm already old compared to her standards," I joked to lighten up the heaviness of what I was saying, but my shoulders felt light despite the immense depth of my admission, and I was so proud of myself for verbalizing my real feelings.

"It hasn't been five days for me." His confession startled me.

"Hmm?" I remembered what Liam had told me, and I had a feeling that was what he was about to share, but I wanted to hear Remi tell his version of the story.

"It's been a year for me, so my current feelings for you feel right on time. Or even overdue. I saw you at Julia's opening party, and I couldn't stop asking Liam about you. I even found you on social media. For me, Thursday was not the start. For me, Thursday was the culmination of a very long year of pining after you."

"Pining?" I giggled. "Oh, Mr. Darcy, you flatter me." I pretended to simper and bat my lashes like I imagined they did in Jane Austen's time.

"It's a big word for a jock." He rolled his eyes. That made me laugh harder. He pretended to sulk.

"You're not just a jock," I told him when I finally calmed down. "And that's sweet. Thank you for telling me that I am falling for my stalker."

"Shaen!" he protested. I cracked up again. "I didn't stalk you."

"Maybe just a little?" I teased. "I'm okay with it. It's kinda hot, and it explains my Stockholm syndrome."

"Oh my God." He pushed the blanket back and moved to get out of the bed. I pulled him back to me.

"Noooo, don't leave."

"Stop being mean." He pouted.

"Fine…" I purred. "Come kiss me."

He complied, and we made out until his phone rang. It was Julia calling to discuss the plans for Wednesday. While he talked to her, I got ready for school and made us both breakfast. As I finished pouring his protein shake into a cup with a straw, he came up behind me and put his arms around my shoulders, kissing the side of my neck.

"I like playing house with you, Shaen Collins."

"I like playing house with you too, Remiel Taylor," I told him back. We stood there for a moment, just existing in our own bubble. No finals, no need for after graduation plans, no anxiety, no funerals to attend. Just us and our bliss, and it was perfect. Even if it was just for the moment.

13

———

Wednesday came quickly, and before I knew it, I was packing up a bag because my ride was coming to pick me up for our drive to Remi's hometown. In the car would be Remi, Sam, Julia, Liam, and Lia. Liam's older brothers were meeting us there, as was our group of friends. Julia had left the younger boys with her parents. I looked through my closet, wondering what one wore to a funeral since I had never attended one before, let alone one for the grandfather of the boy I liked. I knew to choose something black, and I assumed a dress would be the most appropriate option. I ended up picking a dress that I had gotten on a social media market-place secondhand but had never had any events to wear it to before. The dress had long sleeves and a tight high-necked bodice that closed with pearl buttons around the back of my neck. It was open just a bit across the back, and my favorite part of the dress was that it flared out really puffy from the waist down. I felt like a sexy cupcake in it, and I hoped sexy cupcake would still be a respectful vibe. I brought black stockings and a pair of black heels that were a good four inches tall, but I didn't own anything shorter than that. I saw that my phone had buzzed with an ETA text from Liam saying I had fifteen minutes. I proceeded to throw underwear, pajamas, hair care, skin care, makeup, and clothes for the way home into my overnight bag. I then shoved my AirPods and charger into my crossbody purse and ran downstairs to wait for the car.

When they drove up and stopped in front of me, Julia popped the trunk, and I put my bag in with the pile of other travel bags that were already there.

"Hi, Shaen," Sam, Liam's dad, greeted me as I got into the car. He always said my name with extra vowels. It came out Shayennnnn instead of the correct way to say it, which was Shane, and it always made me laugh.

"Hi, Dr. Hennessy," I responded in my most respectful voice.

"It's Sam," he corrected me like he always did.

"Mm-hmm," I murmured, which made everyone laugh. Remi was sitting in the back, so I squeezed between Lia and Liam, who were in the middle bucket seats, and I sat down next to him. He surprised me by laying a kiss smack on my mouth and then reached over to buckle me in. I looked up guiltily and caught Julia's eye as she was turned around watching us. She smiled and said, "If I had a dollar for every time my nephew tried to casually ask about you, I would have a lot of money." She laughed. Remi groaned as his aunt outed him. "So this is a surprise, but it makes a lot of sense, and I'm so happy that my two favorite people are finally together."

"Hey," both Sam and Liam exclaimed together.

"It is what it is. I don't make the rules," she deadpanned. Liam pretended to cry, which made all of us laugh. As Sam merged onto the highway, Remi took my hand and held it tight.

"I'm more anxious about my dad ruining something with us than burying my grandfather," he admitted to me.

"I know." I squeezed his hand.

"Please don't let him get between us. He will certainly try. He isn't... a nice man." He sounded so nervous that I suggested that we listen to music. I handed him one of my AirPods and told him that we had to choose a song for each other to listen to that said something we wanted the other person to hear. He agreed. I chose the first song, which was "Wild Horses" by The Rolling Stones, but it was a cover sung by Miley Cyrus. He seemed confused at first, but then when he heard the words "wild horses couldn't drag me away," he understood my intent, and he smiled. The first song he chose was "Closer" by Tegan and Sara, and I melted when I heard them sing, "It's not just all physical," and then I flushed when the lyrics turned to "all you think of lately is getting underneath me." I pushed against his leg when I heard that, and he snickered. My second song was "Into You" by Ariana Grande, which made him place a kiss on the top of my forehead. His next song was "Candy Shop" by 50 Cent, which made me laugh so loud that we had to take a break because Liam and Lia begged us to tell them what game we were playing. My third song was "Stay" by Kid Laroi and Justin Bieber. He made fun of me by saying that I had a crush on Justin, and I made fun of him back for insinuating that I liked a five-nine and blonde Justin Bieber when clearly I was into a dark-haired, six-three, muscly man. He shrugged, but he looked very smug as he searched for his third song, "All My Life" by Lil Durk, which felt like the perfect song for us to have as our anthem for fighting life circumstances and not letting them get us down. At that point, we were getting close to his house, so for my last song, I chose "Here for You" by Kygo, which made him kiss me softly. Yet it was his last song that reverberated in my body. Honestly, I couldn't make eye contact with him while we listened to it. He had chosen "What If I Told You That I Love You" by Ali Gatie.

Remi's house was huge and in a gated community that screamed megachurch. Remi caught me staring and whispered,

"I would kill to be in your room right now trying not to hear your mom fuck over being here."

I laughed so hard that I had tears in my eyes as Sam pulled up in front of the house and shut off the car. Julia, who was usually so bubbly and had a glass-half-full kind of attitude, turned around in her seat to look at me.

"Listen to me, Shaen, you are a beautiful girl inside and out, and I bet on you and Remi. Every day. Twice on Sundays. Okay?"

I nodded, feeling so confused. Remi had gone super still next to me.

"I am your family. We"— she motioned to Liam, Sam, and Lia— "are your family, and everyone in this car loves you so much. I just want you to know that no matter what you see today or tomorrow, Remi is amazing, not because of where he comes from but despite it." She said that last part so emphatically that I could taste the anger in her words.

"If anything happens, please let it make the two of you stronger, not weaker. Okay? Promise me that."

I had never seen her like this before, and I was suddenly scared to go into the house.

"I promise," I whispered.

"And Remi, we adore you. You are like a son to us, and it pains me so much to see you hurting. We are here for you."

I could hear her silent words "and only you" reverberate through the car.

"Well then." Sam cleared his throat. "Now that we have sufficiently scared the shit out of Shaen, let's go inside."

We all laughed at that, and Remi whispered in my ear, "It's really going to be fine."

I felt sad that he couldn't just focus on what was happening tomorrow, but rather, everything was so strained due to his father's obvious mental abuse.

The house was beautiful, but I didn't get to see much of it

because a housekeeper quickly showed Lia and me to a room in the basement that we would be sharing. Liam and Remi were sleeping in his old room upstairs. We freshened up, and then Remi texted the group chat that dinner was starting. Lia and I gave each other a hug for moral support before going back upstairs. We were eating in a large and elaborate dining room that had dark wood paneling, thick plush drapes, and multiple chandeliers hanging from the recessed ceiling. I had never been somewhere so fancy before. I was already feeling uncomfortable, but the massive cross that was hung on the wall reminded me even more how out of place I actually was. Remi's father was at the end of the huge table, and I was surprised to find that Remi looked nothing like him. Where Remi was dark, his father was fair. Where Remi was tall and broad, his father was more slight and thin. Remi's mother, on the other hand, was dark like Remi, and she was what I imagined Julia would look like if she hadn't added a ton of highlights to her hair. Remi pulled out a chair for me, and his father's head snapped up, and he fixed his green eyes on me.

"Who is this, Remiel?" he demanded.

"My girlfriend." Remi's tone was cold and lacking any emotion. I had heard this sound in his voice one other time before, the night that his father had called him as he sat in my apartment.

"Hmm. Does this girl have a name?" He sounded exactly as I imagined his father would sound. Condescending and fake.

"My name is Shaen." I spoke quickly before Remi was forced to keep playing this weird game his father had going on.

"Hmm." He looked at me again. "I am Pastor John Taylor. Are you a Christian, Shaen?" he asked. I ran cold. What the fuck? Why was this his first question? At this point, Remi couldn't even bring himself to look at me, and I could almost feel Julia's anger coming off of her from across the table. I held my chin high and stared right back at him.

"I am not."

The pastor humphed again. Then, I watched him lift his glass and wait without saying a word. Moments later, Remi's mother rushed over and poured him some wine. So the patriarchy is alive and well, I thought to myself, feeling nauseous.

"Are you Jewish then?" He brought his attention back to me. No one had sat down yet, and I could just feel how much he was loving this power trip.

"Nope." I figured the less I gave him, the better. It felt odd to be doing this weird little dance with a man who had just lost his father, yet he didn't seem that broken up about it at all.

"Let's say grace." The pastor suddenly changed the topic, and everyone sat down. I felt Remi's hand take my left hand as Liam took my right since he was sitting on the other side of me. Remi squeezed my hand as if to apologize. I kept my eyes on him and mouthed, "Wild horses."

He smiled sadly. John lowered his head and closed his eyes, and the rest of the table quickly filed suit. I chose to keep my head up, and my eyes stayed wide open. John began,

"Heavenly Father, bless us and this food and the gifts which we receive from your bountiful goodness. May you watch over my father, who is now released into the arms of Jesus. May we all know the wholeness and peace that my father is now experiencing. Gracious God, help us to love each other fervently. Grow our love so deep that it is able and willing to overcome and forgive a multitude of misgivings. Inspire a spirit of hospitality in each of us and enable us to cheerfully share our home with our guests. And through time, may this lost daughter, Miss Shaen, come to know your love, my Lord. Amen."

I felt like I had been punched in the stomach. If there was ever a way to passive-aggressively let someone know that you do not accept them for who they are, it was exactly like that. One thing my mother had instilled in me was my freedom of belief and expression, yet I had also grown up knowing her disdain for Christianity. I had never known why she felt that way about religion until this moment. Pastor John's eyes opened, and he looked right at me. He looked startled to find my eyes open already, and then I saw it dawn on him that I had never shut them in the first place. I fought the desire to tell him to go fuck himself, and instead, I stared so long and so hard that I forced him to look away first.

Shots fired, I thought to myself as I filled my plate with food and ate. But it all tasted like sandpaper.

This is what hate feels like.

DINNER WAS awkwardly quiet as the pastor didn't say another word to anyone but "thank you" to the waiter when they brought out dessert. There were small pockets of conversation happening around the table, but I chose not to join any of them so as not to draw any more unnecessary attention to myself. When dinner was finally over, Remi's father quickly excused himself, telling us that he needed to complete his sermon for the funeral. He said a general goodnight to the room but didn't look at anyone or address anyone in particular when he left. Perhaps his wife or his son could have used some basic attention, I thought, but I imagined that was not something they received from him often or maybe ever. Both Lia and I offered to help clear the table, but Remi's mother, Miley Taylor, flitted over and told us not to bother because the "staff" would take care of it. She was beautiful, and I could see the similarities between her and her sister Julia in their eye color and bone structure, but it ended there. For one, Miley was dressed much more modestly than Julia. But also, her eyes were devoid of humor or joy. She had seemed very submissive to her husband earlier, and it almost felt as if the pastor had broken it into her.

"Remiel." I heard her soft voice as I got ready to leave the room.

"What, Mom?" He sounded so tired. She paused as if she wanted to say something else, but then she just said, "Goodnight. I love you." And she kissed him on the forehead. He hugged her briefly with a quick "Goodnight" of his own. Then he took my hand and began to lead me out of the dining room. I met the gaze of his mother, and she had an interesting look on her face that I could not decipher.

"Dinner was delicious, thank you," I told her.

"It was my pleasure," she intoned. I imagined she said all the right things and had all the proper etiquette; after all, she was the wife of a famous pastor. It seemed to me that she felt like that was her most valued role. More important than being a mother. Lia went outside with Liam, so Remi and I had the guest room to ourselves for a moment.

"I'm so sorry, Shaen," he bit out as soon as he shut the door, and we were safe to talk. "I knew he was going to do something, but that? Fuckkkkk." He sounded so upset that I pushed for him to sit down on my bed, and then I climbed up into his lap.

"Is this okay?" I asked him, holding his face in my hands.

"Yes. Why wouldn't it be?"

"I wasn't sure how you felt about this while we're back in your home where you grew up and believed other things..." I told him, and my voice dropped off as Remi pulled me down for an intense kiss.

"To be honest, being here makes me want to fuck you in his house just to spite him." He almost snapped. I stilled in his arms, and he realized what he had said. "I didn't mean that, baby. I'm sorry. I wasn't thinking. I want to, I want to do that..."

Remi suddenly seemed very much his age.

"I want that with you, but not to spite anyone. I shouldn't have said that. And I know you're waiting..."

I shut him up by kissing him again. I knew he was overwhelmed by his grandfather dying and having to manage his father and his feelings around that. I knew he hadn't meant it. Remi's hands came up to grip my hips, and he held me down as he ground up on me.

"My eyes. Oh, my eyes." I heard Liam's voice behind us, and I quickly pulled away, breathing heavily.

"Go away, Liam," Remi told his cousin as he pulled his shirt lower to hide his erection.

"No can do, cuz. Uncle Holiness himself instructed me in no uncertain terms to make sure you came upstairs now." Liam was leaning on the doorway. Remi groaned in disappointment.

"He told me, and I quote, 'Make sure Remiel comes upstairs. I worry that he is struggling with the temptation of the flesh.'"

Lia made fake barfing noises and said, "I love how he sent Liam to 'save' Remi when Liam is the one fucking me six ways from Sunday."

We all cracked up at the irony of that statement. Remi sighed as he ran his hands down my arms, hugged me, and then stood up.

"Welp, God calls. Let's go read our Bibles, Liam. We bid thee women goodnight. Please turn away lest we sin," he said mockingly, and we all burst out laughing again.

I slept fitfully that night. I wasn't sure what was keeping me up. Was it the anticipation of attending my first funeral tomorrow, being in a bed that wasn't mine, or was it due to the condescending way Pastor Taylor had spoken about me in his prayer? I wasn't sure.

14

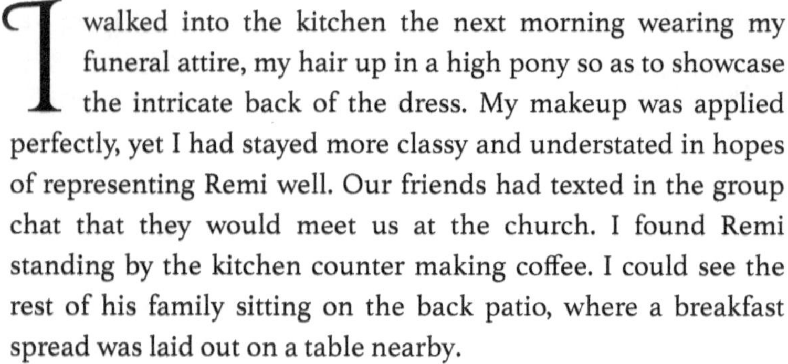

I walked into the kitchen the next morning wearing my funeral attire, my hair up in a high pony so as to showcase the intricate back of the dress. My makeup was applied perfectly, yet I had stayed more classy and understated in hopes of representing Remi well. Our friends had texted in the group chat that they would meet us at the church. I found Remi standing by the kitchen counter making coffee. I could see the rest of his family sitting on the back patio, where a breakfast spread was laid out on a table nearby.

"Good morning." I touched Remi's arm, and he startled as if he had been lost in thought.

"Oh wow." He stared at me. "You look so beautiful."

"You look very handsome yourself," I told him, running my hand down his lapel. And he did. His big, broad shoulders and chest were encased in a black suit that tapered at the waist. He had tried to tame his thick head of waves, but one piece was rebelling, and it fell over his forehead almost into his eyes. He smiled.

"Coffee?" he asked me as the fancy machine finished making him a cappuccino.

"I'm good." I didn't like coffee. The caffeine made my panic attacks come more often, and I did everything possible to avoid them.

"Let's go outside; the women's auxiliary of the church delivered half a restaurant for breakfast out there." He opened the sliding glass door that led to the patio and held it open for me to step out. We went over to the table, and I found a pitcher of freshly squeezed apple and kale juice. I poured myself a cup of that and then took a strawberry streusel muffin and went to sit down next to Liam and Julia. Remi was still at the table making himself a bagel when his father came outside.

"Son, why don't you sit, and perhaps Miss Collins can assist you in making your breakfast," he stated loudly. The muffin I was eating got stuck in my throat. Julia put her hand on my arm. The whole patio went silent.

"No." Remi turned, the knife he had been using to slice his bagel was still in his hand. "I am perfectly fine doing it myself."

What made this even more awkward was Remi's mother was standing right near him, putting together a plate of food for her husband as Remi stood up for himself. His father raised an eyebrow and intoned, "Ephesians 5:22-23. Wives, be willing to serve your husbands the same as the Lord. A husband is the head of his wife, just as Christ is the head of the church."

My shock at what he had just said made a shocked laugh build up inside of me, and I cleared my throat so as not to embarrass myself.

"Fuck your Ephesians, Dad," Remi spat. "In the world I live in, no wife of mine will ever be abused in the name of religion."

Remi's mother flinched as if she had been slapped. His father just calmly took a drink of the iced coffee Miley had prepared for him and said, "I will pray for you, Remiel."

"Please don't," Remi snapped back. He tossed his bagel back

onto the table and told the group of us, "I'm not hungry anymore."

With that, he went back into the house. I wanted to make him a plate and go after him, but I couldn't do that following what his father had just done. Liam got up and grabbed the plate of food to follow his cousin inside, and I was so grateful. After waiting for what I felt was enough time not to let the pastor win by knowing how angry he had made me, I got up and excused myself.

I found Remi and Liam playing Xbox in the basement, still fully dressed in their suits. They had finished off their breakfast, and the empty plates sat on the carpet next to them.

"Clean this up for us, woman." Liam snapped his fingers in my general direction. Remi looked horrified and pretended to slap Liam's shoulder.

"Bro, no." But then he stopped at the sound of my laughter.

"What else do you need, oh holy sir? Do you need me to tie your shoes? Oh, please let me serve you," I replied sarcastically. The boys chuckled. Remi seemed relieved that I didn't appear to be upset over the situation, and the two of them kept playing. I sat down on the couch near them and pulled out my phone to scroll social media. Earlier this morning, I had taken a photo in my dress. My cheekbones looked razor sharp, partially from the lighting and also from my hair being pulled up into a high pony. My full lips were a soft rose pink. My lashes were super long from all of the mascara I had applied. The dress looked so good on my body, and the heels made my legs look longer than they really were. I had originally thought it might not have been appropriate to post my photo the morning of a funeral, but now every fiber of my being wanted to get it out there, so I posted it with the caption:

"I AM WOMAN, HEAR ME ROAR."

Thirty minutes later, @rem22 liked it.

The service for Remi's grandfather started in the church. I had never been to church before, and to me, the room honestly looked like a stadium with its fancy lights, padded chairs, and massive stage. The plan was after the ceremony, the family would then take a limo to the cemetery for the burial. Earlier, Remi had told me that he wanted me to sit next to him during the service, but I had explained to him that I didn't feel comfortable sitting there when it had been reserved just for family. He seemed to understand, and after he was sure that I had a seat with our friends, he went up to the front to sit between his mother and a man who was as tall as Remi and was sporting similar hair too, waves and all. I wondered if he was an uncle, but then, when Remi's father and his brothers got up to carry the casket, the dark-haired man stayed seated. I was sitting in between Rachel and Dee, and I quickly filled them in on the shit that Remi's father had been pulling since I got there.

"What an asshole," Dee hissed.

"Shush!" A woman in front of us turned around, looking highly offended.

"Why don't you..." Dee started.

"We are so sorry," I quickly interrupted and gave Dee a look. The woman turned back around, muttering something about blasphemy and respect. I rolled my eyes.

"Wait till she finds out I'm a lesbian," Dee whispered, and I had to cover up a laugh.

The church was packed; not a seat remained empty. It turned out that Remi's grandfather had been very influential in his own right, and people from all over had come to pay their respects. The pastor's eulogy was well-spoken, as expected, yet very long. I noticed what a good job he did at playing the humble, God-loving son, yet I now knew better after seeing another side of him. His behavior earlier colored everything for me, and his speech left a sour taste in my mouth. I wondered if anyone else realized how much of his speech was fake. At the end of his eulogy, I was zoning out and was startled back to focus when I heard the pastor call up Remi to sing "Amazing Grace." From what I could see of Remi's profile, he looked shocked, and it was obvious to me that no one had asked him to do this or at least warned him ahead of time. I saw him shake his head and whisper something to the man next to him. The man put his hand on Remi's back and said something back. Remi finally stood up and walked begrudgingly up to where his father stood next to the casket. He said something to his father before taking the microphone. The pastor's face didn't reveal anything, and he continued to play the grieving son as he went back to sit down next to his wife. Remi looked over at the band and nodded. They started to play, and Remi began to sing. His voice was velvet at times and crisp at others. It soared with some words and grew huskier at the end. You could tell that he had grown up singing on this stage, and you could also see how much the congregation loved him. People around me were genuinely crying when he finished. I watched him put the microphone back, and then he turned to where his grandfather's casket stood. With his back to the room, I watched him bend his head and quietly sob his goodbyes. My heart twisted in my chest as his grief felt palpable to me. Then, quietly, he left the stage and the room entirely without another glance at his father.

I stayed back at the edge of the crowd during the burial. For someone who could barely handle my own big feelings, being surrounded by so many other people experiencing their big feelings was beginning to feel suffocating to me. The burial itself involved more speeches from the pastor's brothers and then multiple prayers. As the dirt began to hit the coffin, I couldn't take it anymore, so I walked even further away, hoping Remi was busy with family and wouldn't notice me almost by the parking lot at this point. When it was finally over, and my nerves were calming down, I was standing talking with Rachel and Eva when I felt a hand on my shoulder. I looked over to find Remi behind me. Our friends picked up on the emotion on his face, so they quickly said their condolences to him, and then they walked away after we agreed to be in touch once we all got home. I turned back to Remi and saw that he had loosened his tie and unbuttoned his jacket. His eyes were rimmed red, and his hair was a mess from his hands obviously running through it nervously. I immediately went into his arms and hugged him tightly, resting my cheek on his chest. He held me against him, enjoying a moment of peace together until I heard someone behind us say, "Who is this, Remiel?"

Not this again. I braced myself for more drama as I turned around, and there stood the tall man who had been sitting next to Remi at the church earlier. Up close, he and Remi could pass for brothers. Although, I noticed that this man's hair was lighter than Remi's, and his eyes were a bright blue where Remi's were dark.

"This is my girlfriend, Shaen." Remi didn't seem guarded with this man at all the way he did with his own father. He held out his hand and smiled at me as I reached over to shake his.

"It's nice to meet you."

The man grinned, and a dimple showed up in his cheek.

"The pleasure is all mine. I am Dermont Lewis. I'm Johnny's best friend and Remiel's godfather," he told me.

"They grew up together. Then Dermont became a music producer in Hollywood, and Dad stuck with Jesus." Remi made it very clear how he felt about that with the inflection in his voice. "But somehow, Dermont can still stand my dad and keeps in touch with him."

Dermont shrugged.

"Somehow." Then he laughed. He was staring at me. "You look familiar."

"I've never even left my city, let alone gone to Hollywood," I laughed, "so we definitely have never met."

We started walking together to the parking lot. Remi was holding my hand, and as people from his father's congregation stopped him to give their condolences, our linked hands kept getting stares.

"I love how accepting they are," I said sarcastically. Dermont chuckled. Remi snorted.

"So loving," he agreed. "Shaen, drive back with me and Dermont." He pointed to his godfather's Ferrari.

"You don't have to ask me twice." That earned me an approving smile from Dermont. When we got up to the car, I could not figure out how to open the door, and then I gasped as they began to open up like wings.

"So fucking cool," I told Remi excitedly, then clapped a hand over my mouth and glanced at Dermont. He just laughed and told me, "You're fine."

Getting over my embarrassment, I climbed into the back of the car, marveling over the soft leather and all the fancy gadgets. Dermont turned the car on with the push of a button, and I could feel the engine purring under me. Remi slid his hand through the opening between the door and the seat in front of me and put his hand on my ankle, just like he had done last week, his thumb rubbing circles on my leg. I could feel my body relax, and I suddenly felt very tired.

The drive back was uneventful, and I was looking forward to getting the fuck out of this town and away from the vibes going on in Remi's house. Once we got back to the house, I said thank you to Dermont for the ride, and he told me he looked forward to getting to know me better. He and Remi went upstairs to pack up, and I went down to the guest room to gather up my own belongings as Sam had a patient's surgery scheduled for early the next morning, and we needed to get on the road. As I brought my bag upstairs, I was met by Remi's father, who was standing at the landing by the door. I could hear the voices of the people who had gathered in the living room to pay their respects to their pastor, but I could not see anyone in the hallway behind him. I felt nervous butterflies erupt in my stomach.

"Excuse me," I said softly.

"In 1 Corinthians 6:18, it says to flee from sexual immorality. Every other sin a person commits is outside the body, but the sexually immoral person sins against his own body." Remi's father was standing so close to me as he spoke that I could see every gray growing through his hair and the anger in his green eyes. "I know that you do not yet know the Lord, and I pray that you come into a season of accepting Him within you soon, but I hope that you will heed my warning today: do not attempt to lead my son astray from his faith."

I pulled myself up to my full and not-intimidating height, and stared John Taylor directly in the eyes.

"I said excuse me!" I enunciated loudly. "And for the record, the only thing I will be accepting into me anytime soon is your son!"

The pastor looked visibly taken aback.

"And let me be clear, the only person who has led your son away from the lies you forced on him for years was you! I know what you did, and I see how you talk to Remi. I see how you treat your wife. I have personally experienced the abuse of how you hide behind your religion, spewing hateful Bible quotes everywhere you go. I may not know your Lord, pastor, but I do know that how you treat people is not kind. And I don't need to be a believer to know how people should and should not be treated. So maybe look a little less at me and start to inspect what role you may play in the fact that the only reason your son came home in months was to say goodbye to his grandfather. Now, if you'll please move, I am on my way out. My condolences to you." I couldn't believe myself. My heart was beating rapidly in my chest, and I could feel nervous tremors starting in my body. I was not generally a rude or disrespectful person. I also didn't want the parents of the guy who I liked to hate me, but there was only so much I could take before I fought back.

The pastor seemed stunned into silence, and he barely looked at me, yet he moved to the side to allow me to pass. When I looked past him, I saw that I had an audience. Liam, Julia, Sam, Lia, Dermont, Miley, and Remi all filled the doorway. I gulped and almost tripped, but the adrenaline flowing through me kept me walking.

"I'll meet you in the car." I must have sounded so determined that they let me go without saying anything. I wondered how much they had heard.

Apparently, they had heard everything. Julia was crying in between her howling laughter. Sam had dubbed me Queen Shaen. Apparently, Dermont had called me his new favorite person, or so Julia said. Lia and Liam were in hysterics as well. Liam kept reenacting when I said "the only thing I will be accepting into me anytime soon is your son", and then he would throw himself back into a fit of laughter. I was mortified and had my face buried in Remi's arm. Remi, who hadn't said a word since we had gotten into the car. Eventually, everyone quieted down. Julia and Sam were talking quietly as Sam drove. Lia and Liam had both put headphones on and had gone to sleep. Remi had his head leaning against the window, his hand absentmindedly playing with my hair. I sat up to grab my AirPods, hoping he wasn't thinking of ways to break up with me, the psycho who had yelled at his dad the day he had also buried his grandfather.

"Shaen," I heard his voice say softly above me. I kept looking at my phone, where I was pretending to be intently focused on choosing a playlist to listen to.

"Yeah." Here we go. He's gonna dump me in Sam's BMW, and I have nowhere to escape to, and then I'll be alone for the rest of time because no one could ever compete with what I felt for Remiel Taylor.

"Look at me."

I sighed and looked up. I froze when I saw that his eyes were shiny with unshed tears. I reached up to wipe them away with the sleeve of the oversized sweatshirt that I had changed into before the debacle with his dad.

"I'm sorry I embarrassed you," I finally said. He looked surprised.

"Embarrassed? I was so turned on and so thankful and so in awe of you all at once. I was not embarrassed at all. I have never had someone stick up for me to him like that. Ever." Remi took my face in his hands. "You're also so fucking funny, and I love how you just went at him with no fear. God, I just... I just really like you."

Like didn't cut it, and I knew that we were both skirting around it because we were only eighteen and we had just started going out, but at this point, I knew one day soon we would be exchanging I love yous, and it no longer scared me. In fact, it made me feel less alone in life, and I was excited for what was to come for us.

"Well good. I'm glad you're not mad. I can get a little feisty when it comes to bullies, and that is what he is. He's a fucking bully," I said emphatically. "And what is worse is he hides behind his holier-than-thou religious persona to get away with it."

"My tiny, angry pixie." Remi pulled the hood of his sweat-shirt onto his head and then ruffled my hair.

"I'm not tiny," I protested.

"Okay." He grinned and patted his lap. I rolled my eyes, lifted my feet onto the seat, and laid my head down on his thick thighs. I slept better on his lap in the back of a car than I had the night before in a high-end queen bed, and I knew exactly why.

15

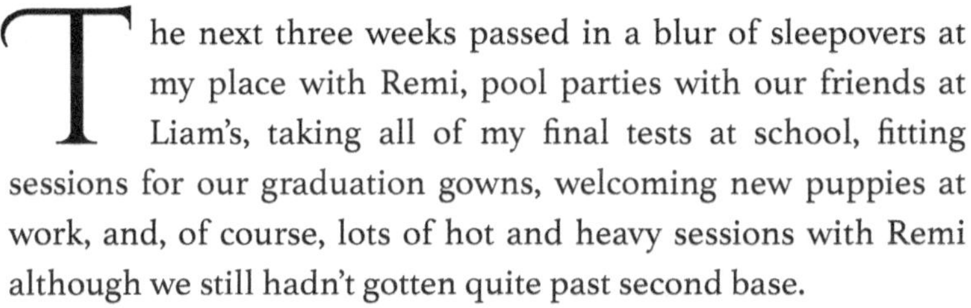

The next three weeks passed in a blur of sleepovers at my place with Remi, pool parties with our friends at Liam's, taking all of my final tests at school, fitting sessions for our graduation gowns, welcoming new puppies at work, and, of course, lots of hot and heavy sessions with Remi although we still hadn't gotten quite past second base.

The morning of our graduation ceremony, I woke up bleary-eyed. I had set my alarm to ring early because I wanted to get up and spend extra time on my hair and makeup before we had to report to school. Yet I had woken up before my alarm rang, and it didn't take long for me to figure out why. I felt the ache in my uterus telling me that little Aunt Flo had decided to show up a day early. Because, of course, she would. Unfortunately, my period always showed up with a vengeance, and it could get really messy if I didn't catch it in time. The problem here was that I was laying with my head on Remi's chest, one leg laying over his, my crotch smack up on his thigh.

"Remi." I shook him gently, yet he still woke up abruptly.

"What's wrong? You okay?"

"I think I made a mess on you," I told him. "And I'm really

sorry. She's early, and she's mad." I winced as another cramp shot up from my butt. I could never figure out why I felt my cramps in my ass, but I did.

"What mess? Who's early? What's happening?"

He was so confused that I laughed and then grimaced again as pain shot down my legs. The pain was only bad on days one and two. I found days three and four to be much easier, and then it was done.

"My period. I'm pretty sure I'm bleeding, and I think I got it all over you," I told him, really hoping I was wrong.

"Ooooh." Awareness dawned on him, and he gingerly lifted up the blanket. Sure enough, I had smeared period blood all over his leg, and my underwear looked like it had gotten into a fight and had lost. Fortunately, I had not gotten any blood on my bed sheets because I had no time to run a load of laundry before going to school.

"Oh my God." I leaned back and covered my face. "I'm so sorry." I was feeling mortified.

"Heyyy." He peeled back my hands. "That's okay, baby. It's just a little normal life, isn't it? Let's go shower, and then I'll get you whatever you need."

"Okay." I hated sounding so vulnerable and whiny, but it was exactly how I felt. One second, I was lying on my back in bed, and the next second, Remi had me up in his arms, kissing my face as he walked us to the bathroom. He turned the shower on, grabbed two towels and hung them over the towel rack, peeled my dirty underwear off my legs, and threw them in the sink. Then he got us into the shower and proceeded to clean all the blood off of us, shave my body, and wash my hair. I stood in the spray of water, feeling it beating on my back, my boyfriend's hands in my hair, and I felt all the stress leave my body. It was as if my muscles were acknowledging how nice it was not to be alone. To have a person to help me face the world. After Remi finished rinsing the conditioner out of my hair, he proceeded to wash his own hair. Knowing we were running against the clock, I shut off the water and shivered against the cool air as Remi opened the shower curtain and wrapped me up in a big towel.

"What do you need?" he asked me, pressing a kiss to my forehead.

"Underwear," I told him.

"Okay, wait here." He left the bathroom and was back a minute later with options—a thong, boy shorts, and hipsters. I took the thong because I didn't want to have underwear lines in my dress.

"Turn around so I can put in my tampon," I told him, peeling open the wrapper.

"Turn around?" He looked offended. "Baby, I've put my fingers in there!"

"Yeah, but this is gross!" I argued.

"It is not. It's normal," he argued back, but he turned around and gave me privacy while I shoved the super-sized tampon into me because I didn't want to risk any leakage happening today. I took some Motrin for the pain and then got to work on my makeup and hair. My dress was white, and I planned on swapping out to a brand new tampon right before I walked at graduation to guarantee I wouldn't have any more bloody mishaps today. The dress was flared, short, and had an off-the-shoulder look, so as I finished my makeup, I applied some bronzed glow to my exposed collarbone and shoulders. I snapped a couple of selfies to send to Lia, who told me I looked "hawt." Finally feeling ready, I left my room to find Remi waiting for me in the living room in his suit, freshly shaven and hair perfectly styled.

"Oh, give me a little spin, gorgeous," he said when he saw me. I obliged him and spun around, my hair flowing around me. When I turned back around, I saw that he had his phone out.

"Did you record that?"

"Hell yeah, I did. You look perfect," he told me as he followed me into the kitchen to make some brunch before we had to leave. We then ate at my coffee table as we watched an episode of *Yellowstone*. When it was finally time to go, Remi grabbed his key fob to drive us to school for the last time. Last week, a delivery service had driven up a BMW X5 SUV to Liam's house. It came with a card from Miley saying it was a graduation present. We figured it was more of a bribe to start talking to his parents again, but other than sending her a thank you text, Remi had not said anything else to both of them since the funeral three weeks ago.

"Let's go graduate." He gave me a grin as he opened the front door. I picked up my bag in which I had packed an outfit for the after-party, tons of tampons, more Motrin, some presents that I had gotten for Remi, my charger, makeup, and a curling iron.

"Are you moving out?" he joked. Remi always made fun of how much stuff I needed to take with me when we went anywhere.

"I'm currently bleeding out of my vagina," I reminded him, calling period privilege. He shut right up.

I couldn't believe the day had finally come. Remi and I had been talking about what life would look like now that high school was over. My new schedule at the rescue was ten to four on Saturdays, Tuesdays, and Thursdays. I had also started a new gig because Julia, after seeing the rescue's social media, had asked me to be her social media manager for her two aesthetics spas. I planned on going in on Mondays to film content for the week and would then work on creating that content on Wednesdays and Fridays. I was really excited about that, and it felt so "adult" to have a full work schedule. I also wanted to get my new car ASAP, and we both agreed that Remi would help me find the right one because he knew so much about cars and because I said I now had BBP, big boyfriend privilege. He liked hearing that and had flexed his arms, showing me how big my boyfriend privilege really was. We also talked about finding our own place to live. I had tossed up the idea of him moving in with me since he slept over every night anyway. My mom was really barely there, and that way, it would give us time to save up more money so our options for apartments could be better. He hadn't said much about that, so it was still up in the air. For the summer, Remi had gotten himself a server job in an upscale steakhouse for Friday and Saturday nights, and he was also going to be a lifeguard at the local public pool three days a week together with Liam. He told me that Dermont had been trying to convince him to record some music, and Sam had been asking him if medical school might be a possibility. Remi had admitted to me that he felt really stressed out because, on the one hand, he wanted to make them proud, but he also wanted to follow his own dreams of going to trade school to learn how to work on cars. He ultimately wanted to rebuild antique cars and sell them. He seemed so excited when he told me about an antique that he had been eyeing and all of the things that he would do to get it running again. I told him that I would support him in whatever he chose. He kissed me then and said, "I really like you, Shaen Collins."

It was his way of sneaking in an "I love you" without actually saying it. I was on to him.

"Do you need to change the plug?" I heard Remi ask, and I realized I had gotten lost in my thoughts on the drive over. We were parking in the parking lot at school as the graduation ceremony would be held in the auditorium.

"The plug?"

"Yeah." Remi motioned to my crotch. "The plug for the blood…" His voice trailed off as I cracked up.

"It's called a tampon, Remi, and I've got a few good hours left before the dam breaks."

"I know it's called a tampon." He looked like a kicked puppy now. "I just wasn't sure..."

"I know." I patted his arm. "And I love that you want to help me. Remind me to change the plug like a half hour before the ceremony starts, and we'll be good to go."

Remi nodded and set an alarm on his phone, looking very serious about it. I had to hold myself back from laughing again because I didn't want to hurt his feelings. He didn't realize that I had been managing not to bleed out since I was fourteen. I snorted at my own joke.

"I've never seen Lia having to deal with this period stuff," Remi said as he grabbed both of our bags, and I took our caps and gowns.

"That's because she takes the pill, so she just keeps skipping the period week and goes months without getting it," I explained.

"And you don't skip that week?" he asked.

"I don't take the pill at all," I told him as we walked into school.

"Will you start once we...?" His cheeks flushed, and I thought how adorable it was that my strong, sexy man had gotten a little flustered at the idea of us having sex.

"No. I don't believe in messing with my hormones. I personally think the pill is very toxic." It was something I felt very strongly about, and up until now, it hadn't been a big deal due to my no semen near me rule.

"How will we prevent a baby?" Remi seemed very concerned about that.

"Well..." We had gotten close to the auditorium, so I kept my voice low. "I can only get pregnant when I'm fertile, and that's only like seven days out of every month. I already track ovulation, and we will either avoid those days or use a condom with a natural spermicide."

He was taking in what I was saying with wide eyes, and it really annoyed me that our education system didn't talk about this properly because not only was he ignorant on the topic, but so were many of my girlfriends.

"I want to help you track," he offered suddenly. I wasn't sure I had heard him right.

"You what?"

"I want to help you track your cycles. I feel like if we're gonna be involved, I should be... involved." He looked so serious that I threw myself into his arms and kissed him all over his face.

"That is the sweetest thing you have ever said to me."

He looked very pleased with himself, then he whispered, "If I squeeze you too hard, will a bunch of blood come out?"

I laughed so loud that people standing in the hallway looked over at us. He set me back down gently and helped me put my bag away.

"I'm not a squishy toy," I said in between laughter. "You can't squeeze it out of me."

"Okay, simmer down, woman, I'm just learning. I've never been around girls who talked about this before, and it's never mattered to me until now." He was laughing at himself at this point.

"I like you, Remi Taylor," I told him, and with that, the principal called us in for one last prep talk before graduation officially started.

The ceremony was long, but overall, it went well. After all of the speeches, we got called up to get our diplomas. Many of the students had a lot of people cheering in the audience when their name was called. When I walked the stage, my friends, Liam's family, and Remi made a lot of noise, but it was still achingly obvious that I only had one real family member representing me. My mom had actually shown up, which honestly had surprised me. When Remi got his diploma, he also received some sort of award for his efforts with football, and that had the entire football team hooting and hollering his name, making Remi flush. Later on, we returned our caps and gowns, and everyone's families were hanging around as the graduation wrapped up. Remi had been cordial to my mom, but later, as she and I talked nearby when Remi was chatting with his extended family, I could feel him hovering protectively, which I thought was sweet. Shortly after, she left to go back to work, so she never had a chance to see Remi's parents, which made me breathe a sigh of relief because it was way too stressful for me to think about them meeting. When we did eventually cross paths, I completely ignored the pastor, even when I heard him try to say something to me. Remi's mother said congratulations, to which I smiled and replied with a simple, "Thank you." Once it was all finally officially over and the families had all left, my friend group and I gathered in the girls' bathroom to get changed. We were going to the after-party on a party bus that would take us to a barn that had been renovated and turned into an event space. The whole grade had chipped in to rent it. The vibe was "country gone wild," so I had opted for a pair of high-waisted, booty-hugging jean shorts, a black tube top, a plaid shirt that I tied up to show off my belly, and a pair of authentic cowboy boots that had been an amazing thrift store find. Then, I gathered my long, thick hair into two braids. After touching up my makeup and stuffing everything into my Mary Poppins bag, as Rachel had started calling it, we left the bathroom in search of the boys. We found Carter, Liam, and Remi waiting for us outside the party bus. Jake would be meeting us there since he had already graduated last year.

"Damn, baby." Remi pulled me up against him and laid a kiss on my lips. "I'm not gonna be able to step away from you all night."

"Afraid someone will steal me?" I joked.

"No, but I am afraid they'll try." He tugged on one of my braids and then spun me to take a look at my ass.

"Goddd," he moaned, shoving his fist between his teeth in a dramatic show of despair. "It's gonna be a long night."

We found seats on the bus, and immediately, Dee started mixing drinks. Everyone, including Carter, planned on drinking tonight. The party was really just for seniors, but since Carter was dating Eva and was on the football team, the people in charge had made an exception and let him on the bus. By the time the bus pulled up to the barn, the energy was already lit, the music was pumping really loudly, and Remi and I were both quite a few shots in. The farm-turned-party area had tons of security features, including a room with lockers where we chose to store our stuff. Then we went into the main room, where we were met by a DJ, a smoke machine, a full, writhing dance floor, and more alcohol.

"We're fucking free, baby!" Liam was shouting. Lia was tossing back Jell-O shots. The lights were flashing, and the air was warm and thick with exhilarated energy. The dance floor felt electric, and I quickly found my way there, fueled by hormones, excitement, and vodka. I was dancing with Lia, Rachel, and Dee as the boys had gone to the buffet to get us food when a guy came over and began to dance behind me. I recognized him from the football team, but I couldn't remember his name. I tried to dance away politely, but he got up close in my personal space and shouted, "You look really fucking hot tonight."

"Th-thanks." I was trying not to be rude, but I was also obviously not interested.

"Do you want to dance?" he asked, leaning near my ear so I could hear him over the deafening music. I shook my head. "No thanks, I have a boyfriend."

The guy looked confused. "A boyfriend? Who?"

"Me."

I felt Remi before I saw him or heard him. The football player, whose name I still could not remember, turned and paled when he saw Remi. Remi wasn't violent, he wasn't scary, and he wasn't known for intimidating other guys, but he was still very much respected by the team, and everyone on it knew that it wasn't a good idea to encroach on Taylor's girl.

"Good taste, Taylor. I didn't know, sorry." The guy quickly ran off.

"See, I told you I can't take my eyes off you," Remi complained half-jokingly. He pulled me closer, placed his hands on my hips, and we began to bump and grind to the music. I had obviously never had sex before, but our dancing felt like fore-play to sex. We were moving so seductively, our hands gliding along each other's bodies, sweat beading up on our hairlines, our movements so in sync that it felt magical.

"I'm so hard for you," Remi leaned down to whisper to me.

"Well I'm soaked for you," I whispered back. I could hear him moan, and his tongue licked his way up my ear, and then he nibbled on my earlobe.

"You cannot say that to me in public," he declared. "I am in pain now." He reached down to readjust himself in his pants while I laughed. He spun me around, so now my back was to his chest, and we kept dancing. After about another hour of that, Eva came back with more drinks and suggested that we go sit outside and play *Never Have I Ever*.

All of our friends, plus more of our graduating class, were sitting around a fire pit. Everyone was in various stages, from tipsy to drunk to almost fully inebriated. I took one of the drinks Eva was holding out. It was a beige-colored drink in a whiskey glass.

"It's called an orgasm," she shouted over the music.

"I like those," I told her, sipping the drink and finding it to be sweet, smooth, and absolutely delicious. "I'll take three more of these orgasms," I announced as I sat down on a cushion that Remi had taken off of a chair and brought over for us to sit on.

"I'll give you some later." Remi thought he was whispering, but all of our friends heard him and burst out laughing.

"Shut up." Remi sounded good-natured about it and was clearly amused that the drunk version of him could no longer whisper.

"Okay," Rachel announced. "Everyone needs a drink. And we will go around in a circle, and you have to say, 'Never have I ever,' and then you say something. If you did it, you drink. If you didn't do it, you don't drink."

Someone passed me another orgasm drink so I could play.

"We know how to play," Dee laughed. Rachel took games very seriously.

"I'm just explaining for those who are too drunk to remember." Rachel held up her beer, and then she sat down next to Carter.

"I'll go first," Lia announced. "Never have I ever graduated tonight!"

The whole crowd whooped, gave each other a high five, and, of course, everyone drank. Liam was next to her, so it was his turn, and I knew he was going to jump right into something crazy that would set the tone for the rest of the game.

"Never have I ever come in public." He smirked at Lia, who took a nice chug of her drink. A handful of the other players did too, and Remi nudged me.

"Don't get any ideas," I hissed. He chuckled.

As we played, a lot of the statements started out harmless, like, "Never have I ever had a crush on Mr. Evans," who was the gym teacher, or "Never have I ever fake cried to a teacher to try to pass a class." Yet the drunker we got, the more raunchy everyone became. People began saying things like "Never have I ever given head in the boys' locker room," or "Never have I ever had sex on school property." If anyone noticed how few statements Remi and I were able to drink to, they didn't say anything.

"Looks like we have a lot of catching up to do," Remi winked at me.

"I'm sorry, but some of these things I am never gonna do," I told him half joking.

"You mean you don't want to break into Mullins's backyard and skinny dip?" Mr. Mullins was our principal. Well, he had been before we graduated. It felt surreal to me that I had finally accomplished the first two things on my list. Graduate and do it as a virgin. I was so proud of myself, especially since I had done it alone without a proper family supporting me.

We continued to play the game for another half hour, and then the group dissipated to go play darts, which did not feel very safe to me being that everyone was pretty drunk at this point.

"I have to change my tampon," I announced to Remi and struggled to get up. He stood first, then I grabbed his hand, and he pulled me up.

"I'll come with you."

I shook my head. "You do not need to babysit me in the bathroom," I joked.

"Yes, I do. The last time we were at a party..." His voice trailed off, and I saw a flash of something on his face that almost looked like regret. I knew I was never going to win, and to be honest, I appreciated how protective he was of me.

"Okay." I took his hand. He smiled, and we told our friends that we would be right back.

In the bathroom, I didn't know if I was just too drunk or if wearing a thong had somehow pushed the string up into me, but I found that the string of my tampon had gotten really wedged up in there. Between the alcohol, my extra long nails that I had gotten done the day before, and the slippery situation of my vagina, I was really struggling to grab the tampon to pull it out. Ten minutes had gone by when I heard Remi say, "You okay in there?"

I wanted to cry with embarrassment and frustration. I washed my hands, pulled my shorts back up, and cracked open the bathroom door. Remi stood there looking edible, hot, and concerned.

"I can't get it out." My eyes welled up with tears, and my drunken brain didn't try to suck them back in like I usually did.

"What do you mean? Doesn't it have like a little tail?" Remi looked so confused.

"Yes." I sniffed. "But the tail got stuck up inside me, and my nails are too long for me to grab it."

"Okay, so I'll do it." Remi made a move to come into the bathroom with me, and I tried to push him back out.

"No way."

"Why not?" He almost looked hurt.

"Babe!" I hissed. "You cannot be serious."

"Do you need it out?"

I nodded.

"And you can't get it out on your own?" he confirmed. I nodded again. "Then what other option do we have?"

"It's just so gross. You'll never think I'm sexy ever again." The alcohol and how nice he always was to me was making me feel so emotional.

"Baby." He took my chin in his hands and tilted my face up to look at him. "Nothing could stop me from thinking you're sexy. This has nothing to do with that. I just want to help you."

I was finally convinced to open the door to the bathroom and let him in, feeling incredulous that this was about to happen.

"We never speak of this to anyone." I was very adamant about the need to keep this horrifying moment a secret.

"Promise." He nodded, grinning at me.

"I'm glad you find this so funny," I grumbled, taking off my shorts and my underwear. He slapped my ass gently and said, "I just want you to realize that I would do anything for you. That is how much I adore you."

I looked up at him.

"You say the sweetest things for someone about to dive into my bloody vagina." I was kidding around, but the truth was that I felt so whole being with him. Just hearing him verbalize how he felt about me was so healing for me and my mess of emotions. I lifted one foot up onto the toilet, and Remi got down on his knees to see better.

"This is not how I imagined it would be going the first time," I murmured.

"What would be?" Remi had his phone out and was shining a flashlight up at me.

"You on your knees down there," I told him. His eyes moved to my face so quickly that it cracked me up.

"Have you been thinking about that...?" He looked so hopeful and excited. I nodded, suddenly feeling shy.

"We're just a few days from our one-month anniversary," I told him. "And obviously not while I'm gushing, but when I'm done, I think I'm ready. If you are?"

"I'm so hard I'm gonna poke a hole into this floor," Remi told me as his answer. I giggled, then stopped as I felt his finger fish around inside of me. A minute later, I felt him tug, and out came my very full and very bloody tampon.

"Oh yay, you did it!" I grabbed some toilet paper and quickly relieved him from having to hold the offending tampon. "Thank you. I'm so sorry," I babbled as I took another one out of my bag. Remi was washing his hands when he said, "No worries, pixie."

And he planted a kiss on my mouth. He tasted tart from the alcohol and sweet from his very own flavor. He watched me through hooded eyes while I inserted my fresh tampon.

"This is gonna sound weird, but I'm so turned on right now." He laughed, sounding embarrassed.

"Do you have a blood kink?" I teased. He waited while I washed my hands, then took my bag and opened the bathroom door.

"Not a blood kink, weirdo." He rolled his eyes. "No, seriously, I get turned on by how comfortable we feel with each other..." His voice trailed off. "I don't know if I can explain it correctly."

"No, I get it." I felt even more emotion for him well up inside of me. "You mean there is something special about us feeling safe with each other."

"Yessss." He seemed relieved that I understood what he was saying.

"I like it too. I feel very safe with you."

He was putting my bag back into the locker I had chosen for the night, and he turned around to pick me up, as my legs went around his waist.

"I like you so much, Shaen Collins, and I am so excited to spend this summer and then life with you," he said before kissing the fuck out of me.

"You're gonna keep me?" I smiled prettily when we came up for air.

"I'm gonna keep you," he confirmed.

We ended up stopping by the buffet and then proceeded to eat our weight in guacamole with chips and burritos, followed by another round of drinks. It was now 3 a.m., and the party was still going strong. After we finished eating, we found ourselves back on the dance floor with all of our friends. I was so drunk at this point, and I kept randomly crying about how much I was going to miss my friends next year. Eva, who uncharacteristically was slurring, kept asking Remi to keep an eye on Carter because she was going to be out of town for college. Their goal was to stay together while he finished school, and then he would join her when he graduated. Lia and Liam waltzed by and made us all laugh when suddenly Lia shouted, "Holy shit!" as she pointed at something. We all turned to look and found Rachel and Jake making out a few feet from us.

"About fucking time," Dee cackled. "That boy has had a hard-on for Rachel for years."

Carter let out a whistle, and Rachel looked over at us.

"Stopppp." She grabbed Jake's hand, and they went deeper into the crowd so we could no longer stare and cheer them on. Liam was handing out shots, and I had a feeling that I was at my limit, so I said no, but Remi took his shot and then kissed me, and probably half the shot ended up in my mouth.

"You guys are so hot together it's stupid," Lia shouted at us.

"You really are," Eve confirmed. "Holy shit."

I got embarrassed, but Remi hugged me, moving us to the music. We got swept into the dancing current, and I let the beat take me. We danced and made out and made out and danced till we were sweaty with dopamine pumping through our veins. I felt high on how tired and happy I was at the same time. Next thing I knew, Lia had gotten up on a table and was dancing on it. The strobe lights kept moving across her face, making her look sparkly. She pulled me up with her, and we jumped up and down on it together, hugging and dancing at the same time. A guy standing near the table handed a blue-colored shot up to me. I tossed it back and mouthed a thank you to him. He smiled and took the glass back. As the DJ switched to a new song, I looked over and saw a girl I didn't recognize dancing up near Remi. At first, he didn't notice because he was talking to Liam, but then she grabbed onto his arm, and I could see her shouting something over the music. He shook his head and tried to take her hand off his arm. But she just held tighter, and then her other hand landed in the middle of his chest.

"Oh fuck no," I exclaimed and immediately sat down on the table to make climbing off of it easier. My head was beginning to pound, and the lights were getting so bright. Was the music suddenly louder? I wondered. Lia jumped down with me, and together we ran toward Remi. I could see him trying to disentangle himself from this girl who had latched herself onto him, but she seemed to have three hands and kept finding him again. Liam was no help because he was just standing there laughing. As I got closer, I heard Remi say, "Please stop touching me."

At this point, I was so livid that I could feel the adrenaline pumping through me, and my hands and lips were tingling.

"Take your hands off of him." I got up in the girl's space and tried to stay calm, but I also wanted to sound like I meant it. She looked at me and laughed. "He wants me," she slurred. "Back off, little girl."

I pushed her.

"No, you back off. When someone tells you not to touch them, Don't. Touch. Them.," I enunciated. She stumbled in her stupidly tall heels.

"It doesn't feel like he doesn't want me to touch him." She tried to fondle him below the belt, but I grabbed her arm before she could, and I squeezed hard.

"I have never hit someone before. But fuck me, you might have to be the first one." I couldn't get up in her face because even in my boots, I was only five-four, and she was probably pushing five-seven, but I certainly tried my best.

"Pixie." I heard Remi from behind me. I turned to look at him, and I felt the girl pull on my braids. Hard.

"Hey!" Remi grabbed me as my head pulled back with the force of her grip, and he stepped in front of me. "Get the fuck out of here." His tone had turned intimidating.

"Seriously, I don't even recognize you, bitch. Leave the party!" Finally, Liam was pissed. I swiped a glass from a nearby table that either contained water or vodka and popped out from behind Remi, tossing it in her face.

"What the fuck?" she screamed, liquid dripping off her chin, and she finally stalked off.

"Let's take a breather." Remi had his hands on my shoulders and was looking at me. Everything was starting to blur. I was so tired and had mixed so much alcohol, and now, with coming down from the adrenaline, I was beginning to feel nauseous, and my heart was pounding. I nodded, and he led me outside, where the night air had grown crisp and felt so good on my over-heated body. Remi took me to the edge of the grass where we found a porch swing. He sat me down and then sat next to me.

"You okay?" he asked.

"I'm sorry. I've never acted like that before." I had to close my eyes because the world was beginning to spin, and I was seeing two of him. Fuck, why did I drink so much?

"Like what?" he asked and began to massage my back. I felt the tension begin to leave my body.

"I dunno, like a territorial girlfriend."

He was quiet for a minute, and then I heard him admit, "I liked it. It made me feel like I matter to you."

I turned myself around and cracked my eyes open.

"You do matter to me. So much," I told him. I paused. "Remi?"

"Yes, babe?" He sounded sweet.

"I'm gonna throw up," I announced.

And I did.

This is what feeling like shit feels like.

16

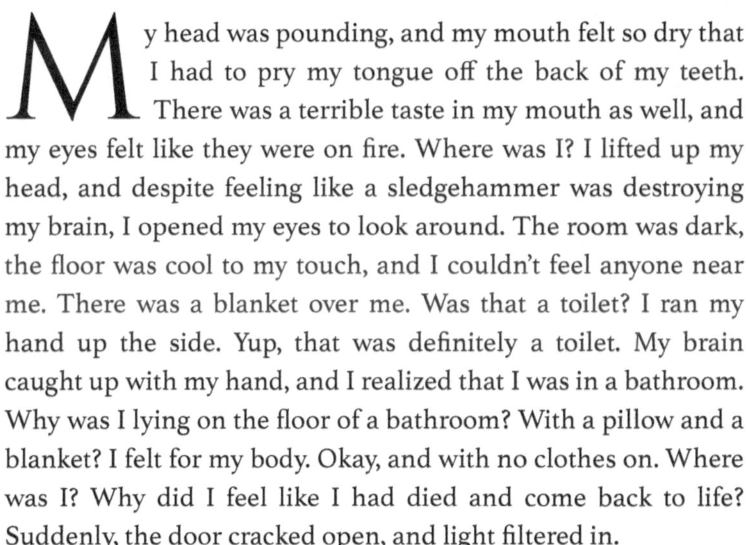

My head was pounding, and my mouth felt so dry that I had to pry my tongue off the back of my teeth. There was a terrible taste in my mouth as well, and my eyes felt like they were on fire. Where was I? I lifted up my head, and despite feeling like a sledgehammer was destroying my brain, I opened my eyes to look around. The room was dark, the floor was cool to my touch, and I couldn't feel anyone near me. There was a blanket over me. Was that a toilet? I ran my hand up the side. Yup, that was definitely a toilet. My brain caught up with my hand, and I realized that I was in a bathroom. Why was I lying on the floor of a bathroom? With a pillow and a blanket? I felt for my body. Okay, and with no clothes on. Where was I? Why did I feel like I had died and come back to life? Suddenly, the door cracked open, and light filtered in.

"Oh, my eyes," I croaked. My voice sounded weird to my ears, and my throat hurt when I spoke. I covered my eyes with my hand, but the sudden movement made me feel so dizzy and made my head throb even worse. The door shut, and the light went away.

"Shaen?"

I knew that voice. That was the voice of... Remi. Remi, who had stood beside me, rubbing my back as I barfed into the bushes at the party. Oh my God, the party! Memories started to assault me. A flash of how I had thrown up every single burrito and chip that I had eaten near the swing that we had been sitting on.

Me trying to get onto the dance floor after and then almost passing out in Remi's arms. Him plying me with water. Me throwing up again in the bathroom this time. Me on a hunt to find the girl who had hit on Remi to tell her what was what. Liam and Remi getting me into an Uber. The Uber stopping on the side of the road so I could throw up yet again. Me crying on Liam's front lawn. Me throwing up once more while in the shower. Remi cleaning up the shower as I laid down, naked, on the bathroom floor. Well, at least now I knew how I had gotten here and where I was. I was in Liam's house. Another memory hit me. Remi bringing me a pillow and a blanket after I refused to get up and go to bed with him. Him whispering good night in my ear, and me saying, "I love you" back.

"Oh fuck." I groaned out loud. My head reverberated with the sound of my own voice.

"Shaen?" Remi sounded really concerned. Maybe he had still been drunk enough not to remember. My brain was in overdrive, and I was absolutely freaking out, but I could not make any more sudden movements because it felt like my head was going to absolutely explode if I did.

"Shaen? Julia is going to run an IV for you, but I need you to put on some clothes."

I jolted awake at Remi's words, and I realized that I had dozed off again; this time, I was leaning up against the bathtub. The cold material felt so good on my body, which felt incredibly hot. I am not okay, I thought. Why am I not okay? Yet I nodded in agreement, my eyes still closed.

"Lift your arms," Remi instructed. I did. He slipped something soft over my head and gently pulled it down my body. Then I felt him pulling shorts up my legs. Next thing I knew, I was in the air. He had picked me up and was cradling me.

"I s-smell," I croaked, turning my face away from him.

"I showered you. You smell like my body wash," Remi whispered. Then he put a pair of sunglasses into my hands. "Put these on. The sun is out."

I fumbled them but managed to get the glasses onto my face.

"What time is it?" I figured it was probably just a few hours later, maybe seven or eight a.m.

"It's three-thirty," Remi told me.

"What?" I was shocked.

"I've been with you the whole time. You were out cold." He opened the bathroom door, and I felt some of the nausea return at the movements my body was making as he carried me in his arms. I felt myself whimper, and he slowed his steps.

"I'm just taking you down to my room. Julia has a bag ready for you," he assured me. His room. In all this time we had been together, I had actually never been to his room. The thought flitted through my mind.

"Okay," I whispered. I was so embarrassed that Julia was going to see me like this. I really didn't remember drinking enough for this kind of reaction to happen, and now Remi had to take care of me, and he would realize what a pathetic burden I was. Everyone would finally see that it was easier to let me take care of myself, just like my mother had. I felt a tear slip out of my eyes as the negative, anxious thoughts that I battled overtook me. I was grateful for the sunglasses so Remi couldn't see how rattled I was. I already knew that even though it had been just about a month of us being together, I could never go back to my regular life. If Remi broke up with me, I felt like I would never recover because now I knew what it was like to have someone care about me. I almost felt like I had been better off not knowing because this experience had been too good. This experience made me feel too whole. It had given me a taste of true happiness, and how could I be expected to return to my empty, lonely, anxious existence once I had lived like this? I was shaken out of my depressing thoughts as my body was placed in a reclining position against some pillows on what I presumed was Remi's bed. I heard Julia's voice talking to Remi in low tones, and then she addressed me.

"Oh, lovie, don't cry."

Well, apparently, the sunglasses weren't enough to cover up my tears. I felt something wet on my arm as she sanitized it with an alcohol wipe.

"Small pinch, and then it will feel a little cold. Okay, honey? You will start to feel so much better as soon as we get these fluids into you. I included some glutathione, so it's going to work really quickly."

I didn't understand what she was saying, but I just nodded, and I felt a blanket cover my legs. I winced at the pinch and then at the cold fluids that began to flow into my arm. I could feel it, and it felt weird.

"Hold still," Remi told me. He was sitting to my left. I turned my head, overwhelmed by how pathetic I felt. I wished he would just take me out of my misery now and send me packing before I kept getting in too deep. My brain was fully convinced that he found me to be way too much to deal with since he had seen whatever side of me it was that had shown up last night. I heard Remi talking to Julia again as she taped the needle in place. I caught drifts of, "Roofied... police..."

"I was roofied?" My brain felt so fuzzy, and my mouth felt like it wasn't saying my words right.

"Shhh." Remi was rubbing my shoulder and tucking the

blanket more tightly around me. I fell asleep with his voice whispering in my ear, but I didn't know what he was saying.

I woke up to the pinch of the IV being removed from my vein and Julia's voice asking, "How do you feel?"

The sunglasses had fallen off during my nap, and I was able to open my eyes. The room was dark, but there was a lamp on, and it didn't hurt me. I blinked and licked my lips. They were still dry.

"Better," I said. My brain was working again. I looked around. Remi wasn't there.

"He's going to break up with me. Isn't he?" I blurted out. Julia looked shocked.

"Why would he do that?" She sat down next to me on the bed and reached over to brush some hair off my face. I shrugged.

"I just feel like whatever hot mess this is, it's not what he signed up for," I mumbled.

"Shaen, what happened last night was not your fault. And even if it was, Remi cares so much about you. He was a wreck last night worrying about you. He's not here because I made him go to sleep since he's been existing on fumes all day." She fussed with my blanket and then handed me a water bottle with a straw. I took a small sip.

"I don't understand what happened. One second, I was fine, and the next second, I can barely remember what happened." I felt so ashamed.

"At first, Remi thought maybe it was the drinking, but then you started to act off. He said you were revved up one second and falling over the next. Then Lia said she remembered that right before this all happened, a guy she didn't recognize had handed you a drink, and they think something must have been in it. So they rushed you home. You were stable enough that they told me they didn't think getting an ambulance was the right move, and I agreed with them. I was here when you fell asleep. Remi never left you, and we all took turns checking on you through the night." Julia filled me in on the events that I couldn't recall.

I made a regretful noise, and she stopped me. "You would do it for any of us."

I nodded. I knew that I would.

"So please accept that we care about you, honey. I know it's hard for you, but you can't stop us," she said jokingly. I gave her a small smile.

"The police said too much time has passed to do blood work because whatever it was seemed to be very fast acting, so it is out of your system by now, but they are looking at camera footage to see if they can get a shot of the guy who had handed you that drink. They're going to come by when they have more information," Julia explained. I nodded again.

"I'm sorr…" I started. She stopped me with a serious look on her face.

"You are like a daughter to me, and my nephew is so happy with you, so I do not want to hear a single apology out of you. You did nothing wrong. The one who should be apologizing is the piece of shit who did this to you." She wrapped her arms around me and hugged me so tight that I felt the love from her pour into me.

"Thank you," I mumbled against her shoulder.

"Do you think you can handle some toast?" She seemed intent on changing the subject. I shrugged.

"Maybe?"

She stood up from the bed.

"I will send Remi in with a slice. We will do one more IV later tonight, but you've got some color back in your face, so I am confident that you are on the mend."

"Okay," I whispered. She blew me a kiss and left the room.

I must have fallen back asleep because, once again, I was

woken up. This time, it was from Remi placing a kiss on my forehead.

"Hiiii," I whispered.

"Hi." He smiled at me. He looked tired, and I felt guilty. "I'm going to feed you some toast. Okay?"

I nodded. Remi proceeded to hand-feed me little pieces of buttered toast until I had finished an entire piece of bread. I was feeling so much better in comparison to when I had woken up in the bathroom earlier. My headache was gone, I felt like I had more energy, and my thoughts weren't scrambled and depressing anymore.

"Um." I took a deep breath as Remi crawled under his blanket and laid down next to me. "Julia said I'm not allowed to apologize," I told him, taking a deep breath and snuggling against his chest.

"She's right." He sounded emphatic about that.

"Well, then, I just want to say thank you." I shivered as I felt his breath on the side of my neck. He had his big body tucked around me.

"You don't have to thank your boyfriend for taking care of you, Shaen." His voice was gruff and full of emotion. I shrugged.

"I feel like I have to. My brain was really fucked up before," I admitted. "And I hate that I keep putting you in a position where you have to take care of me." He looked at me and said, "You're my girl. I want to take care of you."

"I know, but this morning, or earlier, I was convinced you would be sick of my drama and would break up with me, and I was so scared because I can't..." I felt like I would cry again, and I closed my eyes as I felt another wave of fatigue wash over me. I could hear Remi take a shuddering breath near my ear, and right before I drifted off, I heard him say, "I love you too."

Damn it, he had heard me.

Hours later, I woke up feeling even better than before, with most of my energy returned and no more lingering pain in my body. I realized that my bladder was going to burst if I didn't get to a bathroom ASAP. I sat up and got myself out of bed.

"There is a bathroom right there," Remi mumbled, pointing to a door near his closet. The door opened up into a big bathroom with gray marble tile, a huge vanity, and a massive Jacuzzi.

"That tub looks delicious," I told him as I shut the door.

"Let's use it some time," I heard Remi reply as I peed for what felt like a good five minutes. I took my tampon out, surprised that it had held up for so long.

"Can you get me my bag, babe?" I called from the toilet. Remi appeared a minute later, shirtless and in a pair of boxer briefs, holding my bag. I fished around in it and found my tampons. I shoved one in and then took out a fresh bra and underwear. Looking in the mirror, I saw for the first time that I was wearing a shirt with Remi's face on it.

"You told me if I got you one, you would wear it." He grinned. He seemed so happy that I was feeling better.

"I did, didn't I?" I remembered jokingly telling him if he made me a shirt with his face on it that I would proudly wear it. It looked like he had taken me very seriously.

"I got you something too," I told him as I brushed my teeth. He came up behind me and hugged me.

"You don't have to get me anything." He kissed my neck, and I turned around and practically climbed up him. He sat me on the vanity and got between my legs, and we kissed like our lives depended on it.

"I was scared," he admitted against my mouth. I stilled in his arms. I had been too out of it to feel scared. "Your pupils were so blown that your eyes looked dark. And you just... weren't yourself. I don't understand how people keep getting into our private parties and keep hurting you..."

"Hopefully, the police will find something. Did he do this to anyone else?"

Remi helped me climb off the vanity, and I opened my bag again to find his gift.

"So far, it looks like it was just you." Remi's face seemed worried at that knowledge. I had to admit that it was kind of strange that out of the hundred girls there, I seemed to be the only one who had been targeted and that nothing had happened after that. Didn't people usually drug girls with the intention of attacking them after? Something about the story made no sense to me, but I pushed away the nagging feeling and pulled out the gifts. We sat on his bed as I gave them to him. I had gotten him two things. One was a necklace from David Yurman. It had a black leather cord, and on it hung a gold circle amulet on which I had our initials carved: R + S. I had also gotten him a rolling toolbox from Sharper Image that Julia let me hide at their house. The rep I had spoken to told me that anyone who liked working on cars needed one. I handed him an envelope containing the pamphlet for the large toolbox and then a small box with the necklace inside. I nervously watched him open the gifts. He immediately put the necklace on, and then he opened the toolbox brochure.

"Babe... thank you." I could hear how much the gift meant to him by the tone of his voice. I knew he didn't have a lot of support in his dream to work on cars and one day own an antique car shop, but I wanted him to know that I supported him in it, always. He pulled me into his lap, hugging and kissing me. His lips were soft on mine, his tongue snuck out to swipe at the seam of my lips, and I opened for him. Our tongues danced as his hands pulled me closer to him. I could hear him panting, and I had to fight the little groans that wanted to escape me. I knew Julia was cool, but I didn't feel comfortable moaning in her house just yet, if ever. His hands palmed my breasts over my T-shirt, and I could feel my nipples pebbling.

"When will you be done?" He motioned to my general pelvic area.

I counted and then answered, "Probably by Thursday."

"Okaaay." He seemed resigned to wait. I kissed my way down his neck and licked one of his nipples. He let out a sound that had my pussy clenching, and I realized that I was ready for the next step.

"Is your door locked?" I asked him.

"Noooo." He looked confused.

"Go lock it," I encouraged him. He got up, locked the door, and came back. His erection was swelling the front of his underwear. I pulled him back down on the bed and had him sit on the edge. Then I got down on the floor in front of him. Awareness shone in his eyes.

"Shaen, you don't have to..." He started to protest. I made a fist over his underwear and gripped his penis.

"Aaaah." He made that sound again.

"I want to. Is that okay?" I looked up at him, hoping I didn't look like a complete wreck in my T-shirt, messy hair, and bare face.

"Is it okay?" He squeezed his eyes shut for a second and then opened them, looking glassy-eyed with excitement. "How could my first blow job ever, from my gorgeous girlfriend, not be okay?" He had a hand in my hair, and I felt excited at the idea of him leading me.

"Okay, but you have to promise me that if it's not good, you'll give me time to practice." I was so serious, but he let out a laugh that ended in a moan as I ran a hand down his length.

"Baby, you can practice all you want. I volunteer for tribute."

I was rubbing him hard now, and his hips were coming off the bed.

"Take this off." I pulled at the elastic waistband. He listened so quickly, pulling his underwear down and tossing them to the side. Remi's thighs were all hard muscle and had a thin layer of soft hair on them. His stomach was flat, leading up to his defined pecs, and his dick stuck out proudly from his body. I was so hot for him, and I wanted to do this so he could understand how much he meant to me, but I was also so scared. What if it tasted funny? What if I was bad at it? How could I possibly be good at it when I had never done this before? Would I swallow? Would I even let him come in my mouth?

"You're thinking a lot," Remi noticed out loud. "We do not have to do this if you're not ready." He made a move to cover himself.

"No. I'm ready." I was determined. "I'm just an overthinker."

"You? No way," he quipped sarcastically. I pinched his thigh in response.

"Ouch!" he yelped.

"Can anyone hear us?" I asked as I got fully in between his legs.

"No." He was breathing heavily. "My room is in the basement, and ohhhh, Jesus..."

I blew some air onto the tip of his weeping cock and wrapped my hand around the base as I leaned in and gave it a tentative lick. It had a musty, tangy taste and was almost sweet. I could handle that. I took the whole tip in my mouth and sucked briefly. His hips came up off the bed, and I could see him squeezing the blanket on either side of his body as he said my name in a panting, low tone. His penis was too big for my mouth, and I remembered the girls in the dirty books that I read would take what they could and then use their hand for the rest, so I tried that. I took more into my mouth and hollowed my cheeks, moving my tongue and lips on him as I jerked the rest of him with my left hand.

"Oh, dear God, Shaen... I'm going to embarrass myself, baby. But I am literally..." His voice was so deep, and I could feel his fingers gripping the sides of my head now. I moved my mouth up and down his length enthusiastically. He let out a loud moan.

"Shhh," I garbled around him.

"I can't help it," he mewled. I swiped my tongue up the underside of his cock, moved my left hand around the root, then took my right hand and cupped his balls. His thighs stiffened on either side of me. I was so worked up myself that I could feel my body clenching around the tampon. I could feel more pre-cum drip into my mouth, and I swallowed it as Remi's fingers ran over my jaw and then down to softly hold around my neck. He squeezed gently as I took more of him in my mouth and sucked, then ran my tongue around the tip in a circular motion and then went back to getting him as deep as I could without gagging. At one point, I did gag, and that seemed to excite him even more.

"Oh yes, baby, take me. You look so good taking my cock. What a good girl," he panted out in short, loud breaths. I loved that he was so natural at giving praise because I was obsessed with it. I could feel his words like an electric fissure through my body. I sped up the movements of my hand, and I could feel him grow harder in my mouth.

"I'm going to come," he warned. Remi made a move as if to pull out, but I held him in my mouth and gently squeezed the part of his dick that was in my hand as I opened my eyes and looked up at him.

"Ooooh, you're killing me." He tightened his grip on either side of my neck and began to move his hips, taking over. He literally fucked his way into my mouth, his cock getting close to the back of my throat, and I willed myself to allow it. My eyes were watering, and I almost pulled back when I felt him swell and come as he filled my mouth with a warm, salty substance that was too thick for me to call a liquid. He was moaning my name so loud that I was scared the whole house could hear him. As he finished, I felt his fingers touch the front of my throat as I swallowed him down, and the way he clearly loved that made my thighs tremble. He pulled out, his long dick shiny from my mouth, and I watched as it softened on his thigh. His face was flushed, his hair was falling in his eyes, and he had a look about him that I didn't recognize.

"Get up here," he growled. I stood, and he attacked me. He had never kissed me like this before.

"I can taste myself." I heard him say.

"Do you like it?" I asked as he sucked his way down my neck to latch onto my nipple.

"Like it?" he gasped. "I love knowing that it means I made a mess in your mouth. You... you just..." He was at a loss for words, so he switched to worshiping my other nipple. My body was so sensitive due to the hormones from my period that I needed to cover my mouth with both of my hands so no one would hear how excited he had gotten me.

"Baby, I want to taste you." He was down by my waist, hand tight on my hip, kissing the tops of my thighs. I sat up on my elbows to look at him.

"Remi... you can't. I'm..."

"Keep the tampon in, I'll stay up by your clit. I won't go lower." He was almost begging.

"I feel... dirty."

His eyes flickered with amusement.

"Not that kind of dirty." I playfully slapped at his shoulder. "I mean, I feel like this is just gross," I told him. He lay me back against the pillows again and said, "I am obsessed with all of you, and if you want to wait, I will wait. Painfully, but I will wait. But if you let me, I promise I won't find it gross."

I made an "I don't believe you" face.

"I swear, babe. I had it all over my fingers, remember?"

I groaned. "Don't remind me."

He laughed and rubbed my inner thighs with his hands.

"Please, Shaen?"

I gave in and laid back. I couldn't believe this was happening. I had never done anything like this before, and it felt like a really big deal. I knew I was still a virgin and could remain one for as long as I wanted to, but this still felt like a big step in the realm of trust. Of being together. Of connection. I shivered as Remi almost lovingly removed my underwear and tossed them on the floor. He gazed down at me, and I imagined how weird the string of the tampon must look hanging out of me. That couldn't be sexy, right? Yet Remi looked downright ravenous. He had his hands on my thighs, keeping my legs apart, and he was bending his dark head down between my legs. I could feel his breath there, and I was strung up somehow, stuck in the moment of waiting. I felt teased and impatient, and suddenly, after what seemed like an eternity, I felt the swipe of his tongue on my clit, and I knew I would never be the same. It was like a thousand nerve endings went off in my body at the same time. The borderline pain of how tight his fingers were clutching onto my thighs in comparison to the feather-light dance his tongue was making on the most intimate part of my body was blowing my mind. I was a mess for how the flat part of his tongue felt against me, and then suddenly, he sucked, and I thought I might die. I could feel him laugh against my flesh at the insane words coming out of my mouth.

"Rem-Remi... baby... I can't... more. Please, I can't. Oh my God, yes, do that. Oh God, I can't take it."

His mouth was magical on me, which was crazy to think since neither of us had any experience whatsoever, but I guessed this was a result of the natural desire we had for one another. He kept bringing me higher and higher between licking and sucking and then a tiny bite on the side of my swollen clit that had me writhing under him until suddenly I exploded. I felt like I had been flung up above us and was stretched out among the stars. My body was on fire while also running cold. My legs were trembling, and was I crying? I felt like I was crying. The orgasm just kept going as Remi was lapping at me and moaned against me. Him moaning as he ate me was another level of intimacy I had not experienced before. I had never felt closer to another human being ever.

"I love you," I sobbed as the crescendo washed over me, and I collapsed against the bed, sweating and panting. My body was feeling so tight and so loose at the same time. Remi crawled up against me, covering me with his body and crowding me against him.

"I wasn't sure if you meant it last night." His lips were swollen and wet from me. His hair was a mess from my hands frantically grabbing at him, and his dick was hard against my stomach. Again.

"I meant it." I stared at him. He stared at me.

"Is this crazy?" I whispered. He rubbed his thumb against my lips.

"If it is, I want to be crazy with you." He leaned in to kiss me, and I tasted myself on him.

"I love you too," he said against my neck. I smiled, and we fell asleep again.

This is what peace feels like.

WE WOKE up from yet another nap at around six that evening. I took a shower and put on a pair of workout shorts and a tank top. After applying some mascara and a dab of lip balm, I left the bathroom to find Liam sitting on Remi's bed, playing on his phone.

"Oh my God, you look so much better," Liam exclaimed in true Liam fashion.

"Well, thanks," I replied sarcastically.

"No, seriously, you looked like shit for a bit there."

That made both of us laugh, but then Liam got off the bed and came over to hug me. I stood stiffly in his arms.

"Um, what are you doing?" I mumbled; my voice was muffled against his shirt.

"Okay, ice queen, I'm showing some love to my bff because things could have gone way worse, and I'm just happy you're okay." Liam sat back down on the bed. I sat next to him.

"Okay, I get it. I'm glad I'm okay too." It was funny how warm, loving, and cuddly I could get with Remi, but although I loved them very much, I was still my regular old stiff and avoidant of emotions self with my friends. They loved to make fun of me for being out of touch with normal human feelings.

"So you and Remiel, huh?" Liam leaned back on Remi's pillow. I shrugged.

"I really, really like him," I finally said. I didn't love to wear my heart on my sleeve most of the time, but I knew Liam could be trusted.

"It seems like you're both in super deep super quick." He observed.

I nodded.

"Yeah, I guess... Do you feel like that about Lia?" I looked over at him when I asked the question. Lia had joined our friend group in ninth grade, and Liam had flirted with her relentlessly until she finally agreed to go out with him two years later. He had been sleeping with a ton of other girls up until that point but had never dated anyone seriously, so none of us thought it would last. With the exception of two quick breakups, they had made it all the way through eleventh and twelfth grade as a couple.

"I mean, I care about her a lot, and I think she's an amazing person, but you know that I'm going to be in Boston for the next four years, and she's going to be in California, so I just don't see it working out with us being so far apart for so long," Liam admitted.

"Wait!" I sat up and looked my best friend right in the eyes. "You guys are going to break up?"

"I mean, we talked about it briefly. I'll be sad, but we both don't see how it can work with school schedules, being, like, a six-hour flight apart and, not to mention, the time difference. It's just an extra stress that neither of us needs as we go to college," he explained.

"Doesn't sound like you love each other then." I felt bad for them, but it did sound like a breakup would be a mutual decision.

"Love? No way, babe. We care about each other so much, and I respect the shit out of her, and damn her body is..."

I held up a hand. "Nope."

Liam laughed. "Okay, well, I will miss her, but I don't think ending it will break me." He finished in a much more PG fashion.

"Wow." I really thought after two years of being together that they were serious enough to try it long-distance.

"I mean, I hope it doesn't happen, but if you and Remi broke up, it wouldn't be that big of a deal, right? You've been together for what? A month." Liam scoffed. "That's nothing."

"Liam. I know this sounds crazy, but I would literally be unable to leave my bed. Like I would go insane. I would be heartbroken." I shuddered just thinking about it.

"What are you talking about?" Liam suddenly sounded serious. "Shaen, it's literally been like thirty days. You can't be serious."

"I told you it's crazy. But I swear my energy aligns with his energy. I feel like I can't imagine my life without him." I buried my face in my hands, feeling embarrassed for admitting how strong my feelings were.

"Hey." Liam took my hands off my face and held them in his own. "You're my best fucking friend. And you are one of the most emotionally in control people that I know. The fact that you never fooled around with anyone until Remi makes me know how serious you are, and I believe you. If you say you love him, then you love him. That's enough for me. I mean, you love him, right?" He peered at me.

"I do," I whispered. Liam broke up the heavy vibe in the room by jumping into a rendition of *The Lion King's* "Can You Feel the Love Tonight," which made us both laugh. It was a welcome reprieve from all the big feelings he had brought up in me.

Liam's phone buzzed. "Dinner's ready," he told me. I pulled on a pair of socks and followed him upstairs.

"Do you know where my phone is?" I asked as we entered the kitchen.

"I have it," Remi said from where he stood cutting up watermelon. "I texted your mom last night to tell her you were sleeping over here. It's in the pocket of my sweatshirt that is in the living room, but it's probably dead."

I found my phone, and it was, in fact, dead. Liam took it from me and plugged it into a charger in the kitchen. Suddenly, Julia and Sam came into the room, followed by a police officer.

"This is Shaen." Julia pointed at me. Remi stopped cutting the watermelon and came to stand behind me.

"Hi, Miss Collins. I'm Officer Brook. I'm so sorry to hear what happened, but I'm glad you're okay." He shook my hand, and we all sat down at the table. My heart was suddenly racing. The officer didn't waste any time.

"So, the good news is there were cameras at the location last night, and we have clear footage of this man putting a pill into the shot that he gave you," he told us. The room let out a collective sigh. Remi's hand took mine and squeezed it.

"If I show you a photo of a few faces, do you think you would recognize him?" The policeman was now taking photos out of the folder he was holding and began lining them up in front of me. They were all of people at the party last night, in the same lighting and all of similar coloring and build, but the one in the middle stood out to me.

"This one." I pointed to him confidently.

"I know that guy!" Remi exclaimed. Everyone turned to look at him.

"Because he works for your dad." The officer filled in the blanks.

"What?" the room collectively said in unison again.

"Yeah, he's my dad's driver. I saw him yesterday at the graduation. His name is—"

"Blake Summers," the officer interrupted again.

"Yeah. What the fuck, excuse me, what in the world is going on?" Remi was now tripping over his words. The policeman was putting the photos away as he said, "When we saw the video footage of him handing Miss Collins the drink, we obviously kept watching, and we saw that he left immediately. Which is odd because..."

"You would think he was drugging me to take advantage of me," I interrupted quietly.

"Yes." Officer Brook nodded. "But instead, he left right away. He had parked in an area where we could see his car, but we couldn't catch a plate. However, we were able to pick it up later from a traffic cam. The car he was driving was registered to a Pastor John S. Taylor."

Remi stiffened next to me.

"We sent some local police to the house with the photo. The

pastor identified the man as Blake Summers, who is twenty-three, and apparently works as the pastor's driver. We currently have Blake in custody. Both he and the pastor are sticking to the story that the pastor had no idea where Blake was or what he was up to last night. And his alibi did check out."

"I'm so confused." Liam stood up from the table. "Why would my uncle need an alibi?"

"Well, at 4:30 a.m. this morning, Blake Summers texted him and said 'All good,' to which he received no response. This did raise some suspicions. Do you have any reason to believe that John Taylor would wish you physical harm?" The officer directed his attention to me. I looked at Remi, then Julia, and then turned back to the officer.

"I mean, I really don't know him, so I don't know. I don't think so," I stuttered.

"What did he put in her drink?" Remi's voice was tight and strained.

"Benadryl," Officer Brook replied. "Blake said he didn't want to hurt Miss Collins. He just wanted her not to feel good and leave the party."

Remi stood up from the table as well.

"Did he say why?" Sam asked.

"He lawyered up after that." The policeman stood up and gathered his things. "So the investigation is still ongoing, and there isn't anything else for me to share with you at this time, but Miss Collins, if you or anyone else can think of any more details, please let us know. And in the future, after you're twenty-one, of course, please only accept drinks from people you know. Okay?"

I nodded, surprised that was the only mention of all the obvious underage drinking. I was beginning to feel numb. The officer shook my hand again, and Sam walked him to the door.

"Blake doesn't do anything without being told to do it by my dad." Remi looked angry and almost scared. "So what the fuck is going on?"

"Okay, let's say your dad told Blake to do it; tell me why? What is he trying to accomplish?" Liam started putting food onto plates, and I helped him by bringing them to the table. Julia had made fresh garlic bread, fettuccine alfredo, salad, and gnocchi. As confused as I was by this new plot twist, I was also starving, so I dove into the pasta.

"If I'm my dad and I find out that my precious golden boy son is being led 'astray' by a girl..." Remi sat down next to me with a full plate of food as Sam came back into the kitchen.

"And the last I knew of my son was that he was big into purity culture and was taught that girls that drink too much are not godly women. That they are loose with their morals and they're not wife material, then maybe in my twisted logic, if I could make the girl look and act like she can't handle her alcohol, then maybe my precious son would come home. Or, at the very least, break up with her."

"And a graduation party was the perfect opportunity, plus they were already in town." Sam sat down at the table with a plate of food as he agreed with Remi's theory.

"That is so fucked up," Liam announced. "Hey, pass the lemonade, please."

I passed him the pitcher of freshly squeezed lemonade. Julia was so extra, and I loved it.

"Do you really think your dad is capable of that?" I asked Remi as I took another large bite of my food. Remi didn't answer for a minute, and then he replied, "I wouldn't put it past him."

"Neither would I," Julia agreed.

"Am I in danger?" I felt a panic attack begin to slide up my throat.

"Hey." Remi grabbed my hand. "Take a deep breath."

I did.

"Again."

I took another one.

"You are not in danger. I think it was a one-time opportunity where he tried to get the upper hand, but now, with the police sniffing around, he would be stupid to try anything again." Remi sounded so sure and confident that I wanted to believe him.

"I mean, it sounds like this Blake guy is an idiot. He was caught on camera and then was easily identified. Like how dumb of a criminal can you be?" Liam laughed.

"I never want to see your dad again," I told Remi.

"Honestly, me neither," he agreed.

17

Over the next two weeks, I got into a rhythm of my new work schedule. I was having so much fun hanging out with the dogs more often, and I was absolutely loving my new role as Julia's social media manager. As much as I was enjoying my new schedule and was obviously benefiting from the bigger paychecks too, I also missed seeing Remi every day like I used to in school. He was working Tuesday, Wednesday, and Thursday as a lifeguard, and he was a server on Friday and Saturday nights. I didn't work at the shelter on Wednesdays, so I would take my content work with me so I could hang out at the pool. Remi told me I was a distraction, but I knew he loved it. I was developing a beautiful tan, and I kept finding skimpier and skimpier bathing suits at the thrift store that I knew were driving him insane. We hung out every Sunday and Friday until he had to work, and then on Saturdays, I worked during the day, and he worked at night, so we didn't see each other from Friday afternoon until Sunday when he finished at the gym. Remi said he was worried that he was going to lose muscle now that he wasn't playing football, so he had been doubling down at the gym on the days that he could go.

Not seeing him all the time made me feel needy, which my feel-ingless self hated, and my girlfriend self embraced. I had also not drunk any alcohol since the incident at the graduation party, and we hadn't heard anything more about what had happened with the driver, but Remi was still not talking to his parents. My phone buzzed, shaking me out of my thoughts, and I saw it was the chat that we had made for Remi's birthday party, which was tonight.

LIAM

what do we think of strippers?

CARTER

like in general or for the party?

LIAM

both

EVA

Liam no!

DEE

lesbian strippers?

EVA

Dee no!

LIA

I'll be the stripper

SHAEN

ya, no

LIAM

spoil sport

RACHEL

I picked up the cake just now I'm coming over to drop it off Liam.

LIAM

I'm here

CARTER

I'm a fan of strippers and cake

EVA

middle finger emoji

LIAM

ok so my parents are going out with Remi at 4 to "discuss what he'll be doing after the summer is over" which he's gonna LOVE Lol. So be here by 4:15 so we can set up. Then around 5:15 Shaen is gonna pretend to be mad at Remi and that will set the plan in motion for him to come back here all worried and we'll be here with balloons and strippers

EVA

no strippers

SHAEN

What am I mad at him about?

CARTER

he came in you without permission

DEE

say you're mad that you didn't hang out all day

SHAEN

that works

LIA

Perfect

I rolled out of bed to go shower when a voice note came in from Remi.

REMI

Babe, I'm so sorry but after the gym my aunt and uncle are making me go out with them to talk about what I'm doing after the summer. I tried to tell them that it's my birthday, but Sam said his surgical schedule is very busy and this is the only time they can meet so I'll see you tonight? I'm so sorry. Don't be mad.

I giggled as he unknowingly walked himself right into his surprise.

SHAEN

thumbs up emoji

REMI

I knew you'd be mad. Babe I said I'm sorry!

SHAEN

happy bday *heart emoji*

I hated hurting his feelings and acting so bitchy, but my friends were convinced that it would make his surprise so much better, so I stuck to it.

REMI

Shaen it's not my fault. They were really insistent and I can't tell them no when they do so much for me.

SHAEN

k

When I got out of the shower, I saw I had three missed calls from Remi.

SHAEN

sorry was showering. See you later

He didn't answer. We had never fought before, and on my end, this was all fake so he wouldn't guess we were having a party. But it was starting to feel like he was actually mad at me now, which was never part of the plan. I tried to keep myself calm and just focus on the work I had to get done.

I began planning my week's content for the spa. I loved posting before and after photos of lip filler because the results were instantly noticeable and so beautiful. I also planned on preparing a post for Julia's new service, which was an injection that helped get rid of cellulite, and I was working on a video series on the different vitamin infusions that she offered. It was two-thirty when I finished, and I still hadn't heard from Remi. I went into the birthday group chat.

SHAEN

I think I actually pissed Remi off. I was a little too committed to the part

LIAM

ya he's mad

SHAEN

fuck

LIAM

no it's perfect. He's mad cuz he thinks ur mad and that will just make the surprise so much better

SHAEN

are you still at the gym?

LIAM

photo

A very sweaty, muscly Remi showed up on my screen. He was giving Liam the finger as he lifted weights with his other hand.

LIA

damn

LIAM

photo

This time, he had sent a selfie of himself, shirt wet with sweat, blowing a kiss.

LIA

daaammnnnn

RACHEL

get a room

SHAEN

I'm gonna get ready now and then Eva is picking me up to be there at 4:15.

LIAM

aight

After my shower, I put on the new dress that I had found when I had gone thrift shopping last week. It was originally from Anthropology, and it was a deep navy blue color. The length hit right under the knee, and the material was tulle, which was one of my favorites for a girly moment. The best part of the dress was it was strapless and sheer from the waist up, other than some lining over my boob area. It was beautiful and it showed off my tan in the perfect way. As I was finishing my makeup, I put the bronzer and highlighter I had used for graduation across my chest and collarbone again, giving me a gorgeous glow. I left my hair down because I knew Remi liked it best that way. Getting him a gift had been hard because he honestly had everything he needed, and I had just gotten him the graduation gifts. Lia had told me to give him my virginity as a gift, but I didn't feel ready yet, and it also felt kind of cliche. I ended up writing him a long letter and paired it with a date night jar. I had put fifty-two different date night ideas into a mason jar, and I thought it would be fun to choose one a week for the next year. At four, Eva texted me that she was outside. I couldn't wait till I had my own car and didn't need rides from my friends anymore. I made an appointment to go look at used cars on Monday. Remi told me not to buy anything without him because he wanted to confirm that it was a good buy which made sense to me since I knew nothing about cars. When I came out of my room, I saw that my mom was in the kitchen.

"Where you off to?" she asked me.

"It's Remi's birthday," was all I offered.

"You're still seeing him?"

"Yup." I grabbed my bag and opened the door.

"Are you being careful?" she asked me. I turned to look at her.

"You mean so I don't make the same mistake you did and end up with me?" I didn't wait for her answer, I just left quickly before the tears welling up in my eyes could turn into full-blown crying and ruin my makeup.

Liam whistled when he saw me walking in through the front door.

"Damn girl." He was standing on a chair hanging up an arch made of balloons.

"You look so hot." Lia gave me a kiss, which, to my dismay, she caught me wiping off, and she quickly gave me another one.

"Thank you." I spun a little, enjoying the movement of the material around my freshly waxed legs.

We spent the next hour setting up the tables, blowing up more balloons, and putting the food out. I had made three different kinds of lasagna and four types of pie that I had dropped off in an Uber this morning before work. Everyone else had brought other food options too. Liam had put himself in charge of drinks, which I personally still wasn't sure I would be participating in. Dee was managing the music again, and I could hear her setting up the speakers. The house was filled with noise and voices as the whole football team showed up, as well as a bunch of his friends from back home. Then all of his family from Julia's side joined too. We had all collectively agreed that we would not be inviting his parents.

"Okay!" Liam announced, interrupting the hubbub. "Everyone shut the fuck up. Shaen is going to message Remi now, and I need you all to find a spot to hide. Don't come out until I turn the lights on, and then you'll yell 'surprise,' and hopefully he shits himself."

The room laughed, and then the crowd dispersed to find a place to hide. I took out my phone.

SHAEN

so you're just gonna ignore me the whole day?

REMI

I just finished with Sam and Julia. No offense but I'm really not in the mood.

SHAEN

in the mood of me?

REMI

no for fighting

SHAEN

we're not fighting

REMI

it feels like it

SHAEN

well you've been ignoring me

REMI

I'm on my way home. Where are you?

I didn't answer as I crouched down next to Lia, who was now having to calm me down because I realized that I was having my first fight with Remi, and it was all over a misunderstanding, and I couldn't handle the idea that he was mad at me.

"You'll give him a blowie, and he'll forgive you, I promise," Lia told me confidently.

"Lia...!"

"It'll work," Liam confirmed where he hid on the other side of me. "It always works."

"Ew." I tried to shove the unwelcome image of my friends out of my mind's eye.

The house was silent and dark yet buzzing with an undercurrent of excitement when we heard Remi inputting the code to unlock the front door. Then we heard the sound of the door opening. My heart beat heavy in my chest as Liam stood to turn the light on, and everyone jumped up and screamed, "Surprise!"

Remi's face was one of shock. I could see his eyes scanning the crowd until they landed on me.

"I love you," I mouthed. He didn't smile. Fuck, I thought. I waited back as I watched him greet all of his guests, many of whom he hadn't seen since the funeral. Then I waited as he got some food, and then I finally got the courage to go up to him. I stood in front of him silently. He surveyed me with wary eyes.

"So this morning was all a lie to throw me off the scent?" he finally asked.

"I mean, I wasn't lying…"

"So you *were* mad?"

I bit my lip.

"No, I wasn't mad," I admitted.

"You hurt my feelings." His voice was low, his face impassive, but I could feel his pain.

"I'm sorry," I whispered.

"My parents never acknowledged my birthday other than some cake and extra prayer at dinner. I was really looking forward to spending the day with you and celebrating my birthday for real for once," he told me. I felt guilt boil up in my throat. I motioned to the balloons, the pile of presents, and all of the people milling about.

"I love this, and I am very grateful, but I spent the whole day thinking my girlfriend was mad at me."

"I'm sorry. I didn't want to do that to you, but everyone wanted me to make sure you thought I was mad so it would make the surprise better," I admitted.

"Well, it did do that." He bent down to kiss me, and I felt relieved that I was obviously forgiven.

"I'll make it up to you," I whispered in his ear.

"Oh yeah? How?" His eyes ran down the sheer bodice of my dress. "Will you wear this while you do it?"

"If you want me to." I smiled seductively.

"I want you to." He grinned in confirmation and then took my hand to introduce me to his friends and family.

The party was a smashing success, according to Liam. All of the food had been demolished, probably due to the entire football team having shown up. Remi had danced, sang, opened up presents, one of which was a brand new iPhone from Dermont who couldn't make it in person. When it was time for cake, Remi had made a big deal out of blowing out the candles on his cake, and it made me so happy to see him enjoying himself.

Now that everyone had left, I was helping clean up the wrapping paper that was strewn all across the living room. Remi came in and started helping me.

"I'm tired," he announced.

"Okay." My voice trailed off, and for the first time since we had gotten together, I felt unsure of what he wanted. Did he want me to stay over? Did he want to come back to my place? Was he saying he wanted to sleep alone? Was he trying to hint that he was ready to cash in on what I had promised to do for him earlier? The whole party, he had acted like his usual self with me, but the blip we had gone through today was causing extra anxiety to rise up inside of me.

"Remiel," I heard Julia call from the kitchen. He looked at me briefly, then turned around and went to see what his aunt needed. Letting my anxiety fully take over me, I quickly got up and took the last garbage bag outside. Then I grabbed my bag and slipped out through the garage door, hoping to remain undetected. I could feel my heart pounding as I allowed all of my anxious feelings to overwhelm my system. It was getting so bad that I was beginning to feel sick to my stomach. My plan was to walk to the corner and order an Uber there so no one would see me and try to stop me. I had no reason to think that anything was still wrong, but my brain was trying to convince me that I had somehow still ruined everything between us by acting the way I did today. It had felt like he had forgiven me earlier, but now I wasn't so sure. I could feel a panic attack coming on, and I sat down on the curb, trying to calm my breathing. I couldn't cry. I couldn't breathe, but I managed to get some air in through my nose and then blew it out forcibly, trying to regulate myself. After a few minutes, I could breathe somewhat easier, so I ordered an Uber and kept walking to the corner. I saw a call come in from Remi, but I let it go to voicemail. Maybe it was easier to just end this now. If I got in deeper, I would be in big trouble. Already, the idea of him possibly still being mad at me was making me feel physically ill. I knew I would never be able to handle a breakup at any point, but maybe it was best if I just did it now before I fell more in love with him. I knew if I did let it go longer and I grew even closer to him, and then it ended for whatever reason, it would feel even worse than it would now. A single tear found its way out of my eye and made a path down my cheek, dropping off my chin. This is what letting myself feel led to. I didn't like it. I wanted to shove all of my feelings back down to where I had kept them safe up until now. But a small part of my brain told me that now that I knew what feeling happy felt like, if I numbed myself again, I would definitely miss it. Even though feeling hurt, it also felt like so many other good things.

I began getting ready for bed, feeling so much shame about the fact that I had basically run away from Remi. Now that my anxiety had lessened and I could think logically again, I wondered why I had done something so ridiculous. As I lamented how much my unresolved abandonment issues were fucking up one of the best things that had ever happened to me, I heard a knock on the door. I looked through the peephole, and a not-so-happy-looking Remi stood there. My heart felt like it was on its own private roller coaster. I opened the door tentatively.

"What are you doing, baby?" he demanded.

"I don't think I can do this," I blurted out.

"No, Shaen, not that." He sounded so hurt. He walked in, crowding me, so I was forced to walk backward. Remi shut and locked the door behind him. My heart was now beating wildly in my chest. Without a word, he followed me into my room. He shut the door softly because he knew my mother was sleeping down the hall. I felt all of the emotion I had for him begin to ride up in my chest, and it felt suffocating.

"What are you doing, baby?" he repeated softly. Tears welled up in my eyes, threatening to spill over. My lip trembled. I couldn't talk, so I just shrugged. He was so tall and imposing standing there in my room. Looking at me. The hurt and confusion all over his face. Usually, when he was here with me, he would be on my bed, cuddling under the covers. Or on his knees, his mouth on me. Or sitting on my recliner with me in his lap, watching something sports or car related while I read. Or standing in front of the mirror helping me iron my hair when my arms got too tired. I was going to have to move if we actually broke up. I couldn't imagine living in this room by myself with all of his memories haunting me. Remi walked toward me, interrupting my sad train of thought. I didn't move.

"Come here." He opened his arms, and I melted into them.

"What are you doing?" Remi asked again against my hair. I started to cry, but it felt different this time than it ever had before when I allowed myself to cry. Usually, if my emotions got the best of me, I would shed some tears, feel a little sad, and be really quiet about it until I could shove it all away and move on. These sobs that were releasing from me felt like they were emerging from somewhere deeper than usual. I could hear myself making guttural noises that were coming from the very recesses of me. Hot, salty tears were blinding me, my nose was leaking, and my heart... my heart felt like it was breaking. Remi was rocking me, wiping the tears away. Once I began to calm down, he got us under the covers and held me until I finally stopped crying. Now, I found myself lying on his chest, shaking with chills.

"Sorry, I don't know what's happening." My teeth were clattering.

"Your nervous system is trying to re-regulate," he said softly. Remi had been doing a lot of reading about mental health ever since we had talked more about my panic attacks and my fears about people seeing any vulnerable parts of me.

"O-okay." I tried to let my body relax. I felt his warm chest against the side of my body. I focused on his breathing, the delicious smell that was all him, the weight of his hand on my back, and the sound of his voice talking to me. My body eventually calmed.

"Sorry." I felt stupid as I came down from whatever crazy emotional breakdown I had just experienced, and he had unfortunately witnessed.

"Shaen, we're going to fight sometimes. Like for real, not for a surprise party decoy," he informed me gently.

I gave a half laugh, half hiccup.

"And that's okay. It doesn't mean I don't want to be with you, it doesn't mean I don't love you, and it doesn't mean we can't forgive each other." Remi tucked some hair behind my ear and turned my head to make me look at him. "I know you have tried so hard to make sure you don't ever do something that would make someone abandon you again like your own father did, but I promise you not even wild horses can keep me away."

I smiled at his reference to the song I had played for him last month.

"It hurts to love with the possibility of losing, but without the risk, you'd never get to experience the joy of it." He was running his hands up and down my arms now, and I knew it was because he remembered that I had told him about bilateral movements and how they could re-regulate me.

"I will not survive losing you." My voice was barely a whisper.

"I'm not going anywhere," Remi promised.

"You swear?" I knew I sounded a tad needy, but I couldn't help it. I was so scared the rug would get pulled out from under me, and I would be left alone again.

"I swear." Remi held out his little finger to me so we could pinky swear, which made me laugh. "But you have to promise me something." He sounded serious.

"What's that?"

"I need you to choose me."

"I did. I do," I protested. He shook his head. "I need you to choose me over your anxiety and fears of abandonment. I need you to choose me over people telling you to make me mad for a surprise. I need you to choose me... choose us over running away and taking an Uber the second I turn around. Because every day, I am choosing you. Choosing us. We will work out anything that comes our way, but we don't need to add to the regular curve balls that life gives us. Okay?"

I nodded.

"Say it."

"I choose you. I choose us," I told him. He smiled. "Good girl."

The praise ran through me like molten lava.

"Now, let's start the day over." He laid down fully this time and took me with him. I turned on my side to face him, then I took out my phone and quickly typed. His phone buzzed.

SHAEN

happy birthday baby! I love you so much. I can't wait to see you later

REMI

thank you babe! I have to go out with Julia and Sam after the gym will I see you after?

SHAEN

def. I can't wait! Xoxo

He put his phone down and leaned in to kiss me.

"I cannot do that again," he whispered.

"What?"

"Not know where you are. Not know why you ran off. Not sleep next to you. Not have you trust that I am not going to break your heart," he told me, his fingers tracing over my lips, over my jawline, and into my hair.

"I'm sorry," I said again.

"I know you are." He kissed me, and this time, I kissed him back with everything I had. I crawled over him and pressed my body against his. I could feel him hard and desperate in his pants. As I ground my pelvis against him, I could feel his kisses growing sloppier and more excited. I crawled down his body, took his cock out, and showed him how sorry I was.

We slept like the dead after that.

18

"Shaen."

I rolled over. "Shhh. I'm sleeping."

I heard Remi laugh. "Guess what?"

I cracked one eye. "What?" I yawned.

"You're getting a car today!" Remi sounded so excited that I grinned with my eyes still closed.

"Yay." I made a little fist pump in the air because I was so happy about it, but I also just wanted to sleep some more. I was so spent from the emotional roller coaster of last night that I pulled the blanket back over my head.

"I'll get a car later. I'm exhausted," I mumbled.

"Okay, I'm going to the gym, be ready when I get back. We're getting grilled cheese sandwiches for lunch." He pulled the blanket back a bit to kiss my cheek.

"Grilled cheese?" I squealed.

"With Nutella," he promised.

"Barf." Although I loved Nutella, I couldn't imagine pairing it with cheese, but I loved that he remembered my favorite foods. He was still laughing as he left my room, and I went back to sleep.

An hour later, my phone rang. It was Lia.

"All good in lovers world?" she asked.

"Yeah," I sighed.

"Told ya a little mouth and dick action will always fix the problem." She laughed.

"You're so gross. And so right," I admitted, not wanting to get into a full-on detailed conversation about the emotional talk Remi and I had last night, so I just left it at blow jobs. I put Lia on speakerphone as I got out of bed to do my makeup and get dressed, and I listened while she told me about her upcoming trip with her family to Europe. We made plans to get together before she left, and then I finished getting ready. I wanted to be taken seriously at the dealership, so I paired a tight black Skims dupe bodysuit with a pair of gray plaid pants that had a little belt. I then put on a pair of black ankle boots with a heel. I knew they would know how young I was eventually, but I still wanted to appear like a woman who could not be taken advantage of. I was so glad Remi was coming with me because my main source of anxiety when it came to buying my car was that they would sell me a lemon car, and I wouldn't see it coming.

"Honey, I'm home," I heard Remi say jokingly as he came into the apartment. I had texted him the code to the door earlier. I figured it made sense for him to have it since he slept over so often.

"Hi, baby," I called from where I was finishing curling my hair. Remi came into my room looking swole and sweaty. I turned to give him a hug.

"I am atrocious, don't touch me," he warned. I leaned over and licked the exposed side of his pec.

"I licked it, so now it's mine." I winked.

"What?" Remi laughed but sounded confused.

"You know, like when a kid licks his lollipop so no one else can have it," I explained.

"I have a lollipop you can lick," Remi said suggestively and grabbed at his crotch.

"You're gross," I teased. "I'm ready to go."

"I'm gross? You just licked the sweat off my skin," he protested.

"I like it," I told him.

"You do? Good to know." Remi left the room to shower, and I anxiously checked my bank account to confirm again that all my hard-earned savings were still there. I didn't have much of a credit score yet, so I had saved up the full cost of a car and planned on paying the whole thing today. This was a really big deal, but I knew with my two jobs and longer hours, I would be able to replace it sooner than later.

After about ten minutes, Remi came out of the bathroom fully dressed and ready to go. It was unfair how hot he looked barely trying.

"What?" He had caught me staring.

"You look hot," I admitted.

"Well, thanks." He smiled. "Let's go buy my baby a car." He took my hand and led me down the stairs.

"Nope," Remi told the car salesman. "Stop playing games and show us some legit options, or we're leaving."

Damn, bossy, professional Remi was making me horny. I hadn't even test-driven anything yet because Remi didn't like any of the options the guy was telling us about. The salesman finally produced some choices that Remi deemed good enough for me, and I ended up test-driving six different cars. My favorite was a small SUV that was only a few years old with low mileage and was even lower than my budget. After I drove it, I told Remi that I was ready to buy it, but he insisted that the guy pop the hood so he could take a look. When he was done, he came back over to me.

"Do you like it best out of all the cars, baby?" he asked me. I nodded.

"Okay, then do it."

I clapped excitedly. "Yeah?"

"Yeah." He took my hand. "Come sign the paperwork."

An hour later, I had my own car! I got in and turned it on. The engine purred. I could see Remi waiting for me in his car because I was going to follow him to the sandwich shop to get the grilled cheese he had promised me earlier. I ran my hand down the steering wheel. Today was a good day. New car. No fake fighting with my man. And now we were going to eat grilled cheese.

"I did it," I whispered to myself and my new car. I graduated. I was still a virgin, and now I had my very own vehicle. My list was doing well but holding onto my virginity at this point was starting to feel like a technicality. I wasn't sure how I felt about that.

We were finishing up the best grilled cheese sandwiches I had ever had when the group chat buzzed.

LIAM

road trip to the beach house this weekend?

SHAEN

I have work

REMI

Liam we both have work

LIAM

call in sick bitches

REMI

let me see if I can swap shifts with Ben

LIAM

good call

SHAEN

I'll ask my bosses

RACHEL

I'm in

LIA

duh

EVA

hell ya

DEE

can I bring Ashley?

LIAM

who is Ashley

CARTER

her latest girl

LIAM

is she chill?

DEE

she's real good with her tongue

LIAM

and that helps me how?

DEE

she's chill

LIAM

aight

SHAEN

my boss said I can work wed instead of sat so
I'm in

LIAM

fuck ya

LIAM

what did Ben say?

REMI

he said ya

LIAM

how did u convince him?

REMI

I promised him some of your weed

LIAM

gotta do what u gotta do

REMI

this is what I'm sayin

SHAEN

picture

I sent them a photo of me sitting on the hood of my car.

LIAM

sweeet ride baby

LIA

Omg you did it I'm so proud of you!

RACHEL

hell ya Shaen

EVA

ah my baby all grown up

CARTER

is it Remi approved?

REMI

thumbs up emoji

CARTER

she ride well?

REMI

they both do

SHAEN

shut up lol

LIAM

k we leave thurs after Rem and me finish
lifeguarding and then we'll come back sun night

CARTER

good plan

When I finished work on Thursday, I went home to pack. I glanced at my calendar, and I saw that I had ovulated on Sunday, so I was no longer fertile. In about ten more days, Remi and I would be celebrating two months together. Lia had told me that she and Liam had sex the day they had officially started going out. Which honestly made sense for them. Eva, who was a lot more conservative than Lia, had only waited two weeks with Carter. I felt so safe with Remi. Not just physically safe but emotionally understood as well. Free to be me but also supported by him to explore what healing for me meant at the same time. He was also an attentive boyfriend physically. We always talked about what I did and didn't like, and no matter how dirty and bossy he had been in bed, he always cleaned me up and cuddled with me afterward. It felt like I had given so much power to this piece of skin called a hymen. I didn't want it to have so much meaning anymore. I knew how to be safe, and I trusted that Remi would help keep us safe as well. Lately, it had been dawning on me that maybe it was time. My anxiety kept stopping me from saying anything to Remi, and he didn't seem to be in any rush, but I was so curious how much our connection would increase once I knew what it felt like to have him inside of me. To be very honest, I also wanted to know what all the fuss was about. I wanted to stop being afraid of being like my mother. I wasn't. Never was. Never will be. Even if I did have a baby— gulp —I would never do to my kid what my mom had done to me. Before I could chicken out, I texted Remi.

SHAEN

do you have condoms?

REMI

no. Why?

SHAEN

I'm thinking maybe you could bring some on our trip

I was actually shaking.

My phone buzzed with an incoming video call. I nervously pressed answer.

Remi's gorgeous, tanned face filled my screen. He had such a sweet look in his eyes.

"Baby?"

I could hear in his tone that he understood how much this meant to me. I nodded, suddenly feeling emotional.

"You're ready?"

I could hear the kids splashing in the pool behind him. His chest was bare, and he had a lanyard with a whistle on it around his neck. This was such a strange conversation to be having with him at work, surrounded by so many people.

"I think so," I whispered.

"I'll buy some, but you can change your mind. No pressure," he told me.

"Taylor!" I heard someone shout.

"I gotta go. I'll see you soon," he told me.

"Love you," I said quickly.

"Love you too, sweetheart."

The call ended. Sweetheart. That was new. I liked it.

Two hours later, a text rolled in.

LIAM

condoms?????

I rolled my eyes. Apparently, Remi had asked his cousin for help, which was honestly adorable.

SHAEN

they're for my mom

LIAM

nauseous face emoji fuck u for that image

SHAEN

lol

LIAM

see u soon

SHAEN

dancing girl emoji

A few hours later, we were on our way. Remi and I were driving up in his BMW. Liam was bringing Lia, Rachel, and Jake in his jeep. Eva was driving Carter, Dee, and Ashley in her car. We all had various options of food and drinks in the trunk. Sam and Julia had bought the beach house when Liam and I were thirteen. I had always been so jealous of his summers at the beach, and now here I was headed there with my hunky boyfriend and all of my best friends. I was so excited, but it also made me sad because this was a reminder that it was our last real summer together, and time was quickly running out.

The drive took about an hour, so we got there around dinner time. The boys were in charge of bringing all of the suitcases and the food into the house, and the girls began unpacking everything and getting the kitchen ready to cook. I was chopping up a salad when Remi came up behind me and hugged me. I leaned up to kiss him.

"I chose the bedroom down here," he told me. All of the bedrooms were upstairs except for one, which was on the main floor and tucked away in the back of the house. It had a bathroom attached to it and had a huge king bed in it.

"Okay." I smiled.

"'Cause it's private..." Remi almost seemed uncomfortable.

"Ooooh." I laughed nervously. "I just wanted to say that if you're not ready, it's okay." I didn't want to disrespect any of his feelings about this being a big step in the deconstruction of his faith. We had talked about how he felt about what we were doing and if he still had any worries about it being a sin. He had told me that since our conversation after his grandfather had passed, he had done a lot of thinking on it and had even talked to Julia, and he felt at peace with it. He had even let me know that the photo he had taken of me was coming into good use when he jerked off. I had told him that he was gross, but if I was being honest with myself, I was actually flattered, and I was happy that it obviously meant he had really worked through some pretty big stuff from his upbringing that had been affecting him for a long time.

"Oh, I'm ready." He said it so quickly that I burst out laughing.

"What's so funny?" Rachel asked from where she stood, putting together kebabs for the grill.

"Nothing." I was still laughing when Remi lifted me up in his arms and whispered in my ear, "Really, I'm ready. I'm nervous, but I promise I'm feeling one hundred percent about all the stuff around my dad's bullshit."

I kissed his cheek, and he put me down.

"I'm gonna go help Liam get the Jacuzzi ready."

"'Kay, baby." I smiled sweetly at him.

"Jeez, he's just perfect, isn't he?" Rachel waited till he left the room to pipe up.

"What do you mean?" I had finished with the salad and moved on to cutting open some avocados to make guacamole.

"He's just so good to you. I don't know how you did it so quickly, but he seems head over heels." She took a swig of her beer as she picked up the platter of kebabs to bring out to Carter, who was manning the grill.

"I know, looking at it from the outside, it seems fast, but for us, in it, it feels right," I assured her as I measured out the lemon juice.

"Oh, I'm not worried. You two are couple goals." She blew me an air kiss as she went outside to get the kebabs cooking. I smiled to myself. Me? Couple goals? I could have never predicted this turn of events.

"Dinner's ready," I yelled out, hoping the boys could hear

me. They could, and they came piling in through the back door. Liam and Remi were already in bathing suits, as it seemed that getting the Jacuzzi ready had included actually getting into it. Once we were all sitting and passing the food around, Liam said, "Remi, do you want to lead grace?"

Remi froze. His hand that was holding a cup of water got stuck halfway toward his mouth.

"He's fucking with you, baby." I patted his arm as I laughed.

"Bro." Remi punched Liam's arm. "Do not say shit like that to me."

"Aw, poor Remi," Lia teased.

"Ouch. Fuck. Lay off the weights, man, that hurt," Liam whined, rubbing his arm.

"Aren't you the one who literally just told him to start lifting heavier this week?" Carter asked innocently as he passed the ketchup to Jake.

"Semantics," Liam grumbled and bit into his burger. As we all dug in and began eating, Dee said, "I can't believe this is our last summer together."

"Why is it our last summer? We'll all be around next year." Carter was clearly getting nervous about Eva moving away for college.

"Nah, bro, it's the last real summer," Liam agreed with Dee. "Next year, Shaen will be pregnant with Remi's baby. Rachel will be traveling. Dee will probably have moved in with some girl and won't come home on break. Lia will be..." His voice trailed off, and I remembered him telling me he didn't think they would make it long distance. "Well, anyway, we'll all be real adults by then, and it won't ever be like this ever again."

I wondered if him potentially breaking up with Lia was hurting worse than he had originally let on.

"Why am I always the one pregnant in these fake scenarios?" I protested.

"Have you seen Remi? His sperm are probably extra strong swimmers." Carter laughed.

"Can we not talk about my swimmers?" Remi grumbled.

"Listen, you are a virile-looking young man," Carter continued teasing my boyfriend.

"Jesus, Carter." Remi was practically blushing.

"Honestly, virile is such an ick word," Eva told us as she took some more salad.

"What's an 'ick?'" Jake wanted to know.

"Like something that gives you the ick," Lia explained.

"Still no," Jake exclaimed. Everyone burst out laughing.

"It's like your pet peeve. Like the word moist. Or the feeling of suede," I told him.

"Oh, got it." He finally understood. "My ick is people who drive the speed limit."

"Oh em gee. Same," I agreed emphatically.

"She's insane," Remi informed my friends. "She thinks the speed limit is a suggestion."

"Isn't it?" I played innocent.

"My ick is people who bite into Kit Kats," Rachel shared. "Like it's clearly meant to be broken into fourths and eaten properly."

"Yeah, I hear that." Ashley nodded. "My ick is when I wash my face and all of the water rolls down my arms and gets my sleeves wet. It legit ruins my day."

The guys seemed clueless, but all the girls related to that problem and laughed in agreement.

"What's your ick, Remi?" Carter asked.

"People who talk about my semen," Remi told him sarcastically.

"Noted." Carter threw a blueberry at him. Remi tossed it back.

"Children, children." Liam stood up and pretended to keep

them apart. "I propose we go smoke up in the Jacuzzi."

"Fuck yeah!" Lia and Rachel seemed to love that idea.

"We men will clean since y'all cooked," Liam informed us, already beginning to clear the table. He didn't have to tell me twice. I threw my plate out and then went to the room to change into a bathing suit.

I had brought a one-piece that was a dark gray color, but it was far from conservative. It cut up high on the thighs, and it had a corset design in the front, which squeezed my already full chest up so my boobs looked fake. I tied it tight, pulled my long hair up into a messy bun, and took a look in the mirror. If all worked out, I would no longer be a virgin in a few hours. I wondered if I would look different. If I would somehow blossom overnight. Look more mature or knowing? I laughed at myself, cognitively aware that I would probably look exactly the same minus a hymen, but this still felt like such a big step for me that it seemed crazy that it wouldn't show physically. I took a deep breath and left the room to go join everyone outside.

I never smoked when Liam and my friends would light up. Remi smoked occasionally, but as I got into the water, he whispered that he wasn't going to smoke tonight since he didn't want to miss anything later. That made me blush and splash some water at him. He grinned and pulled me onto his lap, his eyes roaming over my bathing suit appreciatively.

"Damn, baby. You look so hot." He ran his hands over my curves and up the corset top to where my breasts threatened to break free. I swatted his hands away as Lia, Liam, and Rachel all climbed into the Jacuzzi. Liam was holding a joint, and the sweet smell of weed wafted over to me.

"You gonna take a hit for once?" Liam sat down next to me.

"Nope." I gave my usual answer. He shook his head and blew some smoke over my head.

"I don't know why."

"'Cause I'd probably end up calling the police on myself," I told him. "You really don't know how bad my anxiety is."

"I think it would help your anxiety." He leaned down and kissed my temple. "If you ever change your mind, I will sit your high with you."

"Aw, thank you. That's the nicest thing you've ever said to me." I laughed.

"Why is she always so sarcastic?" Liam jokingly asked Remi over my head.

"Sarcasm is her love language," Remi agreed. Rachel had put snacks onto a floating tray, and Remi was picking all of the red gummy bears from the candy section and eating them. Lia took the joint from Liam, took a hit, and then passed it to Dee. Liam lowered himself into the water, letting the bubbles get all the way up to his neck before turning to me and saying quietly, "I'm gonna miss you next year."

I looked over at him. His dark blue eyes were rimmed red, and his long lashes were wet from the water.

"Don't go soft on me now, Hennessy." I splashed some water at him. He leaned over and gave me a small hug.

"I'm serious, ice queen." He snagged the candy platter and got us both a pack of Gushers. "We've been best friends since we were what, six? I've never not been in school with you."

"You are so high," I said, trying to push down the emotion rising up in my chest.

"I am pretty fucking high," Liam admitted with a short barking laugh. "But it doesn't make what I'm saying not true. You just don't like thinking about it." He opened up my bag of Gushers, and with his dry hand, he popped one in my mouth. It was just last week that Remi and I had a conversation about Liam's familiarity with me. How he called me babe, hugged me, or even got into bed with me sometimes. Remi had told me that he wasn't intimidated or worried about it. He knew that his cousin loved me as a friend and that we had been thick as thieves for way longer than Remi even knew I existed. I felt relieved to hear Remi say that it did not bother him at all and that he actually appreciated how close we all were. Though, he did add that if Liam ever did do anything suspicious, he wouldn't hesitate before punching him. We had then made out after I had told Remi how hot he was when he went protective caveman over me. I chewed on the Gusher, feeling the bubbling water all over my body, half listening to the conversations my friends were having around the large Jacuzzi, and then turned back to Liam.

"You're right. I am going to miss seeing you every day," I admitted.

"See, that wasn't so hard." He put an arm around me for a quick side hug.

"But I'm not going to miss your lethal farts after Taco Tuesday," I added.

"You always have to ruin it. We were having a moment, Collins." Liam laughed, pulling on my bun, and then dunked under the water to go bother Lia. She shrieked as he bobbed up in the water next to her and crowded her against the wall of the Jacuzzi as he leaned down to kiss her. I was going to miss him and all of my friends. I put another Gusher in my mouth and moved back over to where Remi stood talking to Jake. I leaned against his chest, and his arm snaked around my waist.

"I'm glad you're not leaving," I told him. He smiled and kissed the top of my head. Earlier this week, Remi had finished applying to a local trade school to become a car mechanic. It would take around two years to complete, and then he would have to take a test to get his ASE certificate. In the meantime, in September, he was also starting a part-time job at a local mechanic shop that would work around his school schedule so he could get hands-on experience. I was so proud of him for sticking to his guns and going after what he really wanted to do instead of what everyone else expected of him. Especially his father.

"Dermont called me today." Remi interrupted my stream of thoughts.

"Oh yeah, what did he want?"

"He wants me to come to visit him in California before I start school." Remi's fingers were lightly rubbing over my shoulders, giving me chills in their wake.

"For how long?" I thought about what it would be like without having Remi around for a bit, and I didn't like the sad feeling that came up in me at the idea of not seeing him for a few days. I had been an independent woman for so long, and then a boy made me come and fall in love with him, and suddenly I was a gooey mess over him. It was such a different vibe for me, but I found that I couldn't help it; I loved how I felt about life when I was around him.

"A week." Remi's fingers tightened on my shoulders as he began to slowly massage them.

"What did you tell him?" I felt the stress leave my body from the movement of his hands.

"That I would let him know."

"Do you want to go?" I popped another Gusher into my mouth.

"I think so." Remi popped open a can of sparkling water and took a drink. "We can talk about it later."

I nodded.

Lia and Liam were full-on making out now. Everyone else was just choosing to ignore them. Rachel, Dee, and Jake were still passing the blunt around. Finally, Eva and Carter joined us.

"Y'all were one hundred percent fucking!" Dee laughed as they climbed into the water with us.

"Yeah, and?" Carter splashed some water at her. Eva blushed and climbed in after him.

"We don't kiss and tell," she told Dee.

"Carter does." Liam had come up for air.

"Well, I hope it was good 'cause you guys were in there for a while." Dee passed the blunt to Eva, who shook her head, so Carter took it. All of my friends looked sufficiently high by now. Dee had put on soft music that was playing from the speakers around the pool. There were twinkle lights strung up around the outside area as well, and I felt so relaxed and happy.

About an hour later, we were surprised by a loud, unexpected crack of thunder as the sky opened up.

"Was it supposed to rain?" Liam seemed dumbfounded. We all scrambled to get out of the Jacuzzi and put the cover over it. Then we grabbed our now soaking wet towels and ran to stand under the protection of the screened-in porch. As we got inside, Liam checked the weather on his phone.

"Looks like no more rain the whole time we're here," he assured us. We sat and watched the rain for a bit until Dee announced that she was tired.

"Let's go to bed. We have a long day tomorrow of tanning, swimming, and, in general, doing a lot of nothing." Eva laughed.

"Speak for yourself, we boys will be in the gym in the morning," Carter told her. "These muscles don't build themselves." He ran a hand over his six-pack. Eva eyed his body appreciatively.

"What time do you want to work out?" Remi asked as he held open the porch door, and we piled into the kitchen, leaving wet footprints on the gray tile.

"I dunno? Ten?" Carter took out his phone to set an alarm. "That way, we'll get in a good workout and still have a lot of time to chill with the ladies on the beach."

"Good plan," Liam interjected. "Good night. If anyone needs condoms, Remi has plenty."

The whole room cracked up.

"You're such an asshole," I told Liam as he came over to me, arms spread, and wrapped me up in a big bear hug.

"I love you, crazy girl," he said, pressing a kiss into my hair.

"The feeling isn't mutual," I grumbled, playfully pushing him away. Liam just laughed at me. Even Remi chuckled as he took my hand.

"Okay, my angry pixie, let's go get your beauty sleep."

A chorus of good nights reverberated through the hallway as all of my friends made their way upstairs to their various bedrooms. Remi was still holding my hand as he led me into our room. He shut the door softly and locked it. I stood in the middle of the room, listening to his breathing, wondering if we were really going to do this.

"I don't want to hurt you," Remi suddenly announced.

"You're not going to hurt me." I turned to look at him.

"I will though. Not on purpose. But I know the first time is not fun, Shaen, and I've kind of been dreading that part."

I opened my suitcase, rummaging through my clothes, trying to find my pajamas as I answered, "We don't really have a choice. It's part of the deal; otherwise, I will die a virgin." I laughed as I took off my bathing suit and pulled on my pajama top. Then I took my toiletry bag into the bathroom.

"I'm going to get ready for bed. If you don't want to do it tonight, that's okay. But it's going to hurt no matter how long we wait."

I took my time washing my face, applying my skin care, and brushing my hair. I wasn't upset at him, but I guess I imagined when I was finally ready that he would be all over me with excitement. I didn't envision him worrying about hurting me. It was so sweet, but it felt like a mood killer too.

When I came out, Remi was in a pair of boxers and a tank top and was lying on top over the covers.

"Do you…"

"I'm not…"

We both said at the same time.

"You go first," I told him as I climbed into bed and got under the thick, fluffy down blanket. Remi propped himself up on one elbow and looked at me.

"I love you," he whispered.

"I know," I whispered back.

"And this is a big deal for me, not because of religion or thinking it's bad. I know it's not. But I also know that it can be more than what Carter and Liam make it out to be. It's not just a quick feel-good moment for me, at least not in my mind and definitely not with you." He reached over and ran a thumb over my chin briefly. "This feels like the possibility for a stronger connection between us, which will probably lead to a deeper commitment." He shrugged. "I know this sounds stupid coming from a horny nineteen-year-old, but all I'm saying is this means something to me, and I hate that a moment that will feel so good for me is going to hurt you. I don't like that," he admitted. His face looked sad for a moment.

"I appreciate that." I reached over and took his hand. "And I agree this is not just us wanting to have a good time. This definitely means more. But I have had a lot of time to wrap my head around knowing that one day, I was going to let a man I love do something to me that might hurt me. But Lia said it's not so bad, and Eva said it only took a few times to start feeling good, and I know I'm doing it with someone I trust. I know you'll go slow, and I know you'll stop if I need you to. So I'm not afraid," I assured him. He nodded.

"Okay, well, I need you to be so turned on that you're super wet. That will help." He sounded so serious that I laughed.

"Babe, I'm always turned on around you," I assured him. He looked a bit smug at my answer. He slid his fingers into my underwear.

"Let me check. You know, for science," Remi deadpanned.

"Definitely, science is important." I laughed and then moaned as his fingers swept through the wetness that had gathered at my entrance and then moved higher to circle around my clit. He knew exactly how to touch me and what dirty praise I loved, so I came within minutes, gasping his name and clutching the blanket on either side of me. He rolled over so he was now hovering on top of me, the necklace I got him hanging off his neck. I reached up and tugged on it till his mouth came close to mine.

"I'm super wet," I whispered against his mouth.

"I'm not done with you yet," he whispered back and then kissed me. The scruff on his face was rough against my cheeks, and it drove me wild. He made his way down, stopping to worship my breasts, and then when I was sufficiently worked up, he moved down lower until his mouth was working magic between my legs, and I came again with a scream as my second orgasm wrecked through me. At this point, I was positively aching. I could feel him pulsing insistently against my leg. I grabbed at his hair as he made his way back up to kiss me.

"Baby, please," I panted.

"Please, what?" he teased. He was acting chill, but I could see in his eyes how much he wanted me. I could also feel it in how tense the muscles in his back were.

"Fuck me, Remiel. Do it." I stared deep into his eyes, hoping I looked and sounded sexy. Something about me saying that with his full name seemed to unleash something in him. He rubbed his crotch against my pelvis.

"Are you absolutely sure, baby, because I really, really want to? But I need to know you're one hundred percent sure."

I could feel how thin his self-control was at this point. He felt so tense. The muscles in his arms were strained and bulging as he held himself up so he wouldn't crush me. His need for me was radiating off of him. I reached up to stroke his cheek.

"I'm sure, Remi. Make love to me," I whispered softly. He moaned, his chest vibrating against mine. I felt so much power in this choice to share my body with him. I was giving him something, but it felt like I was taking something too. We were exchanging love, trust, and something I couldn't name. With desperate movements, Remi moved off of me and went over to his bag. In the dark, I saw him take the brand new box he had just bought out of the side pocket, and then he ripped a couple of condoms off. He came back to the bed, taking his clothes off, and from my vantage point, his muscled body was looking so sexy. He reached down and pulled my pajama shirt off. We sat there staring at each other for a minute. His chest was heaving, and his hands were trembling as he ripped the condom open. He fumbled with it at first, but he figured it out and pinched the end as he rolled it down on himself.

"That's hot." I squirmed as his eyes found mine.

"Yeah?" His voice sounded husky. He climbed back over me and kissed me. His lips were full and soft on mine. His tongue was dancing in my mouth. After a few minutes of heavily making out, he lifted his head, panting.

"I love you," Remi told me. "Please tell me if you need me to stop. Okay?" He practically begged. I nodded wordlessly. My heart was pounding with excitement and anxiety from the fear of the unknown. I felt his cock nudge at my entrance. I widened my legs slightly. Remi was watching me carefully, almost looking wary. I smiled and nodded. He pushed in slightly, and I gasped as the head breached my entrance. He stilled. I urged him silently with my hand against his butt. Remi shook his head.

"I'm going slow."

"I'm okay," I told him, my hand was now dancing over his back. He shivered.

"I'm going slow," he repeated. Even though he was barely in me, I could feel the slight stretch, and I could feel how warm he was resting in my entrance.

"Okay." I appreciated how much he cared about me, even if it was dragging out the inevitable. He pushed in a little bit more, and I could feel how much my body had to stretch to accommodate him.

"Oooof." I involuntarily let out a half sigh, half sound of pain. I bit my lip as he stopped again and looked at me, alarmed. I smiled and reached up to brush some hair off his forehead.

"I'm okay," I encouraged him. "It's okay." My heart was racing as I was engulfed in love for him. Sweet, concerned Remi was just adorable.

"I can feel it," he whispered. I knew he was referring to my hymen. I also could feel that he was up against some resistance.

"Please just do it quickly. Waiting is hurting more than just ripping the bandaid off," I begged. He looked at me, his head slightly tilted as if to say, *You sure?*

"Do it," I urged. Remi leaned down and kissed me with so much reverence I felt tears welling in my eyes. I didn't know what this was, but it wasn't what my friends had described. Not one of my friends had told me that sex felt like a connection. Like love. Like transcendence. And I hadn't even really had sex yet; I laughed at myself in my head and then winced as Remi thrust through the thin barrier of skin and bottomed out inside of me.

"Oh!" I exclaimed as pain reverberated through my body. I felt sore, full, and stretched all at the same time. Remi was as still as a statue above me, yet his arms were shaking, and his abs were tense as I ran my hands down them.

"What are you doing?" he breathed.

"I want to feel it." I had my hands between us. I could feel myself, lips spread, wetness seeping around, and there he was deep inside my body. I was surprised at how much of him didn't fit inside me. I circled the root of him with my fingers. He flinched, which caused him to move slightly, and I felt the pain again. Tears welled up in my eyes once more.

"Don't make me move." He looked like he was in pain himself from hurting me. I brought my hands back up to hold onto his arms that crowded on either side of me.

"Can you just do it and finish 'cause…" It felt the opposite of sexy to ask him to hurry. It didn't feel good to admit how much it hurt.

"Shaen. I can't just come if I know it's hurting you." Remi's voice was filled with what almost sounded like shame.

"Don't feel bad. I want this for you, and you do need to move, or my body will never get used to it." I winced as he pulled out slightly.

"Shaen." He sounded unsure.

"I swear it's already getting better." The sharp pain had dulled to an uncomfortable throb. He pulled out more and then slid back in. I felt my body adjusting and stretching again at the invasion.

"S-so tight," he stuttered. It did not physically feel good for me. At least not yet. But what did feel good was watching him lose himself in me. I loved watching him tremble, and I liked the weight of his legs around me. I wanted him to come. I wanted him to be mine for keeps.

"I am yours for keeps," he murmured. Shit, I had said that out loud again. He began to move in earnest now, but I could tell he was still holding back. Which, honestly, I was grateful for. There was plenty of time for a pounding. I just didn't want it right now when it felt like I was being stretched to my limit. Remi had now lasted longer than Eva, Rachel, and Lia had told me their first time was. My legs were cramping, but I was enthralled watching how his face was contorting with how good it felt for him. He was panting now.

"Oh, it's so good, Shaen. So tight. So hot. You're so wet."

I loved when he talked to me like this. I beamed. My vagina felt bruised, and I wondered how anyone came from sex alone, but I also felt strong and feminine with him sliding in and out of me. The idea that this was something so taboo in the world made me feel euphoric. The Christians frowned upon it, Hollywood glorified it, my sex ed teacher had warned about it, and my friends had, quite frankly, cheapened it. This was a connected feeling like I had never experienced. His eyes stared into mine, and then he leaned down and suckled on my nipple and then my neck.

"What does it feel like?" he asked me.

"Uncomfortably full. But also, it feels like one day I won't be able to get enough of it," I admitted. "What does it feel like for you?"

Remi's eyes had now scrunched shut, and his mouth gaped as he moaned his way in and out of me. He opened his eyes again.

"It's so tight. I never imagined it could feel this good. I'm almost there…" He leaned down again and caught my mouth in his. His movements were growing more and more jerky, and he was gasping into my mouth.

"Oh God, I'm close, I'm close." He almost sounded desperate.

"Come in me, baby," I urged him again. And he did; after one more long stroke, his back arched, and he moaned and shook as he emptied himself in me, and it was beautiful.

He collapsed on top of me and lay panting on my chest, his softening dick was still in me.

"Baby?"

"Y-yeah."

He felt heavier all of a sudden.

"Do you mind pulling out? I need…"

"Oh shit." He pulled out and sat back. The condom was covered in blood. Remi stared at it and then looked at me.

"Shaen…" He sounded pained.

"I'm okay, my love. I swear." My love? Where did that come from? "I'm just going to clean up." I sat up and winced. I was kind of pissed that all of my dirty books had led me astray. They always showcased the virgin heroine as orgasming from sex right away and wanting it three times in a row her first night. What a lie. I felt swollen between my legs as I made my way into the bathroom. I peed, and when I wiped, I saw more blood on the toilet paper. I ran the water till it was warm, and then I got a washcloth wet with it and wiped it between my legs. That helped a little. Remi came in holding the full condom. He tied it off and hid it under the tissues in the garbage.

"I'm sorry."

I looked up at him. "Don't you dare do that." I poked him in the chest.

"Do what?"

"Regret it. Stop playing the hero. Losing my virginity is a rite of passage. Are you not gonna give me any babies because labor hurts?" I demanded. Remi's face softened.

"You want my babies?" He kissed the corner of my mouth.

"I want one or two." I kissed him back.

"I'll put my babies in you," he told me huskily. God that sounded so hot.

"Okay, good. So stop being a little bitch about this."

He laughed, picked me up, and brought me back to bed, where I laid my head on his chest.

"If I'm being honest, I can't wait till it doesn't hurt because I want to fuck you so hard," he admitted. I laughed out loud and kissed his chest.

"I love you," I told him.

"I love you too, baby. Thank you."

"For?" I asked.

"For giving that part of you to me."

He was so sweet. I fell asleep feeling so sore and so loved I could barely stand it.

So this is what trust feels like.

19

___

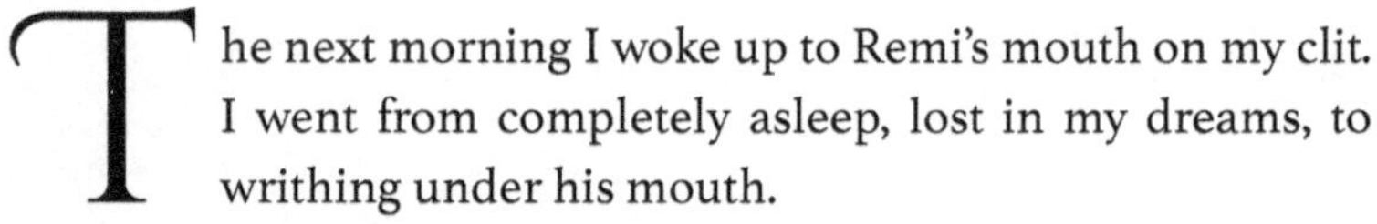

The next morning I woke up to Remi's mouth on my clit. I went from completely asleep, lost in my dreams, to writhing under his mouth.

"R-Remi!" I moaned. "What are you doing?"

"Eating your pussy," he mumbled against my clit.

"I-I can feel that." I laughed. "Oooh." I arched as he sucked on my clit. "But why?" My hands found their way into his hair, and I gripped as he slurped me into his mouth.

"You didn't come last night." He looked up at me.

"I did. I came twice if I remember correctly."

"Not while I was in you," Remi corrected me. I rolled my eyes.

"Hey," Remi admonished jokingly. "There will be no lack of orgasms with me." He dove back down and continued where he had left off. His mouth was so warm and wet against my swollen flesh. I was so sensitive and was still feeling the after-effects from last night. He slowed down.

"I can't hear you."

"Huh?"

"I'm not continuing until I can hear you."

I tried to lift my hips to his mouth. He pulled away.

"Uh-uh," he laughed.

"Remi!" I hissed. "The whole house will hear me!"

Remi licked me from bottom to top. I groaned.

"Be a good dirty girl, and let me hear you." Remi seemed even more confident, if that was possible, now that he had fucked me. Once. He suckled, bit, and licked again. I whimpered.

"Oh, good girl," he said encouragingly. "You looked so good under me last night. You took me so well."

I combusted. When I was done, Remi climbed up my body and kissed me, looking very satisfied with himself.

"Next time, I want you to sit on my face," he said. I gaped at him. "Go back to sleep." He slapped my ass. "I'm going to the gym. I'll be back soon, pixie."

I slept with no dreams after that.

Lia woke me up at ten forty-five.

"It smells like sex in here," she announced.

"It should," I mumbled from under the blanket.

"Holy shit, Shay Shay!" she squealed, using Liam's nickname for me. "Did you finally pop your cherry?"

I turned over and opened my eyes.

"Well, he popped it." I laughed.

"I hope he popped it real good."

"It hurt like a bitch," I admitted.

"Perfect, that means he's big enough to make it good." She grinned. "It'll get better. I swear. Aw, my little baby is all grown up." She lay next to me and wrapped me up in a hug. A few minutes later, she sat up.

"Enough post-coital sleeping, bitch, we're going to the beach." She slapped my ass as she left the room. Why was everyone slapping my butt this morning?

Forty minutes later, I was on the beach with my friends in a skimpy black two-piece bathing suit, my hair was in two braids, and I was wearing minimal makeup. When I was getting dressed, I found a hickey on my breast and two bruises on my hips where Remi had gripped me. They turned me on, and they were clear as day in my bikini, yet I wore them with pride. The sun was hot on my skin, and I felt whole in my body in a way I hadn't realized I would after sharing such an intimate moment with someone. I liked it a lot.

After an hour of shooting the shit with my friends, tanning, and eating copious amounts of fruit for breakfast, we saw the boys running toward us. All four of them looking hot in their bathing suits, their muscles swollen from their workout, but I only had eyes for one.

The boys had brought food from the local deli that was next door to the gym they had gone to, and we all dug in. I sat in between Remi's legs, my back to his chest. Every once in a while, he would drop a kiss on my shoulder. He opened my seltzer can for me, he rubbed my back, and he cleaned the sand off my feet. He was being super attentive and attuned to my needs. I caught Liam watching us. He smiled softly when I shrugged, but he didn't say anything. He obviously knew, and as my best friend, it felt like he was proud of me somehow. After lunch, I napped on a towel on the sand while the boys played volleyball.

When I woke up, Remi was lying on his towel next to me, reading a book about cars.

"Are you reading?" I asked, sounding surprised.

"Good morning, sleeping beauty." He grinned and put his book down. "And yes, I know how to read, Shaen."

I rolled my eyes and sat up.

"Where did everyone go?" I asked, looking at all the empty space around us. Remi pointed to the water.

"Apparently, Sam bought jet skis the last time they were here, and Liam found them."

I shaded my eyes with my hand and looked out at the ocean. It looked like Liam and Lia were on one, Dee and Ashley were on another, and Eva stood in the water up to her waist as Carter swam around her.

"I feel bad that you're missing it." I stood up and brushed the sand off my feet as I slipped on my slides.

"I was not going to leave you, and I got a good amount of reading in." He slung his arm over my shoulders and pulled me close as we walked to join my friends.

"How are you feeling?" He gestured to my lower half.

"I'm fine." I felt embarrassed somehow.

"Hey. Tell me for real." Remi stopped walking and spun me to face him.

"Every step is a reminder of what we did last night," I admitted. Remi bit his lip and turned around from where our friends stood a few feet away.

"I'm gonna need a minute," he explained. I laughed when I saw that he had gotten hard.

"Didn't take much, huh?" I giggled.

"Well, you're standing there looking like a sexy minx, and you just told me that you feel... Okay, that's not helping." He groaned, which made me laugh harder.

"You guys okay?" Eva called. I nodded.

"Be there in a second," I called back.

"Your dad called," I told Remi. He immediately stood straight and glared at me.

"He did?"

"No, but you're soft now soooo..." I pointed to the front of his bathing suit.

"Damn, you're smart." He reached for me, and I ran off, making him chase me. Of course, he caught me in about ten seconds since his legs were so damn long. Then he threw me over his shoulder and ran us into the water as I shrieked and begged him not to. The next thing I knew, I was being tossed into the cold yet refreshing water, and I came up sputtering.

"You fucker." I splashed him, and he cracked up.

"Does my pixie not know how to swim?" He swam circles around me.

"You know that I know how to swim!" I exclaimed, throwing more water at him, which just made him laugh harder. Eva and Carter joined us.

"Who naps in the middle of the day?" Carter teased.

"I was tired."

"You would be with monster dick over here keeping you up."

"I don't have a monster dick," Remi muttered, rolling his eyes.

"Bruh, we've all seen it." Carter lay on his back, floating in the water, the sun shining bright on his face.

"What do you mean you've all seen it?" I sputtered. Eva had brought over two floaties, and I leaned my chest and arms on one.

"In the locker room. Showers after the game," Carter explained.

"Why were you staring at my dick?" Remi asked slyly. "Something you need to share with the class, Carter?"

"It's hard to miss, Remiel." Carter shot back.

"Touché." Remi lifted his hands in surrender and swam off to where Liam was sitting on the jet ski and was shouting for his cousin to join him. Dee, Ashley, and Lia began to swim over to us as Remi got on the other jet ski and roared off after Liam.

"Is it really bigger than normal?" I asked Carter, which made Eva giggle.

"Bruh." Carter stared at me right on. "I'm not one to say anything that would hurt Little Carter's feelings, but I swear Remi is bigger than all of us." He had his hands cupped over the front of his bathing suit as if to protect his penis from hearing about the competition. Eva snorted.

"Your dick is just fine, babe," she reassured him.

"Only fine?" Carter pouted.

"It's exquisite," she corrected dramatically.

"That's better." He grinned and then turned back to me. "But seriously, the dude is blessed."

I wondered if that was why I still felt so sore. I had no experience with any other penises, obviously, so this was all I knew.

"It's a good thing," Eva told me. "He's gonna be able to do so many fun things."

I laughed. "You make it sound like it's an amusement park."

"It kind of can be." Eva winked as Lia and Dee came over.

"Where is Rachel?" I asked, changing the subject.

"Oh, she and Jake had a fight earlier, and they walked off and haven't come back yet," Dee explained.

"I hope they're not angry fucking out here," Lia said. "Sand up in your coochie does not sound fun."

"Where could they possibly be fucking out here?" I asked, looking around at the beach, which offered very little privacy.

"You'd be surprised how creative you can get when you want some lovin'." Lia laughed.

"Where's the craziest place you've done it?" Ashley asked. Ashley was bi, so she had been with boys and girls.

"I went down on a girl in a Walmart dressing room," Dee piped up.

"At the movie theater," Eva confessed.

"How?" I wanted to know.

"We were in the back row, and I sat on his lap and had a coat over me. We thought we were being so chill about it, but it was probably so obvious." Eva cracked up describing it to us. Carter was looking all smug.

"It was obvious 'cause you're so damn loud, Ev."

She pushed him but didn't argue.

"I fucked a guy in a cemetery," Ashley told us.

"That's so creepy," Dee told her.

"You're just jealous." Ashley leaned in and kissed her.

"Liam and I fucked in a confessional booth at his uncle's church," Lia admitted.

"Holy fuck, Lia."

We were all bent over howling when Liam and Remi came back to join us.

"What's so funny?" Remi wanted to know.

"Apparently, Liam and Lia had…" I started.

"Sex in your dad's church," Lia finished the sentence for me. Liam reached over to high-five Lia.

"Hell yeah, we did." He seemed so proud of himself.

"At my pop's funeral?" Remi asked, looking perturbed.

"Bro. No! At Christmas the year before." Liam seemed appalled at the question.

"Oh yeah, that's when I was shocked you guys were even kissing." Remi seemed annoyed at himself. "I wore a purity ring and everything back then."

"Yeah, you did." Liam laughed and patted his cousin on the back. "And look at you now. Tearing up pussy and everything." Liam seemed to remember it was me who he was talking about, and he leaned over and said, "Respectfully, of course."

"Of course." I nodded, laughing and blushing as he fist-bumped me.

"Anyone hungry?" Carter asked. We all agreed that we were starving, and together, we went back to the house to get ready for dinner.

Eva, Carter, and Rachel, who had shown back up with a very satisfied-looking Jake, were on dinner duty tonight, so I went back to the room to shower and change. I knew the group had plans to hit up the local club later, and I was feeling wary about it since shit had gone down at the last two parties I had attended, but I got dressed to go either way. I decided to wear a pair of ripped jeans and a cream corset halter top. I was doing my hair when Remi came in and closed the door.

"Oh fuckkkkk," I heard him say. I turned around.

"What?"

"What do you mean, what? You look so hot." He came up behind me and peppered some kisses up the back of my neck. I shivered.

"Well, thanks." I kissed him back and then finished doing my hair as he sat on the bed and told me about his plans to visit his godfather. Apparently, Dermont had bought him a plane ticket for the end of August, and the plan was for Remi to stay with him for a week. He seemed excited to hang out in California, and I was excited for him, but I knew I was going to miss him too.

"Does your dad know you're going?" I asked and stood up to leave the room because I was so hungry my stomach was rumbling.

"I don't know. I have no plans to talk to him, especially knowing that he tried to hurt you." Remi took my hand and opened the bedroom door.

"Well, we don't know that for sure." I wasn't defending the pastor, but the fact is we did not know one hundred percent what had actually happened.

"Listen, I know. Proof or not," Remi told me. "And he's an ass anyway. I'm done with him."

"No argument from me." I got up on my tippy toes and kissed his cheek.

"Hottie alert!" Lia announced as I came into the kitchen. Liam whistled as Ashley said, "I'd tap that."

Dee fake slapped her.

"What?" Ashley pretended to be confused.

"I'm right here," Dee laughed. "Shut up."

"I got you something." Liam was pulling a packet out of his pocket.

"My birthday isn't until September, Liam." I reminded him.

"Oh, I know." He looked over at Remi. "She's a psycho for her birthday, so just start preparing now."

Remi nodded. "Noted."

Liam handed me the small package, the size of a pack of travel tissues but thinner. It was black, and in white letters, it said "Cup Condom."

"You cover your drink with it so you can stay safe tonight. There is enough in there for all of us to have one," Liam told me.

"Oh my God, thank you. I actually love this. I was feeling a little nervous about tonight." I hugged him and slid the "gift" into my small bag.

We ate quickly and then called an Uber so no one would have to be the designated driver tonight.

The club was so posh that there was a bouncer with a list of names on it. Liam had called ahead and got us into the VIP section using his parents' names. The beach club community was tight-knit and wealthy, so his last name meant something up here. I had no idea how Liam had also managed to get us drinks, being that we were all under twenty-one, but he did. We all popped a cup condom onto the glass and then stuck a straw through the top. I stuck to one drink only, so I was feeling good but fully in control as well. The dance floor was packed, yet we found a spot to squeeze into, and we all began to move with the music. Remi was all over me as we danced, and I loved it. If I was dancing in front of him, we were chest to chest, my hands around his neck, and his hands were on my ass. If I was standing with my back to his front, then his hands were firmly around my waist. At one point, we ended up making out in the corner, completely lost in the music and our lust.

"I swear I could take you right here," he rasped in my ear. I imagined what that would be like. Me up against a wall in the corner of a packed club. The lights flashing, the energy palatable, and him pumping into me, hands on my waist, gripping tightly, his mouth on mine.

"It would be hot, wouldn't it?" He could see the cogs in my mind going. I dipped my head, suddenly feeling shy.

"It would be hot," I admitted.

"Do you think you'll be able to go again tonight?" Remi had to shout over the music because it was so loud. I did a kegel to test out my level of soreness.

"I think so." I blinked up at him as the strobe lights flashed over his face. "You're so hot."

"No, you're so hot," he murmured in my ear and sucked my ear lobe into his mouth. Suddenly, Liam knocked into us as he danced nearby with Lia.

"You love birds ready to go? I'm horny, and public fucking is frowned upon," he asked.

We all knew he would definitely do it if it weren't illegal. I laughed and nodded. "Yeah, let's go."

Back at home, Remi joined me in the shower, where I got on my knees and blew him until he was holding himself up against the shower wall with one hand and gripping my hair with the other.

"I want to come inside you, so let's stop." He gasped, pulling me off of him. I stared up at him, the water spraying down into my face.

"Oh fuck. Okay, finish me. I'll just get hard again," he acquiesced. If I hadn't been so eager to make him come, I would have cracked up. It only took a few more twists of my hand and suckles of my mouth for him to explode down my throat. I stood up on shaky legs, and he picked me up to take me out of the shower.

"I want you to sit on my face," Remi told me as we dried off.

"I don't know..." I felt weird about it. I wasn't heavy by any means, but what did sit actually mean? Hover? Or literally use his face like a chair?

"Come on, baby, you're gonna love it," Remi urged. He laid down on the bed and urged me to get on top of him.

"What do you mean by sit?" I asked nervously.

"Smother me with your pussy. If I need air, I'll tap out." Remi looked so serious, but when I began to laugh, he joined me. I loved how even our intimacy was full of laughter and coupled with feeling the lighter side of life. I widened my thighs around his face and lowered myself till I felt his breath on me. I grabbed onto the headboard and braced myself. Sure enough, with the first lick, I had to hold on for dear life because, in this position, he had access to my body in a way that was going to weaken me completely. Remi immediately put his tongue inside of me and started lapping at my juices.

"Ooooooh, Jesus," I moaned.

"You don't even believe in him," I heard Remi mumble against my skin.

"I-I know, it just felt like an appropriate thing to say while you eat me out," I panted. I felt Remi's chest shake under me with laughter. His hands reached up, and he grabbed two handfuls of my ass. His fingers were really close to my butt hole, and I wasn't sure how I felt about that; however, all cognitive thought left my brain as Remi went to town. He licked, sucked, nibbled, and completely wrecked me as he did it. His fingers dug into my flesh, and I could hear him moaning in between licks. The fact that he loved doing this as much as I liked receiving it made it so much hotter for me. I was grinding my pussy against his mouth, and I knew his face must be soaked. I wondered how he was breathing with my body so fully seated on his face. I could feel my orgasm barreling toward me, and with the next suck, my legs tightened on either side of him, and I came so hard I had to throw my head back and yell his name. I collapsed backward and saw Remi's face sit up from between my legs. Sure enough, his whole chin was wet from me. He used the towel from our shower to clean up his mouth.

"Fuck, baby. That was so hot." He sounded gleeful.

"Proud of yourself?" I asked weakly.

"Oh definitely." He repositioned us so I was under him, and he was in between my legs. I watched him take a condom from the pillow next to me and roll it on.

"You're getting good at that," I told him. He winked at me, and with his hand, he guided his cock between my legs. I braced myself for the pain again, but this time as he slid in, it just felt like a throbbing bruise rather than a pain I couldn't ignore.

"Okay?" Remi peered down at me, holding himself still. I nodded. He began to move, and I was happy to see that it didn't hurt as bad as last night. It wasn't quite pleasurable just yet, but it definitely was better. The best part again was watching Remi completely lose his shit in me. He was going faster and deeper than last night and was breathing so hard as he talked to me.

"Fuck, Shaen, you feel so good around me. Look at you taking me. God that's so hot. You're so tight."

Suddenly his hand went in between us, and I felt his fingers flick my clit.

"Oooh." A delicious feeling went through me. Remi watched my face as he moved his fingers over me again. That felt really good. As he strummed my clit, he began to fuck me in earnest, so hard that the headboard was shaking.

"Still okay, pixie?" he asked with teeth clenched as he looked down to watch where he slid in and out of me. I nodded. My whole body was focused on the amazing things that were occur-ring between my legs. Remi's ministrations to my clit were allowing my body to relax, and without feeling so tense, I was able to focus on the feeling of his cock hitting my G-spot. It was so good that it almost hurt, but it was different from that of last night. It was an intense feeling. Almost like how perfect it felt to itch a mosquito bite that you couldn't quite reach all day, and then the relief you got from finding the right spot was the best and weirdest way I could think to describe how it felt to chase this orgasm that was about to hit me. It felt different than my usual orgasms. This one felt less sudden, and the start to it was more drawn out. I knew it was going to come, and I knew when it crashed, it would take me under.

"You're such a good girl letting me fuck you like this," Remi growled. "You are doing such a good job."

Oh fuck, lights pricked the edges of my eyesight, and I had to shut my eyes as the orgasm decimated me. It felt like it just went on and on till I had to remind myself to breathe.

"Oh-oh." I opened my eyes in wonderment at the new pleasure I had just discovered, only to watch Remi's face contort with the intensity of his own release. His hips stuttered above me, and then I felt him unload inside of me, only stopped by the condom. When he was done, he gripped the top of the condom, pulled out, and rolled over onto his back. His chest was sweaty and was heaving as he breathed quickly.

"Wow." He looked over at me, and we both burst out laughing.

"Yeah, wow," I agreed.

～

THE NEXT MORNING, I woke up to an empty bed and a quiet house. A note from Remi sat on the night table.

"You looked so peaceful, pixie. So I didn't want to wake you. Went to the gym. Be back soon. Xoxo, Remi."

I smiled and then picked up my phone. The group chat had been active.

RACHEL

going to starbies with Dee and Ashley anyone want anything?

LIA

1 venti iced coffee. 3 pumps vanilla, 2 pumps hazelnut, drizzled caramel and cold foam.
Thank u bestie!!

EVA

I'll have a shaken espresso with oat milk, cinnamon and 1 pump of white mocha

LIAM

we're good. Thanks rach

REMI

speak for yourself

RACHEL

what do you want?

REMI

can you get Shaen an iced vanilla chai tea latte with sweet cream foam?

RACHEL

yup. Also you win best bf award

LIA

I need tampons anyone have?

DEE

Ashley has in her pink bag. It's in the bathroom.

CARTER

Aw poor Liam won't be getting any

LIAM

u think aunt flow stops me? Booooy

CARTER

blood droplet emoji *eggplant emoji*

LIA

it helps with the cramps

CARTER

tmi

LIAM

u literally started this conversation lmao

REMI

can y'all work out? I'm almost done and I'm gonna have to wait for you idiots

EVA

I have a masseuse coming later. Who wants one?

CARTER

raised hand emoji

LIAM

raised hand emoji

RACHEL

Jake does but I'm good

DEE

Ashley will

EVA

k. @remi do you think Shaen will?

LIAM

lol no way she hates being touched

REMI

she likes when I touch her

LIAM

I know we heard

REMI

middle finger emoji

I laughed and then sat up when I saw that my drink was sitting on the night table, right next to the empty condom wrapper. Whoops. I couldn't even muster up the energy to feel embarrassed because it just felt so good to have taken this next step with Remi. I took a sip of the tea.

"So good," I said out loud to the empty room. Then I got up to pee, brushed my teeth, washed my face, and put on a bathing suit. I stopped to admire the tan I had gotten yesterday. I always felt so much better when I was tan. Grabbing my drink, a dirty book, and my phone, I went out to the pool. Eva and Lia were lying out by the pool and called out a good morning when they saw me.

"I want to have a lazy day today," I told them. "Like Uber Eats food, then we do nothing for the rest of the day and maybe end off with a movie?"

"That sounds perfect," Eva agreed.

"Liam wants me to come with him to visit a friend of his later, but other than that, we have no plans," Lia told us.

"I think Dee and Ashley are renting a boat this afternoon," Eva remembered. Rachel and Jake walked out to the pool, and we told them about having a lazy day. They liked the sound of it too. Lia attached her playlist to the speakers, and we sat in the sun like that for an hour until the boys got back.

Remi made us avocado toast for lunch. We were alone and eating it by the pool as Dee and Ashley had gone off on the boat, and Lia and Liam had gone to visit a childhood friend of his that he had made from his summers spent here. Liam and Ashley had already gotten their massages before they left, so Eva, Carter, and Jake were inside with the masseuse. Rachel was in her room on the phone. I was sitting in Remi's lap, licking avocado off of my fingers, when he leaned closer to me and said, "I didn't know I could feel happy like this."

I turned to look at him. "What do you mean?" I asked.

"You know how I grew up," Remi started. I nodded.

"Yeah."

"Well, it was a lot of pressure on me once I found out what my dad had done to my mom, that he had abandoned his child, and just that everything I thought was true was possibly a lie. I felt like not only would I need to figure out what I did want for my life and what did actually matter to me, but it also felt like everything would be shadowed by my parents feeling like they had failed me somehow. I mean, what fucked up trauma is that?" Remi laughed at the irony of what he was saying. "For example, if Liam decided he didn't want to be a doctor anymore but instead he wants to do something else, Sam and Julia wouldn't be disappointed and think they failed him, right?" He looked over at me.

"They would support him in whatever he chose," I agreed.

"Exactly. But here, with this, my parents are wondering where they failed me. They're praying for me to come back because they think if I don't, I'll burn in hell. This is not about them not supporting me, that's way too simple. This is them believing intrinsically that I am a reflection of a failure of theirs because I am not living the life they chose for me."

I patted Remi's arm as he took a deep breath.

"Yeah, it's fucked up." I nodded.

"For a while, it felt like I would get stuck either going back to their life to make my parents happy, or I would forever live not fully happy because I would be... missing something... maybe. I can't really explain it. But then I found you, and I know this sounds so corny." Remi's eyes seemed to beg me to take him seriously.

"But you're legit the best thing that ever happened to me. I feel like I'm able to realize who I really am because I don't have to pretend to be the pastor's kid, or the football player, or anything else in front of you. I can just be me... and that makes me happy." His fingers were now playing with my hair nervously. I turned around to be able to fully to look at him.

"You're mine for keeps." I smiled.

"Same." He bent forward and kissed my lips gently. I felt that kiss for the rest of the day.

ON SUNDAY, we woke up early because we had to pack up and clean the house before we left after dinner. Rachel had baked fresh blueberry muffins for breakfast, so we were all gathered around the table, stuffing our faces with muffins and talking about the timeline of when we would all be together again. Liam wanted Remi and I to fly to Boston to visit him around Halloween, but I didn't know if I would be able to afford to take off work and buy plane tickets. The good news was that everyone would be coming back home for Christmas and New Year's, but after that, we probably wouldn't see each other until spring break and then, of course, next summer. Lia was wiping away tears as she finished her muffin.

"I don't like this," she cried.

"Yeah, it fucking sucks," Carter agreed. I was again feeling very grateful that Remi had decided to stay home. The school he was attending was literally a half hour from his house. Remi looked over at me and squeezed my hand. He knew I was going to miss my friends, particularly Liam.

"Soooo," Dee said, changing the subject. "This may seem weird, and there is zero pressure to do it, but as you know, I'm adopted, so my dads got me a kit to do that anonymous DNA test thing to see if I have any siblings, and they accidentally got two, so I wanted to give it to you, Shaen. In case you ever want to see if you can find your dad." She seemed uncomfortable as she took the envelope out of her bag. "But again, no pressure at all. It's all anonymous, so even if you do it, he wouldn't know who you are unless you choose that option. Basically, everyone is given a number, and if he happens to be on the website, he would get an email that a number matched with his DNA, and he can choose to view it or not, but he can only view it if you agree for him to see it," Dee rambled. The whole room had gone silent. I took the envelope that Dee held out to me and held it against my chest.

"That's really nice, Dee, thank you," I told her quietly.

"Can I hug you?" she asked. I nodded. She leaned in and gave me a quick hug and then let go.

"Do you want to do it, hun?" Liam moved next to me immediately. He knew how not having a dad my whole life had really messed with me. I hadn't ever really wanted to talk about it, but he had picked up on plenty over the many years of our friendship.

"I'm not sure yet. But it says here that it doesn't expire till next summer, so I have time," I told him. He gave me a quick hug too.

"Okay, it's not allowed to be awkward." I laughed. "I don't have a dad, and Dee has two, kind of selfish if you ask me... but anyway, what are we doing today?"

That had everyone laughing.

"I LOVE YOU. Call me when you get home," Lia called out the window of Liam's jeep as Remi reversed his car out of the driveway. I waved until we couldn't see them anymore. We spent the day on the beach snorkeling and riding four-wheelers. Then we had dinner at a local Thai place, after which we said goodbye to each other. I knew that we would still be hanging out for the rest of the summer, but I was feeling very nostalgic knowing that this was really the last big trip we'd be doing as a friend group before everyone left for college. As if he could feel how heavy my thoughts were, Remi put a hand on my knee as he drove.

"That's the same company I did my DNA test with," he told me, referring to Dee's surprising gift from earlier.

"Oh yeah? Still no matches?"

He shook his head.

"I've given up at this point. I'm okay not knowing. I have you and Liam's family. That's good enough for me."

I smiled up at him. "Me too."

The next thing I knew, I was being carried from the car into my apartment.

"We're home, baby," Remi whispered. I woke up groggily.

"What time is it?" I asked.

"Nine." He sat me on my bed and then put our bags down.

"I'm gonna shower and then sleep 'cause I have to go to work early to film content for Julia tomorrow," I told him. He nodded, standing awkwardly in the doorway of my room.

"What's wrong?" I asked as I peeled my clothes off and put them in the laundry.

"Where do you want me?" he asked awkwardly. "Here... or do you want a night alone? I can go if you do..."

"I never want a night alone." I went over to where he stood and wrapped my arms around his waist. "I know we haven't talked about it again, but I want to live together eventually." I kissed his chest and peered up at him; this lack of confidence was not usual for him.

"You okay?"

"Yes." He smiled at me, seemingly back to his normal self. "Let's go clean you up." He swatted my ass as he walked behind me to the bathroom.

After we showered, I popped us some fresh popcorn and drizzled melted chocolate on it.

"I would have never thought to do this, but holy shit, it's good." Remi was inhaling the popcorn.

"Right. It's the perfect mix of sweet and salty." I took another handful and pressed play on the next episode of *Yellowstone*. So much for going to sleep right away. After we finished the episode, I cleaned the now-empty bowl and brushed my teeth. Remi was lying in bed doing something on his phone when I crawled into bed next to him. Then my phone lit up with a notification. It was from my social media app, and it said that @rem22 had tagged me in a post. I swiped up to open the app and saw that he had posted a photo of us.

"Liam sent it to me," he said softly. I blinked. Liam must have taken it the morning after we had sex for the first time. I was in my black bikini, sitting in between Remi's legs, leaning up against his chest. Remi's body is angled toward me, his head leaning down, and my face is looking up at his. He is smiling at what I'm saying, and the sun is shining down on us. I can see the water behind us and how the wind is blowing through my hair. What stops me in my tracks is how obvious his love is for me. It's all over his face. In the way he is looking at me. At how his body is around me, protecting me. Our energy is palpable from the photo, and it takes my breath away for a second.

"Oh." I am suddenly at a loss for words.

"Is it okay that I posted it?" Remi asks. I can tell that he is misunderstanding my silence. I take a look at the comments that are suddenly rolling in.

JULIA_INJECTOR_RN: oh my god my favorite couple. I love you both

LIAM_HEN: photography credit

LIA.B: you guys are so sexy *swoon*

CARTER.9: *eggplant emoji* *water droplet emoji* *hot panting face emoji*

RACHEL_BAKES_12: I miss you guys already

DEE*rainbow emoji*: invite me to your wedding

EVALUVSCARTER: oh my gawwwwd

I shared the photo to my stories and typed on it, "I fucking love this man," and I added some heart stickers before pressing "Share." Then I saved the photo to my phone and made it my wallpaper.

"Okay, so you like it?" Remi laughed, sounding relieved.

"I love it," I corrected, pushing him back on the pillow, and I climbed on top of him.

"Okay, good." His words cut off as I kissed him with everything I had. Quickly, we discarded our clothes, and I got up to get a condom from his bag and lock my door. I came back to the bed and handed him the condom. He made quick work of putting it on, and I climbed back on top of him. Remi looked up at me.

"You'll be okay like this?" he asked, worrying about me as usual. I nodded.

"Okay, good because, fuck, you look good on top of me." He guided his cock between my legs and took my mouth in his as he thrust up into me. He felt different from this angle. It was slightly deeper, but it also hit a new place inside me. Remi sat up slightly, taking me with him so that I was sitting in his lap and his back was against my headboard. This way, he was able to guide me in my movements above him. He was holding onto my hips, and as I lifted up, he helped me, and as I shifted back down, he thrust up. We got into a rhythm of movements until his breath was coming out in short grunts, and I was sweating around my hairline.

"You close?" he asked me. Although it didn't hurt anymore, I still felt very stretched and tender, so I wasn't sure if I was going to be able to get there without help, and I told him so. Remi reached over to my night table and pulled open the drawer. He grabbed my vibrator and turned it on. As soon as he put it on me, my eyes rolled back, and I shuddered.

"Come on me, Shaen," he ordered. His mouth had found my nipple, and he was working it between his lips. Then he let go and began thrusting into me as he kept the vibrator on my clit. His movements kept knocking into my toy, but I could feel myself getting there, and I began to moan louder. Suddenly, Remi moved his hand.

"Wh-what are you doing?" I demanded. The wave of the orgasm that was about to hit me moved away, and I lost it.

"Beg me." Remi's other arm was across my back now, holding me down on him as he rutted his way up into me.

"Beg?"

"Beg me to let you come." His eyes shone with a glint of an emotion that I couldn't decipher.

"Babe... no." I couldn't possibly. The vibrator turned back on, and I sighed with relief when he put it back on my clit. I rocked against his cock and my toy as I chased my pleasure. Just as I was about to come, Remi moved the vibrator off of me again.

"Fuck." I was feeling frustrated now. "Why!?" I slapped his chest.

"Beg. Me.," he enunciated, sounding breathless.

"Please," I heard myself say.

"Please, what, pixie?" He was not playing around, and I half hated it, half loved it.

"Please let me... come," I whispered.

"I can't hear you."

"Oh my God, let me come, Remiel, make me come!" I sobbed. The vibrator was on me in a second, and this time, he didn't stop as the orgasm hit me. In fact, he fucked me harder through it, and we came together.

"Oh my Goddddd," I groaned, "I love you so much!"

"I love you too, Shaen," he panted. "Fuckkkkk, I'm coming."

He pulled out when he was done and then looked at me seriously.

"When are you ovulating next?"

"I didn't even get my period yet," I laughed. "I'm not due till July twenty-secondish."

"So we're safe right now?" he confirmed. I nodded.

"Okay, can you download the app you use so I can track it with you?" he asked as he got up to dispose of the condom.

"Okay. What's your password?" I called.

"615526," he called back. I put in the password, and his phone opened up to the favorites screen in his contacts. I saw that I was on his favorites list, and he had me saved as Pixie *sparkle emoji* *heart emoji*. That gesture made my heart skip a beat. I swiped out to look for the App Store, and as I did, I saw that the photo of us was the background of his phone too. Just kill me, I thought, he was so sweet.

"6/15 is the day we met, and 5/26 is the day I got to kiss you for the first time," Remi explained, coming back into the room. He was stark naked, and he laughed when he caught me staring.

"Like what you see, pixie?" he asked, his voice sounding throaty.

"I really do." I smirked as he got into bed next to me. I proceeded to show him the app and where I input May and June's periods so July would pre-populate.

"I've been taking my temperature every morning, and I track that too because I'm not going to just trust an app," I explained.

"Text me your temps, and I'll input them into my app too," Remi told me, fully serious. I leaned over and kissed his cheek.

"I don't know how I got so lucky with you, baby," I told him, lying on his chest.

"I'm the lucky one," I heard him say as I drifted off to sleep.

20

The next month passed in a blur of sex with Remi, getting together with our friends as often as possible, working at the rescue, creating content for Julia, watching *Yellowstone* with Remi, and reading dirty books where sometimes the scenes made me so horny I had to stop and jump Remi. We also spent time discovering new music, cooking our favorite foods together, and playing house, as Remi liked to call it. There were many late nights laughing under the covers. I had even brought Remi to a thrift store for the first time and in turn, I joined him at the gym once, but I hated it. I had also gotten manicures with the girls, FaceTimed with Lia on her family trip to Europe, consoled Dee through her breakup with Ashley, helped Eva shop for school, and in general very much enjoyed our last summer together. It was now the last week of August, and everyone was leaving tomorrow, including Remi, who was flying to LA to spend the week with Dermont. I had been dreading this day for weeks now. Instead of allowing myself to sit with my feelings for too long, I focused on writing letters to my friends and choosing a little gift for each of them. We had done our last barbecue together to officially say goodbye at

Dee's house last night, and tonight I was going over to Liam's house where Julia had invited me for the last family dinner before Liam went to follow in Sam's footsteps and attend Harvard Medical School. As much as Liam liked to fuck around, he was actually really smart, although you would never catch me telling him that and inflating his already very healthy ego.

I parked next to Remi's car in the driveway and grabbed my overnight bag. I was sleeping by Remi tonight as he and Liam both had early flights tomorrow morning, so Sam and Julia would be driving both of them to the airport. I knocked on the front door and then walked in.

"Ah, my favorite girl." Julia came out of the kitchen and kissed my cheek. "How are you holding up?" she asked me as I made my way to the basement door to put my bag in Remi's room. I felt a familiar lump rise up in my throat, and I swallowed it back down.

"I'm okay." I smiled brightly. I had been doing such a good job of learning to feel my feelings. I hadn't been reverting back to what Liam called my ice queen persona as often. I had been feeling safer navigating my feelings and sometimes even verbalizing them. In turn, it allowed me to feel happiness on a deeper level than I had before. But now, that sadness, loneliness, and fear were creeping in, I was feeling like I needed to fake it again. Because otherwise, I would feel suffocated by these hard feelings. Feelings I didn't want to be experiencing altogether.

"I'm a mess," Julia told me. I stopped to hug her.

"I know. Me too," I admitted. She pulled away, and I saw the tears in her eyes. "I'm selfishly so happy that you and Remiel will be here this year."

"Same. I just have to get through this next week."

"Oh, to be young and in love." She smiled and then rushed back to the kitchen as the oven timer started to beep. "Dinner will be ready in twenty," she called.

"I'll be right back," I told her and then made my way downstairs. Remi's door was closed, and I rapped on it gently, but there was no answer. When I opened it, I heard the shower going.

"Babe?" I called. He didn't respond. My anxiety got the best of me, and my mind worried that something had happened to him, so I tried the door to the bathroom, and the handle turned. I opened the door a crack and felt relieved when I saw that Remi was alive and well and was just showering. I was about to shut the door when I heard him moan. He hadn't seen me as he was facing the water, his left hand was on the wall of the shower, and his right hand, oh, his right hand was moving quickly on his cock. The realization of what I was seeing ran through my body, and while I felt guilty spying on such a private moment of his, I also felt a clench between my legs as I realized how turned on I was by it. I peered back around the door and watched with bated breath. Remi's hand was moving quickly, root to tip, and occasionally, he would pause to gently rub over the head. His grip was so tight, I wondered how it didn't hurt. His movements were growing sloppier, his moans louder, and suddenly, his body stiffened, and he bent over as he came. I quickly moved back as he stood up, and I gently shut the door.

"Fuck," I whispered to myself. That had been so hot, and now I had to sit at a dinner table with Liam and the rest of the family with my soaked underwear and my fluttering pulse. I sat myself down on Remi's bed and looked at my phone, trying to pretend like I had been sitting here the whole time. As I heard the shower turn off, I opened my social media app and went to post a new photo that I had taken of us. I had snapped it last night in portrait mode, so the whole background was blurred, and we were just a silhouette, but you could clearly see that Remi was kissing me and that my arms were up around his neck. I posted it with the caption: "With you I am safe enough to be me," and I tagged @rem22. Suddenly, the bathroom door opened, and Remi came out, a puff of steam following him, and a white towel wrapped around his hips.

"Hi, baby!" I smiled as he came over for a kiss. "Are you packed?"

"Pretty much. I just need to put in my toothbrush and stuff like that." He pulled a T-shirt and a pair of jeans on and then ran a brush through his wet hair.

"Ready?" He held his hand out for me to take and helped me get up from his bed.

"Yup, I'm starving." I held onto his hand and followed him out of the room.

"You owe me a show," he said quietly as we walked to the stairs.

"Huh?" My heart sped up. Had he seen me?

"It's only fair." He winked at me. "You saw mine, so now you need to show me yours."

"Oh my God" He had seen me! I hit his arm as he cracked up. "It was an accident!" I protested.

"Well, pixie, I can guarantee that tonight when I watch you make yourself come, it will one hundred percent be on purpose." He bent to kiss my lips quickly, and then we joined the family for dinner.

"Julia, you outdid yourself." Sam leaned over to kiss his wife as he took a look at the massive spread of food she had made.

"She outdoes herself every time." Leo, one of Liam's older brothers, laughed as he poured himself something to drink.

"This is true," Sam agreed. We all ate as we chatted and laughed, but as we finished the meal, I could feel my mood shifting as I acknowledged the feeling of impending doom that was hanging over me. All of my friends were leaving me. My boyfriend was leaving me. My best friend was leaving me. I could feel a panic attack crawling its way up my throat.

"E-excuse me." I stood up quickly as breathing became difficult. My fork clattered down onto my plate, and I rushed out of the room. I found myself sitting on the floor of Remi's room, knees pulled to my chest, my body curled around myself as I rocked to self-soothe.

"Breathe, Shaen." I could hear Liam's voice through the buzzing in my ears. I was pulled into his arms, and when I opened my eyes, my vision was hazy, but I could see Liam's concerned face in front of mine.

"Deep breath in, babe," he instructed.

I tried.

"Okay, and out."

I tried again. Suddenly, I burst out crying. It felt like it was coming from that place again. That scary, empty space inside of me. I was cradled in Liam's lap, sobbing as he murmured that it was okay, and he was here. I heard Remi come into the room. He had been in the bathroom when I had left the table and hadn't seen me freak out.

"What the fuck... Shaen?"

I felt him crouch next to me, and Liam handed me off to him, but he didn't let go of my hand.

"She has panic attacks," I heard Liam say.

"I know." Remi's voice was soft. "Shaen... honey."

I was numb now. I was no longer panicking; I wasn't crying either, I was somewhere in nothingness where none of my sad feelings could touch me. I didn't answer. I felt Remi turn to Liam.

"Can you get her an ice pack?"

"Yeah, I'll be right back."

And he was. I felt Remi pull the collar of my sweatshirt down a little, and Liam placed the ice pack on my chest. I wanted to stay in the nothingness, but I knew I had to come back. I felt the cold ice, and I focused on that. I could feel that. What did I smell? Remi's cologne and spice. I breathed it in. I squeezed the muscles in my legs in and out. Then I wriggled my toes. I felt my nervous system calm down until the ice on my chest grew painful. I sat up and took the ice pack off.

"I'm sorry." I was so embarrassed. I thought I had made so much progress with this, and yet here we were. Again.

"Don't be sorry." Liam was crouched right beside me. "You did nothing wrong."

"I'm supposed to be strong," I said, hiccupping from all the crying I had done earlier.

"You are strong," Remi told me, stroking my cheek.

"I've always taken care of myself." I looked up at him, my lashes wet with unshed tears.

"I know, baby," Remi said softly.

"And you will continue to do that." Liam was still holding my hand, and he squeezed it. "But you also have us to take care of you too. Okay?"

"Okay," I acquiesced.

Liam turned around while Remi helped me get into pajamas, and then they both tucked me into bed.

"I'm going to go get her a plate of dessert and a hot tea," Remi told Liam.

"I'll wait here with her." Liam climbed into the bed and lay next to me. I curled up into him.

"Do you remember the day we met?" Liam asked me softly, his fingers running circles on my back.

"You were eating glue." I giggled.

"You're still sticking to that lie?" Liam sounded horrified. "I was not eating glue. But I did sit down next to you at circle time and told you that my name was Liam, and you told me that your name was Shaen, like Shane, not Shay-en, and I never left your side ever again. And I never will," he told me gently.

I sniffed. "But you are." I hated sounding so pathetic, but I hadn't prepared to be this broken up over my best friend moving a few hours away.

"I'm not. I'm going to text you so much you'll end up blocking me," Liam said emphatically.

I laughed at that and wiped away a tear.

"I'll be back soon, Shaen. Plus, we will talk every day. I promise." He bent to kiss my temple. "And I'm leaving you with the next best option." Liam gestured to Remi, who was walking back into the room holding a plate and a mug.

"Next best my ass," Remi snorted. Liam got off the bed and winked at me. I laughed again. He bent down and hugged me.

"I'll come say goodbye in the morning. Okay?" he said softly. I nodded, not trusting myself to talk again.

"Love you, Shay Shay."

"Love you too."

He left the room. Remi brought me a fork and a hot cinnamon roll. My system was shaky and depleted after my panic attack, and sugar sounded like the perfect solution, so I ate the whole thing and washed it down with the tea.

"Don't judge me, but I'm too weak to go brush my teeth," I murmured, my face in the pillow.

"You're perfect even with dirty teeth.," I heard Remi say as he turned the light off and rubbed my back until I fell asleep. Later, I woke up to Remi's arm slung across me, and my bladder was begging me to go pee. I had to extricate myself from my boyfriend's sleeping embrace, and when I finally got out, I went to use the bathroom. While I was there, I washed my face and brushed my teeth. The clock on the night table read 2:30 a.m. Remi would be getting up in four hours to leave. My heart clenched at the idea of it, and I crawled back to lie next to him. His body stirred, and he whispered, "Baby?"

"I'm here."

"You okay?"

"Yeah..."

Remi's hands reached for me and pulled me closer. I immediately felt his erection against my stomach. His mouth found mine, and I poured all of my crazy emotions into this moment. I was absolutely ravenous for him, my underwear was soaked, and my breaths were gasping against his mouth.

"Do you want to come?" I heard Remi whisper in my ear. I nodded frantically. I knew that the best way, not the healthiest way emotionally, but the fastest way physically, to push away all of these lonely, abandoned feelings down was to flush my system with oxytocin and dopamine.

"Okay." Remi pulled away, moved the blanket off my legs, and motioned to me.

"Make yourself come."

Was he really sticking to what he had said before dinner? That felt like a lifetime ago. I didn't want my fingers. I wanted his mouth and then his cock. I could tell from looking at him, though, that there was no point in arguing. My bossy, horny Remi was here, and if I was going to come at all, I knew it had to be of my own volition.

"It's going to make me so hard, baby," he told me huskily. "Pull your underwear down."

I did and waited for further instruction. I was by no means a submissive person, but I found that sometimes letting all of my anxiety go, not having to wonder what was next, and allowing him to take the driver's seat was such a relief to my brain.

"Run your hand down to feel how wet you are," was my next instruction.

I did.

"How wet are you?"

Remi's voice was making me wetter.

"I'm soaked," I told him and was rewarded with a groan.

"Did you get wet when you watched me jerk off earlier?" he

asked. I flushed. "Yes."

"Good girl."

I was rewarded again.

"Take your fingers and run them through your wetness and then move them up to your clit," he ordered. I did that too, and I could hear how wet I was as I moved my fingers around.

"Do you hear that?" Remi asked. Of course he would point it out. I flushed again and turned my head away.

"Look at me." His tone was stern. I looked back at him.

"That's for me. You made that for me. So I can slide inside you. Right, Shaen?"

I nodded exuberantly.

"Your body wants me to fill you. But you're so tight, so you need to be so wet to take me."

"Y-yes."

"You're doing such a good job."

That reward again; my body blossomed from the praise.

"Rub your clit. Show me what you do when I'm not there, and you want to come." Remi's voice was now right by my ear, but he wouldn't touch me. I ached for him.

"I know you do," he responded to me.

Shit, I kept saying things out loud that were supposed to remain thoughts. I had to stop doing that! I moved my fingers up and began to spread my wetness all over my swollen clit. I watched Remi's eyes following my movements, and I could see on his face how much he liked it. At first, I was rubbing hesitantly, but as I could feel myself growing wetter and more desperate, I really began to masturbate in earnest. Remi made an appreciative sound that spurred me on. I was so close, and my hips were almost thrusting off the bed.

"Yes, like that. You're doing so good." Remi's voice set me off.

"Oh, oh. Remi," I called breathlessly as I came.

"I'm right here."

I turned, and his mouth descended on mine as I came down from my orgasm. My body was buzzing in the aftermath, and I needed more.

"Please," I whispered against his mouth. He lifted his head to look at me.

"Do you need me to fuck you?" he asked. I could see the head of his cock slipping through the slit of his underwear.

"Y-yes." I kissed him again. He rolled over to grab a condom. When he came back, he turned me over.

"Be a good girl and take me like this," he murmured. We had never done it in this position before. I was breathless as he held me in place, and I waited on my hands and knees. I felt him line himself up behind me and guide his dick into my soaking wet channel.

"Oh J-Jesus," he stuttered as he bottomed out inside of me. Remi felt huge this way. He pulled out and slammed back in. I could feel the embers of my orgasm sizzling and coming back to life. I was losing my mind as he fucked me. Suddenly, he lifted me up, so I was still on my knees, but now my back was up against his chest. I could feel how sweaty and out of breath he was. Things felt much tighter now. Remi had one hand pressing down against my pelvis, and as he rutted inside of me, his hand kept pressing down, and it made things even tighter and more intense. His other hand came up to squeeze a little on each side of my neck. I could still breathe, but the little bit of pressure on my arteries was causing me to really focus on taking deep breaths. It was making me be fully aware and in the moment. All I could think, feel, breathe, see, and exist was Remi's thick cock penetrating me over and over. The sound of his grunting and him telling me I was doing so good, I was taking him so well, I tasted so good, I was his good girl, set me off into an orgasm like I had never experienced before. I found myself crying as I came down, his hands loosening off of my neck as he poured himself into the condom inside of me. We both lay there after, completely speechless at the cosmic explosion we had just experienced together.

"Baby, should I cancel the trip?" I heard Remi ask softly.

"No! I swear I'll be fine," I insisted.

"You sure?"

"Yes." I wanted to say no, stay with me, never leave me, I love you! But I was a big girl, and I could live without him. It was only a week.

I woke up again to the rustling sounds of Remi packing up the last of his things and zipping his suitcase closed. As I sat up, trying to tame my hair down with my hands, Remi came over to me with my pajama shirt.

"Here put this on. Liam wants to come in and say goodbye."

I lifted up my arms and let Remi pull the shirt over my head, and I smoothed it down my body. Then I felt around for my shorts, and I pulled those on too. I took a quick bathroom break to brush my teeth again, and I heard Liam come into the room. He and Remi were talking in hushed tones when I came out of the bathroom, shutting the light off behind me.

"There you are." Liam forced a grin, but I could see the worry behind it.

"What's wrong?" I asked, looking from him to Remi and back to my best friend. Liam came over and picked me up in a big hug before putting me back down and tilting my chin up to look at him.

"We're just a little concerned that maybe it's too much for all of us to leave on the same day," Liam admitted.

"Last night was a fluke. I swear I'm fine." I smiled as big as I could muster. "Remi will be back in seven days, and I've decided I will take off work for Halloween. I'll take the train because it's cheaper than flying, and I looked it up, the train ride from here to Boston is super cool. So I'll see you in exactly sixty-six days."

"I can pay for a flight, Shaen..."

Liam knew I hated when he offered, and never in our entire friendship did I ever let him pay for more than a coffee or a game of bowling.

"The train is cool. I want to do it," I interrupted. Liam held his hands up.

"Well, it sounds like you have it all figured out." He opened his phone and scrolled on his calendar to October thirty-first, and he put a big notification on it that simply said, "Shaen *pumpkin emoji*." Then he made a new group chat with just Remi, him, and I.

"If you need us, promise you'll text. I don't want you to..." His voice trailed off when I hugged him.

"I promise. I will be okay. I'm so excited for you. You're going to have the best time! And you're finally becoming a doctor." I infused as much happiness into my voice as I could muster. Liam kept his arms around me for a solid few minutes and then leaned down and kissed the top of my head.

"I'm going to miss you." His voice sounded raspy now, and I just gave him one more tight hug in response. I had chosen not to go to the airport for this exact reason. I didn't want to have all of these heightened emotions in front of a bunch of strangers and then have to keep them in check for the entire hour ride back with Julia and Sam. I preferred to do it here. In Remi's dark room, which smelled like him, and I could hide in until I was ready to come out.

"Love ya. Talk to you soon." Liam said one last goodbye and then left the room, gently closing the door behind him.

"Well, one down, one to go," I said brightly, that fake smile back on my face. Remi just gathered me in his arms, I wrapped my legs around his waist, and I cried into his shirt.

"You've broken me," I whispered. "I used to be able to keep it together before you came along."

Remi's hand smoothed over my hair.

"No baby, I'm putting you back together," he murmured in my ear. "Just like you are for me." Remi rocked me until I stopped crying and then put me down so he could wipe the tears from my eyes with his thumb.

"I will be right back, sweetheart. Okay? Maybe sleep here until I'm back?" he offered. I shook my head.

"I have work, and all of my stuff is at home." I couldn't possibly stay here with reminders of him and Liam everywhere I looked. No, I would tough it out in my bedroom just like I had for the last almost nineteen years of my life.

"Okay. Well, text me, and I'll FaceTime you every night. I love you, pixie." Remi bent down to kiss me. I let myself drown in it for a minute, and then I pulled myself together.

"Go. You don't want to be late. I love you." Then I watched him take his suitcase and leave the room, shutting the door behind him. I felt all of the strength I had been holding on to completely leave my body, and I promptly crawled back into bed, my hand clutching Remi's T-shirt that smelled like him, and I fell back to sleep. Alone again.

I woke up with a start, feeling drool drying on the side of my mouth. Ew. I wiped it away and looked at my phone. Holy shit, it was already 1 p.m.! It was Wednesday, and I had no work, but I still felt so out of sorts, having completely missed half the day. My phone was full of missed calls and text messages. Three missed calls from Remi, two from Liam, and one from an unknown number. I toggled over to my text app.

I opened the chat I had with Liam and Remi.

> LIAM
>
> boarding now. All good?

A half-hour later:

An hour later:

Another hour later:

I felt so bad having slept through all of this, and yet a part of me just wanted to roll over and block it all out again. Instead, I quickly texted back:

I didn't want them to know I had just woken up and was acting like a pathetic mess since they left. I rolled out of bed, took my pajama shirt off, and stuffed it into my bag. Then I pulled Remi's shirt on. It engulfed me, and I pretended it was him hugging me. I snuck out through the side door so no one in

Liam's family would catch me doing what felt like a walk of shame, with me getting out of bed in the middle of the afternoon. I drove home in a daze, stopping at a local juice place, and bought myself a coconut açaí bowl. The apartment was empty and quiet when I got home. Of course it was. I ate the açaí bowl in my bed, then shut all the shades in my room and went back to sleep.

The sound of my phone buzzing woke me up yet again. It was now 3 p.m., and Remi was calling.

"Hey." I cleared my throat before answering in order to make it sound like I was fine and not sleeping the entire day away.

"Baby?" I could hear music in the background, and then I heard Dermont shout, "Hi."

"Hi! How was the flight?" I infused a chill, happy tone into my voice.

"It was good. I slept for most of it," Remi told me. So did I, I thought. "Dermont picked me up in his Maserati, Shaen. This car is sick! I'm gonna send you pictures."

I could hear how excited he was, and it made me genuinely smile.

"So he's like rich, rich, huh?" I asked, sitting up and turning the light on in my room. I heard Dermont laugh at that.

"Pretty much." Remi was grinning, I could hear it. "What are you up to?"

"Oh, nothing really. Just got some errands done, and I'm thinking of going thrifting for some more work-appropriate clothes because Julia wants me to start modeling for some of her skin care and facials in the spa." Julia had asked me to do that, that was true, but I was lying about going anywhere today, and I felt bad doing it.

"Hell, yeah, she did, baby. You're so gorgeous." Remi sounded so confident that it put a smile on my face.

"Thank you, Remi," I replied softly.

"Well, we're just getting to Dermont's place, so I'm going to shower, but FaceTime me before you go to bed, okay, Shaen?"

I could still pick up on some of the worry in his voice, and I felt bad that I had put it there.

"Will do, love. Talk to you soon." I amazed myself at how cheerful I sounded. I was such a mess. After we hung up, I forced myself to take a shower and put on real clothes. I worked for an hour creating some more content for Julia and the rescue, and then I looked through my social media feed. It was full of pictures of my friends on flights, taking selfies with their new roommates, and documenting the process of setting up their dorm room. I was interrupted from my sad little pity party by a text from Carter:

CARTER

how you holding up?

SHAEN

not good

CARTER

ya same

SHAEN

I'm sorry

CARTER

I'm going into a movie with Jake but if you need anything let me know

SHAEN

thanx

At five, I ventured out of my room to check the fridge. My mom had obviously had visitors over as some leftover pizza, still in the box, and two beers sat alone on the shelf.

"Fuck," I exclaimed to the silent room. Then, I took my keys and drove to the grocery store to pick up some real food. I decided I was going to make some Rice Krispie treats to cheer myself up, so I got the ingredients for that and the makings for a taco salad. As I walked back into the apartment, Liam Face-Timed me. I answered, and his face filled up my screen.

"Hi, baby!" he exclaimed. He must be out at a pool hall because I could see people playing in the background. A guy with long, sandy brown hair poked his face in next to Liam.

"Who is baby? Is that your girlfriend?" he asked, waving hi to me. Leave it to Liam to make friends within minutes of getting to a new place. People gravitated to him because he was loud, funny, and super confident.

"Nope. This is Shaen, my best friend," Liam told the guy.

"Well damn, is she single? 'Cause she is hotttt." The guy peered back over Liam's shoulder.

"She is not single." Liam turned the phone away. "Don't be looking at her."

I cracked up.

"I see you're already making friends?" I propped my phone up against the paper towel roll and got to prepping my taco salad while Liam and I talked. He told me all about his flight, his dorm, his roommate, and his schedule. He sounded happy, which made me happy. I was sitting down getting ready to eat when Liam said, "I don't know what to do about Lia."

I stopped mid-chew. He had been successfully avoiding this conversation with me for weeks.

"What do you want to do?" I asked. Liam squeezed his eyes shut for a few seconds, and when he opened them, I was surprised to find them shiny.

"We've been together for a long time, you know? If we were in the same school or even the same state, I would stay with her, but how am I supposed to do it like this?" He ran a hand through his already messy hair. "I had to go here. I couldn't go to school in California... you know that."

I nodded. Liam's plan was to become a surgeon like Sam, and the best place for him to do that was Harvard. Him going to the same school as her had never been an option for them.

"So she's in Cali, I'm here, and not only do we have crazy schedules, we also have a three-hour time difference. I don't know how I'm supposed to make that work... also am I supposed to be celibate till Christmas? My dick will fall off, Shaen." Liam seemed particularly distraught over that last part. I laughed until he made a fake crying face.

"Listen, if this were me and Remi, I would do anything to make it work. I'd either wait and stay celibate, or I would move and transfer schools. Or make it work in our own schools. I would visit, I don't know... my point is she seems okay. She knew you were going to Boston since ninth grade, and she never applied to anything but the school she's in when she could have gone to other schools in your area." I took a big bite of my salad and chewed while Liam wrapped his head around what I was saying.

"Fuck, you're right," he finally said. "Do you think she's just waiting for me to break up with her?"

"I don't know, Liam, why didn't you talk to her about this ever since you both got acceptance letters like a year ago? It's not like this happened out of the blue," I told him. He rolled his eyes.

"Shaen, we did talk about it, but we never came to any conclusions because every time we tried to talk about anything, we ended up fucking." Liam laughed.

"Well, maybe that's all it was. A high-school fling that was based on being a mostly physical relationship. Maybe it's not meant to go further than this." I didn't want to be the reason they broke up; she was also my friend after all, but it was starting to feel like it had run its course.

"Shit, you might be right." Liam seemed sad. "Well, I gotta go, but call me tomorrow so I can figure out what I'm going to say to her."

I nodded.

"Bye, hottie," I heard from off-screen. Liam punched him, and the guy yelped and then laughed.

"Bye, Liam."

I felt a little bit better after our call. He and I were forever, and I knew we could and would maintain our friendship through all his years of college and medical school. That was one thing I knew for certain.

After eating way too many Rice Krispie treats, I took a long shower and cried the whole time. Crying in the shower felt safer for me since it was easy for me to pretend it wasn't happening. What tears? No, that is shower water. I laughed at my own idiocy and got out to dry off. For some reason, out of the blue, a lot of my lonely feelings that were surfacing today felt like they were stemming from my "no one loves me, never had a dad" issues. When I was twelve, I had mustered up the courage to ask my mom about him. We were doing family tree work in school, and mine was so empty that I was embarrassed. When I discovered that my birth certificate only had my mother's name on it, I asked who my dad was. All she said was he had been a lot older than her and wasn't interested in another family.

"He didn't even want you, Shaen. Just let it go," she had told me.

Those words had fucked me up more than I was able to verbalize at twelve, but now at close to nineteen, I was aware of the damage they had done to my ability to feel my feelings, to feel loved, and to accept that emotion was a safe thing to express and experience.

The envelope Dee had given me last month sat on my dresser. Taunting me. Maybe he would want me now. Maybe my mom wasn't telling me the truth when I had asked her about him years ago. Maybe I did have a whole other family who would want to know me. I would never know if I didn't try. Deciding it was now or never, I quickly ripped open the package. I filled out all of the paperwork and then swabbed my cheek. I packed it all back up before I could chicken out and placed it in the return envelope. I decided I wasn't going to tell anyone that I had done it. First, let me see if any relatives popped up first. I didn't want any drama around it before I knew for certain. A lot of my angst seemed to dissipate with making the decision to try to find this elusive father of mine. Feeling a lot lighter and more peaceful, I got into bed and FaceTimed Remi. It was 10 p.m. for me, which made it seven in California, and sure enough, when Remi answered the call, it was still sunny out where he sat by the pool.

"Hi!" He wasn't wearing a shirt, and I got a nice eyeful of abs and chest as Remi got up and walked inside.

"Hi yourself." I smiled as I laid down and got cozy in my blanket.

"I miss you." Remi was sitting on a bed now and had propped his phone up on something.

"I miss you too."

Remi's eyes roamed over my face and down to where he could see my cleavage.

"The things I would do to you if I were there," he whispered into the phone.

"Oh, yeah?" I smiled, biting my lip.

"Yeah." Remi leaned forward as if to say something else when the door behind him opened, and Dermont poked his head in.

"We're going to leave in twenty. Oh, hey, Shaen." He waved at me, and I waved back.

"Hey, Dermont."

"I'm taking your boy to a car show, and then we'll be catching dinner at Nobu."

I had no knowledge of what he was saying, but I nodded and said, "That sounds amazing. I hope you have a great time!"

"I know you're going to sleep. Call me tomorrow before you go to work. Wake me up." Remi sounded regretful.

"I will, baby. Good night." I kissed the screen, and he seemed pacified.

"Love you, pixie."

I was scrolling social media before I officially went to sleep when the text came in.

REMI

If I was there I would pull your tank top off but not all the way, instead I would tighten it around your wrists to keep your hands above your head. Then I would lick and suck your nipples until you were begging me to make you come. But I wouldn't. Instead, I would kiss everywhere but your pussy. I would kiss your thighs and your belly. I would leave little love bites all over you. I would lick my way all over the sides of your lips until you were leaking down your legs making a big mess. You would be moaning and begging and only once you were completely losing it would I finally touch you. My tongue would be all over your clit and I would fuck you with three fingers. You would be so worked up that you would come immediately. Your legs would tighten around my head so hard that I would have to pry them apart to get up to your mouth and I would kiss you so you could taste what a mess you had made. And you would love it.

I gasped, reading his filthy text. My body was thrumming with desire. Another text came in as I was reaching for my vibrator.

REMI

video yourself for me. I know what you're doing

Oh, my kinky man. Could I do it? I hesitated. A third text came in.

REMI

be a good girl and do it for me

Fuckkkk. I left the light off, so the only source of light was a little bit of moonlight that was streaming in from the window. I propped my phone against the water bottle on my night table, then swiped to the video feature and pressed record. I lay back on my pillow, lifting up my tank top so he could see the slope of my breasts. Then I shoved my underwear down, leaving it around my ankles. I opened my legs, turned on my vibrator, and touched it to my clit.

"Oh fuck," I groaned out. I immediately was not focused on doing anything special for the recording. All I could think about was the dirty things Remi had described doing to me and how much of a good girl I wanted to be for him. I came almost imme-diately. Fireworks shot off behind my eyelids, and my hips lifted off the mattress on their own accord. Instead of removing my vibrator, I fought through my heightened sensitivity and kept it on me. I moaned Remi's name as I thought about him sitting at his fancy car show next to his godfather and typing that dirty text to me under the table. I imagined he was here next to me and was watching me pleasure myself. He would be working his cock as he stared at me with his eyes only half open. His abs would contract as he moved his hand up and down himself, squeezing and jerking. I came dramatically, calling out to a God

I didn't believe in, alone in my bed but not feeling so alone anymore.

I couldn't bring myself to watch the video, so I quickly just sent it to him and then deleted it off my phone. It sat there unread until I fell asleep. The next morning, I woke up to a string of texts:

REMI

I will never be soft ever again.

REMI

how are you so hot?!

REMI

I need to jerk off but I'm in nobu. This place is bougie AF

I laughed at his use of bougie. Then I blinked at the text sent twenty-four minutes after his previous message.

REMI

ok I jerked it in nobu's fancy bathroom and I'm still hard. You've ruined me pixie.

Two hours later, the last text of the night had come in:

REMI

photo

It was a picture of him lying in an unfamiliar bed, one arm was up behind his head. The other one was down between his legs. I couldn't see everything clearly, but I knew what he was doing, and it got me wet all over again.

THE NEXT SIX days passed in a blur of work, loving check-ins with Remi during the day and dirty text threads at night, calls with Liam, and time spent impatiently waiting to hear back from the DNA company. It was officially September 2nd, six days before my nineteenth birthday, and I was waiting in the airport to pick Remi up. I had worn my tightest body suit and a pair of jeans that did great things for my ass. I had also baked fresh oatmeal cookies and brought them with me. After waiting for about a half hour, I finally saw him walking through the crowd toward the exit. He was easy to spot as he was almost a head taller than everyone around him. Remi's face lit up when he finally saw me, and he began to walk faster. I ran the last few feet and threw myself at him. He caught me and lifted me up as I tightened my legs around his waist. We immediately began making out until people around us kept grumbling about getting a room.

"Oh my God, never again," Remi told me when he let me back down to the floor. "Next time you come with me." He took my hand, and we walked to where I had parked my car. As I drove home, he ate the cookies and told me all about his trip. Apparently, Dermont had convinced Remi to record a demo of a song. Remi told me that he had done it to humor Dermont, but he could never see it through as an actual career.

"LA is just so pretentious," he said. "I would never fit in."

"Big word, babe," I quipped.

"Right, look at me being all smart." He grinned. "But seriously, everyone has a boob job. Dermont had me meet some of the people he works with. They're all fake. The women just laughed at everything I said because they thought I was hot, not because they actually cared."

"Hot women laughing at what you're saying?" I pretended to be aghast. "That sounds terrible."

"There's my sarcastic girl." He reached over and ran a finger down my cheek. "I missed you so much, baby."

I kissed his finger as it passed over my mouth.

"I missed you too. The first day, I was such a mess that I realized we will have to be together forever because I literally could not handle it." I gripped the steering wheel at my confession.

"No complaints from me." Remi took my other hand, kissed my knuckles, and then continued to hold my hand in his.

"So Dermont took me shopping, check it out." Remi pulled up his sleeve and showed me some fancy watch from a brand I knew nothing about.

"Wow, that looks expensive. That's so nice of him." I glanced at it as I took the exit off the highway.

"Yeah, he likes to spoil me. I can't even stop him. He won't hear of it." Remi shrugged. "He's always been like this."

"Is that kind of extra for a godfather?" I asked.

"I don't know. It's all I've ever known from him," Remi told me. Something tickled the back of my brain, but I didn't know what felt off, so I ignored it.

"Pull off here," Remi said suddenly. I looked around. We were by a local hiking area. The parking lot was empty and surrounded by trees.

"Okay, low-key kind of creepy. What's up?" I parked and looked over at him.

"I can't wait," he said, unbuckling my seatbelt.

"Rem, I'm ovulating today," I told him regretfully.

"I know, baby. I get notifications on my phone. There are lots of other options other than fucking." He winked at me and then climbed into the back seat of my car. "Come here, sexy." He motioned with his finger for me to join him. I sighed.

"I'm afraid we'll get caught." I hesitated.

"I'll make it worth it if we do," he promised. I gave in and climbed into the back, where he pulled me onto his lap and began kissing me.

"You. Drove. Me. Crazy.," he enunciated between kisses. I knew he was referring to my little homemade video.

"How many times did you watch it?" I giggled.

"Seven million," Remi responded without hesitation. "I've had a perpetual hard-on since you sent it."

"You're so crazy." I laughed again as he began to unbutton my jeans.

"Yeah, crazy for you," he mumbled. His mouth was on my breast, over the thin fabric of my bodysuit. The material was growing darker as it got wet. I moaned as he finally got my jeans undone, and his fingers slipped passed the body suit and into my underwear.

"Who is this for?" he asked in a sultry tone, watching my face closely.

I could feel how wet I was as his fingers easily breached my opening and began to pump in and out of me.

"Y-you. It's for you," I groaned.

"You're fucking right it is." Remi's mouth was near my ear now, and he began telling me in detail what he was going to do to me when we got home. I came embarrassingly fast all over his hand, and then, of course, he licked it all off of each finger. I rewarded him with a blowjob. We did not get caught.

21

Wednesday, September 9th, I woke up late since I didn't have to go to work. Remi had slept at home since he had gone to orientation for his new school the day before and had needed Sam to fill out medical paperwork for him. But since Sam had been on call, he got home late, and by the time they finished, I had already fallen asleep. So Remi had texted me that he loved me so much and would come by tomorrow morning. Well, tomorrow morning was here, and I was officially nineteen. I smiled. Happy birthday to me, I thought to myself. I sat in meditation for thirty minutes before I got up to start my day. The friend group had already been busy.

LIAM

I'm first. HAPPY BIRTHDAY to you Shaen! I love you so much! Did my present come yet??

LIA

happy birthday shay shay! Go check the front door

I played it. In it, she was singing "Happy Birthday," and told me she wished she could hug me so tight because she knew how much I loved that.

I went to the front door, and an Uber Eats order sat there next to a box. Lia had sent me my favorite drink from Starbucks and a birthday cake pop. The box was from Liam. Inside was the newest iPhone, a necklace with a stone on it that looked suspiciously real, and two train tickets to Boston for the day before Halloween. I was blown away by his generosity and his refusal to listen to me when I told him not to spend money on me. I took everything into my room and then went back into the group chat.

Yesterday, Liam finally broke up with Lia. Not that any of us had wanted it to happen, but it felt like they had both been dragging out the inevitable. Afterward, he had FaceTimed me, looking defeated and sad. He had told her that he cared about her too much to keep her stuck in a relationship that could not progress right now. She had cried, which we had all expected. I had been worried that she would have left the group chat, not out of spite but to preserve her mental health, but I was pleasantly surprised to see that not only was she still in the chat, but she was still acting like her usual self. I looked at my phone. It was 10:30 a.m., Liam was still in class, so I would have to wait for his break to call and yell at him for spending so much money on me.

When I went into the kitchen to make myself some breakfast, I saw that my mother had ordered me some pancakes from a local pancake shop that had a birthday breakfast option. The pancakes were made with sprinkles and a white icing drizzle. She had put a sticky note on it that said, "Happy Birthday Shaen, Love, Mom." There was also a birthday card on the counter with a hundred dollar bill in it. My mother wasn't a bad person, she just wasn't everything I needed her to be as my only parent. I shook off the negative thoughts and dug into the pancakes. As I finished up, licking the icing off of my fingers, I heard the front door open.

"Happy birthday, baby!" Remi's face lit up when he saw me. His arms were full of balloons, flowers, and five gift bags.

"Oh my God, you're already overdoing it." I laughed. "You didn't have to get me anything." I got up on my tippy toes to kiss him.

"Are you crazy? I wanted to get you everything." He went into my room to put all the bags down on my bed and then picked me up. I wrapped my legs around his waist, kissing him until he pressed me up against my closed door and moaned appreciatively as he ground his pelvis against mine.

"Do you want to fuck first or open presents first?" he whispered in my ear and then licked the side of my neck. I cocked my head, thinking.

"Ummmm. Let's open presents first because that will go faster, and then we'll have more time to…" My voice trailed off as he put me down.

"To do the dirty?" Remi winked at me. I laughed.

"Exactly."

"Okay, sit down," Remi said in his bossy voice. "I got you a present for each one of your senses."

He showed me the bags. On the outside of each bag, he had written something. The first one said "Taste," the second one said "Touch," the third one said "Sound," the fourth one had "Smell" written on it, and the last one said "Sight." I clapped excitedly.

"Oh my God, how did you even think of this?" I got up on my knees to kiss him again. Remi shrugged, smiling modestly.

"I love you so much," he told me as if that was the explanation for him being able to come up with this amazing birthday experience.

"I love you too." I beamed up at him as he handed me the taste bag. Inside was a card that read,

Happy birthday my love. You are so sweet, so generous, so gorgeous, and so creative. My life was lacking so much before I met you. I am so lucky to be able to call you mine. Love a+f, Remi

I felt my eyes burn with unshed tears as I pulled a box out of the bag. In it sat a box of chocolates from a brand called Pierre Marcolini.

"They're from Paris," Remi told me with a kiss. I had no idea what the high-end brand was, but I could tell that they were very pricey. The box itself was heavy and embossed with gold lettering. When I opened the cover inside, nestled on silk, sat six gorgeous, hand-crafted chocolates.

"They almost look too pretty to eat," I told him, hesitating.

"So do you, but that doesn't stop me." Remi laughed when I fake-hit his arm. I picked up one of the square-shaped chocolates that said "The Citron" on it in gold letters. When I took a bite, a cacophony of flavors burst in my mouth.

"Holy shit, that's so good," I moaned. I held out the other half to him.

"No baby, they're yours," Remi protested. I put the chocolate in between my teeth, and then I brought our mouths together. I pushed the chocolate into his mouth with my tongue. He kissed me as the chocolate melted in his mouth, and I pulled away, panting.

"Damn," he said, licking his lips, looking torn between his desire to keep kissing me and his excitement in watching me open the rest of my presents. He handed me the second bag that said "Touch" on in. In it was a gift certificate for a couple's massage.

"This is amazing, Remi," I breathed. "I can't wait to go." I hugged him and then took the third bag. For "Sound," he had gotten me tickets to see Justin Bieber.

"Babe, this is too much!" I looked down at the printed tickets.

"It's not enough, baby," he corrected me. I hugged him again, this time closing my eyes as he rocked me gently for a few moments. I was overwhelmed because this was by far the most anyone had ever done to recognize my birthday. The fourth bag, "Smell," contained a perfume that I immediately sprayed on myself.

"Thank you. This smells delicious," I told him, sniffing my wrist. Remi beamed. Knowing him, he had picked everything out himself. In the "Sight" bag was an eye mask made from a very soft gray leather.

"Baby, this is the opposite of sight." I laughed. I faltered when I saw the look on his face. His eyes had darkened, and he was almost looking at me hungrily.

"I know." He nipped his way up my jaw and then kissed me deeply. Our tongues danced until I was panting. Remi pulled my pajama shirt off of me, running his hands up to the underside of my breasts, weighing them in his palms. His thumbs ran over my nipples, beading them. Then he bent his dark head and ran his hot tongue over them. I arched my back, moaning his name. Remi took the eye mask from me, and while maintaining eye contact, he slipped the mask over my eyes. Everything went dark.

"Can I fuck you like this?"

Without being able to see him, his voice sounded deeper and more gravelly. I was painfully aware of his breath on my collarbone and his fingers seared into my hips. Holy shit, this was going to incinerate me. I nodded slowly, biting my lip.

"Also..." Remi paused. I waited with bated breath.

"You're not fertile right now, so I was wondering if I can go in you bare?"

I froze as he began to pull my shorts down. He would find me naked beneath them. I let out a gasp as his thumb found my clit and began to strum my sensitive flesh.

"I want to come inside you for real, baby." He was sucking on my earlobe now, sending shocks through my body. I nodded frantically.

"Yes," I moaned.

"Yes, what?" he demanded.

"Yes, come inside me." I was almost there. His fingers were now pumping in and out of me, climbing me higher and higher.

"You look so good in my mask." His voice was near my face, and I could feel his breath on my cheek.

"You make me so hard, Shaen. I'm so proud of you for taking

me like this." His voice was even deeper now. My breath was ragged, and my body was throbbing. His mouth took mine, and I cried out his name as the pleasure almost bordered on pain as I sat between that space of crazy and completion until I finally exploded under his fingers.

"Yes, baby, take it. Oh, good girl," he groaned above me.

I could feel tears seep out of my eyes as I experienced my first orgasm without sight. Losing one sense enhanced the others, and it had been so intense. I laid there trying to catch my breath, my body thrumming with desire for him. I heard his zipper make a noise as he opened it and then a rustle as he took off his clothes. Suddenly, I was up in his arms, and he was walking with me. The next thing I knew, my back was against my cold bedroom door, and his warm abs were pressed against the front of my body. I hooked my legs around his waist and my arms around his neck as I held on.

"Hold tight, birthday girl," he rasped, as I felt his bare cock slip inside me. I blinked behind my eye mask. Oh. He was so much warmer this way.

"Oh my God, you're so wet." His voice was full of wonder as he began to move in earnest. His hips slapped against mine as his cock slipped in and out of me. I was soaked and so tight that he was frantic inside of me. I felt his hand reach in between us and he began to work my clit again.

"Oh, you're doing so well," he moaned in my ear. "Take me, Shaen, take me."

"What do you see?" I asked him, my voice almost stuck in my throat. His hips stuttered at my words and then regained momentum.

"You're soaked. I can see you all over my dick, your legs, and I can feel you dripping down my balls," he moaned out. I gasped and squeezed. I was rewarded with another groan from him.

"I can see myself disappearing inside of you. You take me so good, baby, so good." His breath was coming faster now. His tempo was messier. "You're so soft inside. So tight. So wet."

I felt his hands leave me, and then his fingers were inside of my mouth.

"What do you taste?" he rasped against my lips.

"Me. I taste me," I cried.

"Y-yes." His mouth was back on mine, and his fingers returned to my clit. My back was feeling uncomfortable against my door, but the pinch against my spine added to how good this was.

"You look so good with me inside you." He was making loud moans now as if he couldn't hold back.

"Oh, oh my God, I'm coming," I cried out. My body clenched around him as I came, and he rutted inside of me a few more times until I felt the hot spurts of his release against my walls as he finished inside of me. I lifted up the eye mask, blinking at how bright the lights felt. Then I watched as he gently pulled out of me. Some of his cum followed, and it smeared against my lips and upper thighs. I reached down and ran a finger through it before I pushed it back up inside me.

"Oh, Godddd." He closed his eyes for a second as if he couldn't handle seeing it.

"Do you have a breeding kink?" I giggled as he carried me to the bathroom and started a shower for us.

"I don't think so," he laughed. "But I'll admit there is something primal about seeing my cum in you."

I hugged him.

"This was the best birthday I've ever had. Thank you," I whispered.

He kissed me so passionately that we ended up fucking in the shower. Then again on my bed, first in missionary and then finishing with him behind me. After the third round, we collapsed on my bed.

"I'm dehydrated, woman, don't touch me. I need a break," he whined. This made me laugh so hard that my abs hurt. We ended up falling asleep in each other's arms, his cum drying on my thighs, his love bites all over my chest, and my heart so full of joy I thought I might burst.

This is what love feels like.

~

THE NEXT DAY, I worked late because my bosses had asked me to take the last shift tonight. As I finished up for the day, I tucked all the doggies in for the night.

"Goodnight, babies," I cooed as I made sure each one had what they needed before I closed all the kennel doors and shut off the main lights. It had been an amazing day because three dogs had gone to their "furever" homes today. I locked up and pulled my jacket around me as I stepped into the crisp air that night had brought. I hadn't been able to find parking in the lot next to the rescue this afternoon, so I had to walk one block over to get to my car. The streets were basically empty this late at night, so I walked quickly to get to the warmth and safety of my car.

"Miss Collins," a familiar voice called out as I approached my parking spot. A voice that immediately sent prickles of fear down my spine. I turned around slowly.

"What do you want?" I asked coldly as Pastor John Taylor stepped out of his Lexus and began to approach me from across the street.

"I just want to talk," he told me.

"I have nothing to say to you." I fumbled with my car keys. Why was he here? Why was he waiting this late at night near my work? How did he know where I worked? He had to know that we had suspicions that he had something to do with his driver drugging me all those months ago. I began to panic. Was he here to hurt me?

"Don't come closer!" I shouted. The pastor stopped walking.

"I'm not going to hurt you." He seemed offended that I was acting so afraid of him.

"Why should I believe that?" I sneered. "Why are you here?"

"I want to talk to you about Remiel." He was still standing several feet away, but he was talking loud enough for me to hear him. "I figured if he hasn't left you by now, then maybe we can work together to help him."

I flinched at how callously he referred to his son breaking up with me. I also found it pretty out of touch that he thought I would ever entertain helping him.

"What could he possibly need help with?" I tried to reach for my phone inside my bag without the pastor noticing, but I kept coming up short because my hands were shaking so much.

"I know that you are not a woman of faith, so perhaps you won't understand this."

Remi's dad was using what I recognized as his *pastor* voice with me. It made me feel like he was talking at me instead of to me, and he was using a tone as if he thought I was stupid.

"But Remiel had such a strong relationship with the Lord before, and it pains me to see him struggling like this."

"He's not struggling," I replied strongly.

"That's the enemy at work," the pastor said confidently. "We need to help him cast out this evil spirit and assist him in coming back to Jesus. Where he belongs."

"Do you hear yourself? You sound fucking insane," I yelled at him. Suddenly, it felt like the world had gone into slow motion. I saw the pastor mouthing, "Move, move!" and he began waving his hands. I turned to my left and gaped as a car came barreling down the street, swerving dangerously. I tried to get around to the other side of my car, but my legs felt like they were stuck in quicksand. I managed to get myself to the front of my car, but suddenly, pain took over my body. I felt myself get flung up into the air, and then the next thing I knew, I was crashing onto the hood of the car that I presumed had just hit me. I found myself sprawled on the cracked windshield, staring into the lifeless eyes of the driver, who was contorted in a weird angle over the steering wheel, blood dripping down his face. I couldn't take my eyes off of him as I thought in a detached way how sad Remi would feel when I didn't come home tonight. Then I realized that I could no longer breathe. Despite the cold air I had noticed earlier, I now felt warm. I felt peaceful. I floated off into a numb oblivion and could no longer feel my body.

So this is what dying feels like.

22

My mouth was painfully dry, and my body hurt so badly that I couldn't even shift my legs without pain radiating through me in a way that made my brain ache. I could hear a beeping sound that was reverberating through my skull and was giving me a terrible headache. Where was I? Did I drink too much last night? What was happening?

"Oh, try not to move, honey," a voice sounded above me. I cracked open an eye. My other one refused to open. A woman in blue scrubs and a ponytail was smiling down at me.

"Who the fuck are you?" I croaked.

"I'm your nurse, Sloane," she told me. "I was told your name is Shaen?"

I nodded, and my entire body screamed in protest. How did she know my name?

"How bad is your pain on a scale of one to ten?" Sloane asked me as I squeezed my eyes shut again.

"Eleven," I managed to say. "It's an eleven."

"Can I get some more morphine in here?" I heard her voice vibrating through my whole body. I felt a prick, and a delicious stupor took me back again.

Wherever I was, it was giving me weird dreams. I could hear a man shouting my name. I couldn't see his face, but he quickly morphed into a black, intimidating cloud of smoke that was scaring me. I tried to crawl into a little hole that I found in the corner of this weird place I was in, but then I heard someone calling me Ice Queen. I wanted to tell him that the ice queen was broken and wasn't coming back, but I couldn't talk. Suddenly, everything shifted, and I was petrified. Of what, I didn't know, but it felt like the whole room was watching me. A whole room of dead, unseeing eyes. Watching me, unblinking. I wanted to scream, but I couldn't. Suddenly, I heard my mother's voice. The words "he didn't want you, Shaen" began to reverberate and echo around me. Over and over and over. I could finally use my vocal cords, and I had to scream to cover up the sound of her voice. I just screamed and screamed until my throat was raw and dry. "I love you, pixie." Who was that? I felt something that seemed safe and warm and good press into my awareness, but I couldn't figure out what it meant. Then I fell deeper into nothingness, and everything disappeared, and all I could hear was the sound of my beating heart somewhere off in the distance.

"Shaen?" My mother's voice was urgent and high-pitched above me. Was I late for school? Why was she waking me up? She never did that. I cracked my eyes open. Her face was leaning over me. Why was she crying?

"What?" Why did my voice sound so weird? I was so tired. Maybe she'll let me stay home today. "I think I'm sick." I forced the words out and they sounded so rough and guttural.

"Oh, Shaen." She was legitimately sobbing at this point. I didn't know what to do with that, so I just closed my eyes and let the nothingness take over me again.

"Shaen." Sloane was back again. "Hi, honey." I opened my eyes again. My face hurt. I looked down. I had a blue gown on, I was under a white blanket, and I had a wire coming out of my arm. No, not a wire, an IV. My brain sluggishly caught up. I was in the hospital. Oh my God, I had been hit by a car! My eyes snapped back to my nurse in a panic.

"You remember?" she asked softly. I nodded. "What happened?"

"Let me get your doctor." She patted my arm very gently, and she stepped out of view.

"Hi, Shaen." I turned my head slowly to look at the tall man next to my bed. He had chestnut-colored skin and was wearing a white lab coat.

"I'm Dr. Nick. How are you feeling?" he asked.

"Like shit," I managed to say. He chuckled. "I can imagine. You are a very lucky girl."

Am I? I felt stuck, lying in this bed, riddled with pain and confusion.

"What happened?" I repeated. The doctor clicked his pen and then looked at me.

"Like I said, you were very lucky. The man who brought you in said a drunk driver came out of nowhere and hit you head-on."

"What man?" I interrupted.

"We were actually not sure who he was to you. At first we assumed he was your father, but then he left pretty quickly. We didn't even mention this to your mother," Dr. Nick told me. "His name is..." The doctor scrolled on my chart that was housed on a tablet in his hands. "Ah, here it is, John Shane Taylor."

Shane? That must be a mistake. Was I hearing things?

"He's not my father... he's..." Oh my God, Remi. How long have I been here? Had anyone let him know what had happened and where I was?

"Oh, interesting. We just assumed you were related, so when we thought you might need a blood transfusion, we asked him what his blood type was..."

"A blood transfusion?" I interrupted again.

"You didn't end up needing it," the doctor reassured me. "But it turns out you both have an AB negative blood type, which is the rarest blood type. Less than one percent of the population has it. I guess that was just a lucky coincidence."

Warning bells started going off in my head. Nausea rose in my throat, but I swallowed it back down. Dr. Nick continued telling me what had happened.

"So the impact of when you were hit caused you to fly up several feet in the air and then come slamming back down on the hood of the car."

"The driver was dead," I murmured, remembering the lifeless eyes staring at me.

"Yes. He wasn't wearing a seat belt, and his head took the brunt of the crash on the steering wheel when he hit you, which severed his spinal cord. He was dead on impact," he explained. "Apparently, John Taylor said he saw it happen and called 911, but there was a twelve-car pileup on the highway that had a lot of emergency services responding to it, so EMS told him it would take around ten minutes for an ambulance to get to you. John didn't think you could wait the ten minutes, so he risked moving you, and he carried you to his car. He got you to the hospital in six minutes."

The pastor saved my life? This story was getting crazier and crazier.

"What was unique about your injuries was you came in presenting with crush syndrome. But you hadn't been crushed. We think the force of hitting the hood of the car caused traumatic rhabdomyolysis due to a muscle reperfusion injury."

"Huh?" I was so lost.

"Basically, the force of pressure to your body damaged muscle tissue and released a bunch of toxins into your body, so you came in with respiratory failure and cardiac arrhythmias. At first, we thought you must be bleeding out somewhere, so we checked your blood type to prep for a transfusion during possible surgery, and that's when we saw your potassium and uric acid levels were elevated, and we realized that your body thought it had been crushed."

"So, what did you do?" I asked weakly. No wonder everything hurt like a bitch.

"We administered saline through a central line. The saline dilutes the toxins in your blood and protects your kidneys," he explained.

"So I'm okay?" I felt so scared to hear his answer. The doctor reached for my hand and squeezed gently.

"You are okay, Shaen." He smiled. "Like I said before, you are very lucky. You will be in pain as the bruising and swelling heal, but the worst is over. You can go home tomorrow."

I nodded, trying to process everything he had said.

"Has my boyfriend been here?" I asked.

"I don't think so. But your mom slept here both nights. She just stepped out, but she said she'll be back. Your phone is over there if you want to call your boyfriend." Dr. Nick pointed to the portable hospital bed table.

"How long have I been here?" I braced myself for his answer.

"Today is your third day."

Holy fuck. I took my phone and pressed the cracked screen. It was dead. Fucking great. I wanted to call Remi, but I didn't know his number by heart. I actually didn't know any of my friends' numbers. I felt tears well up in my eyes as I fell back to sleep.

I HAD something to ask my mom, but I couldn't remember what it was. She was helping me climb up the four flights of stairs, which was proving to be absolutely impossible in my current state. For once, I was appreciative of my mom being a nurse because she said she would manage all of my medicine and had handled my discharge instructions. I finally made it up one flight when I heard a strangled voice call my name. I turned my head, my body protesting painfully, and saw that Remi was standing at the bottom of the stairs, staring up at me in horror.

"What the fuck happened?" he ground out. His face was covered in a few days of hair growth, he had huge bags under his eyes, and his lips were dry, looking almost like he had forgotten to drink water.

"Hey! Calm down," my mom snapped. "She cannot be stressed or aggravated right now."

Remi ignored her and bounded up the stairs, taking them three at a time. He stood in front of me, still staring. His hands were reaching out toward me, but they were not yet touching me. It seemed like he was too scared to or almost like he didn't believe that I was real. I knew that I looked terrible; I had seen myself for the first time this morning. I had stitches in my hairline, the entire left side of my face was mottled with bruising, my eye socket was swollen, and my eyelid was scabbing over from a cut.

"I was hit by a car, and I was unconscious for like two days, and my phone was dead, and I don't have your number memorized." Tears began to flow from my eyes, tracking down my messed-up face.

"Oh baby, baby..." Remi's voice quivered as his eyes welled up, seeming only seconds from crying with me. "Can I carry her?" He directed the question to my mother without looking at her.

"Be very careful, her entire body is bruised," she replied sternly.

"I'm always careful."

I could tell he was still not a fan of Amy Collins. He gently put an arm under my legs and very slowly lifted me up while supporting the side of my body with his other arm. I curled up against his chest, taking a deep inhale of his familiar scent. He carried me as slowly as possible, pausing to make sure I was okay at each landing. When we got to the apartment, my mother unlocked the door and watched as Remi brought me to my room. Surprisingly, my mother had already set up the bed with a pillow support system used for patients who were post-op, so I didn't have to fully lay back.

"I need a shower." I felt so gross and dirty.

"I'll..." my mother started.

"I got it," Remi said, talking over her. They both stared at each other until my mother backed down.

"I'm going to go buy some soup for you," she said to me, using a gentle tone I had never heard from her before. When she left the room, I said in a half-hearted tone, "Nothing like almost dying to remind your mom that you still exist."

"That is not funny. Don't say that," Remi said strongly. He was sitting by my feet, his face in his hands. I heard him make a sobbing sound, and I could see that his body was shaking.

"Remi," I called his name faintly.

"I didn't know where you were." He was hoarse. "I called and called. You weren't here. You weren't at work. Your car was abandoned one street over. I couldn't find you. Every time I came here, no one was home. I called the hospitals, but because I'm not family, they wouldn't tell me anything. I was losing my mind..." His voice shook as he looked over at me. My heart lurched at seeing him like this.

"I love you so much," I murmured because I knew there was nothing else to say. We were both traumatized, and there wasn't anything I could say that would make it better. He leaned closer to me, and I gingerly ran my fingers through his hair.

"I can't lose you." He turned his head and kissed my hand.

"Never," I promised. Something was tugging at my memory, but I couldn't quite place what it was.

Remi cried again when he showered me. The whole left side of my body, from my shoulder down to my ankle was cut up, swollen, and bruised. I had an ugly red scar forming from where the central line had been.

"You are so brave," he whispered to me as he gently washed my hair, avoiding the stitches. "You are so strong," he said as he poured water down my body and rubbed away the glue left from the medical tape that had been holding the IV in place. "You are so beautiful," he told me as he brushed my hair after I had gotten out of the shower and put on a soft, oversized T-shirt. Then he placed a gentle kiss on my lips in between each bite of chicken soup that he fed me. After I finished the bowl, he put on high-frequency music that the internet told him had healing vibes and then helped me get comfortable against the pillows. I fell asleep feeling safe for the first time in four days.

I woke up to hearing him talking to my mother. He was explaining that Julia would be dropping off a red-light therapy lamp soon. Julia had several red-light therapy options at her aesthetics spa. She used them for their healing properties and for reducing inflammation. I wondered how Remi had convinced her to bring such an expensive contraption to my apartment.

"I don't think we should have so many strangers over here while Shaen is still recovering," I heard my mother say. Remi snorted in response.

"Julia is not a stranger."

Remi was always so respectful and polite to people, but I

knew his current attitude with my mother was due to him knowing what had gone on my whole childhood. It honestly felt like yet another way that he showed how much he would do to protect me. There was a knock on the door, and the next thing I knew, Julia was on her knees beside my bed.

"Oh lovie." She had tears in her eyes. "I'm going to make it all better."

After pressing a kiss to my forehead, she began unpacking all the goodies she had brought. First, she gave me a B12 shot and told me about a study that showed that B12 increased wound healing, especially in the early stages. Then she unpacked a tub of an all-natural ointment that she used to help heal bruising after injections at the spa, and she very gently dabbed it on all of the bruised areas on my face. While she was doing that, she had Remi make me a turmeric tea, and she explained how it would help combat inflammation. Lastly, she put together the red-light lamp. It had a stand that she set up at the side of the bed, and it had a movable arm that held the lamp portion, so she was able to bring it down and have it hover over my body. She placed a sleeping mask over my eyes and had me rest under the lamp for twenty minutes. When I finished, she swung the lamp back over near the wall.

"I'm going to leave this here. I showed Remiel how to turn it on, and he knows what settings to use for your face and what settings to use for your body." She was sitting on the bed and holding my hand. "I also put some groceries in the fridge. When you're healing, it's very important to eat based on your blood type. Sam said you want to focus on tofu, seafood, dairy, and green vegetables. He said that people with AB negative tend to have low stomach acid, so I want you to avoid caffeine, alcohol, and deli meats for now. I also bought you a bunch of bottles of celery juice, and I want you to drink one a day." As she talked,

Julia opened a bottle of said celery juice and handed it to me with a metal straw in it.

"Save the turtles." Remi noticed and laughed.

"That's a very serious thing, Remiel." Julia turned to him. "Sea turtles have been endangered since 2001."

He held up his hands in surrender.

"Okay, okay, metal straws it is." He winked at me. I laughed and then groaned at how much it hurt to do so. The words "blood type" were bouncing around in my head, tugging at a memory that I couldn't quite grasp.

"How's the celery juice?" Remi asked. I held out the bottle for him to take a sip.

"Hmm, it's kind of tangy." He licked his lips. I felt so bad for how tired and stressed out he looked. I wanted to tell him to lie down and take a nap, but I already knew that he would refuse.

"Are you taking any pain meds?" Julia asked me.

"They gave me some Percocet." I pointed to the bottle on my night table. "But I don't like the way it makes me feel."

"They can also slow down the healing process," Julia agreed. "I put some natural pain remedies on your dresser. If you want to try that, you can."

For two people in the medical field, she and Sam certainly knew a lot about natural healing, which I really appreciated. All three of us looked up as someone knocked on the front door.

"Are you expecting anyone?" Remi asked. I gestured to myself.

"Who would I have invited over? Also, my phone is still broken. I can't get it to turn on." I tried to smile at him since I couldn't handle laughing.

"Touché." Remi opened my bedroom door, and there stood my annoyed-looking mother and a frantic-looking Liam. My eyes welled with tears.

"Liam?" Julia sounded surprised.

"I got on the first flight," he told his mother. Then he got a good look at me. I had never seen Liam really cry, ever, until now.

"Shay Shay." His voice was strangled, sounding like his throat was swollen with emotion. He swallowed, and his Adam's apple bobbed. I shrugged, my own feelings welling up inside of me because I knew that he had just dropped everything and ran to me as soon as he had heard what had happened. Liam crawled onto my bed gently and hesitantly kissed my cheek that had no damage. "Who do I need to beat up for you?" He wiped away a stray tear before it dripped off his chin.

"He's dead," I replied.

"Oh well... that's good because otherwise I'd be in jail right now."

"Liam!" Julia sighed.

"Mom. Look at her." His hands were trembling as he reached over to hold one of mine. "Remi didn't tell me he couldn't find you until yesterday. When you didn't answer my texts, I thought you were mad at me for spending so much money on your birthday present or something. And I was studying for a test, so I was offline a lot, but then when Remi called me and said he didn't know where you were, I've been going out of my mind ever since."

"I'm sorry," I whispered.

"You shouldn't be. I'm just still processing." Liam kissed my fingertips and then curled his fingers around mine. "Fuck." He exhaled. "I'm so glad you're going to be okay."

I squeezed his hand as Julia leaned down and kissed my temple.

"I love you. I'll be back tomorrow. Text me if you need anything."

"Thank you." I managed a small smile. "Love you too."

I could see my mom stiffen when she heard that. I imagined it felt odd to hear your daughter say that to someone whom you had never met before. Julia stopped in front of my mother.

"Shaen is just a gem, as I'm sure you know. We adore her."

I blushed. My mom nodded and replied, "I know."

She did not know, and it made me angry to hear. Remi must have noticed my change in temperament because he quickly announced, "Nap time."

My mom glared at my boyfriend, but she left and shut the door behind her. Remi lay down on the bed, resting near my feet, as Liam was stretched out next to me on my right side. Then we all got some much-needed sleep.

The next morning, I already felt a massive difference in my energy. All of Julia's magical remedies were working. Remi had already had me do two more red light sessions, and he had applied more of the healing salve, being meticulous so as not to hurt me. Liam had whipped up a mix of tofu and spinach for me to eat, and I sat in bed, taking small bites of it. The apartment was otherwise quiet since Remi had taken my broken phone to Apple to have them switch it to the new phone that Liam had bought me for my birthday. We couldn't back up my current phone since it was so smashed it wouldn't turn on, so we needed the professionals to do it. My mom had gone to work for the first time since my accident. Liam was sitting next to me, looking through a dating app. I appreciated that he was acting like his normal self around me. Everyone else was treating me like a glass doll to some extent.

"I haven't fucked anyone in weeks," he groaned. "It's torture."

"No possible options at school?" I asked, taking a sip of my celery juice.

"I kind of don't want to shit where I eat anymore," Liam told me. "I don't want to be in a relationship. I just wanna get some and then not see them in class the next day. Ya know?"

"Yeah, that makes sense." I peered over at his phone as he scrolled through photos. "Wait, I know her."

"I'd tap that." Liam clicked on her profile. "Well hello there, Sloane."

"She was my nurse."

"No shit." Liam was fixated on a photo of her at the beach. "I can play nurse and patient." He basically purred.

"Ew, if you're hard right now, that is so gross." I tried to push him away, but I was too weak.

"She's hot. And she's a nurse." Liam grinned at me. "I'm gonna hit her up."

"Tell her I say hi," I said sarcastically.

"I will. While she's riding me." He laughed.

"You're actually disgusting." I rolled my eyes.

"True," he agreed.

"Sooo," I started.

"Uh oh, that doesn't sound good." Liam put his phone down.

"I haven't told anyone this, but the reason I was standing outside of my car the night of the accident was because I had just left work and was walking to my car, and Remi's father was there. He said he was trying to convince me to help him bring Remi back to religion or whatever." I scoffed.

"Wait, what the fuck are you saying?" Liam sounded shocked.

"Yeah, and he saw the accident happen, and apparently, the ambulance wouldn't come in time, so he brought me to the hospital himself. The doctor told me that he left soon after."

"That is crazy, Shaen! Why haven't you told Remi?" he exclaimed as his phone buzzed.

"I don't know," I admitted. "I will soon." That persistent feeling that I was forgetting something pressed into my awareness again, and I grew agitated from being unable to figure out what my brain was trying to tell me. I suddenly felt a wave of exhaustion come over me.

"I'm gonna nap," I told Liam.

"Okay, we'll talk about this again when you wake up. Sloane messaged me back, so I'll be here flirting. You sleep, babe." Liam patted my good shoulder, and I smiled as I closed my eyes.

When I woke up, Remi was back. I could hear him talking to Liam in the kitchen. I dragged myself out of bed and very slowly shuffled my way out of my room. As soon as the boys saw me, they both jumped to help me.

"Stop." I held up a hand. "You both have to go back to school, so I need to get used to taking care of myself. You can't be here babying me all the time."

"I took the week off," Remi informed me as he took hold of my hand and began to guide me to the living room.

"I have to go back tomorrow," Liam told us regretfully.

"I'll be okay." I flinched as I sat down in the chair. My body hurt so fucking bad; I was still surprised nothing was broken. "What are you guys eating?"

"Cereal." Liam held up a bowl of Captain Crunch.

"Can I have some?" I asked as Remi gently laid a blanket over my legs.

"Nope." Liam shook his head. "We ordered you crab rolls and a spinach salad." He unpacked the Uber Eats order and brought me over a plate of food. "I'm pretty sure Captain Crunch is not on the blood type list that my mother left." He and Remi laughed at how strict Julia was being with me as I recovered. I watched as they poured themselves another bowl and pouted.

Blood type. The word finally clicked inside my brain. I remembered the weird gut feeling I got when the doctor told me that my blood type was extremely rare. I still wasn't clear on why the medical staff had asked the pastor what his blood type was when they had a blood bank in the hospital, but the fact was they had asked, and apparently, he has the same rare blood type as me. Which, I told myself, was 99.9 percent a complete coincidence. Just like the fact that his middle name was Shane. That had to also be just a weird cosmic twist of the universe telling me to go fuck myself, right? I pushed the weird thoughts into the recesses of my brain and took a bite of my food. When all the flavors hit my taste buds, I moaned because this was the best thing I had eaten in the last five days.

"Jeez, Shaen, I'm still here. Calm down with the sexy noises." Liam pretended to blush. I gave him the finger.

"What is your blood type?" I suddenly asked the boys.

"Fuck if I know." Liam shrugged. "I've never asked."

"I know what mine is because I'm O, so they're always asking me to donate." Remi was slurping the leftover milk from his bowl.

"My roommate sounds like that when he eats girls out," Liam told us when Remi put his bowl back down.

"I don't even want to know how you know that." Remi looked so disgusted that it made Liam crack up. While they were laughing, I had warning bells going off in my head. I remembered a bit from science class because our final had been on blood types. If Remi's dad was AB negative, that would mean Remi would have to be A, B, or AB, depending on what his mom was. There was no possible way he could be O, even if his mom was O, because O blood type paired with AB would always end up as either A or B. Something wasn't adding up.

"You okay, pixie?" Remi noticed the confused look on my face.

"Oh yeah, I'm fine. I just never understand what Carter is saying." I lied and referenced our group chat, where our friends had been checking in on me constantly. Now that my new phone was activated, I had been able to catch up and respond to everyone's well wishes.

"No one does," Liam assured me. "Hey, guess what? I'm meeting up with Sloane tonight."

"To fuck?" I asked.

"No, to do my taxes," Liam replied sarcastically.

"That was fast but here is to getting some! Hell yeah!" I tried to show that I was excited for him without moving my face too much because it still hurt.

"You think she'll wear her stethoscope while she…"

"Nope, nope. Blah blah," I quickly drowned him out.

"Fine." Liam pouted. "But if she does, I'm telling you about it after."

"Or don't." I grimaced, already knowing that we would definitely be getting a fully detailed description when he came back. "I need to pee." I changed the subject, and Remi came over to help me up and then waited for me in the hallway while I used the bathroom. As I washed my hands, I avoided looking at myself in the mirror. The swelling was already coming down, but as the bruises healed, they were turning all sorts of colors, and I was still too banged up to want to look at myself. When I came out and Remi helped me back into the main part of the apartment, I saw that my mother was standing in the kitchen.

"You're back early," I observed feeling surprised.

"I came home to check on you." She was pouring me some celery juice, and I didn't have the heart to tell her that I had already had some. I stood uncomfortably in the kitchen sipping the juice when Liam came out of my room with his wallet and keys.

"We're going to my mom's spa to pick up an ultrasound facial machine from her other location. She wants us to bring it here, and then she'll come by later to do it for you. She said it heals bruises really fast," Liam told me.

"Okay." I waved. Remi kissed my cheek and left with Liam.

"Mom," I said, holding myself up against the kitchen counter. "Am I the result of a rape?"

She literally tripped over nothing as she walked toward the living room. Then she spun around, her eyes wide with something unspoken.

"No. Why would you ask that?" She seemed suspicious.

"Am I named after him?" I whispered. My body was beginning to tremble. My mother's eyes narrowed.

"Why are you asking me that?"

That wasn't a no. My stomach plummeted.

"Mom. I'm nineteen, and you have always avoided this topic. I mean, to be honest, you've been avoiding me my whole life too." I breathed in and out slowly, trying to avoid a panic attack. My mother looked at me with an unreadable expression on her face.

"I wasn't avoiding you on purpose." She swallowed heavily.

"How do you avoid someone by accident?" I retorted. I slowly walked to the living room and lowered myself down into one of the chairs as gently as possible.

"I-I wasn't avoiding you. I was just trying to work so I wouldn't give you the life my parents gave me." She was more flustered than I had ever seen her. "Growing up, we never had enough food, and sometimes the electricity would be off when I came home from school. I never had anything that I needed, and I just wanted to make sure that we never lived like that." She shrugged. "Clearly, I fucked up."

I gaped at her, silent. We never had conversations like this. I had never heard about her childhood, ever.

"I didn't name you after him. I just naively thought that if I named you Shane, but I spelled it differently, maybe his wife would realize what he had done and would leave him. I wanted to punish him." She said it so quietly that looking at her, I could see the fifteen-year-old who had been hurt and abandoned, and I was flooded with empathy for her.

"Did she?" I asked. My mother shook her head, and after a minute of silence, her posture changed, and she seemed resigned to tell me what she had been keeping from me all of these years. My heart was beating so fast that I felt nauseous.

"I grew up in this area, but my parents sent me to church camp about an hour from here. The youth pastor and his wife were in their twenties and lived at the camp for the summer. When Shane found out that I didn't believe in God and that my parents had only sent me to a religious camp because it was free, he took a special interest in me." My mom wrinkled her nose like she could smell something bad. "He would meet with me at night to talk about God and read the Bible. All the girls thought he was cute, and I was already an outsider because I wasn't from their area. I didn't have stylish clothes, and I knew nothing of their religion, so I used it as..."

"Clout?" I offered.

"What's clout?" she asked.

"Like influence or to be popular," I explained. My mother nodded.

"Yeah. The girls were all jealous that he spent so much time with me, and when they would say something about it to him, he told them that Jesus had told him to help me." She rolled her eyes. "The first time his hand accidentally brushed across the side of my chest, I thought it was an accident." Her eyes lowered in shame. "Once I realized that it wasn't an accident, it had happened so many more times that I felt scared to bring it up. I was stupid." She sighed.

"You were groomed, Mom. You weren't stupid," I spat, feeling so angry for her. She shrugged once more, and again I could see that scared fifteen-year-old trapped inside of her.

"The accidental touching turned into running his foot down my leg or resting his hand near my chest, but I never stopped him." My mother couldn't even look at me. "Nothing else more than that happened that summer. But then I went back in December because the camp was doing a weekend event for Christmas. At that point, I could see that Shane's wife was pregnant; she had a small bump, but I didn't know how far along she was. Anyway, I wasn't... I wasn't raped." She could barely say the word. "What happened was the night before the weekend was over, Shane told me to come to his office. I went willingly. He told me that I was so beautiful, and that meant that God favored me. He wanted to know if I would do something with him to honor God."

"Mom..." I whispered. "You don't have to tell me if you don't want to."

"I've never told anyone this before, and now that we're here, I'm going to say it." She seemed determined. I nodded, clutching the blanket in my hands.

"I didn't know what I was agreeing to, but once I realized what he wanted, it was too late." She winced at the memory. "But I didn't say no, so... I wasn't technically raped."

The trauma was obvious in her words.

"Would he have stopped if you had said no?" I asked gently. She paused, and suddenly, tears appeared in her eyes.

"No," she said breathlessly.

"No, he wouldn't have," I agreed softly.

"Well." She sighed. "The one good thing I got out of it was you."

I couldn't believe what I was hearing. I had grown up wondering if she wished she hadn't had me.

"When I realized that I was pregnant, I looked him up in the phone book, and I called him on his work number. First, he tried to pretend that he didn't remember me, but then he got furious with me. He told me never to call him again and to 'take care of it.' That confused me because he always preached about choosing life and taking care of the less fortunate. Yet he hung up on me after he told me to abort you. I have never wanted to hear another word about God ever since because I realized it was all a facade."

"But you didn't abort me." I said it like a statement, but it was really a question. She shook her head.

"I could never," she said simply. I was feeling like I needed to cry, so I took some deep breaths to shove the emotion back down until I was alone later and could process in the safety of my room.

"When I gave birth to you, I tried to contact him one more time. I wrote him a letter telling him that I had you, but I never heard from him, and I never contacted him again." She was silent for a moment, and then she added, "If you want to change your name, I will understand. I now see how strange it was to name you that." My mother looked defeated. Tired. Unsure.

"I actually like my name," I told her. She smiled wanly.

"I like it too. I'm sorry I never told you about this, and who your father was. It's honestly really hard for me to talk about Shane Taylor."

My world began to spin. She never called him John, but I was a million percent certain that I now knew who my father was, which meant that I was in love with my brother.

This is what fear feels like.

AFTER ENDING the most life-changing conversation my mother and I have ever had, I faked needing to use the bathroom so I could leave the room before I had a complete breakdown in front of her. I locked myself in there, turning on the sink to mask the noise before I fell to my knees and began to wretch into the toilet. My face was aching from the effort, and when I finally rested myself against the cold, smooth seat, I felt so weak that I could not even move. I had sex with my brother. Remi was going to leave me. I was going to be alone. I would never recover. Maybe I shouldn't tell him. He would never know. I almost listened to myself and my jumbled mess of thoughts. But then I realized if I don't tell him, then we will never be able to have kids. No, I'll have to tell him. Maybe he'll love me enough to stay with me? Could his love for me change that fast? Am I disgusting for even considering this? He's going to leave me. He's going to leave me. He's going to leave me. I am going to die from heartbreak. How was this happening? How was this terrible, evil, misogynistic man my father?! A man who had raped my mother. It felt like the universe was conspiring against me. This was so unfair! I felt the bile rise in my throat again. It burned as my stomach churned endlessly. I lay there unaware of how much time had passed when, suddenly, my brain sluggishly remembered two very important details. For one, Remi had type O blood, and two, last week, I finally got the results of the DNA kit Dee had given me, and I had not received any matches. Since I knew that Remi was registered on that very same website, that could only mean one thing: the man Remi called Dad was mine, not his.

This is what sadness and confusion feel like.

WHEN REMI and Liam came back, I pretended to be asleep because I didn't yet know what to say to Remi. "Hey, I thought you were my brother for a second, but it turns out your dad, who is actually my dad, raped my mom when he was twenty-six and she was fifteen, so I have no idea who your dad actually is, but at least we're not blood siblings," just didn't roll off the tongue very well. After about an hour of faking sleep, I felt Remi shake me gently.

"Baby, Liam left to meet Sloane and it's time for a red-light session and some Motrin," he said quietly. Was this going to be it for us? Even though we weren't related, would it be too weird to know that his real mom was married to my real dad, who he had thought was his real dad up until I would tell him that he wasn't? Would this destroy our relationship? Would he be mad that I didn't tell him about his dad being the one to save me after my accident? Well actually, my dad.

"Fuck," I said out loud.

"I know it hurts. I'm sorry to wake you," Remi said sweetly, having no idea what was actually bothering me. I blinked up at my beautiful boyfriend, trying to savor the moment before I had to absolutely wreck his current reality.

"We have to talk," I said, knowing that my tone sounded ominous. His face paled.

"What's wrong?"

"Can you help me sit up?" I asked. He gently lifted my body, so I was sitting up but still leaning against the pillows. "Okay, I need to tell you something, but I need you to listen to the entire story before you freak out." I was twisting the blanket nervously between my fingers.

"You're already freaking me the fuck out, babe." Remi's eyes darted over my face, looking like he was trying to read me.

"Sit down," I said hoarsely, patting the bed next to me. He sat immediately.

"Are you breaking up with me?" He looked like he was going to cry. Tears flooded my eyes.

"No, I will never do that." I gulped out. "But I need you to listen."

He nodded anxiously.

"I love you. I love you so much, and nothing I'm about to tell you will change that, but I hope it doesn't change it for you. Please promise you won't do anything out of anger. Okay?" I begged. Remi didn't answer, his lips were now squeezed in a thin line. I took a deep breath.

"The night of my accident, I worked late, as you know, so I was walking to my car after I closed up, and your..." I paused and swallowed loudly. "The pastor was there, and he called my name."

Remi's body jolted in shock.

"Did he hurt you?" he hissed. His fists were clenched by his sides. I shook my head.

"No. He was there to try to convince me to bring you back to God," I explained.

"How does he know where you work?" Remi sounded skeptical.

"I have no idea." That knowledge had creeped me out too. "But he was waiting for me. I yelled at him to stay away from me, but suddenly, a car came out of nowhere, and I tried to run." My eyes filled with tears again. "I couldn't get away fast enough. I remember getting hit and being thrown in the air, and then I fell onto the hood of the car. I felt like I was dying, Rem." A sob escaped, and Remi took my hands in his.

"We don't have to do this right now, sweetheart," he told me gently.

"We do." I sniffed. "I don't remember this happening, but the doctor told me that the pastor brought me in because the ambulance couldn't get to me fast enough."

Remi looked shocked.

"Who knew my dad had it in him?" he said sarcastically. My heart skipped a beat thinking about what I was about to tell him and not knowing what the outcome would be.

"So when I came in, I had weird symptoms that ended up being due to crush syndrome, but before they knew that, the doctors thought I might have internal bleeding, and they checked my blood type. The hospital didn't know who the pastor was to me, so they had asked him what his blood type was. The doctor told me that we were a match." I paused, gauging his reaction. Remi looked confused.

"Okay. So?" he asked, running his hand through his hair.

"What is your dad's middle name?" I suddenly inquired.

"It's Shane. I know you would think I'd hate the name, but honestly, no one calls him that anymore," Remi told me. I nodded.

"Yeah, well, the doctor called him John Shane when he was telling me the story, and something felt weird to me. Like while I was so out of it and in crazy pain, my brain latched onto this information and just wouldn't let it go. So earlier today after we talked about blood types, I finally asked my mom if she had been raped and is that why she never told me who my dad was. I knew I was definitely going out on a limb, and everything could have been some weird cosmic coincidence, but I asked anyway."

Remi's eyes bore holes in me as he stared.

"And she finally told me who my dad is and the story around it," I whispered.

"Who is he?" Remi's voice rasped. The fear growing in his eyes was mirroring how I felt inside.

"My mom went to a church camp when she was fifteen, and the youth pastor groomed her until one day, he convinced her to have sex with him. When she told him she was pregnant with me, he told her to have an abortion. She wrote him a letter when she gave birth to me, but he never responded."

"Are you my sister?" Remi's voice was strangled, and his face held so much anguish that it made me want to cry again.

"Please tell me that my dad is not your dad, Shaen. Please don't do this to me. I love... I love you so much. I-I can't..." He hiccuped as tears began to run down his face. I reached out to take his hand, but he flinched and pulled away.

"Shane Taylor is my dad," I blurted out. Remi let out a painful breath and turned his body away from me.

"But he's not yours." I completed what I felt was the worst part of my story; my body was so tensely wound up that the physical pain running through me was excruciating.

"What?" Remi choked out. "What the fuck are you saying?"

"I'm saying that I ran the DNA test that Dee gave me, and you did not pop up as a match, and your blood type is O, but your dad's is AB negative... like mine." My voice trailed off as Remi sat up straight.

"I can't have O if he's AB negative." He also remembered our science class. I shook my head. "No," I agreed.

"So, who is my dad?" Remi sounded so lost that I wanted to comfort him.

"Can I hug you?" I asked tentatively. Remi paused.

"You're really not my sister?" he asked, biting his lip nervously.

"Your mom is married to my mother's rapist, but no, I am not your sister," I confirmed; my tone sounded bitter. Remi seemed to space out as he tried to process what I was saying.

"For the record, I wouldn't be able to stop loving you even if you were technically my brother," I admitted. That caught his attention, and he stared at me, his face unreadable.

"Could you?" I asked. "Could you have stopped loving me? After everything we have been through?" My voice broke, and my heart was racing in my chest. I knew what I was saying was extremely taboo, but I couldn't imagine being forced out of love with someone who felt like my soul mate.

"Well, you're not my sister." Remi's voice sounded strained, like it was painful to talk. "So it really doesn't matter."

"It does matter. It matters to me because, for me, I would

always keep you. I wouldn't care. I'm in too deep," I confessed. I was thankful we weren't actually being faced with this terrible reality, but I needed him to know the truth, no matter how crazy it may sound. Remi closed his eyes and pressed his hand against his forehead as if he were in pain. After what felt like an eternity, but in actuality was probably just a few minutes, he choked out, "I could never stop loving you."

I couldn't stop the tears then. They rolled down, making tracks on my face. My lips quivered as Remi leaned in and pressed a soft kiss to them.

"Honestly, everyone can go fuck themselves, Shaen. I am keeping you forever, no matter what." Remi sounded so certain that I started crying again. He rocked me gently.

"Don't cry, sweetheart." He kissed me again. When I finally calmed down, I looked up at him.

"Remi, you need to call your mom."

He sighed.

"I know, and I need to do it now because if I don't, I'll never do it." He pulled his phone out of his pocket; his hands were shaking slightly. I squeezed his shoulder silently, telling him that I was here to support him. Remi pressed the button to FaceTime his mother. After three rings, her face appeared on the screen.

"Remiel?" She sounded shocked. "Is everything okay?"

"I know that your husband is not my father, and I need you to tell me the truth. Who is my father?" Remi just laid it all out there without skipping a beat. I could see his mother's face pale, and her eyes opened in complete shock.

"Wh-what are you talking about?" she stuttered. "Come home, Remiel. Let's talk in person."

Remi surprised me by laughing. A cruel, sharp sound.

"Yeah, no thanks. That is not my home. I'm going to ask you one more time, or I'm going to tell D-Dad." He fumbled over the word. "I'll tell him what I know."

His mother sighed, looking resigned.

"He did this to himself." His mother's demeanor suddenly changed from docile and submissive to that of a scorned, angry woman.

"What do you mean?" Remi spat.

"Your father has a thing for younger women," Miley told her son in a matter-of-fact way.

"He's not my father," Remi corrected. His mother sighed again.

"Like it or not, he raised you, Remiel. I'll call him what I want to."

She said it with an element of sass that I never expected from her. She continued telling her story.

"Soon after we got married, we were the youth pastors at a camp, and I caught him touching one of the campers inappropriately. When I confronted him about it, he told me he had never done something like that, and how dare I accuse him of something so terrible. Then, of course, he quoted Ephesians 5:22-24, where it says, 'Wives, submit to your own husbands, as to the Lord. For the husband is the head of the wife even as Christ is the head of the church, his body, and is himself its Savior. Now as the church submits to Christ, so also wives should submit in everything to their husbands.'"

Remi clenched his hand. I knew how much he hated his father and how he used his stupid Bible quotes to abuse the people around him. Oh, my father, I corrected myself in my thoughts. Wow, this was going to be very complicated. Either way, Remi hated when the pastor used religion to control and gaslight him and his mother. Miley herself seemed to grimace at the memory.

"I was so angry, especially since your father rarely touched me. He was never interested in intimacy with me, and whenever

I asked for it, he used to tell me I was being needy and that was not behavior worthy of a divine woman."

"I'm sorry, Mom," I heard Remi say. I was startled at his immediate change in mood. He seemed less angry and more empathetic toward her now.

"I did something bad, Remiel, and your father can never know. Promise me." His mother seemed hesitant. Remi nodded. "I promise," he assured her.

"I was so lonely in my marriage and starved for intimacy. I knew what I had seen him do with that girl, and I was scared that I didn't really know what kind of man I had married." Her voice wavered in obvious shame. "What you don't know is that I knew Dermont first. In fact, I had met John through Dermont. We had gone to school together, and it had always been Dermont that I wanted, but he wasn't religious, so my parents would have never approved. When I met his friend, Shane, that's what everyone called him back then, who wanted to be a pastor, I knew my parents would love him and it would keep Dermont around, so I ended up going out with him and not Dermont. Well, after we were married for a little bit, your dad was off on one of his church business trips, but I was always so suspicious of them, and I worried that he was really meeting up to hang out with girls or even worse. Anyway, that night, Dermont was in town, so we met up for dinner. I usually never drank, but I did that night, and I ended up confessing to Dermont how I felt about him and what was going on with Shane... John." Miley paused to take a drink of water with a shaking hand. Remi seemed glued to the phone.

"One thing led to another, and I stayed at Dermont's hotel. It was that night that I conceived you, Remiel," his mother confessed.

"What?" Remi's voice was barely a whisper. He looked over at me, his whole face showed his disbelief. "Do they know?"

Miley shook her head. "Your father can never know, but Dermont knows. I made your father sleep with me the next night in case I wound up pregnant, and for a while, I pretended that maybe you were really John's baby, but once I saw you, I knew. With your dark hair and facial structure..." Miley's voice trailed off for a moment, and then she refocused. "Dermont can't stand your father. He has begged me to leave but you know I can't. The only reason he pretends to still be John's friend is so he can continue being around you and have a relationship with you."

"I can't believe you," Remi bit out.

"I know I should have remained faithful," his mother cried. "I never did it again."

"No, not that," Remi corrected her. "I can't believe you stole a happy childhood from me, and for what? It's obvious you aren't happy, and you saw how he has always treated me. Did you stay with him even when you knew that Dad raped a fifteen-year-old girl when you were two months pregnant with me?" he all but shouted.

"How do you know that for sure, Remiel?" she demanded. It seemed that she was still in denial.

"Because I know who his real kid is, and I will never tell you or him who they are." Remi shut down her question immediately. I was so happy that he didn't even say "she" because he had to know that I never wanted them to figure out who I really was.

"I honestly just feel sorry for you, Mom. I wish you would leave him because I don't plan on coming home if he's there. Ever," Remi told her. She started to sob and kept saying she was sorry, that she didn't think she had any other choice.

"I have to go, Mom." Remi hesitated, then quickly said, "Thank you for telling me." Then he hung up and looked over at me.

"I don't even know what to say." Remi sounded numb.

"I know." I reached for his hand, and he held it tight. We were interrupted before we could say anything else by Julia knocking on the door.

"Hi, lovie." She came in with a smile. "Ready for a nice little face massage?" She gestured to her facial ultrasound machine. I nodded.

"Thank you, Julia," I told her.

"Anything for you, Shaen. You're family." Julia smiled. I flinched at the word. The meaning of *family* had gotten rather clouded today. Remi helped me get comfortable while Julia set up the machine. He was typing on his phone while Julia worked her magic, and then when she was done, they both left the room to get some food ready for me. His phone sat next to me and lit up with a text from Dermont, which said, "We need to talk."

I closed my eyes. Today was starting to feel like too much for me to handle. Only sex or sleep could save me from this emotional mess, and since, obviously, sex was off the table with my body still in so much pain, sleep would have to do.

23

____

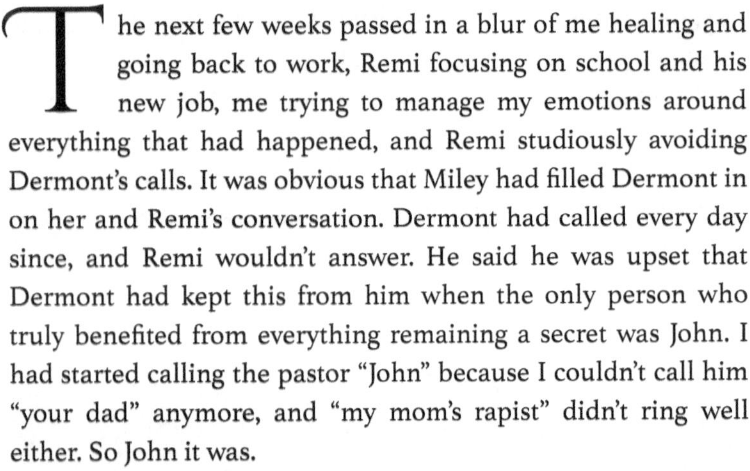

The next few weeks passed in a blur of me healing and going back to work, Remi focusing on school and his new job, me trying to manage my emotions around everything that had happened, and Remi studiously avoiding Dermont's calls. It was obvious that Miley had filled Dermont in on her and Remi's conversation. Dermont had called every day since, and Remi wouldn't answer. He said he was upset that Dermont had kept this from him when the only person who truly benefited from everything remaining a secret was John. I had started calling the pastor "John" because I couldn't call him "your dad" anymore, and "my mom's rapist" didn't ring well either. So John it was.

Together, we had decided that my mom could never know who Remi's mother was married to, which was going to be difficult to hide forever, but we would certainly try. Remi was talking about changing his last name. He said he didn't want to have the last name of a rapist who he wasn't even related to.

Remi was considering taking on Liam's last name or Dermont's. So it would either be Hennessy or Lewis. The fact that my mom hadn't seen the pastor at graduation or said anything about Remi's current last name was nothing short of a miracle.

Another change that had happened since the accident was that yesterday, I had moved out of my mom's apartment. After another week of resting, I had begun feeling well enough to leave the house and felt up to going to Remi's place for dinner. After we ate, Sam and Julia approached us and asked if we would consider moving onto their property. They had a small loft apartment over the garage that Liam's oldest brother, Levi, had been living in, but he had moved out in August to live with his girlfriend, so it was currently empty. The apartment had its own separate entrance, which was great for an element of privacy. The stairs opened up into a big room that had a small kitchenette, a huge bed, a small couch in front of a large TV, a big bathroom with all of the amenities, and a walk-in closet. As if that wasn't enough, Sam had told us that they didn't want us to pay them rent. Instead, they wanted the two of us to put eight hundred dollars a month into an investment account so that in a couple of years, we would have a down payment saved up to buy our own place. Of course, I had tried to fight them on that, but they wouldn't budge. So yesterday, Remi, Carter, and Jake spent the day helping me load up their cars with everything I wanted to keep and drove it over to our new place. I couldn't go to sleep until everything was put away, so we stayed up until 3 a.m. unpacking all of my belongings. The last thing I did was change the linen to something new that I had bought specially for our new place. We made love quietly in our new bed and then fell asleep, feeling like the puzzle pieces of our new life that had been disrupted by the chaos of the last few weeks were finally falling into place. The next morning, I was in the shower when I heard the front door open, and Remi call, "Honey. I'm home."

I grinned to myself, loving how that sounded. When I heard him come into the bathroom, I peeked around the shower door.

"Hi, baby." I smiled.

"Will you be ready on time?" he asked. I nodded. We had something very exciting planned for today.

"Definitely." I quickly got out, dried my hair, and got dressed.

The group chat was active as I got into the car, and Remi drove us to the tattoo shop.

LIAM

I can't believe ur getting ur first tattoo without me *crying face emoji*

LIA

send pics as soon as they're done!

EVA

Shaen did you decide what you're getting yet?

CARTER

please tell me you're getting a dick

RACHEL

eek tattoo day!

DEE

duck ya!

DEE

fuck

LIAM

my babies losing their tattoo virginity I'm so proud

REMI

i have no idea what Shaen is getting, she won't tell me

CARTER

it's most def an outline of your dick

EVA

shocked face emoji

SHAEN

you'll see *tongue out winking face emoji*

"I spoke to Dermont today," Remi suddenly told me.

"What?!" I was shocked. He shrugged. "He wore me down with his daily phone calls."

"I mean, he was persistent." I laughed. "What did he say?"

"He said he understands why I'm upset at him, and he's so sorry but that he loves me so much, and he's so happy that I now know and that he wants to fly here to see me if I'm open to it." Remi parked the car and turned to look at me.

"Are you open to it?" I asked.

"I told him I was only okay with it if you would be there with me, and he agreed."

We got out of the car, and I gave him a hug.

"I'm proud of you," I told him as I got up on my tiptoes to kiss him. "I know it's hard, but I can see that he loves you, and you honestly deserve a happy ending."

"It's not an ending, my love, this is the beginning." Remi took my hand and kissed my knuckles before walking us into the tattoo parlor. We had decided that although we were young and still had a lot of time to figure out all of the details of our life together, we wanted something permanent on our bodies to profess our love for each other. We hadn't shared what we would be getting; instead, we wanted it to be a surprise. Since I had never gotten a tattoo before, I was a little bit nervous about it. After signing a bunch of paperwork and showing the tattoo artist what I wanted, they sat me down in a chair and got to work. I was pleasantly surprised to find that it didn't hurt as much as I had thought it would, and it was over quickly. I took pictures of it while I waited for Remi to finish. Once he was done, Remi paid, and then we went back out to the car. We sat there for a minute, and finally, Remi asked, "Ready?"

I nodded.

"You go first," he urged. I lifted the sleeve of my sweatshirt to reveal my tattoo to him. It was along the side of my right arm. I had chosen a fine-line tattoo, all in a simple, lowercase font that said, "I feel you for keeps."

Remi obviously knew about my challenges with feeling my feelings, and lately, he had been helping me with identifying feelings that I wanted to avoid and started helping me feel safer experiencing them. We did deep breathing together every night, and he joined me for meditation sessions in the mornings. I wanted to include that aspect of my healing in my tattoo, and then I had chosen the "for keeps" part because saying "I keep you" was something we said to each other often, and I felt that it represented our love for each other really well.

"I love it, baby." Remi's eyes shone with emotion. I leaned over to kiss him.

"Let me see what you got." I was getting impatient to see what he had chosen.

He complied and pulled up his sleeve. I gasped as feelings of love and happiness flooded through my body. Remi's right arm, wrist to elbow, was covered in pixie dust. A few tears found their way out of my eyes and rolled down my cheeks.

"I love it, Remi. It's perfect," I told him. He reached up to wipe away my tears.

"And I love you," he told me before kissing me and completely taking my breath away.

Scratch every other feeling I ever had before this one. This flow of emotion, love, and trust, this is what happiness feel like.

EPILOGUE

The sun shone through the gap in the curtains and cast a sheen of light on Shaen's naked back. Fuck she was so hot, and she literally did not seem fully aware of how crazy she made me on a daily basis. I leaned over and kissed the tattoo on her arm. She stirred and turned over. The blanket shifted and fell, revealing her bare breast. Her nipple, a dusty rose color and already beaded, was just waiting for my mouth. I latched on and suckled. She moaned, and I felt her fingers clutch at my hair. I switched to her other breast, and she moaned again.

"I'm supposed to be the one waking you up. It's your birthday, Rem." Her voice was husky with sleep, and I grinned as I let her nipple pop out of my mouth.

"This is the best birthday present I can give myself," I told her as I made my way lower down her body, stopping between her legs. She was already soaked for me, just like she always was. It made me so hard knowing how responsive she was to me.

"What a good girl you are. You're already so wet for me," I told her, chuckling as I watched her grow slicker from my praise.

I blew some air across her labia but didn't touch her. I watched her lift herself up, trying to find my mouth with her pussy.

"You want my mouth, pixie?" I asked, blowing more air across her.

"Y-yes!" she said loudly. I laughed. "You'll have to ask nicely," I told her. She groaned. She hated and loved my games.

"Please," she said sweetly.

"Please what?" I teased. She let out a frustrated sound and then said, "Please lick me."

"Lick you where, Shaen? Use your words." I blew more air right on her clit, and her hips moved, seeking more but came up empty as I pulled away.

"Remi!" she whined. "Please lick my pussy... Sir."

Sir? That was new. My dick was steel, and I pushed against it with my palm before saying, "What a good girl you are for asking so nicely."

She mewled, panting slightly, and let out a moan as my mouth latched onto her. Her taste flooded my mouth. Her honey was thick around my tongue. I licked, sucked, nibbled, and swallowed her essence. She was fucking herself up against my face, making a mess in the three days' worth of facial hair I had grown since we had gotten to the beach house. I made an appreciative noise against her. I had one hand on her hip, holding tightly, and with my other hand, I had three fingers fucking into her warm, tight channel. I could not wait to bury my entire length into her. She was growing wetter and louder, and her movements were more stuttered, as if she could barely hold herself together. I knew one sentence that would drive her right over the edge. As I flattened my tongue and ran it over her sensitive bundle of nerves, I groaned out, "You taste so good. I can't get enough of you. You're such a good girl."

She exploded, moaning my name and tugging at my hair, which stung in such a good way. As she trembled in the aftershocks of her orgasm, I kissed my way back up her body. I knew she was not fertile, so I didn't bother with a condom. I kissed my way into her mouth; her lips were so plump and soft against mine. I knew she could taste herself on me, and it was always such a thrill for me. Her hands reached in between us, and she grabbed hold of my throbbing cock. I moaned; her fingers felt so good on me. Shaen put the tip of me inside her, and with a quick movement of my hips, I slid home. She was soaking, tight, and incredibly warm on my dick.

"Oh God," I moaned, biting her shoulder as the feeling of being inside her washed over me. I would never get used to how good fucking her felt. It wasn't just physical; it was how intensely close we felt and the energy we exchanged as we fucked. You would never catch me admitting this to anyone but her, but sex with us was so much more than just feeling good. She felt good in my soul. Fucking her was beautiful. She was beautiful. Our love was beautiful. It wasn't lost on me that last year, this was the exact bed that I had taken her virginity in, and now here we were so much more experienced. Even closer and that much more in love. My cock was deep inside of her, my hand was squeezing the sides of her neck slightly, and she was urging me to fuck her harder.

"Harder, Remi, more, more, more. Don't stop." She was moaning loudly.

"Baby, all of our friends will hear you." I laughed as I kissed her to keep her quiet.

"I don't care." She was almost there, I could tell. I circled my hips and fucked slightly shallower, making sure I kept hitting her G-spot. She slipped her hand in between us, and I felt her rubbing her clit. She was so fucking hot when she did that, and I could feel my own orgasm creeping up on me as I felt her hand moving on herself.

"Be a good girl and come for me. Come now, Shaen," I

demanded in her ear. She broke apart for the second time. Her pussy was squeezing my dick so hard that between the pressure, watching her completely lose herself to her own pleasure underneath me, and feeling the sharp edge of her engagement ring scratching at my back, the euphoria took over me, and I unloaded myself inside of her.

"I'm keeping you forever, pixie," I whispered as we fell back to sleep.

"I'm keeping you too," I heard her murmur against my chest.

This is what it feels like, I thought to myself as I breathed in her delicious smell and gently kissed the top of her head.

This is what it all feels like.

THE END

ACKNOWLEDGMENTS

Wow. I'm over here writing this knowing you, a stranger (and hopefully now a friend and fan) will be reading it. At the end of my book. The book I finally put out there. See, I've been writing since I was a kid. I wrote three full books in high school but never did anything with them. My father actually kept a bunch of old computers not knowing which one houses those books I wrote so long ago. I did have some poems published in magazines but nothing like this.

I knew I had to do this though. Reading is one of my best friends. I have read thousands of books. Reading was always a safe space for me—thanks to my mom for bringing me to the library for the first time—like I am sure it is for you. It's a place for my brain to go to when it needs to check out or desires a place to fall in love with characters that feel so real you cry when it's over. Right?

I hope you loved Remi and Shaen as much as I loved creating them. I really do. And I hope my book is one you to return to when you need a slice of safe space to *feel* in.

Now onto my thank you's. The obvious place to start is with my husband and my daughters. And to be honest, it's to say thank you for leaving me alone while I wrote this book in 30 days and then supporting me while I edited it endlessly for months. I love you.

To my siblings for cheering me on and to my brother Meyer, who was a dog groomer when he passed, all of the dogs in here were for you. To my Facebook and Instagram friends who have been so supportive and, honestly, kept me going until the last sentence was written.

To my friends, my beta readers, my arc readers, my editor, my proofreader and my cover designer, thank you. This is real because of you!

And to you, my readers. I can't wait to see where we go together because this is only the beginning.

I feel you for keeps.

XOXO
Rae

ABOUT THE AUTHOR

Rae Lloyd is a romance author with a deep passion for the written word. Having been an avid reader since a very young age, she was inspired by the thousands of books consumed since childhood. Rae's dream of having her writings published has finally come to fruition. She can be found writing in between living life with her three daughters and her husband. As well as hanging out with her many adorable pets, baking gluten-free desserts, or cultivating beauty in her wig salon. With many stories brewing in her mind, stay tuned for more to come.

To stay in touch and receive all book updates subscribe to get emails on https://www.raelloyd.com.

You can also find Rae on Tiktok and Instagram @raelloydwrites.

You can join Rae's Facebook group called Rae's Readers

9 798990 084100